CORRUPTED MOONS

MOONLIGHT IN GLENWOOD

BOOK TWO

LITA HUNT

AYNSLEY J. FRASER

ISBN 979-8-9870098-4-0

Cover by Tina Fulton

Edited by Ashley Chapman

Beta Readers and Contributors

Disc, Duck, Flicka, Hay, Mono, Rhianne, Kung Fu Alan, Lou, Ro, and A. Sherriff

Special Thanks To

Darren at Imperial Outpost Games for chasing people away so we could write, Aynsley's parents for giving up their dining room on a Sunday, and Lita's parents for the use of their library in a pinch.

All our various caffeine providers this wouldn't have made it to paper without you.

For everyone who told us we can't, we did.

PROLOGUE

Evie
October 26th, 2018
Night Claw Residence, Glenwood, CA

E vie could feel the transformation just under her skin, trying to force its way out as her bones threatened to crack under her weight. While werewolves didn't *have* to run on every full moon, most did need to transform at least once a month or face the consequences. She hadn't gone for a run since August. The longer Evie pushed it off, the more moonburnt she became and the more fragile her patience grew. Sure, the last few months had been intense. But how had she gotten herself into *this* state? Again...

She'd been planning to 'give in' to Laika's pushing for a run when she got home from work tonight. Her best friend would have kept her out for hours until the moonburn faded. Werewolves always ran better in packs anyway, even packs of two. Instead, Laika wasn't home; she was out on a date with a possible serial killer! That was the final straw for Evie's shaky control.

Someone was yelling at Evie, trying to drag her from her panic.

She tried to ignore them while she curled up on the floor. But Shelly, her newish roommate, wouldn't stop frantically calling her name. They'd only been roommates for a short while. Despite Shelly being a werewolf as well, she had almost no experience dealing with pack problems. Or in Evie's case, some bad self care. Thankfully, Shelly should be smart enough to bail if Evie lost her control to the point of a frenzy.

Wait... her second new roommate, Tor, was very human and wouldn't know any better.

Evie needed to hold herself together. She pulled her knees up to her chest, then wrapped her arms around them for dear life. The action wouldn't actually stop her from shifting into a wolf, but she felt safer and more in control. Through clenched teeth Evie begged, "Call Laika."

"Okay," assured Shelly. Her footsteps retreated, likely to follow the instructions given. Only Laika would be able to handle an out-of-control werewolf. She'd done it before...

Evie racked her brain for a solution that wouldn't put anyone but herself in danger until Laika arrived. Her best friend would come home for a situation this bad. But she needed to buy time... maybe the basement? The doors of her rental house were reinforced with dwarven magic, making them highly resistant to werewolf strength. If Evie got herself to the stairs, then she could make Shelly lock her in. They only kept holiday decorations, the washing machine, and dryer down there; nothing that couldn't be replaced.

However, this plan would require uncurling and that was the only thing keeping Evie sane. How had she gotten this stressed out? Why hadn't she just sucked it up like an adult and taken care of herself? Yes, life had been insane since September. She'd had to adjust to having two new women in the Night Claw pack house after years of it being only herself and Laika. Yes, she'd agreed to share a room with Laika so they could all afford the rent, but it wasn't all that bad. Then again, the interviews and debates that raged until they'd agreed on a plan were still causing Evie problems. She hadn't managed to shake Becky after turning the half elf down as a roommate; if anything, the woman was everywhere.

Anger surged through Evie unbidden as her inner wolf again tried to escape. She needed to keep her mind calm and stop focusing on her problems. Her new roommates were still way better than if Evie had been living at home. She'd spent over a decade running away from the Belle family name and now it was starting to nip at her heels. No! Evie was trying to banish the bad thoughts and not invite more into her head. Everard Belle could stuff his 'concern' for his daughter where the sun didn't shine.

Evie needed to move. Her tenuous control was fraying at the edges and she'd just have to gamble uncurling. Her fear of hurting someone outweighed her need to stay on the living room floor. Forcing herself to roll onto her stomach, Evie set her blurred vision on the basement door. She reached out to drag herself towards the safety it promised. The distance looked so long... longer than it should be. She needed to focus on happy thoughts because each inch felt like a mile.

Her day job was a safe topic because it really wasn't that bad. For years Evie had come into work, kept a smile on her face as she dealt with her boss' Hollywood drama, fetched him coffee, taken notes at appointments, and just been the nameless assistant... Arik knew her name now, though. He and his stupid 'Project Moonlighter' had consumed her every working day. Why had she agreed to write that stupid screenplay? She wasn't a writer and wasn't even getting paid for her efforts... shit, she was doing it again...

A shudder ran along Evie's spine and the joints of her fingers bent in the wrong direction. Long claws were trying to push up from below her nails. NO! She needed to hold it together because Shelly hadn't come back yet. Evie didn't know where Tor was either, and a frenzied werewolf could kill a human easily. "Shelly," she croaked, "Have you called Laika?"

Evie wouldn't have blamed Shelly if she'd run rather than stick around and deal with this disaster. She couldn't bring herself to look anywhere but the basement door. Her silver eyes stayed locked in place as Evie started to use her knees to push forward. Imagine if those idiots in the Blood Fang pack could see her right now, crawling across the living room on her stomach praying she didn't end up as a call to the GPD. Would she even be able to show her face on another job if MOONS was forced to contain her? Moonlighting was already proving to be harder by the day...

She'd put in the time and paid her dues handling situations exactly like this for as long as she'd worked for MOONS. The Night Claw pack was finally starting to get some recognition and a chance to rise out of the bottom ranks. Evie and Laika's usual jobs were easy to the point a trained police officer with a stun gun could do them. If supernaturals hadn't been involved, Night Claw's jobs wouldn't even have warranted a call to SWAT. But through her terrible luck of being the only known empathic werewolf in Glenwood, she'd gotten the call to that job which normally only senior moonlighters would receive. Nothing had gotten easier since then.

So far Evie had seen glass skeletons that were once a party, watched an amusement park and its guests crumble away at her feet, and had literal air pressure trying to crush her. This whole Glenwood Anarchist situation was so far outside of her skill set. She'd wanted to prove that Night Claw was useful, but now Evie was just so scared... No! She was doing it again.

Evie was running out of time and not moving fast enough. She'd made it only halfway across the living room. With a pained groan, she started using her hands to pull herself forward again. Her fingers had a thin layer of reddish fur and claws instead of fingernails. Shit, when had that happened? The claws dug into the floor, sinking so deep that she'd leave gouges in the carpet. Great! How was she going to afford repairing that? Her strained control snapped for a moment as Evie's muscles tightened, followed by the cracking of bones and joints. She was losing this battle...

Where was Laika? Evie's best friend was supposed to be here, and she always knew what to do... Laika was supposed to save her from herself. Irrational jealousy surged through Evie even as she tried to force it back. Since last month, Laika had become obsessed with her new 'friend', the creepy emotionless void of a vampire named Alfred. Werewolves and vampires were historical enemies, so why was Laika going out on a date with one? Especially one as ominous as Alfred? He might be the Glenwood Anarchist for all they knew and that's why he'd let Laika and Evie join the case. So he could prevent them from connecting him to all the murders! Once Evie got through tonight, she could focus on proving her claims.

Words reached her ears, but the blood rushing through her head made them incoherent. Shelly had to have reached Laika... and once her best friend was home, everything would be fine. Evie's hand brushed the basement door and she felt a surge of victory course through her veins. Yes! She could- Oh no...

Fur erupted from her skin as the wolf overtook Evie. Twisting and cursing, Evie let out a pained howl.

CHAPTER 1
MOONDRUNK

Laika
October 26th, 2018
Night Claw Residence, Glenwood, CA

Laika was furious on the inside, even if she was playing it cool outside. She'd been texting Alfred since September, trying to feel out if she liked him. Yes, their first meeting had been at the scene of a murder... but that just added to the excitement. Him being a vampire was different from Laika's usual. But he was a full time moonlighter, knew a ton about magic, and he was hot. She wanted to test the waters. However, Evie had turned every opportunity into a disaster.

After a series of non-dates, Laika had finally asked him out. She'd been looking for a place for her and Alfred to go for their first real date all week. Repeating his plan of Longtooth Steakhouse felt too easy, so she'd spent hours looking for vampire-friendly restaurants and a park that was open after sundown where they could take a walk.

Alfred had agreed to the entire plan when he picked her up an hour ago. That was another bonus: he had his own car, unlike Laika.

Right now Laika was supposed to be sitting across from Alfred, staring into those blue eyes and pestering him with a hundred questions about magic. Before they'd even ordered food, though, Shelly started ringing Laika's phone non-stop until she'd finally answered. The brunette was in full panic about Evie because her stupid pack-mate had pushed herself too long and hard. Evie's body forced a shift as her inner wolf demanded to be freed. But her mind continued to fight against it, leaving her stuck mid-shift on the living room floor.

Now Laika was on her way home to go pick up Evie and drive out into the middle of nowhere. They'd have to just hope they didn't run into any wolves or get into trouble with some park rangers on duty.

The worst part was that Alfred had been her ride. So now, once again, he was taking her home to handle Evie instead of enjoying dinner. And as petty as it was... Laika felt spiteful about how good she looked today! She'd spent an hour styling her dark hair up beautifully. The sage green dress she wore complimented her tawny skin tones and even her makeup brought out the amber in her eyes. Laika was a straight 10 out of 10 for her date... only to have it all go to waste. She was going to drag Evie through the literal dirt on this run.

"I'm so sorry. I swear I didn't plan this," Laika apologized for the tenth time. She turned her gaze towards Alfred, eyes brimming with sincere apologies.

"I know," Alfred replied as he sped them down the streets of her neighborhood. "A simple no would have sufficed, by the way. If you did not actually want to go to dinner with me."

"No, I really want to go out with you!"

"Are you certain about that? I am starting to wonder if you were just leading me on to get on my case." His playful jab chipped away at her stormy mood.

"I wouldn't do that!" Laika knew that this looked bad for the third time in a row. Any sane person would drop her at the door and never look back. An amused sound answered her as Alfred pulled his town car along the sidewalk in front of her home. This wasn't like last time; Laika couldn't drag her feet about going in the house just to talk a bit longer. Evie needed her help *now*...

"I know it wasn't the plan, but after I take care of Evie's run, can we pick back up where we left off?" Laika fumbled with her seatbelt as she tried to find a way to salvage this terrible date. "It will only be a few hours... I'll buy you a drink to make up for this whole mess?"

"Just a few hours?" Alfred sounded skeptical as he checked the screens to see how bright it was outside.

"Yes, I promise," Laika begged. A moment of hope blossomed as he didn't outright say no. She rushed to take advantage of the opening. "It'll be a longer run than normal because she put it off, but it won't take the whole night."

The vampire paused, grabbing his helmet as he seemed to consider her words and again checked how close to sundown they were.

Fingers undid her seatbelt, but Laika didn't go for the door just yet. She turned her gaze on Alfred, hoping he'd hear the sincerity in her words. "Please? I was really looking forward to going out with you."

"I suppose I am better company after the sun goes down," Alfred finally agreed.

Laika stifled a laugh. "You're fine company all the time. I-" Her words were cut off as the sound of a strangled howl hit her ears. Color drained from her face as she remembered why she was back home.

There was a distinctive click of Alfred's helmet, followed by a series of louder clicks as the door locks disengaged. Her door opened with a flurry of motion as Laika propelled herself out into the cool autumn air. The sun was low in the sky, casting long shadows from the surrounding houses, and her flats slapped against the paved walkway as she sprinted to the door. Laika was so focused on that howl that she barely heard the sound of the car doors closing, or the footsteps following in her wake. The heavy wood of the front door cracked against the wall as Laika called, "Shelly! I'm here, what's going on?"

"Over here," answered her roommate. Shelly was sitting on the floor in front of the basement door with Evie's head on her lap. All the furniture was pushed along the walls and Laika could see broken pieces of the coffee table.

Evie was half curled onto her side. Red fur had started to burst through the pale skin of her hands and arms. Her limbs looked painfully twisted, but that wasn't unusual. Shifting reshaped their very bones. The problem was that it didn't seem like Evie was moving closer to one form or the other.

"Shit... How long has she been like this?" Laika was kneeling next to her packmate, but the question was for Shelly.

"Maybe five minutes? It happened right before you got here," the answer tumbled out as Shelly tried to not let her panic show. "Laika, I've never seen someone get stuck! What do we do?" Being completely honest, Laika had never seen someone stuck this badly either. A situation like this called for Luca's wisdom. She hit her father's number on her phone.

"I need to get somewhere safe," rasped Evie through clenched teeth. She was conscious still with limbs spasming randomly every few seconds. "I'm... holding back the change."

"You're what?" gasped Shelly, "Don't be crazy! You need to give in and shift right now."

"But... I might frenzy... our neighbors," replied Evie. There was a sliver of panic as she cracked her eyes open to plead with Laika. She understood what her friend meant. An uncontrolled shift in the middle of a suburban street could be bad for the houses around them. They lived in a predominantly human area as well. Someone could get bitten or Evie could even get shot by a scared neighbor. They needed help.

Unfortunately, Luca wasn't answering his phone and Laika had to make decisions on her own. She assured Evie, "I understand. We just need to get outside of Glenwood."

"I'm coming too," Shelly added as she relinquished Evie. She found her shoes, sliding them on as she scooped up Evie's discarded purse. Rummaging through, Shelly pulled out the keys and turned back to her roommates. Laika had lifted Evie up, frowning as she felt the trembling of the stalled shift under her hands. How could she let it get this bad? They'd been distracted with work, but Laika was normally better about enforcing runs.

A jingle caught Laika's attention and she eyed the proffered keys. "Sorry Shelly, I need to keep a hand on Evie just in case. You need to grab the cooler from the kitchen and you're going to have to- You don't have your license yet, do you?"

"No, I failed my first test," admitted Shelly. "But I could drive anyways?"

"Or I could, as I am a licensed driver with a car big enough for everyone," proposed Alfred, pulling attention to himself. He was standing in the shade of the doorway with his helmet still on.

Laika jumped at the sound of Alfred's voice, looking up in surprise. She had completely missed him following her to the door in her haste. Feeling a tad embarrassed for him witnessing yet another scene of werewolf drama, Laika tried to wave away the offer, as helpful as it was. "That's very kind, but you don't have to. If Evie goes into a frenzy, I don't want you to get hurt."

For a moment the vampire didn't move and then he said, "I will be fine."

"We don't have time for this," Shelly interjected with her panicked expression, "If he can drive then let him drive!"

"I believe we are agreed. I will go open the doors then." Alfred nodded as he left them to carry Evie.

Laika realized she was outvoted and hoped that her packmate would keep it together. There was no way a vampire could take a frenzied werewolf, especially in an enclosed space. She brushed past Shelly, heading back to the town car, trusting the woman to lock up the house. Evie uncharacteristically hadn't said anything during the whole exchange. As Laika hauled her packmate into the back seat of the town car she was met with a confused werewolf. Her friend was lost in her pain from the half shift.

"Don't worry, we're getting in the car and we'll be in the woods in no time," Laika reassured.

The front doors opened as Alfred slid into the driver's seat and kicked the car to life. Shelly followed a moment later, sliding into the passenger's seat. She hesitated as she was greeted by monitors instead of a windshield. Glancing between Alfred and Laika for direction she asked, "Maybe I should sit in the back?"

"No time, Shelly, and you'll be happier for a seat between you if Evie gets her claws," Laika answered quickly before Alfred could.

The doors closed and monitors whirred to life. A familiar metal click echoed as Alfred removed his helmet. "Is there a particular place we need to go?"

"No, just somewhere away from town with a forest for cover," Laika hesitated before continuing. "We can get in alot of trouble if we go running without a license in a state park, and private land is a whole mess..." Laika felt like she was babbling. Alfred was a senior moonlighter, he probably knew this already.

"I may know of a place. I will get us there as quickly as possible," he answered simply, before throwing the car into gear. He drove them out of the suburbs barely following the speed limits before reaching the foothills.

Alfred's car bounced along a dirt trail. Laika's ears could hear the gravel and sticks pinging off the metal. She owed Alfred so many drinks and thanks for this. He hadn't been kidding when he said he knew somewhere in the middle of nowhere. There was nothing but trees on either side as far as the cameras could see.

The town car came to a soft stop and the doors unlocked. Alfred made no move to pick up his helmet, even as the locks on the doors clicked open. There was no light on the cameras other than the head-lights. Shelly scrambled out from the passenger seat and pulled the back door open. Holding her hands out, she took hold of Evie's legs to help drag her from the backseat. Between her and Laika, they got their friend about thirty feet from the car.

"Okay," Laika touched Evie's arm while leaning in close to speak, "you're somewhere safe now. Shift and go running. I'll catch up soon."

Evie let out a groan as her body started rapidly contorting again. Wavy red fur spread like wildfire as her limbs twisted the rest of the way into the four paws of wolf form. A few minutes later, Evie shakily pulled herself to stand on four paws. She shook scraps of fabric from her shredded work clothes in every direction. Her silver eyes flashed towards Laika, but the red wolf tore off into the woods at top speed.

Cursing, Shelly kicked her shoes off and took off after her. "Evie, wait a moment!" The brunette werewolf was pulling her shirt over her head as she disappeared into the underbrush. That left just Laika and Alfred in the clearing now. She held back to make sure her pack-mate didn't circle back for the only non-werewolf in the area. As she approached the town car, Alfred got out.

"Any issues?" he asked politely.

"No, Evie's off to run now. The first hour she'll be wild, but she'll calm down."

"I am glad to hear that. I shall stay here while you join your packmates."

Scrutinizing his face, Laika had to fight a frown. She'd imposed so much on Alfred. And yet he didn't seem at all put out. "You can head back to town and I can call you after the run?"

Alfred wasn't deterred. "I believe it would be best if I stay nearby. This is no trouble."

"It'll be boring standing out here, and I don't want you to feel obligated..." Her demand that they continue their date after the run hadn't meant she wanted him to have to stand around literally waiting on her.

"I have a book," Alfred countered.

Laika protested, "But we'll be hours out here."

"I assure you I will stay with the car. I have no intention of following you as you run."

Laika shook her head, "No, it's not that. You'd never be able to keep up with us on four legs. I just... don't want you to feel stuck out here waiting on us."

"If I go home, I will sit on the couch and read a book waiting for your call. Assuming you even have a connection out here. There is little difference to me and a much longer wait for you. Go join your friends." Alfred gave her a warm smile before he turned back to the town car, ending the conversation as he did.

Laika stared after him in surprise, but he hadn't left much room for her to disagree. She watched Alfred climb back into the car and close the door before she got moving. A full moon had only been a couple days ago, so there was plenty of light for Laika to see by. Evie and Shelly were long out of sight, but she'd be able to track once she shifted.

Even with the blacked out windows on the car, Laika stepped into the underbrush of the forest before undressing. Clothes and shoes were kicked off into a heap on the forest floor. Minutes ticked up until four dark paws joined the rest running off into the dark.

Pine needles and wet earth assaulted Laika's nose when she took her first deep breath. She could smell other werewolves, likely Evie and Shelly, but it was too vague for her to track them by scent. Her large ears took over the job of finding her friends. They weren't making as much of a cacophony as before when Evie went tearing through the underbrush in a mad dash. A snapping to her left made Laika's ear twitch. Then the faint sound of fur scraping by leaves and twin breathing hit her ears. She'd found their direction.

A smirk crept onto Laika's muzzle as she lowered herself to the ground. The pair weren't moving anymore, which meant it was time for her favorite game of stalking Evie. Her friend had never been a rough-and-tumble, wild wolf type. Evie didn't even know how to hunt. So getting the drop on her would be easy.

Swift strides closed the distance between Laika and her friends.

They didn't have much of a head start, which meant it was only a few minutes before they were in view. Evie's red fur looked fiery under the moonlight and she rested in a bright patch of light. That wouldn't do... Her friend needed to run for a while to erase the damage of the moonburn.

Crouching down, Laika took aim.

Shelly's brown eyes looked up in alarm and soft grey ears swiveled around frantically. She was far more alert than Evie. Her reactions were too slow though.

Laika sprang!

Her dark frame pounced on Evie and sent them crashing into a flurry of fur. Laika gave a mock growl as she took her packmate to the ground. Teeth gnashed as the two descended into a snarling mess of play bites and kicks. Evie never stood a chance before she got pinned.

There was a whine of discontent as Evie tried to shake Laika loose. Her fur was splattered with dirt and mud. The complaints would still be rolling about muck in her hair days from now. But anything would be worth it if that meant Evie got into the spirit of the run.

Bouncing up onto four paws, Laika danced away a few steps to hide behind Shelly. The grey wolf let out an uncertain whine. Her eyes swept from one friend to the other. Meanwhile, Evie had found her paws again while glaring at Laika. As much as Evie might want to, she would never tackle the skittish Shelly. So she tried to circle around the grey wolf in her attempt to catch Laika.

However, the dark wolf was quicker on her feet and soon the pair were running circles around Shelly. Flashes of teeth were taunting as Laika stayed just ahead of Evie.

With a growl of frustration, Evie's fangs clicked together as she just barely missed Laika's tail.

Amused howls forewarned Laika leaping over Shelly with a mighty jump. Laika landed on the other side before nudging her nose into her grey friend's side. Her tail whipped behind her as she took off into the trees.

Laika was the bait for her own game of chase. She did anything to keep Evie moving for as long as they needed to. She circled back time and time again with playful snaps before speeding away once more. This was the most fun part of being a werewolf: running through the trees at top speed with her pack on her heels. Well, maybe not top speed... Laika never could run full out against anyone. No one could keep up.

When a stray rabbit crossed their path, the dark wolf tried to push her friends into a hunt. Evie turned her nose up in the air; she refused.

Hours stretched out behind the group of werewolves, tracked by the moon climbing higher into the sky. Finally, Laika swung them back the way they'd come, slowing her pace at the same time. Even she felt satisfied by the amount of running and playing tonight. Laika came to a stop once she found her clothes from earlier. On a branch above the pile was a thick blanket fluttering in the light breeze. The distraction allowed Evie to tackle her from behind.

The mess of claws and jaws continued until Shelly appeared, dragging one of them off the other by the back of the neck. Huffing breaths turned into the sounds of the shift taking effect. Three wolves became women who were laying on the forest floor.

A glorious feeling of loose muscles clouded Laika's mind. She always felt so relaxed after a run. If it wasn't for the fact they had someone waiting on them, her jelly limbs would've stayed right here and taken a nap...

Or maybe not. She felt her stomach rumble as a reminder of the dinner she had not gotten to eat. With a sigh, Laika rolled into a sitting position preparing to pull herself to her feet. The world lurched to the side for a moment. "Oh! I'm *so* moondrunk!"

Giggling erupted from a very naked and cuddly Evie laying at her feet. "I'm not. I never get moondrunk."

"Liar!" Laika hissed before descending into giggles of her own.

Shelly stumbled around a tree, throwing her arm up to lean

against the bark. She had managed to pull her clothing on, but her shirt was backwards. "Did we go running too long?"

"No! We barely ran… but it was a nice run," Laika answered. She stretched her limbs as she finally stabilized her balance. Right now the werewolf was not blackout moondrunk like her packmate rolling on the ground. "Maybe we're just a little moon-tipsy?"

"Yeah," agreed Shelly. Her brown eyes fell to Evie, who was trying to claw her way up a tree. "But she's really gone."

Together the women were able to get Evie wrapped up in the extra blanket. No one questioned that it hadn't been there when they left. Another sign that the girls were out of sorts.

Evie complained, "I want my pants!"

"You tore them up," hissed Laika while trying to tie a knot in the front. The blanket was a dark blue and long enough to cover her friend up well. This would do until they got home.

"Where are we?" Evie looked around. Her eyes studied the trees as she clung to Shelly affectionately.

"I don't know," admitted Laika with a shrug.

Evie looked aghast. "You just took me to the middle of the woods? How are we getting home!?"

This was a very normal interrogation after her friend put off running to this level. She did it multiple times a year instead of just taking a weekly run. For someone so good at self care, Evie was a moron about indulging her wolf.

Laika corrected, "I didn't take us anywhere. Alfred said he knew somewhere."

"It's a nice somewhere," Shelly added, holding out both hands to the redhead.

"You let a mass murderer take us out into the middle of the woods alone?!" Evie seemed startled by the realization. She ignored attempts to get her up from the ground.

"What?" Laika tilted her head in confusion. She'd pulled her dress over her head and remembered to put underwear on.

"Oh," laughed Shelly, "Evie's been complaining all week your new boyfriend is murdering half of Glenwood to get your attention." The brunette had redressed in her jeans and fixed her backwards shirt, even if the latter's buttons were offset by two.

"That's true," Evie agreed with a vigorous nod, "But she's not dating him, she's being stalked by him."

There was a long pause as shock overtook Laika then she burst into laughter. "Oh my moon Evie, you have been watching way too much trashy TV! That doesn't happen in real life!"

"Yes it does! You've got a stalker!" argued Evie.

Before Laika could answer, she heard the click of a door on the other side of their foliage barrier. Her tipsy thoughts wandered to if Alfred had heard them from inside the car. How many times now had they insulted him while in earshot?

"See, he's coming to get you now!" Evie threw her hands in the air while trying to stand. Her balance toppled her back into the dirt.

If Laika had been less tipsy, she would've scolded her friend harsher. Getting into a shouting match seemed like a terrible idea. "Shhh Evie, you're being *way* dramatic. Isn't she, Shelly?"

"So dramatic, but you both totally are the most dramatic people I have ever met. Now come on! I'm starving!" Without waiting, Shelly got both hands under Evie's arms and hefted her up.

When they stumbled back to the car, they looked more like a trio of muck monsters than werewolves. Their clothing was streaked in mud and bits of leaf litter. Laika and Shelly each had an arm around Evie, half carrying and half dragging her.

Alfred was leaning against his car with a book in hand. He glanced up at them and Laika caught a surprised blink. She hadn't left him with any warnings about her state on returning, especially since none of them could walk a straight line.

Unbidden, a grin spread across Laika's face due to him actually waiting. She slipped free of the tangle of wolves by handing off her burden to Shelly. Long strides closed the distance between them and she came to a stop in front of Alfred with a laugh. "You really waited. I'm sorry if we were gone too long. Are you okay?"

"Of course I waited," responded Alfred. He held up a beaten looking paperback, but the cover was unreadable in the dark. "I did have a decent book to entertain me."

"What book? Is it about magic? Or some fancy mystery?" Laika pressed curiously, but it faded quickly.

Before Alfred could answer, a whine echoed from Shelly. "Laika, did you bring the cooler?"

"Yes! I feel like I'm going to faint!" Evie seconded with pleading eyes. "I'm so hungry."

Laika twisted to look at her two friends. They had gotten more wrapped around each other with every step. "Oh... no, I totally forgot. Uhh..."

"Are you all alright?" Alfred's voice pulled her attention back. "No one had a cooler previously."

Laika sent her whole body spinning back to look at him. Her world felt off kilter immediately and her balance faltered. Wild arms fumbled to grab anything for balance and a gloved hand came to the rescue.

"Are you alright?" asked Alfred again.

"Sorry, sorry!" She cracked up into laughter, allowing herself the few steps forward to lean on Alfred. "They're just a little moondrunk; nothing's wrong."

"Ah. That does explain the... change in demeanor." Alfred did not push her away.

Laika appreciated the lines of his face while enjoying the feel of his heavy leather coat. Despite herself, an accusation tumbled out. "Are you stalking me?"

"What?!" Alfred looked like he had more to say, but he was cut off.

"I'm hungry!" Evie yelled, dragging attention back to her. "Can we please go get something to eat?"

"Of course. If everyone could get into the car then I can take you home." Alfred muttered something she didn't understand before taking a step back from Laika to get the doors open.

After much stumbling, all three women found themselves safely belted into the town car. All of them were loud and giggling at every word. Chatter about the run consumed them while they drove through the trees and back onto the empty streets.

As the edge of the Glenwood appeared on the screen, Laika prompted her friend. "Evie, didn't you have something to say?"

"About?" questioned Evie.

"You know... that apology you owe?"

Evie pouted and pulled herself to lean over into the front seat. "You accepted my apology already!"

"Not me," chastised Laika. "You need to apologize to Alfred for last week... and tonight."

"No," Evie half hissed, sulking back into Shelly's embrace.

"No?" Laika shot a glare at her friend, "Why the hell not?"

Evie's suspicious gaze met her friend's, "You know why?"

Laika began to gear herself up into a fight she didn't want. This was getting ridiculous, like some weird vendetta.

"Can we get burgers?" Shelly interjected quickly.

Laika's stomach rumbled in answer.

"Of course," agreed Alfred as he detoured them off the path to home. He pulled into the first open drive-thru with anything resembling food. Soon the town car grew quiet with the sounds of werewolves attempting to devour their body weight in burgers.

"Thank you," Shelly mumbled finally once she'd emptied the brown burger bag, "I felt like I was starving."

Alfred's lips formed a tight line. "You are welcome."

Laika was beginning to wonder if they were pushing the edge of his patience tonight. He seemed tense as they finally reached the street of their house. As soon as the town car shifted into park, she undid her seat belt and slid herself to press into Alfred's side. She dropped her voice extremely low. "Are you okay?"

Again Alfred seemed surprised by the contact, but he heard her clear enough. "Yes, I am fine."

"So where are we going?" Laika asked. She heard the back door click open.

"Going?" Alfred managed to turn enough to look down at her.

Laika took advantage of the space to curl up closer on the front seat. "We're going out, right?"

"Is that a wise choice? You are a tad more drunk than expected."

Sorrowful eyes peered up at him, "But... I really want to go out?"

"Nowhere is open for dinner," countered Alfred.

"I ate already, we could go get drinks."

The edge of Alfred's lips twitched up. "I cannot take you to a bar like this."

"Why not?" Laika took stock of how dirty she was and embarrassment colored her features, "I could go clean up."

"I am more concerned about the moondrunk than your attire," teased the vampire. The tension in his shoulders was fading away.

"... but?" Laika's voice was bordering on a whine.

Alfred held up a hand to settle the werewolf back down. He reached past Laika to the glovebox and retrieved a silver flask. "Perhaps we can compromise on a drink in the car before you go inside? We can try again next week for dinner?"

"No," declared Laika but she stole the flask out of his hand. "We are not waiting another whole week!"

Alfred seemed amused. "Did you have another plan in mind?"

"Yep, you're coming over for Halloween to help me pass out candy and then we're going out to the bar."

"I see-"

Laika pressed a finger to Alfred's lips to cut him off. She noted that his skin was cool to the touch. "And! You need to wear a costume because I'll be in costume for candy, and you'll look really silly without one."

"I suppose I can agree to that," Alfred mumbled. She could feel he'd relaxed now that it was just them in the car.

Laika cheered and attempted to take a drink from the flask. But he snatched it back out of her hands.

"Hey!" Laika argued, still reaching for it.

"Do not drink from a flask without having someone else drink first. That is basic safety," Alfred scolded, but he had warmed up again. He sipped the amber liquid inside and then offered the container back. "Would you like some whiskey?"

"LAIKA! HURRY UP," Evie interrupted the enjoyable mood by screaming from the front door. "WE'RE GOING TO BINGE MOVIES AND SLEEP ON THE COUCH!"

Laika groaned. Why was her friend trying to trash her fun again? All she wanted to do was have a meal or a drink with Alfred and see if their connection was still there in person. "Can we go somewhere else? I just don't want to go home tonight."

"Are you sure about that?" Alfred looked concerned as most of the happy energy faded away. "I will not be upset if you just want to go to bed."

"Please," Laika pulled on his collar, dragging him down to her eye level, "I have spent my last week walking on eggshells in my home. I do love Evie like a sister, but she drags out times between runs until she's almost unbearable. I'm just sick of taking care of her right now. Can we just go *anywhere* else and hang out?"

There was sympathy in his blue eyes. "Of course. We can find somewhere away from here, but please do let me know when you are ready to go home."

"Thank you!" Laika threw her arms around Alfred in a bone-crushing hug.

- ☾ -

October 27th, 2018
A Blissfully Dark Place, Glenwood, CA

Laika had a moondrunk hangover. Before she even opened her eyes, the first twinges of a headache were forming. Whenever she'd asked her family why werewolves got moondrunk in the first place, the answer was always a vague 'overflowing of spirit.' Which...didn't help on mornings like this. That was the least of her problems, as Laika realized this was not her bedroom when she looked up.

The room was unfamiliar, from the bare walls to bland furniture. Laika was alone, tucked under the covers, and still wearing her dirty clothing from last night. Waking up with her underwear on was always a good sign, but where the hell was she? She remembered running in the woods, devouring burgers, and not getting out of the car. Everything after that was a bit hazy.

Her eyes were adjusted enough to the dark that she was sure no one was in the room with her. Laika called loudly, "Hello?"

Silence responded to her question until a door opened to the right, but she couldn't see anyone in the shadows. A faint click of a switch sounded as light cut through the dark. A lamp next to the bed came alive with soft yellow light. Alfred stood in the doorway, "Good morning. Did you sleep alright?"

"Where am I?" Laika asked. She recalled refusing to get out of the car and him agreeing they could go somewhere else. But as Laika remembered, they'd gone to a park to drink and talk.

"My spare bedroom. You passed out on me, and it was nearly sunrise by then," explained Alfred. He didn't come any closer, lingering in the doorway. She wondered if he could tell she was starting to panic due to the unexpected change in plans.

Laika threw the covers off and demanded, "Why didn't you take me home?"

"You asked me not to, but if you are ready, I can drive you now." Alfred seemed unconcerned by the inquisition. Laika felt her cheeks grow hot as his words brought up a memory of the night before. They'd been sitting on the bumper of his car, and she'd been complaining about the week in detail to the point of begging him not to take her home. How embarrassing could this get? Laika had been a drunken mess.

"Oh... that's right. I remember now," she admitted and started to search for her phone. She needed to get a ride home quickly and regroup.

"Your phone is sitting to your left. I managed to find a charger for it last night, so you should have some power," Alfred added. Between keeping his distance and generally helpful demeanor, Laika felt one of her worries start to cool back down. She'd taken more advantage of his patience last night than the vampire had of her. The embarrassment over her current state was only growing.

Laika fought to keep her composure. "Thanks. I need to let my friends know I'm alive."

"Your phone started ringing early, so I did silence it, and I sent Shelly a message that you were still asleep from my phone," Alfred explained as she gripped her lifeline to her pack.

Laika checked her messages and the time. She'd slept through most of the morning and had a few missed calls from Evie and Shelly from a couple of hours ago. They'd dropped off to just Evie demanding a response, likely after Alfred had texted them. She owed her friends some proof of life.

LAIKA

I'm fine, I crashed at Alfred's last night.

EVIE

When will you be home?

She'd get back to her friend when she had an answer. For now, she had to focus on determining how much of a mess Moondrunk Laika had made for Sober Laika to clean up. She crossed her legs and turned her attention back to Alfred. "Okay, I have a couple of questions."

"What would those be?" Alfred's calm demeanor cracked the barest fraction of an inch, revealing his amusement.

"Are you stalking me?" Laika kept her face completely serious, waiting for his answer. She hadn't considered it a concern, but Evie had put it in her brain after the run last night. Waking up at his place hadn't helped her shake it, so she needed to address it. As much fun as Laika was having with this whirlwind of a relationship, she didn't want to get hurt again. Her last relationship had messed her up for years.

He stood silently for a moment as if contemplating his answer. "No. I am not stalking you, but I am courting you for the possibility of a relationship."

"Courting?" Laika echoed with a dry tone, before a snort of laughter ruined her stoic expression. "Are you always this formal?"

"Only when I am being exceptionally serious about a subject."

"Good," Laika tilted her head back and looked at the bland ceiling again. There was fun in teasing someone stuffy, but being able to relax and enjoy themselves was important too. Especially since he was apparently serious in his pursuit, and Laika believed him.

He'd kept his distance by casually leaning against the door frame, allowing her space while she questioned him. It hadn't gone unnoticed by Laika that Alfred was putting extra effort into keeping her comfortable despite the question. He prompted her to continue, "Do you have any other questions?"

"Yes, did we sleep together?" Laika felt like she knew the answer. She was still wearing her filthy outfit on his clean sheets. Now that she was paying attention, she could see that Alfred was wearing the same suit as the night before.

Alfred was again serious, "No. I do not take advantage of drunk girls."

"I wasn't that drunk," protested Laika, but she was pleased by the answer. Given how impulsive she normally was and how much worse she could be moondrunk, mixed with how hot Alfred was, it wasn't like it would've been hard to convince her...

"You were quite drunk," disagreed Alfred. Despite his neutral expression, she knew he was enjoying teasing her.

Laika wasn't sure if this morning would have been less or more embarrassing if she'd just woken up naked in bed with him. Her honor had been maintained as a woman who waited longer than the first date... but only because her date had put her to bed safely. That embarrassment flare started to heat her cheeks again, and she quickly changed the subject as her stomach grumbled, demanding food. "Where can I clean up, and what's for breakfast?"

"There is a small bathroom behind you," Alfred pointed to a plain door on the back wall. She saw a flash of his fangs at the second answer. "However, I have nothing you will eat in the kitchen."

"Really? Not even bread for toast?" Everyone had a loaf or milk in the fridge; they were staples of any single person's life.

"Unless you developed a taste for blood last night, I do not tend to keep food around for the living." He gave a hint of a shrug, reminding her that he didn't need to eat and their dinner dates were mainly for her. Alfred was there for the company.

Laika wasn't upset by that, but she wouldn't be herself if she didn't take the opening to jab at him. "Really? But what if you get a craving for waffles?"

"That seems unlikely because I have never had a waffle before," explained Alfred. Again he seemed to be perfectly honest, but how could that be the truth?

Laika looked shocked as she scrambled up to her feet. "Seriously?"

"Yes?" Alfred pushed himself out of his leaning position, but he stayed at the doorway.

Laika glanced at the bathroom and then down at her clothing, which limited their options from most of the best places. "Okay... do you want to go to Waffle House? I still owe you a meal and breakfast is better than dinner anyways."

"I would like that," he answered. She got a full smile that showed off his teeth for the first time.

Laika immediately got the feeling that this wasn't something that just anyone got to see. Maybe she'd drag this day out so that they did make it to dinner tonight?

CHAPTER 2
HALLOWEEN

Evie
October 31st, 2018
Night Claw Residence, Glenwood, CA

Evie felt great today. Since her run on Friday night, she'd been indulging in a bit of self care. The monstrous hangover she'd woken up with on Saturday had faded pretty quickly after some food. Rejuvenated, she'd felt so much more like herself than she had in weeks.

She'd kept her cool when Laika didn't return all night and day. Her worries about Alfred the suspicious vampire hadn't gone away, but she realized screaming at her packmate wouldn't do any good. To avoid thinking about Laika, Evie took herself out to a nice club and found some fun company for the night. Anything in the name of self care, naturally.

Halloween was one of those holidays where Arik bounced from fancy party to fancy party. It was the perfect time of year to be seen and to rub shoulders with all the big names who could make projects happen. Not the sort of thing you took a no-name junior assistant to.

If Arik didn't have some current Hollywood fling going, he took his head assistant, Tony, or his manager, Natasha, as his plus-one.

And now Evie was enjoying a rare day off. A quiet morning to herself, an indulgent lunch, and some movies on the couch. The recipe for a relaxed werewolf.

Or at least, that was the normal way of things.

> ARIK
>
> Evie, your costume is here. If you arrive by 2:55 we will have just enough time to get to the party at the Barone's
>
> It is the place to be!

> EVIE
>
> What?

> ARIK
>
> Your costume!

Evie tried not to talk to her boss disrespectfully with their new joint project. So she glared at her phone, looking for any answer that wouldn't get her fired.

> EVIE
>
> I don't know what you're talking about.
>
> It's my day off!

> ARIK
>
> You're coming to my parties as my platonic +1!

> EVIE
>
> No... I'm not...

> ARIK
>
> Why not?
>
> All your favorite actors will be there from all those movies you like!

> EVIE
>
> You don't even know what movies I like?!

ARIK

I asked Tony!

Evie frowned and wondered why the elf was putting in this much effort. She already had a costume for tonight, superhero themed of course. Plus, she already had a Halloween tradition of going out with Laika to their favorite bar for spooky themed drinks.

> EVIE
>
> I have plans already tonight.

A picture arrived, clearly meant to entice Evie into joining him. She groaned loudly at the image of a classic Black Widow costume.

> EVIE
>
> Very original.

ARIK

Do you not like this one?

There were other redheads but she seemed to be the most popular.

> EVIE
>
> Black Widow is fine and I like her as a superhero

ARIK

Perfect, be here at 2:55

> EVIE
>
> Nope, it's my night off!

ARIK

But Evie! Think of what this could do for our screenplay!

The truth finally came out.

Evie knew the detailed costume probably cost him a few thousand at least; the rush fee alone would be more than her week of pay. Way too much for just a party. But Arik had been looking for a way to reward her for 'saving him' at Hot off the Presses. He'd been ignoring that it was *his* magic that actually did the saving. Yes, Evie had carried him over the finish line, moved a few cars, and held his hand when he needed the comfort. She'd be dead if Arik hadn't been there when the attack hit. As far as she was concerned they were even, and it was completely against the rules for him to monetarily compensate her anyways.

No doubt this was some weird mix of guilt and Arik's single track mind. Evie took a deep breath before responding.

> EVIE
>
> I already have a costume, I already have plans, and I don't want to be confused as your latest girlfriend.
>
> Have fun tonight, but do it without me.

There was a few minutes of silence before Arik responded.

> ARIK
>
> I understand, keep your phone on at least!
>
> I might have some questions about the screenplay tonight.

> EVIE
>
> Fine

Evie knew that was the best compromise she'd get out of someone so self-centered. But it *was* better than being dragged back to work on her day off. She put her phone on silent for a bit after checking the clock.

The front patio needed to be set up for candy goers and wasn't going to do it itself. Evie went to find their folding chairs and table from the basement. She went down the steps carefully, pausing to cast a wary eye towards the iron door at the bottom. Who knew what Fred, their gruff dwarven landlord, kept in there... The door was creepy enough.

First up were towering stacks of boxes labeled with Laika's handwriting in bright red and green marker. Bypassing them, Evie spied their card table on the back wall and the chairs on another wall. More hands would make fewer trips into the dark room, but she'd put money on Laika coming home in a whirlwind of her own. Hooking her arm around some folding chairs, Evie grabbed the little table and dragged the mess back up the basement stairs. The metal chairs bounced on each step, making noise that would have woken the dead. Thankfully, the racket instead summoned a werewolf.

"Need a hand?" Shelly's face poked through the doorway at the top of the stairs. She looked disheveled with unbrushed hair and an oversized shirt. Maybe she was still in the middle of her costume prep because the woman didn't have a trace of Halloween makeup on yet.

Evie nodded, dragging the chairs up to offer them to her roommate only to remember the time and curse. "Shit, sorry Shelly. I didn't mean to wake you up."

"It's no problem. I took the night off work anyway." Shelly waved quickly, before reaching out to take a chair in each hand. "You guys said we'd be out late?"

"We usually stay out until last call," confirmed Evie.

"And where are we going?"

"Hair of the Dog, a werewolf bar near GPD." Evie made it to the top of the stairs. She was glad to not have multiple trips up and down now.

"Is it a mixed crowd on Halloween?" worried Shelly.

Evie paused to study her roommate. She could feel the anxious waves coming off Shelly right now. "Is that a problem?" She knew enough to know her roommate wasn't the most social person unless there was a computer screen between her and the other person. A rowdy Halloween crowd might be a bit too much.

"No," Shelly quickly added, "I just wanted to know what I'm

dealing with. Fragile humans while drinking or just tons of rowdy werewolves."

"It's mostly the latter, but the crowd is our age on a night like tonight. The young, childless werewolves of Glenwood."

They made their way onto the front patio to begin setting up a place, and Shelly stayed quiet. Together they put four chairs and a table in front of the door. Everything was covered with some black tablecloths. Evie still needed to get the bags of treats out of the kitchen, but they'd be ready for any trick-or-treaters soon.

"Is Tor coming out?" Shelly asked as she smoothed the last piece of black plastic into place.

"She's at work, but we're expecting her anytime now," answered Evie. Again there was a ball of nervous energy coming off her friend. "Can I ask what you're really worried about?"

Shelly sat down in one of the chairs with a heavy sigh.

"You don't have to tell me," offered Evie, sitting next to her.

"I just don't have any experience hanging out with people my own age." Shelly turned beet red, trying to hide her face.

"Yeah… I can tell. Same for humans, vampires, and pretty much people in general?"

Shelly sounded anguished as she admitted, "I was pretty sheltered before coming to California. My dad liked to keep me and the rest of my family on a short leash."

Evie reached out putting a hand on Shelly's shoulder. "That sounds pretty rough. My father was the opposite; he was never around at all and just left everything up to my mother."

"Didn't you hate your mother? I remember you saying something about that during TV a few weeks ago," asked Shelly.

"My mother was the worst and my father just let her be that way. He's been calling me almost every day for weeks now, but I cut them out of my life years ago," explained Evie.

Shelly had a thoughtful look. "Do you want me to erase your contact information from the web? So he can't find your phone number anymore?"

"You can do that!?" Evie again wondered if her roommate was a criminal.

"I can put in the requests for the takedowns. I know where to go since I did the same for my new number when I left home. I didn't want my dad to be able to find me." Shelly shrugged and there was a resigned energy coming from her.

"That's really tempting, but I'll pass for now. Why are you hiding from your family?" Evie knew it was nosy, but this had been bothering her. Just a few weeks into their new living situation she'd grown suspicious there was some family drama afoot.

"I was barely allowed to leave the house as a kid and even when I got older I wasn't allowed off the compound. He believed that his daughter shouldn't associate with anyone he didn't personally approve of." Shelly sat up in her chair finally, "I was a prisoner of my own family."

"What? Did you come from a cult?" teased Evie. Silently she worried she was right.

"You don't know it's a cult when you're born there. And I think it's more like weird werewolf separatists that want their werewolf utopia in the middle of rural America," Shelly continued quietly.

Embarrassment hit Evie in waves almost strong enough to knock her over. "Oh... you win. My family is crazy, but yours sounds certifiable. No wonder you don't know how to interact with anyone in real life. No one socialized you as a kid."

Shelly laughed sadly, "Yeah. So I'm trying to catch up now, and that means weird traditions of dressing up in underwear and animal ears to go drinking."

"You don't have to dress like me and Laika," responded Evie, waving her hands in front of her with a grin.

"Oh thank the moon. I really didn't want to wear that cat costume that Tor brought home for me." Relief was evident on Shelly's face.

"You don't like it?" asked Tor. She'd appeared on the steps of the front porch, the other women too engrossed in their conversation to notice her arrival.

Deep reds colored Shelly's face at being caught talking ungratefully about the costume. "Um... no it's just that..." She trailed off, struggling to find the right words.

Evie came to the rescue, "Tor did you get her underwear and ears or what?" Given how her roommate dressed when she went out for the night the question wasn't an unreasonable one.

"It has full coverage from the wrist to ankle. She told me she didn't want her cleavage out on display, so it's a full body leotard with ears and a tail," explained Tor. She joined them at the table taking one of the seats. As she sat she asked, "Is it like, racist if you dress as another animal when you are a werewolf?"

Laughter broke the tension as both Evie and Shelly started cracking up. Once she caught her breath, Shelly finally admitted, "No, that's not the problem. It's just kinda skin tight... and I can't go out in public like that."

"Tor," scolded Evie breathlessly, "Why would you get something like that for Shelly?"

"She asked for something that didn't leave her uncovered, it's all I had in my closet that didn't show off skin," shrugged Tor. But as the werewolves stared at her, the human woman's face dawned in realization. "Oh... You don't want to show off your body at all..."

Shelly nodded, "I'm sorry, I didn't want to be ungrateful for your help."

Tor waved it off, taking no offense, "Do you want me to drive you to Walmart and we can pick up a shapeless bag in some theme? Or I can do you some zombie makeup and you can wear your ripped jeans?"

Evie watched her new roommates discuss options and she felt relief at how quickly the problem had been settled. All four of them were so different, but they'd struck a harmony in the house. The energy in the house had shifted from a dynamic duo to a loving family which reminded her of visiting the Lowell's house. Evie hated to break the moment, but she had to bring up a sour topic. "Hey, can we talk about Friday?"

"You mean when you shifted in the living room?" asked Tor. She hadn't been there for the dire events of that night, but she'd been told what happened when everyone got home. Off to the side, Shelly visibly flinched at Evie's words because that had been roughest on her.

"Yes," confessed Evie, "I wanted to apologize for causing so much drama." The living room had been in a disarray when she'd been dragged to the car that night. By the time the werewolves got home, Tor had put everything back in place and had snacks.

Tor shrugged, "No harm done."

"I'm just glad you're okay," agreed Shelly, "I've never seen someone half shifted. It looked so painful." The uncomfortable reaction suddenly made sense to Evie. Her new friend wasn't upset it had happened; she was just grossed out. Which was extremely reasonable.

"Uh..." Evie had prepared a whole speech about how she'd try harder to not let that happen again. How she was so sorry for putting them in danger and was ready to put her pride to the side and deal with their anger. The quick forgiveness threw Evie off. "So you're not planning to move out?"

"Do you think you're the only person I know who's pushed a run too long?" asked Shelly, for once the person with more experience. She placed a hand on Evie's arm reassuringly, "No, I'm not moving out, but I *am* going to join Laika in forcing you to go out once a month."

Tor gave her a smirk. "Thanks for the apology, but I wasn't even there so not much point in being mad. Besides. I paid in advance, you aren't getting rid of me. I used to have to deal with Jones getting blood all over the sheets. Do you know how annoying it is to get blood out of silk?" The women laughed together as Tor poked at her ex-boyfriend again. Evie had realized that the vampire and the human had a much longer-term relationship than Tor claimed with each of these stories.

With that, all concerns were settled and neither party was mad at Evie. Damn, she'd gotten so lucky finding these two as roommates.

- ☾ -

Laika
October 31st, 2018
Night Claw Residence, Glenwood, CA

L aika dashed through the door at top speed after getting out of work late. A bunch of the college guys hadn't shown up today, causing the warehouse to be understaffed. She'd had too much extra work making up for them ditching. At least their next shift Boss would chew them out, while she'd get a day off. There was no way Laika would make it home in time on foot, so she'd sprung for an Uber despite how expensive it was. The driver made good time, but the sun was already dangerously low on the horizon.

"Hi Evie, hi Shelly, hi Tor!" Laika said in a rush as she sped through the living room.

"Hi Laika?" Shelly's voice answered in a daze. "Is something on fire?"

Evie scoffed before Laika could answer. "No, she's just late, late for a very important date." There was a pause as Evie raised her voice to make sure Laika could hear, "Not too late to switch it up to an Alice in Wonderland theme. Instead of that tired old thing."

From where Laika stood in the bedroom, pulling clothes from the closet, she shouted back. "It's not tired! It's classic! And hilarious!"

Cursing under her breath, Laika wondered why she didn't set this out last night. Instead. here she was digging through piles of clothing, expecting a knock on the door any moment... "Evie! Help!" Laika cried. A sigh came from the living room, followed by footsteps down the hall. A moment later, nails tapped rhythmically on the door frame as Evie entered.

"Why are you ransacking our closet?"

Laika turned sheepishly towards her packmate. "Have you seen my costume? I can't find it anywhere."

"Oh really?" Evie tipped her head to the side, mischief on her face. She was already dressed up in a clingy red corset trimmed with a giant golden 'W'. Smoothing her star-spangled blue skirt, she continued, "That's because I hung it up in the bathroom after I ironed it. You're welcome."

Laika was on her feet in a flash, throwing her arms around her packmate. "Evie! You're the best!"

The hug only lasted a minute before Laika's feet carried her to the master bathroom. Sure enough, hanging there was the bright red costume she'd been looking for. Her hands seized it and set to getting ready. "What were Shelly and Tor wearing?"

"Tor is a princess I think. Shelly's a lady knight," Evie answered. She waited at the door frame.

"That's a princess?" Laika questioned. When she'd seen the tight black costume, it had looked more like something for bedroom time than for going out.

"It has a tiara, it's a princess," defended Evie. Tor was going to be popular at Hair of the Dog tonight. "Okay, so no one is moving out. I'm going to get us set up to hand out candy. You get us drinks and chips once you're ready?"

Laika agreed before pulling open her makeup bag. There wasn't much time left as her phone gave the 5 minutes until sunset warning with a ring. She needed to put up her hair as well. Distracted as Laika was, she'd barely registered the comment about people moving out. Before Laika could press on the subject, Evie moved to the bathroom door and hit her with another bombshell.

"There's one more thing." Evie dropped her voice so it wouldn't carry, "I got from Shelly that she's hiding from her family."

"What?" Laika almost smeared bright red lipstick up her cheek.

"Yeah, they sound like some werewolf supremacists from the south. I think she escaped and got as far away as she could."

"Are we expecting them to show up at the door?"

"No," assured Evie sincerely. "I don't think they know where she is. But if any werewolves show up looking for Shelly, then we should just say we don't know her."

Their silver and amber eyes met in the reflection of the mirror. Their new roommate wasn't one of their pack and she had made it clear she never wanted to be one. But that didn't matter. Laika agreed, "Yeah. Never heard of her." Then Evie left her alone to put the rest of her makeup on. Laika was fast, but not fast enough. She was still pulling her stockings up when she heard the doorbell ring. Her phone confirmed her fears. It was past sunset.

"Coming!" she called, more for her roommates than anything. Then again, perhaps the caller would be able to hear her. Her suspicions were starting to form that Alfred was a lotus vampire based on his hearing. Not that she'd asked.

Precariously balanced, Laika shoved her foot into her shoe and rushed pulling her stocking the rest of the way. There was the tell-tale sound of ripping, and she cursed. Her neat stockings now had rips from her hasty movements, but there was no time to do this over. Maybe he'd think it was part of the effect?

With a flourish of red fabric, Laika took off down the hall. She could hear voices at the door and worried it was Evie picking a fight... She rounded the corner, thrilled to be wrong as Shelly stood at the door, chatting calmly with Alfred.

"Why would you think that women never wore armor in the past?" Alfred asked as he studied her costume.

"Because there's no pictures of it?" shrugged Shelly.

"I suppose noble women did not, and they are the most likely to be painted or drawn," his attention was drawn to Laika as she appeared. Alfred's blue eyes took in every inch of Laika, and he seemed to approve. "Hello."

"Hey!" Laika exclaimed, excited he'd actually shown up to hand out candy. She'd doubted he'd been serious about this pale imitation of a makeup date. All four roommates and her boyfriend going to a bar wasn't exactly romantic.

Shelly gave Laika a confused look. "What the hell are you supposed to be?"

"What do you mean?" Laika teased, twirling to show off her red cape. In proper Halloween fashion the short skirt of her costume also flared up, revealing her long legs. She'd put effort into looking good today in hopes they'd get some one on one time back at Alfred's apartment... If she wanted time to just talk or more, Laika hadn't decided yet.

"I mean, why are you dressed like a hooker about to visit her grandmother?" Shelly retorted.

"You look hot," Tor added from where she sat on the patio. She gave Laika a playful wink.

Laika looked down at her short dress and red cape. Everything was a few years old, but still in good repair. Except for the ripped tights she'd had to replace every year when they inevitably got destroyed at the bar, of course.

"Červená Karkulka," explained Alfred, still leaning in the doorway.

"What?" All three women asked.

"The red riding hood," he clarified, and Laika could see how amused he was at the outfit.

Laika studied Alfred to figure out what he'd dressed up as. Again he was wearing his heavy daylight coat, but it was open showing off he had on another suit. Actually, he looked the same as the last time they'd met up. A small frown tugged at her lips.

"What is the matter?" Alfred inquired.

"You're not wearing a costume!" Laika complained, throwing her arms up dramatically.

"Ah." He didn't appear apologetic. "One moment." Alfred reached into a pocket, pulling out a small white half mask. The effect was simple, but as soon as he put it on, his suit and coat added to the Phantom of the Opera feel.

Laika studied the costume with intense scrutiny, letting silence reign for a beat. Finally, she snorted with laughter. "This feels like cheating! It's the one time of year you can dress up as anything. Do you not like dressing up?"

"I have no issues with dressing up," answered Alfred. He adjusted the mask carefully, unphased by the question. "But I do not follow the modern traditions. As lovely as you look, I do not believe I could pull off an outfit like that."

"I guess not." Laika could barely respond between bouts of laughter.

Evie came storming up the basement stairs with a fifth chair in hand. She ignored the happy mood with piercing questions. "So I take it you're coming out to the bar with us too? Or did you just show up for candy duty?"

"I invited him to go with us," Laika quickly defended. She could already feel her annoyance growing again. They'd had a really good week with no fighting, and five minutes in it was falling apart. This wasn't even the first time one of them brought a date to the bar on Halloween.

"I just thought we were having a girl's night," Evie admitted.

Before any tension could grow, Alfred offered, "I can leave if there is an issue."

Laika wanted to say no, but she stopped long enough to check on how her friends were reacting. They hadn't actually discussed it being girls only. Her attention settled on Evie because half of their Halloween tradition was the redhead not coming home for the night.

"What? Of course you're coming with us," Shelly answered for the group. "I'm selfishly excited 'cause if you're sitting at our table, most of the creepers will stay the hell away."

"I believe I can function fairly well as a shield and designated driver for the night," agreed Alfred. All eyes fell on Tor and her fishnet covered legs which rested up on the edge of the table. Any defense against the masses of drunken men tonight would be welcomed.

Laika's eyes stayed on Evie, who didn't look happy at the news. But before her packmate could voice any more dissent, Laika stole the extra chair. "That settles it then!"

"Yeah, fine," Evie agreed sullenly.

"Do you want to help me finish setting up?" Laika asked Alfred as she approached him in the doorway. The vampire nodded as he moved to let her pass.

"I guess I'll go get us snacks," mumbled Evie, heading for the kitchen.

Tor got up to follow, "I'll help."

Laika let them go, ignoring whatever tantrum her friend was having now. Maybe Tor could help calm it down. Once they were outside, Laika set up a fifth chair around the table. She fussed with the spacing to make sure everyone had some leg room and they could see any kids approaching.

"I do like your costume," Alfred quietly added as he took his seat. He'd chosen one on the end, closest to the wall. "The absurdity was not lost on me."

"Oh really?" Laika took the chair next to his and leaned her elbow on the candy table.

"You are both Red and the Wolf." Alfred chuckled at their shared joke.

"Yes! Thank you for understanding!" That spark shot through Laika again as he kept up with her sense of humor. "Your costume is still cheating. I'm pretty sure you've worn that suit to one of our many attempts at a date so far."

"Not this one. You did say we would be going out to a bar. I did dress down a tad for that endeavor."

She watched Alfred pull off his daylight coat to hang on the back of the folding chair. Then his gloves and leather leg guards were removed. There were so many more steps for his gear compared to her just tossing on a vest. Laika found herself asking,

"Do you always wear a suit everywhere? Even to, like, the grocery store?"

"I rarely have a need to buy groceries and I would just keep my coat over my outfit for the day. But to answer your actual question, yes. I do wear suits all of the time."

She blinked at the mostly straightforward answer. No other moonlighter Laika could think of wore a suit to work. The closest would be Aaron and Owen with their police uniforms. Curiously she asked, "Why?"

"I find them comfortable and usually appropriate for any situation."

"Dress clothing is not comfortable," Laika rejected while shaking her head.

Alfred disagreed. "If you have cheap dress clothing, then yes. It can be dreadful unless you have something tailored to you and your movements."

Laika laughed. By now trick or treaters were starting to fill the streets with their parents. A steady stream ran up the path with eager hands and rushed thanks before heading to the next house. Shelly sat down and was happy to take charge of the actual candy bowl to heap a large handful on any kids that approached. Eventually, Tor and Evie rejoined them at the table as well. Drinks and snacks were dumped before Evie picked up her phone to text. For the most part she ignored them unless a question was asked directly to her.

Annoyance grew in Laika, but she tried not to act on it. She was enjoying conversation with the others. But she'd really like Evie involved as well, not a repeat of their Longtooth dinner.

Thankfully, a phone rang cutting off any argument from brewing. Alfred pulled his cellphone from a jacket pocket checking the screen. "Excuse me," he apologized, "I need to answer this."

Before Laika could even ask if everything was alright, her own phone started ringing with the MOONS number on caller ID. That was strange, since the dispatcher usually called Evie's phone first. "Aren't we off for the night?"

"I put us on the no job list," Evie agreed. Then her phone began ringing, still in her hand.

That made three calls in the span of a minute. Laika looked between the vampire already on a call and her friend answering MOONS. Her own phone had cut off once Evie answered. What the hell was going on?

INTERLUDE - BUBBLING

The Anarchist
October 31st, 2018
..somewhere in Glenwood, CA

T oday was the last ritual in the summoning. The Anarchist sat on the edge of the circle, carefully braiding her hair so it would stay out of the way. Excitement surged through her veins, creating shaky fingers.

"Are you ready yet?" The voice was starting to sound impatient.

"Almost," the Anarchist dismissed them. She had gotten used to the voice as more like background noise than a real person to talk to. She wanted to look her best at the end of this ritual. So she took her time fixing her hair and checking her features in the mirror. The circle was already complete, the components in place, the epicenter picked, and no one was any closer to finding her.

Even her Love hadn't really found the trail yet, as much as they tried.

All of the Anarchist's preparations were going to finally pay off! As long as she managed to cast flawlessly tonight, all the blood on her hands would be worth the victory. Soon she'd be able to tell her Love about all the sacrifices she'd made for them...

"Hurry," whined the voice. "I want to be free."

Again the Anarchist ignored them; she'd be happy to get them out of her head. She had a different vessel in mind. Her thoughts drifted back to her Love. Fate had brought them together many times over the last few months, after she'd spent so much time watching from afar. Granted, the destined meetings had ended in lackluster ways due to others' interference...

Both mystical and love life plans kept being upended right at the precipice of greatness. The Anarchist had barely reached the minimums with the last two rituals. But she *had* reached them. She was leaving nothing to chance this time. Tonight she'd succeed far beyond anyone's expectations and prove her father was wrong.

There would be no one to cut her ritual short this time, either. All the moonlighters would be distracted with the holiday, off at frivolous parties, or policing the frivolous people at those parties.

And her Love would be nowhere near the effects either this time. Last time she'd let her mind wander too much before casting. The Anarchist had meditated on her carefully selected target for at least an hour beforehand. Given the distance between the location and her Love's home, there was no way her Love would be a first responder again.

"Now?" pressed the voice in her head.

"Now," agreed the Anarchist. She began to clear her mind and focus on the task at hand.

Magic sparked from her fingertips, begging to join the circle. It came so quickly now, as it belonged with her. Soon it would be jumping from rune to rune, powering her spell. After tonight, all of this power would be hers as long as she got this right.

A coppery smell began to taint the air surrounding her as the spell flickered to life. Everything was going to be perfect. Blood would flow...

CHAPTER 3
BOILING

Laika
October 31st, 2018
Cold Blooded, Glenwood, CA

L aika tried to push the gnawing feeling in the pit of her stomach aside. She'd been counting the hours until midnight since opening her eyes this morning. Nothing had happened all day. So right before their phones rang, she'd almost forgotten that 364 hours ago, Hazel Amadori had predicted there would be another attack in Glenwood. No matter how crazy the senior moonlighter had sounded that night in the interrogation room, Laika hadn't been able to let go of that oddly specific number which worked out to be October 31st.

When Evie and Alfred's phones went off in rapid succession, Laika gripped the edge of the table. She couldn't listen to both calls, so she settled for Evie. Focused on her eavesdropping, she'd been distracted when Alfred apologized and grabbed his coat. Laika should have been disappointed that another one of their date attempts had fizzled out. But she pushed it to the side long enough to change out of her costume and hurry into the car.

An unknown voice on the phone had told them to report to work. She hadn't been the stoic Julie that Laika knew, but another woman who sounded more frantic. There were no details on the job, just that there was an emergency and all active moonlighters were needed. Night Claw had been given a location to report to and nothing further.

But when the Saab pulled around the corner to their destination, Laika saw two Glenwood Police Department Cruisers pulled up in front of a storefront and her stomach twisted even more tightly.

A small group of people crowded around the front of one of the cars. From this distance, Laika recognized Aaron Leavonsworth and Owen Kirkland, who worked as the MOONS' liaisons. But it was the last group member that had Laika feeling ill.

"Shit... Do you think this is another Anarchist attack?" Evie hissed as she threw the Saab into a parking space.

Laika stared at a long black daylight coat wrapped around a woman with blond hair. If Hazel was here, then another attack was all but confirmed. The vampire had saved both Evie and Laika during previous attacks. Hazel had thrown around some big magic to save Laika from falling to her death at Sync Holes Amusement Park. And arguably, Evie would have been crushed to death by the air pressure that ravaged downtown Glenwood. She'd probably been responsible for saving people when the cell phone towers started rusting people as well. Hazel was on loan from LA MOONS and was one of the most powerful and complicated people Laika had ever met. After their last interaction, she scared the werewolf.

Finally, Laika opened the car door and answered, "Yes." Despite how much she wanted to be on the big cases, now Laika wished she was elsewhere. So she forced her attention solely onto the officers, prepared to ignore the vampire.

If it was all moonlighters on deck, then why weren't they here? There were at least a half dozen packs above Night Claw in the ranks who would get called to the center of the action before them. Why weren't the liaisons with those packs on this busy night?

"Ever the fast bunnies," Hazel greeted them first. Evie responded politely with a wave as they reached the group. But Laika kept up her armor of indifference.

Owen saved them from any more awkward silence. "You got here fast. Did you see Blood Fang's car on the way?"

"No," Evie answered with a shrug. Neither of the members of Night Claw was excited to hear that both packs had been called to the same spot. What the hell was going on tonight? This didn't feel like the center of an attack on a level with the others. Everything seemed calm, but there was tension surrounding the group that even Laika could feel without any magic.

Standing next to the GPD cruiser, Laika surveyed the scene around them, letting the conversation fade into the background and looking for the source of the call. In the flashing blue and red lights, she could see an open doorway across the street. The door was hanging open and a light emanated from inside, but it came from the floor and upwards. Then Laika realized the door led to stairs that likely went to a basement. But other than the faint hum of lights... there was no sound coming from across the street. No talking, no music, not a single sound to indicate life.

Laika attempted to strain her ears more, searching for anything, but all she caught were the soft sobs coming from nearby. Sitting on the curb behind the GPD cruisers were two girls in their early twenties at best. Barely able to drink by Laika's guess, and they were dressed in the usual Halloween fare: a pair of sexy nurses covered in fake blood, ready for a late night. Then again... Laika glanced back at the open doorway and found bloody handprints on the door. That might not be fake, but neither looked injured as they cried quietly to the officer talking to them. Someone else's blood? What the hell had happened here?

"Such a waste, isn't it?" Hazel chimed in, her gaze following Laika's to the bloodstained pair.

Laika couldn't help herself, no matter how much Hazel had creeped her out. "What's a waste?"

"The blood splatter. Everyone knows you don't go directly for a vein; it's just a waste."

"Oh…" Laika's fragile stomach twisted again. She'd forgotten that to Hazel, a scene like this would be the same as someone throwing a carton of milk over the girls. "It's not their blood, is it?"

"No, bunny, it's not their blood," agreed Hazel. Apparently Laika's nickname was back to 'bunny'. Once more, the vampire seemed the picture of competence at the crime scene. Not the raving lunatic who'd scared Laika back in the interrogation room. "I suspect it belongs to their dates for the night. Perhaps I should check."

Again Laika couldn't stop her morbid curiosity, "How?"

"With a bit of taste, I'm sure one would oblige me. If the blood sings, I'll know what the caster wants," explained Hazel.

"The caster wanted blood? Can you find them with that?" As much as the idea of Hazel licking blood off of two terrified victims grossed out Laika, if they could find the caster, then it might be worth trying.

Hazel burst out into laughter. "Oh no, my silly bunny. Our golden lion already savagely descended on the ritual with shining claws. She shredded it beyond my ability to trace the source now." There was a note of wistfulness to her words.

"Shredded… the ritual?"

Owen clarified, "Melinda already shut down the ritual." He was still scratching away on his clipboard as he continued, "This is the edge of the affected area. She was the closest to the scene and called in the attack herself. Before we even managed to call anyone else, Melinda said she broke it."

"All the claws and no consideration," griped Hazel. This news at least explained why no one was panicking: the attack was already over.

"Then why are we here?" Evie's confusion was evident.

Hazel answered for the officer, "To clean up the bloody mess. If you'll excuse me, I need to go on the hunt again."

"For the caster?" asked Laika hopefully. Even if the ritual was broken, maybe there was still a way to track them.

"No, we have bigger problems now than a two-bit magician with borrowed power," Hazel sighed as she gave them a dramatic bow.

This time it was Owen's turn to press, "What does that mean?" But they got no answer, just a wave while Hazel stalked to her car. He tried again, clearly torn between chasing her down and letting her go, "What does that MEAN?"

"It means you've got a pest problem," Hazel called back, "Don't forget, bunnies, don't let your eyes wander, or heads will roll!" With that, the vampire moonlighter was gone.

Owen lowered his voice and whispered to Laika, "Is it racist if I call her batshit crazy?"

"Does she turn into a bat?" Laika shrugged.

"Do you think she'd even answer the question if I asked?" countered Owen, then his eyes went past Laika. "Finally."

She followed his gaze to Blood Fang's horrible soccer mom minivan parking behind the Saab, and it took all of Laika's restraint not to groan as all the doors flew open. Five figures piled out, every one of them wearing a moonlighting vest. This night was shaping up into an absolute living nightmare if she was going to have to deal with all of these meatheads.

Working with Daniel and Joey wasn't bad, the former being as silent as the mountains he rivaled in size and the latter being a harmless ditz. But the other three members of Night Claw's main competition were a different story.

Ace Deerling was the leader of Blood Fang and, as far as Laika was concerned, had the biggest stick up his self-righteous ass. He played at being the knight in shining armor stereotype, but he'd been nothing but an asshole to Night Claw since their first jobs together. She'd gained a begrudging respect for Randall after their joint research sessions with the Moonscent girls. But Thad would sour that goodwill the moment he opened his mouth to throw out some misogynist barb at them.

She was prepared for the blonde man to start spitting vitriol any minute, but in theme with tonight, Thad was uncharacteristically silent with his lips pressed in a thin line. All of the other werewolves looked grim... Did they know something her pack didn't?

There was no time to ask as Owen began to bark orders, herding the werewolves into a tight group around the hood of the GPD cruiser. The Night Claw pack was bunched shoulder to shoulder with their most hated rivals, Blood Fang. Ace had strategically placed Daniel and Joey between Night Claw and the rest of his pack. All five members being at a single job didn't happen often, and never to work with Laika and Evie.

Her attention was pulled back to their MOONS liaisons starting the brief. Normally Owen would have made a sarcastic quip or been scolding them all just to get along. Instead, he looked dour. His eyes went between the stairs and his partner. Aaron's brows were furrowed, and he looked more unsettled than Laika could ever remember seeing him.

"There has been another magical attack, centered on a vampire club in west Glenwood." Aaron's tone was grave.

"Twisted Cross?" Laika interrupted, panic and relief flashing through her at the thought. They'd left Tor safely back at the house with Shelly, but Tor had talked about the huge party the bar was planning for Halloween.

"No, this place is more underground than that. But the distur-bance sent most of the vampires on the scene into a blood frenzy," continued Aaron, watching them for any signs they didn't understand.

Every single werewolf knew precisely what that meant.

Werewolves could frenzy when they were in danger or had gone too long without a run. But their blood-drinking, supernatural cousins only lost control like that when they were hungry. Both types of frenzies were destructive, but a vampire's would be focused on only one thing... Anyone in that club with a pulse would be lucky to make it through the night.

Laika's eyes were drawn back to the crying girls with a dawning realization. They'd been at a party with a vampire who went into a frenzy. She knew now what was waiting downstairs. Aaron laid out the details. "Senior moonlighters have been sent to the epicenter of the attack. The Dark Wind and Swift Shadow packs have established a perimeter of the most affected areas. Melinda is still on the scene for triage, and Klímek is working on threat containment. We have that part handled, but some vampires escaped before MOONS got on the scene."

"Why aren't you there with them?" Evie asked. It was a good question. These two were the most experienced liaisons on the force. Well, the only liaisons really.

"Because senior moonlighters don't need us to coordinate with the rest of the police force. Detective Gibson is pinch-hitting as their point of contact. We're responsible for your packs and the clean-up," Owen answered quickly, barely looking up from the clipboard he was hastily writing on.

That was a surprise. Detective Gibson was notoriously antagonistic to both the liaisons and the entire concept of MOONS. Why would he help when he hated moonlighters, and especially werewolves, so much?

There was a look of dismay from Ace. "Respectfully, I don't believe we need two liaisons if resources are stretched this thin."

"You're correct," Aaron interjected. "We are splitting your packs into two teams, and one of us will be going with each team. Our job is to track and contain anyone who has broken the perimeter."

"We are pre-authorizing hybrid forms. Don't worry about the paperwork right now; I'll ensure everything is filled out after we have this under control." Owen set his pen down, shuffling a monstrous stack of papers back together. Seven werewolves worth of paperwork was on that clipboard, but for once he wasn't badgering them all to get it in order.

Laika fought to keep her expression neutral. Just back in August, she could count on one hand the number of times that they'd been sent to a combat situation that would require hybrid forms. The total had doubled in two months. Hybrid forms were a combination of human and wolf traits; when Laika shifted, she gained a head of height and doubled her size in fur-covered muscle. Unlike her pure wolf form, hybrids stood on two feet with massive clawed hands. Mixed with a muzzle full of fangs, hybrid werewolves became a lethal weapon that required extra sign-off.

"Ace, you're going with me," Aaron continued, "Joey and Thad will be with us as well. We'll be taking on the first target, which is in the building behind us."

"I'll be taking Daniel, Randall, Laika and Evie. We've got a report of an erratic vampire from three blocks over who is contained in a restaurant freezer," Owen looked grim as he scanned the group.

They'd broken the packs into two teams based on power needs: muscle, speed, and tracking for each team, with Evie being the odd one out. An empath wasn't very useful for tracking or reading in a fight like this. And based on who they were sending with Night Claw, they'd done their best to minimize any disputes. Laika should probably applaud how thorough they'd been.

Behind them, one of the girls had broken their silence to start screaming. "It's not a vampire! It's a monster! A monster!"

A chill ran down Laika's spine. She still hadn't heard a single thing from the building. Looking towards Evie, her unspoken question was met with a tiny shake of her head. Evie's empathy must not be picking up signs of life either. The woman then spoke up, "Hey... How long ago did they get out?"

All eyes turned to Evie, wary and worried.

Owen answered, "About thirty minutes ago now. Hazel confirmed no one is alive downstairs."

"It killed everyone!" shrieked the partygoer between heavy sobs, "Even the other vampires!"

"Other vampires?" Aaron looked startled by that. He quickly broke from the group to gently ask the girls a few more questions.

"I wasn't aware this place was a vampire bar... that might change things," Owen explained as he took a step back to call into the station on his radio. Laika heard him asking for clarification on the address and name of the building.

Thad spoke up. "Most vampires don't feed on other vampires even when frenzied. That doesn't make sense unless we're dealing with the Iris Court."

"Excuse me; they're cannibals?" Laika exclaimed.

"Kinda," answered Thad, "But frenzied, an iris would prioritize living blood over vampires."

An unease fell over the group.

"I... I don't hear anything downstairs. I was listening in case something came up the stairs but... It's still absolutely silent," Laika added, feeling sick. Any other day she'd be excited at a mission this unusual, but this night just kept taking turns for the worst. What was next?

Owen rejoined the conversation. "I thought Glenwood didn't have an iris population?"

"It's Halloween. They're probably in from one of the surrounding states for the big LA parties." Aaron clearly wasn't happy about his statement as he returned as well. Whatever the crying girls had told him, he was noting it down. Finally, the officer ordered, "Small change of plans, both teams handle this one together. Ace is the field leader, and I'm calling into the perimeter for backup."

"We can handle one vampire," Ace disagreed, "Get the second team moving and leave this to me, Thad, and Joey."

Thad quickly shook his head, "No. If that's an iris downstairs, then we want all the help we can get."

At the rebuke from his packmate, Ace backpedaled with an uncertain tone, "If you say we need both, then." He took the change of plans in stride by turning to the building and advanced slowly, edging closer to the passage before shaking his head. "This is too narrow... Hybrid forms won't fit down these stairs."

"I might be able to," Laika offered and moved up to look. She read the name on the blood-stained door, 'Cold Blooded.'

He'd been right; this place wasn't built for seven-foot-tall were-wolves. The passage wouldn't even let people walk two at a time. Her focus swept back to the survivors as the unnamed officer loaded them into his cruiser. No wonder so few people had made it out.

Ace frowned as he calculated how to proceed. "I need Evie to stay human until we're down there. Your powers might be able to pinpoint the target before we see them and it'll be easier for you to tell us if you can talk."

"Okay, that's fair," agreed Evie.

"Joey, Laika. Owen said there is a receiving door in the back alley. You two circle around and check if it's still locked up." Ace looked more to Laika than his packmate when giving the order. Laika didn't feel the usual bristle of annoyance when he started commanding her pack around. This situation was beyond their petty rivalries. Apparently, Evie felt the same, as her packmate nodded quickly.

Ace continued to bark orders. "I will take point down the stairs; Daniel, you stay behind me to cover the door. Thad, Evie, use your powers to identify and communicate any threats. Randall, cover them."

Everyone acknowledged by falling into place quickly. Laika shifted into her hybrid form after stripping out of her sweats and shirt; her clothing went back into the Saab for later. Now she crept along the edge of the building above Cold Blooded with Joey on her heels. They were the fastest and quietest on their feet, even against supernatural hearing.

She didn't love Ace's plan, but she wouldn't be the cause of the pack's inability to work together tonight. So, Laika had agreed. No matter how bad their rivalry was, Blood Fang wouldn't let anything happen to Evie while they were split up.

There was a stench in the air that Laika couldn't place with her terrible sense of smell. It was foul, like rotting food and spoiled milk. There would be dumpsters at the back of the building that were likely the culprits. But the rancid smell would make it impossible for Laika to pinpoint anything. The building remained unsettlingly quiet as she took the final corner to the back.

The alley looked unremarkable. Plain grey concrete walls and faded asphalt greeted the pair of wolves. It looked identical to the receiving dock at the warehouse. The ground sloped downwards into a ramp, which made sense for an underground club. The decline would allow trucks to back in and be on level with the kitchen or backroom. At the bottom a faint glow emanated out from a few windows atop a closed stainless steel roll-up door. She could also see a secondary door just big enough for a person to fit through. Maybe where packages were delivered? There was a sliver of light from a small window in the center but no handle adorned the outside. They wouldn't be opening that door easily from out here...

Laika pointed to the roll-up as their entry. Given the height of the hybrid wolves, fitting through anything human-sized would be a hassle anyways. Thankfully, Joey understood the plan and the pair quietly slipped down the slope on light paws. Something was wrong here, besides the lack of sound and nauseous smell coming from the nearby dumpsters. She spied dark paint covering the windows, blocking some of the light from inside. Had they painted over the windows to keep the sunlight out? While Joey worked on getting a grip on the door, Laika stood up on the tips of her toes to get a better view. She realized that the windows weren't covered in paint... the dark red-brown stains were blood. There was blood on the inside of the windows. But they had to be 8 feet off the ground? How did it splatter up that high?

A hand landed on Laika's arm, causing her to spin violently, but it was only Joey. He'd been unable to open the door on his own. Forcing her fear back under control Laika regained her composure, she nodded and took up a space next to him. Humans could lift a roll-up, so a single werewolf shouldn't have a problem even if it was locked. However, the metal didn't budge when Laika turned her muscles to the problem. This wasn't an issue of strength... something had blocked the tracks, making it impossible to move.

Well shit, how were they going to get inside now?

Joey and Laika continued to strain for another minute before she felt something cold and wet seep between her toes. Looking down, Laika realized they'd bent the bottom of the door only to release a river from inside. With the light from the gap, she could see the same dark red color and her breath caught... she was standing in a pool of blood.

Like a startled animal, Laika leapt a full foot in the air and backward, causing even more blood to splatter up. In her panic she'd forgotten Joey, but the other wolf landed at her side. He had a disgusted grimace on his face, an expression they shared as the pool of blood continued to spread before them... nope.

Laika turned her attention to the other door, resigned that bending through that would be better than this.

As she'd observed before, there was no handle on the outside of the secondary door. Someone had to open it from the inside for entry. However, there was a narrow window down the center with a wire mesh between the glass panes to secure it against exactly what the werewolf was planning. Usually the cracking of glass and the amount of time it would take to get through the wire was enough of a deterrent for criminals. But when you had claws as sharp as Laika and permission to break and enter, she didn't hesitate to put her fist through the fragile window. Shards tore at her skin even through her fur; the little cuts would fade away in minutes as her werewolf powers included enhanced healing. She tore the mesh layer apart as though it had been no more than wet paper. The second pane of glass fared as well as the first against Laika's strength. Hopefully, Owen wouldn't ask her about the back door when he cataloged the damage.

Joey nudged her shoulder in celebration of a successful plan. She doubted he'd rat her out to Owen for the minor destruction of property.

Laika was thankful for her extra long hybrid arms as she reached inside. There was a chain at the top, which she spent only 30 seconds trying to slide free before ripping it off the door in annoyance. Claws weren't great for fine dexterity, but they worked well on turning the thick latch of the deadbolt. She congratulated herself as she found the inside handle, but as her palm settled down... Laika didn't find cold metal. Instead, she was met with something cool and lumpy. What the hell?

Carefully Laika tried to feel out what she was touching and realized there were knuckles and fingers... Again Laika sprang backward at lightning speeds, not caring if glass or wire ripped open her arm. There had been a *hand* on that door handle...

The force of Laika's action had been enough for the door to creak open. It silently swung outwards, revealing everything she'd been fearful of. There was a hand and an arm down to the elbow hanging off of the door... but the rest of the person was missing.

What the hell had happened here?

CHAPTER 4
BLOOD

Evie
October 31st, 2018
Cold Blooded, Glenwood, CA

E vie was walking between Daniel and Thad, trying to focus on any emotions ahead of them and not the long streaks of blood on the walls. The large man in front already had to hunch his shoulders to move, so she couldn't see anything past him.

"Their weaknesses are pretty straightforward, but we'd be better off with a witch in the group," explained Thad. He was mostly talking to Randall at the back.

Uncharacteristically, Evie tried to engage him in the conversation. "What do we need?"

"The big two weaknesses are weapons made of ironwood and dead man's blood." This was perhaps the most agreeable conversation Thad had ever had with Night Claw.

"That might as well have been in Greek," Randall groaned. "The idiot version?"

Giving his friend the stink eye, Thad explained in more detail.

"There are a ton of types of wood that are ironwood. But most are pretty toxic to work with, so no one has a sword of it laying around. You could probably find one at a well supplied witch shop."

"And the second one?" But Evie didn't hear the answer as her breath caught when Daniel cleared the bottom step, letting her see the entrance.

The frame was fully wooden and carved to look like an arch of flowers. They looked like hundreds of roses, with a small plaque declaring this place "Cold Blooded" in fancy script.

"So this is a rose bar then," Thad announced as though it was the most obvious knowledge in the world. But given the flashy archway, even Evie begrudgingly agreed.

The scent of blood wafted over Daniel's shoulders, making Evie's skin crawl. How many bodies were likely just laying around? She could see Ace pause for a moment before disappearing into the dim room. Daniel cleared the doorway and stopped a few steps into the room. He held up a hand as he checked the immediate area. When no shadows jumped out, he let the other three in.

Evie swept around, taking in the state of the bar. Earlier tonight, this had been a cozy place. This far underground the lack of windows was a little less creepy. Evie thought it would be a nice place to spend a few hours. Unlike Twisted Cross, the lighting was a warm, incandescent yellow, and bright enough to allow you to see each other. No strobe- or blacklights to light the dance floor.

Across the room was a heavy wooden bar along the corner of the far wall, with mangled stools lining the outside. A stage and a dance floor dominated the center of the room, littered with smashed tables and chairs.

Blood splattered the broken furniture and there were dried drag marks across the ground. But not a single soul living, dead or undead, was in this bar. Something had moved them all out of the main area. This looked like the set of an 1920's gangster hideout in a horror movie. Beyond creepy...

Evie took another step forward getting closer to her 'bodyguard' while being careful of the debris. The door to the women's bathroom was blocked by a cracked table to her right. No emotions radiated from behind there, but she was struggling to pick out anything beyond the cloud of hunger staining the area. To her left was a pile of upended tables and chairs, which had been thrown into the booths.

Laika appeared from a swinging door that must have led to the kitchen. Even from this far away, Evie could see her packmate was pale as a ghost and for some reason unshifted. She'd wrapped what looked like a chef's jacket two sizes too big around herself. Ace moved to meet Laika with hurried steps. She was saying something to him in whispered tones, but her words weren't carrying across the dance floor so Evie moved forward towards them. She wanted to know the details of the kitchen, since that's where most of the bloody marks had been headed.

Quiet steps led her across the dance floor until she could hear Laika's low voice. "There's no way the iris went out the back. The door was completely blocked with the... Joey and I couldn't force it open."

Ace frowned, his eyes moving towards the other door on this side of the club. The men's restroom hadn't been checked yet, and it wasn't blocked like the other one. He took a cautious step towards it as he continued to talk to Laika. "It didn't come up the other stairs either. Which means it's either still in here or there is another way out."

"Joey is checking for survivors... But I don't think anyone in that mess could've..." Laika trailed off as she spotted Evie. She gave a quick shake of her head, while moving to block her line of sight to the kitchen. Clearly her packmate did not want Evie to go into the back.

Evie's lips pulled down into a frustrated frown. She could handle whatever nightmare Laika was trying to spare her. After all, she still had the glass people crowding her dreams. This was her job and no matter how uncomfortable, she would do it. "I'll go help Joey. I'll be able to sense if someone is al-"

Something heavy slammed against wood with a loud crack.

All heads snapped looking for the source of the sound.

The door of the women's bathroom flew outward in multiple directions, torn apart as a seven foot tall creature pushed through. Every finger was tipped with long, curled claws that ripped through the blockage like paper. A massive maw hung open, showing off rows of razor sharp teeth while pitch black eyes on an otherwise human face searched for those who had disturbed it.

"Oh shit," yelled Thad, trying to backpedal away. "That's not an Ir-"

But it was too late, as the creature swiped a massive hand forward.

Randall threw up both his arms to protect his head, hoping to stop the blow. But the power of the swing crunched his bones as easily as the door before. Momentum carried him into Thad with another sickening thud. They kept moving with no chance to catch their footing or counter until they crashed against the wall, leaving a crack in the drywall. The pair slid to the floor, leaving the wall tinged with streaks of red.

How had they walked past their target!?

Realization hit Evie like a slap to the face. Someone had blocked the restroom for a reason when trying to escape! That had been the only place someone could be hiding...

Evie wanted to scream, but her mind latched onto the last warning from their vampire expert. This wasn't an iris. She was completely sure that's what Thad had been saying before the hit. What the hell was this thing?

"That's a peony," Laika whispered, and all the pieces came into place.

The vampire opened its mouth in a silent snarl, blood dripping from a mess of needle-like fangs. All of its jaw was stained with blood along its throat. Evie realized why it was 'smart' enough to be quiet: something had torn its throat into a bloody mess. Similarly clawed feet dug into the wooden floor, pushing the peony forward to follow its victims.

But the huge form of Daniel intercepted the creature by throwing a right hook. He had no time to shift forms this close to the target, but he kept swinging to keep all attention on himself.

Nothing seemed to phase the vampire as each hit was shrugged off. Evie felt something wrong with its emotions. Hunger was the overwhelming winner, but there was fear and maybe sadness as well. Why would it be sad? Unless it... he was aware but not in control?

Daniel got a hand around the peony's wrist. A kind of resolved panic was coming from the werewolf, knowing he couldn't hold this forever. But maybe he could hold on long enough for the rest to react.

The daze wore off Evie as she realized she'd been watching, not helping. She needed to shift, and now! Silently she prayed her shift would go as fast as before. But as the wolf rose to meet her call, the speed was her usual. "Damn it!"

Ace and Laika burst past her. They hadn't been as stunned as Evie and their shifts were already taking effect with every step. Thankfully, no matter how annoying Ace was, his skills were always well practiced. A copper furred hybrid practically erupted from his skin in mid stride. Meanwhile, Laika would only need another minute before she was ready. Her legs were already done shifting, which was how she kept her pace while coming to Daniel's aid. Again Evie cursed at herself for how slow she was at shifting. The fight would be over before she even got there.

Finally, there was an opening as one of Daniel's swings didn't connect with the peony's jaw, but glanced to the side. That was all the peony needed to break through with his maw opening wide. Razored death aimed toward Daniel's shoulder, ready to rend it to the bone.

Even with her half-shifted vocal cords, words fumbled into a screamed warning from Evie. But just before contact, the vampire stopped. His bite turned into a silent snarl of distaste. With her empathy she was certain that disgust had appeared for just a moment.

Instead, the peony grabbed with claws at Daniel's arm, jerking it backward with a sudden pop. His shoulder dislocated with a startled yelp and he stumbled away, trying to prevent more muscle damage. Daniel wasn't far enough away when the other clawed hand connected.

The peony had removed his biggest threat from the fight as Daniel's head cracked into the wall.

Evie watched in horror as Daniel fell with his arm at a wrong angle and disappeared into the piles of toppled booths. She didn't have time to pursue him because the rest of the werewolves left standing attacked in a fury of motion.

A copper furred fist slammed into the side of the peony's jaw, cracking teeth into each other as his maw snapped shut. Another powerful swing quickly followed, but clearly Ace didn't have a plan beyond swinging wildly yet.

Evie tried to catch Laika's attention. They couldn't keep swinging blindly because raw power wasn't in their favor. But her packmate was just circling, trying to tear away at the vampire's balance.

"Ugh..." Randall was stirring from where he'd fallen with a dazed expression. Regeneration was his actual power and that was coming in handy right now. Blood Fang's pack had such an annoyingly good mix of abilities among them. His shaky hands closed on Thad's shoulder to pull him back towards the safety of the bathroom.

Finally, red fur rippled up Evie's arms as she finished her shift into hybrid form. The snaps gave way, allowing her clothing to accommodate the bulky frame. She felt thankful she'd left the Wonder Woman costume at home.

Frustration was coming in waves from the other wolves as they made no progress. Evie wanted to avoid the blows being traded because they had injured on the field. Another bad swing could kill Daniel, who couldn't defend himself. But that would leave them down one more pair of claws...

A howl heralded Joey's arrival as he burst out the door from the back. When his eyes took in the peony before them, Evie felt his fear almost overwhelm the young man. However, he didn't stop and threw himself into the melee with claws drawn.

Now Evie could go after Daniel and try to come up with a plan. The others seemed to realize what she was doing because they tried to force the vampire back to the center of the floor. She skirted around the edge of the brawl while leaping over debris with quick motions.

At the edge of her vision, Evie could see a whirlwind of claws trying to take chunks out of their target. One would dart in for a feint with short swipes, only for another to strike when the peony moved to retaliate. Again the cycle continued when the missing werewolf started their feint. Usually these tactics were effective at keeping an opponent off balance, but one mistake here would result in disaster.

Nothing seemed to be having much effect on the frenzying, relentless vampire. Again Evie felt like he had an edge of sorrow or guilt to the hunger coming from him. As she reached the broken pile of furniture that concealed Daniel, Evie had to turn her back to the fight, trusting her empathy to keep tabs on the rest. Joey and Laika's speed matched with Ace's strength should be enough, especially when Evie joined in as well.

Flashes of pain accompanied the thuds of flesh and claws connecting. Evie stopped being subtle, choosing to throw chairs and tables out of her way. She needed to stop wasting time now.

Ace stumbled into view for a second. Several hits had struck home, leaving his fur slick with running blood and fingers at the wrong angles. He let out a growl before dragging his thumb down the side of his neck. It was answered by a sharp bark of acknowledgement.

Evie looped her arms around the fallen Daniel she'd dug out, but as she lifted him enough to pull free, her hands nearly slipped. Her allies were reading determination, but her mouth hung open aghast. They had not been authorized for lethal force. Night Claw had never been on any job where it was allowed. What sort of madness was happening that Ace was signaling to kill the peony?

The poor vampire might be trapped in a spell and out of control! Evie spun around looking to her packmate for help. Laika must've been of the same mind because she stumbled to a stop, her eyes going wide. She clearly hadn't expected this response either when they outnumbered their target four to one.

While Night Claw may have been stunned by the order, nothing stopped Blood Fang from flying into action.

Ace barreled forward directly at the peony. He looked like a large bulldozer, smashing everything in his way to pieces. His hands pulled up high like he was ready to rend down with heavy slashes. The vampire rose to meet the challenge, preparing to enter a grapple match. But the copper werewolf dipped lower right before they connected, and the peony's swings missed. Instead, both his wrists were imprisoned by the muscled manacles of Ace's super strength.

Laika sprung into motion, aiming for her ally rather than her target. But she didn't reach them in time to prevent what happened next. Trying to rip free of the Ace's grasp, the peony found the hybrid's grip to be unyielding as he lost the battle of strength. He threw his head back in a silent roar of frustration.

Joey had been waiting for this moment, as he pushed off the nearby rubble for extra speed. Like a grey arrow he flew forward, managing to get one hand on the peony's shoulder. Claws dug in, giving him enough leverage to get to the other hand on the vampire's neck.

Before Joey could finish his maneuver the peony's leg shot up, kicking Ace squarely in the gut with all his force. Bones cracked and the werewolf let out a pained gasp. The once iron grip was now glass, and the vampire ripped his hands free. Mere inches away and completely dazed by the hit, Ace couldn't defend.

Claws seized Ace by the neck then hurled him towards the bar. The force of the throw dislodged Joey enough that the grey werewolf joined his packmate a moment later. Wooden planks couldn't hold up to the force, so both men smashed into the wall in a heap.

Evie could feel so much guilt coming off the vampire, she was sure now. He didn't want to kill or maim anyone. She needed a plan that would put him on the ground, not under it.

When the peony looked towards his latest victims, he was met by a snarling Laika appearing in his path. For a moment he looked like he was taking a half step back before squaring his shoulders to return the snarl with a silent roar that splattered blood everywhere.

Cursing, Evie almost dropped Daniel onto the bathroom floor in surprise. She had hoped to tend to him safely, but there was no time now. Only her packmate was stupid enough to take this vampire on single-handedly after he'd dropped five combat-ready werewolves.

"Go!" A voice rasped, as dark hands streaked with drywall dust took hold of Daniel. "I've got him." Randall looked unsteady, but Evie took the offered help before bolting back to the fight.

She needed a plan, and she needed one now. Nothing creative or world changing was coming, likely due to the pure fear that clouded her mind. They might die here if they weren't more careful. Evie saw Laika was getting pushed back with every swing. Evie relented; she didn't have time to be fancy, and an old faithful would have to do tonight.

A sharp bark demanded attention, but she waited until Laika glanced her way before making a gesture of her own. There was an answering nod from her packmate before the peony blocked Evie's view. She'd have to trust Laika to understand and follow through.

Sound had caught the peony's attention, identifying Evie as the next threat. Dozens of cuts barely bled from the earlier assault. But he didn't look at all exhausted or even slightly winded. His shoulders squared, preparing for a head on assault like the one from Ace.

This time, Evie dodged to the side and threw her clawed hand out. The fingers of her right hand wrapped around the vampire's wrist. Then her left hand snaked underneath to grip the tricep. Her weight and momentum pulled him off balance, while Evie swung around to the vampire's back. Her arms clamped around the peony's chest like a vice, hands gripping each other like a seatbelt, restraining the enraged monster.

Thousands of times she'd practiced this two-man take-down. If she could get him on the ground, then she could prevent any more death tonight. Her muscles strained to hold the lock in place as the vampire tried to wrench free of her grip. While Evie may not have Ace's raw strength, from here she had control. Claws gripped the wooden floor for extra stability and she used her weight to slow the peony. She reminded herself to trust that Laika was coming.

Her faith was rewarded when her packmate darted in view, sliding on one knee. The dark furred wolf threw her arms in a bear hug around the peony's knees. Just another second and the pair would be able to twist him to the ground.

There was no warning as the peony threw himself backwards.

Laika's arms never got into place before Evie heard a crunch. Then the pain registered as she felt her skull crack against the wall. Her ribs protested as they were crushed by the peony's full weight and for just a moment she blacked out.

Evie's eyes groggily pulled open, surprised she was even alive right now after the blow. On the ground in front of her, Laika was groaning while trying to pick herself up. Both packs of wolves were down; all seven of them laid low by one vampire in a blood frenzy.

Her mind caught up with the world; where was the vampire?!

In her daze, she could hardly focus on the emotions rolling off him, but he was definitely not in the room. Did fear send him running? Why? They had all fallen and he could take his fill... but he hadn't wanted werewolf blood earlier...

"He's going up the stairs!" Randall's voice was as ragged as the man himself. He scrambled out over the broken pieces of the bathroom door. A hand was pointing towards the open door they'd come through earlier.

Fear flashed through Evie. The vampire hadn't bitten Daniel. He hadn't bitten any of them, despite having ample chances. Werewolf blood was unwanted, but if he was still hungry then he'd gone after the only living non-werewolves in range.

Evie let out a pained roar as she pulled herself to her feet. Aaron and Owen were in danger, and she doubted even their bullets would help. As if heralded by her thoughts, gunshots rang out.

The next minute passed in a blur as Evie tried to move at lightning speed up the stairs, chasing the vampire. She was vaguely aware of her packmate pushing in front and taking steps 4 at a time. Even various members of Blood Fang were trying to react despite how broken and bloodied the group was.

Finally, Evie managed to drag herself back to the street.

A frightful scene was waiting for her. Owen struggled in the air with his feet completely off the ground as the peony dove for his neck. There was no last minute save happening this time. No amount of speed would get anyone there before Owen had his throat ripped open.

Blood splattered to the asphalt a moment after as the vampire's fangs broke the skin. Then he coughed and gagged like acid had just touched his tongue, before throwing away the officer ungracefully. Owen twisted in the air before smashing into his cruiser's window. The glass cracked out like spider webs, but held in one piece. Apparently wolfkin blood wasn't wanted either.

Evie managed to force herself into action. She needed to check on Owen to make sure he hadn't cracked his spine, then spirit her friend far away from this peony because all of them were so outmatched.

"Aaron!" Randall yelled, pulling attention back to the peony who hadn't dallied after his first failed attack. The unshifted werewolf had followed them up the stairs, and she could see at least Ace back in his human form following. They'd be no use like that.

Everything fell to her and Laika, but Evie didn't know what they could do beyond swinging wildly. Which seemed to be her packmate's plan, as Laika tried to scramble forward after the peony. But fatigue mixed with all her injuries slowed down Laika too much.

Neither of them had even made it halfway there when the vampire got his claws on Aaron.

Officer Leavenworth had his gun drawn at the ready. As soon as his partner wasn't in the way anymore, he'd started opening fire. Bullet after bullet slammed into the vampire's chest, but his frenzied charge didn't pause. Then the chamber clicked empty...

Evie felt terror coming off their friend and it was magnified by her own fear. Laika, Ace, Randall, and even Owen's emotions were all mixed together, which completely overwhelmed her into inaction.

Fangs tore into the junction between neck and shoulder, and a relief flickered off the peony. This was something he could use to sate his hunger. The struggling human in his grasp wasn't capable of putting up any fight.

Then the hunger cut off abruptly.

No one had seen or heard the approaching hybrid werewolf. Blonde fur covered her forearms as she surprised the entire group. One moment the peony was buried in Aaron's neck, and the next his head rolled to a stop, bumping into Laika's feet. The hybrid's other arm was cradling Aaron so she could apply pressure to his wound.

Stunned silence hung in the air for a moment. Another werewolf appeared, sprinting down the street. Evie recognized him as Mike, a member of the Dark Wind pack, the highest ranked group of werewolves in Glenwood. He was in his human form but dressed in moonlighter's gear: a tactical vest with netting for the sleeves, with matching pants and boots. Evie realized the blonde hybrid was also wearing similar gear that had stretched to accommodate her. Suddenly, she felt ridiculous standing there in a bargain-priced vest. Her sparkly orange stripper shorts were on the ground from her shift, but they wouldn't have made Evie feel better.

"What are you doing?" snapped Mike. "Shift human now. I need a cellphone; mine was smashed."

Up close she could see he was covered in cuts and bruises. That made some kind of sense since she knew Dark Wind was working tonight too. Had they broken the perimeter to come save them?

Evie wasn't the only person to reach this conclusion as shame crashed down onto her from the surrounding werewolves. Finally, she managed to regain her human form and rushed forward with her phone. The screen was sporting a new crack from the wall slam, but it still worked.

Taking the phone in hand, Mike didn't thank her as he started dialing a number from memory. "Go help Mary," he commanded before heading for the car window where Owen was twitching.

"Yes sir!" The only other person with them was the werewolf holding Aaron, so Evie rushed over desperate to follow directions. "What can I do?"

Mary handed over the officer and switched out their hands. Blonde fur was covered in blood from the still bleeding injury. Once free, she shifted herself back to human and waved Laika over as well. A stern tone demanded of her packmate, "Phone, now."

Laika mutely gave up her cellphone.

"Don't take your hand off that," Mary said before moving, "If you do, then he doesn't make it until the ambulance gets here. Understand?"

"Yes," Evie responded by doubling her efforts to staunch the flow. She wanted to cry, but held herself together. This wasn't about her.

"Are you okay?" Laika whispered. But her focus was on the senior moonlighters who were standing to the side, making calls.

"I'll be alright," choked out Evie, "You?"

"We lost." The words were bitter as they rolled off Laika's tongue.

"I know, did all of Blood Fang make it?"

Laika gave a short nod, "Yeah. Thad's still out cold, but I can hear Daniel and Ace talking about him downstairs."

"Thank the moon." Evie felt relief for the first time since they'd stepped onto this hellscape of a job.

Mike called out loud enough for everyone to hear. "Melinda is on the way with the paramedics. When she arrives you do what she says, no fighting. If Melinda says you're going to the hospital, then you are."

A chorus of 'yes sir' echoed back at him from everyone, even Owen who had regained consciousness. Mike leaned back to Mary, whispering something that made Laika flinch.

"What?" Evie asked in a hushed tone to her friend, frowning at the reaction.

"He told her to be nice," answered Laika.

Mike got their attention again. "There is another incident three blocks west and I need to head over now. Mary is going to do another sweep of your injuries just to be safe. Be careful; the streets might not be completely clear yet." With a wave he headed towards the next attack.

Silence hung once more until the man was out of earshot. Then Mary's rage flared up enough to surprise Evie and a lecture followed. "Seven! There are seven werewolves here and you lost a fight to a peony!"

"Hey, hey," Owen tried to interrupt. He was sitting on the ground with Randall fussing over him now.

Mary rounded on the fallen officer, "You shut up, you've been coddling them and this is what happened. You and I both know that with seven werewolves they should have taken that monster down in minutes then been off to the next fight."

"How?" Laika's frustration led to her outburst.

"Because you're a damn werewolf and your blood is poisonous to peony vampires! It takes a mouthful at most to do the damage you need for a clean decapitation!" Mary was red in the face as she half screamed the answer back. She looked about the same age as Mike with a short crewcut.

Evie wondered if this was what it was like to be dressed down by a drill sergeant.

"Oh," Laika mustered. She looked even more defeated than before, "We didn't know that."

"Clearly, you lacked the basic knowledge and abilities needed to handle even a moderate threat like this. When Melinda gets here, anyone who isn't going to the hospital needs to go home. I have enough work to do tonight and I'm not babysitting a bunch of puppies who can't do their jobs. Got it?"

No one responded, but the collective wills of the two young packs had taken enough of a beating they wouldn't dare disagree.

"Good." With that, Mary took off to follow her packmate towards the next attack.

Owen tried to rescue the mood despite how easily he'd been shushed earlier. "Okay, that was harsh. But try not to take it to heart too much. Everyone makes mistakes."

"How many of your mistakes nearly got your friends killed?" Ace surprised everyone by cutting in. Between him and Daniel, they'd carried Thad upstairs on the biggest piece of a flat table they could find.

No response was forthcoming as sirens began to sound in the distance. Mercifully the ambulances were arriving sooner than Evie had dared to hope. They were probably already on their way to the epicenter when one detoured to them.

Night Claw escaped the need to for a trip to the hospital, but both officers and most of Blood Fang were not so lucky. Anyone who wasn't in desperate need of a paramedic was going to follow in the minivan with Randall driving.

Before Ace climbed into the passenger seat, he looked back at the two women left standing next to the GPD cruiser. All of his usual hatred for them was replaced by a tired respect when Evie made eye contact with him. Evie had felt a strange kinship with Blood Fang when she heard the man speak exactly what she felt earlier. Tonight they hadn't been rivals. They'd been allies, and lost together.

CHAPTER 5
CORRUPTED

Evie
November 1st, 2018
Glenwood General, Glenwood, CA

"I'm fine," Aaron said by way of greeting when Evie and Laika entered his hospital room.

Evie didn't agree with his assessment. Her eyes kept jumping from the bandages that were tinged red to Aaron's neck brace. She thought he looked like a mummy still in costume from last night. "You don't look fine."

"You look like hell warmed over," added Laika. She was holding a bouquet of flowers with a big 'Get Well Soon' plaque in the middle.

"Honestly, I'm fine," Aaron echoed himself trying to brush off concerns. Between the ashen color of his skin and sunken in eyes, nobody believed him.

"Don't listen to him," Owen spoke up. He'd been sitting in the armchair in the corner, and had gone unnoticed until now.

Evie could see that Owen was still wearing his uniform from last night, and he gave off an aura of tired frustration. She was sure he'd spent the whole night in that chair. The pair looked like they'd been at a Halloween party gone wrong between the mummy and the uniform.

Owen continued, "He's just on the good painkillers right now."

"Did you need surgery last night?" Evie asked, but she dreaded the answer. Her guilt was doing a good job of giving her worst case scenarios already.

Aaron attempted to shake his head, only to remember he was wearing a neck brace. "No, just some stitches. This looks a lot worse than it actually is. Melinda was one of the paramedics last night and she got the bleeding stopped before the ambulance made it to the hospital."

"Then why are you wearing a neck brace?" Laika cut in.

"So he stops trying to rip his stitches. The nurse put that on him after the second time someone had to fix them," grumbled Owen.

Evie could feel her packmate's growing worry. They'd both been terrified they would find out Aaron didn't make it through the night. Mike and Mary never gave their phones back, so they hadn't even been able to text Owen for an update. Even using Shelly's phone to call GPD had gotten them nowhere.

Night Claw had shown up at the hospital expecting the worst, armed with a bottle of whiskey to grieve with Owen. When the receptionist downstairs had given them an actual room number and not condolences, they'd rushed to the gift shop. Evie spent way too much money on frilly flowers so that they could sneak in the whiskey as a get well gift.

Again Evie found herself staring at the bandages wrapped around Aaron's neck and shoulder. She felt guilt swelling up. Mary's lecture had robbed her of sleep last night. If she'd only been faster or smarter or stronger, then Aaron wouldn't be laying in a hospital bed.

"I'm so sorry!" Evie blurted out the words. She heard Laika rush out an apology as well.

Laika continued, "We should've known better!"

"It never should have gotten up those stairs!" agreed Evie. She could feel tears trying to form, but fought them back. Just like last night, this wasn't about her.

"If I'd just been faster," Laika lamented, her hands were curled around the vase of flowers tightly.

Between Evie and Laika's rapid fire apologies Aaron struggled to respond. Finally he held up his hand to stop them. "Woah, woah, calm down."

Both women shut up for a moment.

"Owen told me about what happened after I lost consciousness last night when Dark Wind showed up to help. You both need to know I don't blame you," Aaron explained calmly.

"But-" Evie's protest was cut off by a quick wave of Aaron's hand.

"No, we were far too close to an active scene. When I sent you after that vampire then I should have moved at least a block back. This is exactly why we have strict perimeters at jobs," Aaron stated.

He forced himself to sit up straighter.

Owen leapt from his chair when he saw Aaron move. He hissed, "Knock that off!"

But Aaron pushed Owen off as he gave Evie and Laika reassurance. "Last night caught us all off guard. It's not your fault I got hurt. I've told every member of Blood Fang who's come through that door the same thing."

He gestured at the bedside table where three cards and a teddy bear already sat. Evie opened her mouth to argue again that it was her job to keep someone as human as him safe. But Aaron cut her off with the same sentiment.

"I signed up as a MOONS liaison knowing that it would put me just behind the frontline of supernatural situations. All of which could kill me. I knew what I was getting into, and me being an idiot who didn't back off when I should have isn't your fault," Aaron concluded.

"I'm not taking back my apology," Evie replied. She made a snap decision, moving forward to throw her arms around her friend. Laika followed into the hug.

Evie was just so glad that Aaron was alive and clearly fine enough to lecture them. This was much better than the chewing out from Mary last night.

"What are you doing?!" A nurse screeched.

Evie looked up to see a short woman in blue scrubs storming into the room. Her ginger hair was pulled into a loose ponytail which matched her fiery aura.

"Oh here we go again," muttered Owen as he sulked back to his armchair.

"Get your hands off of him, he's healing," shrieked the nurse as she pushed herself between Evie and Laika. The new presence forced them to let go of Aaron or risk hurting him.

"Abby. Chill out; a hug isn't going to kill him," scolded Melinda, who had followed the nurse in.

The tall blonde witch was dressed in a clean, white doctor's coat. She was the only witch moonlighter that Evie had seen in Glenwood. Why was she here? She was a stark contrast to the petite ginger nurse. Melinda's heavily tattooed skin only heightened the difference when standing next to Abby's perfectly unmarred porcelain complexion. They looked almost comical together.

"But Doctor, he's healing right now and they have super strength," disagreed the newly-dubbed Abby.

"And? Do you hug with your full strength every single time?" Melinda shrugged.

"Yeah," Laika quickly agreed, "We weren't about to hurt him."

Evie could feel how annoyed her friend was. She had her own frustrations at being pushed away as well. But she tamped those feelings back down, forcing a polite smile on her face. Putting a hand on Laika's arm, Evie pulled her friend back to give Melinda room.

"Are you okay?" Evie asked Aaron.

Aaron had laid back against his pillows. "Don't worry about me. I'm fine."

"No, you're not," corrected Melinda as she stopped at the side of Aaron's hospital bed. She picked up the clipboard hanging there to check last night's records. Meanwhile, Abby busied herself with collecting Aaron's current vitals. They were a well oiled machine of movement and never got in each other's way.

Melinda's eyes scanned the chart quickly. She handed it to the nurse before continuing, "You got bitten by a peony last night and fed on. You aren't going to be doing 'fine' for a while."

"You're lucky you didn't get turned from that," Abby added. She gave Aaron a sympathetic pat.

"What? That's not how you get t- Nevermind," Melinda interjected.

Evie was beginning to understand why Owen had been so put out when Nurse Abby appeared. So far she'd been pushy and clearly not qualified to be dealing with supernatural medicine.

"So what's wrong with me then," Aaron asked as he tried to ignore the crowded room.

Melinda's eyes followed Aaron's and she frowned again. "All of you out. I can't discuss medical conditions in front of you."

"I need to-" Owen started to disagree, but he was getting up from the chair he'd claimed since yesterday.

"Nope," the witch shut him down, "It's literally the law. I'll even need you out, 'Officer Kirkland'."

Owen put his hands up in a show of defeat before grabbing Evie and Laika's shoulders to steer them out of the room. "Alright, alright, 'Doctor Vaas'."

As they were pushed towards the door, Laika leaned in to whisper to Owen, "Doctor? I thought she was just a paramedic."

"I went to medical school," Melinda answered in a bored voice, before the officer could speak.

"Laika," scowled Evie quietly. Laika's face flushed and her aura reacted the same. She couldn't believe her friend had done that. Especially after scolding Evie at Longtooth! Another few choice words came to mind, but Owen cut her off.

"Yes, Melinda is our stoic doctor stereotype. Keep moving." Owen started to push them out of the room again.

But he and both women stopped in their tracks when Melinda returned her attention to Aaron. "I solved your mystery, by the way."

"What?" Evie pushed her way back in. She ignored any attempts by Abby to get rid of her; werewolf strength trumped humans when Evie was paying attention. Laika followed her as the pair moved to the empty side of the hospital bed.

"Which mystery?" Aaron asked. His eyes were firmly on the blonde witch.

"Your rituals," answered Melinda. She held up her clipboard for all of them to see.

The backside of it wasn't a blank brown; instead it had a five pointed star in a circle. Each point was marked with a different color. Evie wasn't exactly sure what this was called, but she'd done enough magic research last month to be a little informed. These were the five elements of witchcraft that all witch magic came from. A click of a camera broke Evie's attention. She realized Owen had joined them to get a better view. He was documenting everything with his phone.

"By my count, there are five attacks now?" Melinda waited for confirmation.

Laika listed off the places, "Yeah, the apartment building, the network towers, the amusement park, the cafe, and the club last night."

Evie's eyes widened as she realized what Melinda was implying. Five elements to five attacks. Could it really be that simple? Just a circle of witches wreaking havoc on Glenwood for unknown reasons? A moment later Melinda confirmed some of Evie's suspicions. "Each one was a corruption of an element. Lightning for fire, rust for metal, and so on."

"Why would anyone do that?" Owen pressed eagerly.

Evie could feel threads of hope starting to build in everyone around her, even herself if she was truthful. But the emotion collapsed as fast as it appeared.

"I don't have a clue," Melinda shrugged. "There's nothing I know about that needs that much negative build up. None of the major circles are claiming any knowledge either, but they aren't known for being truthful."

"Damn," swore Owen.

Aaron had pulled himself into a sitting position again. He wasn't as easily defeated by the news. Instead, he started rapid fire questions, "Who would know? Do you have anyone we could ask? Maybe an official inquiry could loosen some lips?"

Melinda frowned, "Go ask Alfred. If anyone knows about a corrupted murder ritual then it's him. He's probably got the original scroll once he remembers it."

"Yeah... That makes sense," Owen agreed, typing notes furiously on his phone.

"What? He-" Laika started, before whipping her head around to look at Owen. "That makes sense?"

"Isn't that a little concerning?" Evie spoke up, feeling both her own discomfort at the wording... and annoyance at the excitement spilling from Laika. Why wasn't she weirded out by this?

Both Melinda and Owen turned to Evie, and in almost unison they said, "Why?"

"Because Alfred knows all the murder rituals?" she replied. Evie was starting to wonder why only she was having a reasonable reaction.

"He's Glenwood's magic expert. If he didn't know all the murder rituals then he'd be pretty shit at his job," Owen answered. He seemed satisfied with his notes before closing his phone.

"Once we have a lead on the exact rituals, Alfred can usually find them in a couple days," added Aaron. "We could ask Miss Amadori as well, she's still on loan. I don't know if rituals are her magical specialty or not."

Both Officers and Melinda were completely unconcerned by this revelation that someone in MOONS had access to deadly magic. Evie couldn't get her head around it. Only Abby seemed as horrified as Evie, and that wasn't helping. Laika had gone completely silent at the full explanation; she was patting her pockets looking for a phone that didn't exist. Frustration built up in her friend, which only pissed Evie off more.

"Okay. We need to get out of here and let Aaron rest," Evie declared. She took Laika by her elbow, dragging her out of the hospital room.

"Thanks for visiting," Aaron called behind the retreating women.

- ☾ -

Laika
November 1st, 2018
Glenwood General, Glenwood, CA

L aika felt like her head was going to explode from all the questions she had. Why didn't she have her phone? She'd had all the pieces already and just been too distracted to fit them together. Hadn't she been sitting in GPD when Aaron read out the report? Which, if Laika thought about it, was exactly how Alfred wrote text messages too.

Alfred was on the Glenwood Anarchist case. He'd been able to get Laika on the case as well. That only made sense if he had some pull in MOONS or GPD, and the resident magical expert fit the bill. How had Laika missed this? All her 'clues' from the last few weeks about what type of vampire he was needed re-examined. Lotus didn't exactly scream magical expert.

She was pulled out of her own head by a sound. Laika heard shoes on the linoleum floor following her, and she looked up. Owen had been finally shooed out of the room. He was jogging to catch up with her and Evie. His easy grin was back in place even as he scolded them. "Slow down! You both should be taking it easy today anyways."

"You're one to talk," Evie shot back. "We half expected you to be laid up too after last night. You didn't exactly hit that windshield gracefully."

Laika surveyed Owen, looking for indications of his own wounds. Wolfkin did not have the blessing of werewolf healing. He'd heal just as slow as a human; however, he'd take a hit better than them. "Are you okay though? You did get bit, and thrown into the cruiser..."

Owen's hand raised to wave away the concern. "Once Aaron was stable, Melinda got me squared away. I'll be sore for a few days, but I'll be back at work tomorrow. You'll still have me." Glancing back to the room they'd just left, Laika opened her mouth to ask how long Aaron would be stuck here. Her question was cut off as a warm voice rang out down the hall.

"Laika! Owen!"

Laika turned towards the source, her expression lighting up as she spied a friendly face. Keisha was all but bouncing up the hall, with Randall and Jaci in tow. While she wasn't thrilled to see her rival from Blood Fang, the Moonscent girls were a welcomed sight. "I'm so glad you both are up and moving! We heard about last night... Oh! You must be Evie! Laika's told me all about you!" Keisha moved forward to offer a hand to Laika's packmate.

Randall came to a stop as well, looking a little awkward. "Hey... You guys doing alright?" he asked quietly.

"Yeah, just checking on Aaron... You?" Laika answered with a bit of awkwardness of her own. Conversation was easier when they just sniped back and forth. But she felt a bit of kinship with Blood Fang after last night.

"Most everyone is home now, but Daniel had to stay. Keisha and Jaci asked for a ride to come visit, so..." Randall trailed off with a shrug.

Laika took a moment to introduce Evie to the two young girls. She'd told her packmate about them plenty of times before, since they'd started running together twice a week and going to the library for research. Keisha took the opening to ask, "So any luck on that ritual yet?"

"How the hell do you know about the rituals?" snapped Owen.

His face veered sharply into disapproval. Eyes moving from one werewolf to the next, they settled on Laika. He'd found his culprit.

"How could I not know about the Glenwood Anarchist case?" Keisha countered. She looked unashamed of being caught.

"Yeah, right. I'm going to go check on Daniel. Try not to announce every detail to the entire building while I'm gone," scoffed Owen. He gave Laika one more piercing look before retreating down the hall to where Daniel was resting.

"I mean, it's our case," muttered Evie. But she kept her voice down low while the officer was still in earshot.

Randall wasn't as subtle as he caught up. "Excuse me, what? How did you get on that case? You're not qualified!"

All of that kinship Laika had been feeling shriveled up. She gave him a superior smirk. "Clearly we're more qualified than you. We're tracking down leads on break-ins to pinpoint exactly which rituals are being cast."

"Like Pixie Dust?" Randall latched on to the thought quickly.

"Yes, like Pixie Dust," Evie confirmed. She looked just as pleased as Laika felt at having one up on Blood Fang.

He sulked as he pulled out his phone, likely to rat them out to his packmates. "But that was just as much our case," complained Randall.

"That's so cool," Jaci cheered.

Keisha was also having the opposite reaction of Blood Fang. "Does that mean all the research we've been doing at UCLA helped?"

"Oh yeah it did," Laika praised. Owen had warned her off sharing too many details, but Keisha and Jaci had gotten her into the library the first time and every other time Laika had asked. She'd also conned Randall into pulling books for them. So without the Moon-scent girls' help, Laika knew she wouldn't have half as much standing right now. "If you two hadn't helped, then I couldn't have helped Alfred find the connections. Plus, Melinda was able to look at the rituals and details and let us know they were corruption based. We're so close now."

"Corruption?" Randall questioned. He couldn't hide how interested he was in the conversation even when annoyed at them.

"Yes, she said they were a corruption of the-" Laika began.

Randall finished for her, "-of the elements." Then he went back to his phone typing more furiously than before.

"Don't you even dare," Evie snarled, squaring up for a fight in the hallway.

"What?" hissed Randall.

"Don't you even think about trying to swipe our case. Just because Thad has some legit vampire knowledge doesn't mean anything. This is a circle of witches and you aren't getting our case," argued Evie.

Laika was momentarily surprised since just last night her packmate was peddling the theory that Alfred was behind everything. Now the culprits were witches?

"Hey, if we're more qualified, then that's your problem not mine," shot back Randall.

"Knock it off," Keisha got in the middle of them. She stamped her foot for attention then purposefully gestured around them.

Patients were peeking around the doorways to see who was shouting. Nurses were giving them wary looks and even a lone security guard had started towards them. Jaci had fallen silent, fidgeting with her glasses to avoid the attention directed at them.

"We should be going anyway. We already checked in on Aaron," Laika explained. Embarrassment was likely glowing on her face at how quickly they'd devolved into a fight. When the girls who couldn't legally drink were the most mature, then Night Claw had failed today.

"Let me know if you need back into the library," Keisha offered. "I'll make Randall drive me."

"No you won't," muttered Randall. He'd crossed his arms defensively, but stopped fighting.

Laika would put money that Keisha won that battle of wills.

CHAPTER 6
RECOVERY

Laika
November 1st, 2018
Night Claw Residence, Glenwood, CA

All Laika wanted to do was go for a run. She had pent up energy and no physical outlet for it. Her muscles ached from being tossed around the night before like one of her bags of moonbeans. Maybe not the best comparison... Family business or not, Boss would've chewed her out if she'd handled the coffee deliveries to the warehouse even half as rough. Werewolf healing fixed cuts and scrapes, but bruising lasted much longer. Evie had gone to the shed in the backyard where she could paint in peace. Laika was jealous her friend had a stress hobby that was easy to do at home. There wasn't even anyone to talk to since Shelly retreated back to her bedroom and Tor was out.

Laika tapped away on her aging laptop that had been purchased in her freshman year of college. The brick of metal and plastic weighed a ton and was a decade out of date. Even casual web browsing made its fans whir as loud as an airplane taking off. For all her keen hearing, that was just white noise to Laika now. But it had sent Shelly fleeing the living room after the laptop achieved lift-off for the fourth or fifth time.

So now Laika sat by herself, trying to read Evie's 'screenplay' to pass the time.

"This is terrible," Laika groaned aloud, emphasizing each word with a dramatic click of the backspace key. She sprawled across the couch with her laptop perched on her chest. Walls of text dominated her screen, and she wasn't sure she could call this a real script given how bad each page was.

Laika thought with how much trashy TV Evie watched that she could write an interesting story. Not to mention how many real moonlighting jobs they'd been on before! But nothing in the screenplay seemed believable. Her fingers danced across the keyboard, replacing sentences with a few of her own. She added some witty dialogue, exposition, and bam! The scene was passable.

Editing was something to do, since Laika was phoneless. She was sure that even if she had her phone, MOONS wouldn't be calling her in for jobs for a while. By now Owen had surely taken them out of rotation and Night Claw would be relying on their day jobs.

For once Laika really couldn't, or more honestly wouldn't, argue. Last night's fight had been rough... but even worse, the tongue lashing she'd received from Dark Wind had hurt more than any broken bone.

Throwing her hands up to cover her face, Laika let out a wordless growl of frustration. She'd fucked up so badly, people had gotten hurt and her heroes had seen it all! Retrieving her phone from Mike and Mary was a daunting task. She considered sacrificing her phone to the gods of pride and avoidance. But Laika couldn't afford to replace her phone any more than she could afford to replace this behemoth of a laptop.

KNOCK! KNOCK!

Laika sat up on the couch, surprised to hear someone at the front door. She'd heard a car park a few minutes ago, but Evie's car was in the driveway so she'd assumed it was for a neighbor.

"One moment," Laika called loudly. She shifted her laptop to the coffee table then smoothed her clothing while standing up. Usually, she'd jump over the back of the couch for fun. But Laika's muscles protested even stretching enough to stand.

"No rush," replied the tired voice of Alfred. He hadn't spoken loudly, like he'd assumed Laika could hear him through the door. That forced Laika into fast action; she practically sprinted for the door. She hadn't forgotten that Alfred was called out last night to the scene. Without her phone she'd had no way to check up on him, unless she wanted to wander the streets of Glenwood trying to find his apartment.

"Hi," Laika greeted him, pulling the door open with more force than she'd meant. Despite the twinge in her shoulder from the explosive action, warmth spread across her face.

Alfred waited on her doorstep, "Good evening, how are you doing?"

"Fine! How are you? Sorry I didn't text you, my phone-" Laika's words were cut off as her phone appeared. Alfred had pulled it from his pocket, like a magic trick.

"Is this your phone? Or is this one Evie's?"

"That's my phone!" exclaimed Laika. She gratefully took her missing lifeline, quickly tapping for the notification screen. A full battery greeted Laika in the top right and only a handful of messages were waiting on her.

"Can I leave Evie's with you as well?" Alfred asked as a second phone appeared.

"Of course! How did you end up with-" Laika's gaze finally turned to him, but her words cut off abruptly.

Alfred looked pale, paler than normal, with dark circles around his eyes. He wasn't wearing the leather coat Laika had grown accustomed to. There were no cuts or bruises on his face, but she couldn't see anything hidden under his full suit.

"Are you okay?" Laika asked, every word was dripping with worry.

"I am fine," assured Alfred. He gave her a tired smile, "I had a long night."

"I heard you were at the center of the attack?" Laika pressed, before taking a step back to clear the doorway. "Come in and rest for a bit. You can tell me about it?"

Alfred looked back at his car parked in front of the house. He hesitated, "I was on threat containment last night... However, you have your girl's night tonight if I recall correctly."

She reached out to grab the jacket at his wrist gently. Laika contemplated just dragging him through the doorway, but she explained instead, "Tor's still at work, Shelly's playing a game, Evie is out back painting. Pretty sure trashy TV is getting a late start tonight."

"I really should be heading home before it gets late," Alfred persisted.

"You shouldn't be driving when you're so dead on your feet," Laika pressed, not letting go of his jacket sleeve yet.

Finally, Alfred turned back to her with an amused expression. "I am always dead on my feet."

"Perfect, so you can come in and tell me all about last night," Laika pleaded, but she couldn't conceal her laughter.

"I suppose I can stay until your girl's night begins," he agreed. Alfred allowed himself to be pulled over to the couch. Without all his heavy daylight gear, it was less of a dance to get settled.

Laika took a seat next to Alfred on the couch. She looked expectantly up at him. Before she could pester him again about the night before, he disarmed her with a question.

"Did you get injured last night?" he asked. His blue eyes were scanning her bruises carefully.

"I barely escaped a concussion. I got a ton of scratches and a few deep cuts but they're already healed up," answered Laika. She lifted the bottom of her shirt to show off pink skin where fading scars had been.

Alfred glanced at her side before he leaned back on the couch. "I see. I am glad that you were not seriously wounded. Michael made it sound like Night Claw was barely held together last night when he arrived."

"Michael?" Laika questioned with confusion on her face. She didn't know anyone on the GPD force by that name... Had he been a paramedic?

"I believe he goes by Mike with the younger packs," clarified Alfred.

Laika could feel tension draining out of the vampire as he got more comfortable on the couch. But he was still paying attention to everything she said.

"You talked to Mike? Ah... That's how you got our phones." Understanding clicked in Laika's head as she put the puzzle pieces together. But that meant Alfred surely knew all about what a mess last night had been. She felt her face grow warm with embarrassment, as she mumbled out her words, "We got lucky. Daniel got the worst of it... aside from Aaron."

"Both Daniel and Aaron have received any treatment they need. You should not blame yourself for their condition," Alfred reassured her. He reached his arm out to wrap around Laika's shoulders.

There was a flash of surprise across Laika's face at the arm; so far she'd initiated all their contact. She was starting to think Alfred just wasn't the touchy feely type. But he'd provided her exactly what she needed right now; a little bit of affection before she spun herself back up.

"But I should have known better. I thought a peony was an iris!" Laika explained, she felt stupid all over again.

"How many iris and peony have you previously met?" Alfred asked.

"...do you count?" Laika queried knowing she hadn't met any

others. He had given her the opening to prod about the type of vampire he was.

"Are you assuming I am an iris or a peony in that question?" Alfred deflected, his arm pulled her a little closer to his side.

Laika retorted, "Clearly a peony." Mentally she was thinking iris since she'd struck peony off her mental murder board tracking clues about his court.

"Then no, I do not count." Alfred's court remained a mystery, but he seemed unperturbed by the question.

"OH!" Laika remembered now what she'd been dying to ask him since talking to Owen earlier. "How long have you been MOONS' magical expert?!"

Alfred flowed with her change in the subject, "43 years last September, as much as Benjamin and I disagreed about it at the time. He admitted at his retirement that I did, in fact, know more about magic than him."

"You've been a moonlighter for 43 years? How long has MOONS even been around?" Laika curled up against Alfred's side, so she could stare up at him. They hadn't snuggled up like this before and she was enjoying the comfort.

"43 years last September," answered the vampire with a small shrug.

"So the entire time? You didn't say anything!" Laika half scolded, but there was a grin spreading across her expression. "Next thing you'll tell me that your moonlighting ID number is like... #0001 or something."

"I am #0003, because Nilani talked Benjamin into her crazy idea a day before myself," answered Alfred. Laika recognized Nilani as the name of Moonscent's alpha. How old was she if she'd started Glenwood MOONS so long ago? Alfred reached into his jacket and pulled out his wallet. A moment later he handed Laika his moonlighter ID.

Laika grabbed the old plastic ID. The style was similar to hers with his name at the top and an id number below. As Alfred had promised, his read '0003' making him the third person to join Glenwood MOONS. She wanted to see his picture, but it had faded with time, barely showing even an outline of a person.

"How do you get away with not needing a new picture?" Laika quizzed. She held onto the card, still checking the details against her own.

"At this point, every officer I work with has inherited me from their predecessor. They stopped asking for an id after a while," Alfred responded. He took his ID back and put away his wallet.

Laika was cuddled up on the couch with Alfred and he was telling her fun facts about himself with every answer. This was much better than dinner at a restaurant. Silently Laika counted this as their first real date. She started gearing herself up for more questions, only to be cut off.

"I believe I have entertained you enough to warrant the story of what happened last night. I saw the report, but most of the events down in Cold Blooded are missing due to Mr. Bellamy being unconscious for them," Alfred interjected. His tone wasn't stern, but he left little room for her to redirect them.

Laika bit her lip; she needed to tell him the story or say she wouldn't. Either might be an end to their cheerful night.

"If you do not want to tell me-" Alfred began to say.

"No," Laika interrupted. She leaned her head against his chest and pulled her feet up onto the couch as she collected her thoughts. "I'll tell you. I'm just not proud of how the fight went or how everyone got hurt."

"In your own time then," Alfred replied softly. He repositioned his arm so it curled more around her waist than shoulders now.

Laika sighed heavily. Then she explained what happened from the time they parted ways on the porch until she'd passed out in bed. She hadn't told Evie about the scene in the kitchen yet. But she told Alfred about the pile of bodies she and Joey found jammed up against the exit. People who had been trying to escape when they were cut down, humans and vampires.

When it came to details that made Laika look like a terrible moonlighter, she didn't sugar coat them. Including rushing into the fight, not helping Ace with his plan, or how stupid she'd been about the wolf's blood.

Alfred had listened to Laika's story patiently. He'd remarked on a few moments of the tale and asked her reasoning for the final attack. There was no judgment, just him trying to understand her. At the end he reminded her, "No one expected you to know that werewolf blood was poisonous to peonies. Or even that the creature you fought was a peony."

"But-"

"No one expected you to know. You had a vampire expert on scene and he made a bad call on the type of vampire. He lacked the details he needed. Before he could fix his mistake the fight broke out and he was the first one taken down," Alfred reasoned out. His tone was soothing and his logic undeniable.

"I guess, but-"

Alfred interrupted her again, "Should someone have checked the bathroom? Yes, but there was a whole pack of werewolves who made the same mistake. Next time every single one of you will check the coat closet, bathroom, and storage room before clearing the area. No one died. Count yourself lucky that your bad luck did not end with more than one body bag. Learn from this and move on."

That had been a command. Laika didn't know what else to call it, despite the fact that his tone was kind and soothing. But it didn't have the same sympathy that Aaron had when he'd tried to free her from guilt.

"I really screwed up though," Laika admitted as her shoulders slumped.

"Yes, you did," agreed Alfred. His hand moved to run soothing circles on her back, "But you were not malicious in your actions. You cannot change it now."

"So I need to learn from it?" Laika replied dramatically.

Alfred matched her levity, "Yes, and try not to do it again. If you run into another peony?"

"I slit my hand open and stick it in their mouth?" snarked Laika while wiggling her fingers in his face.

"If I were a werewolf then I would have the same plan," Alfred answered. They both laughed at the ridiculous thought.

Laika's phone began to beep, breaking her attention from Alfred. She spied the time as her fingers dismissed the alarm. That was the warning that trashy TV was starting in 5 minutes. Usually it was the signal for everyone to grab their dinner and settle in... but it was still just the two of them in the room.

"Oh... It looks like everyone is running late," Laika mused, eyes flicking to her messages to see if Tor had sent anything. Nothing, which meant the stunt show was running long. "One second, let me just kick off the DVR."

There was a soft sound of agreement from Alfred, but Laika's focus was on the remote sitting annoyingly out of reach. She was loath to uncurl from her comfortable position. The wolf stretched out her toes to grab the remote. At least there was no Evie here to complain, and hopefully Alfred would find it as amusing as Laika did.

The remote retrieved, she quickly clicked through all the menus to set up recording on all the shows for tonight. It wouldn't be the first time they had a delayed start, it just meant they'd stay up a bit later... and it meant she could enjoy a bit more of Alfred's company.

A few minutes later with all the shows successfully scheduled, Laika set the remote back down on the couch next to her. "There we go, so where were we-"

As Laika's gaze turned back to Alfred, she realized why he had been so quiet. He had fallen asleep with his head resting on the back of the couch. She couldn't be sure exactly when he passed out, but it had been while she fussed with the DVR.

The normal warning signs of someone dozing off simply weren't there with Alfred. He already didn't breathe and he was always very still. If Laika had been paying attention, maybe she'd have noticed when his hand stopped moving. But now she studied the sleeping vampire, wondering if she should wake him up. Then she looked around at the lack of roommates for TV time and decided against it.

Laika laid her head back down and picked up her phone. She checked her missed messages while she snuggled up. When the rest arrived, she'd wake Alfred and send him home. For now, Laika caught up on the news about micro quakes the night before, probably caused by the Glenwood Anarchist.

She hadn't been paying attention when the backdoor opened and closed.

"I'm so sorry, why didn't anyone come and get me? I just lost track of time out in the she-" Evie was yelling as she barreled through the kitchen, but her words died off as she entered the living room.

Laika felt Alfred jolt awake before she had time to shush her packmate. He sat up, quickly dislodging her from their comfortable position. For a moment his eyes were unfocused before the vampire took in the situation and settled down.

"Evie!" scolded Laika as she caught herself by grabbing onto Alfred's shirt. Thankfully, the material didn't rip, so she stopped her fall into the coffee table.

"What the hell is going on here?" screeched Evie. Her face was turning red as she took up an aggressive stance.

"Nothing?" Laika had no idea why her friend was yelling. Until a moment ago she'd been waiting on Evie to show up. Now she was wishing the redhead had stayed in the shed if this was how she was going to act.

"It doesn't look like nothing!" hissed Evie.

Dramatically Laika pointed her finger at her packmate as she spat, "Get your mind out of the gutter."

Color drained out of Evie's face as she raced forward. For a moment Laika thought her friend was going to launch herself in an attack. But she stopped short, grabbing Laika's arm.

"Why are you bleeding?" Evie screamed, before leveling a glare at Alfred.

Laika looked at her hand seeing it was stained red with fresh blood. But she wasn't bleeding? Had she cut herself trying not to fall? The answer became clear when she spotted a growing spot of red on Alfred's shirt.

"Why are *you* bleeding?" Laika asked in shock.

"I am fine," Alfred assured as he buttoned up his suit jacket, hiding the blood.

"But you're bleeding," she disagreed. Part of Laika wanted to push his hands out of the way and pull his shirt off to see how badly hurt he was.

"I know," again Alfred tried to soothe her, "But I promise I am fine. I cannot bleed out from an injury like you."

Laika never took her eyes off the vampire but she demanded, "Evie, get the first aid kit."

"He said he's fine," Evie shot back. She'd backed off a few steps but was in a huff with her arms crossed.

There wasn't time for Laika to deal with both Alfred's wounds and her packmate's drama right now. She made a choice to ignore Evie. "Just stay there and let me get the first aid kit, then I'll take you to the hospital," Laika started making plans. She leapt up from the couch. Where was the last place they'd had the sparingly used red box?

"Laika," Alfred forced her attention back onto him. He didn't reach out and grab her but he pinned Laika in place with his eyes. "I do not need the hospital; they are of very little use to a vampire. I promise you I am fine."

"But you're not?" Laika gestured with her hand, only to frown at the blood staining her fingers. She wanted to wash her hands, but she worried what would happen if she left the room.

As if reading her mind, Evie took hold of her wrist. She had paper towels in hand, and was wiping the red away with a look of disgust. "Just let it go Laika," her friend warned before her voice dropped to mutter, "This is not normal."

"Please take my word that I am healing and not in need of aid. I have overstayed my welcome. I should head home and allow you back to your girl's night." Alfred pushed himself up to his feet, hand patting his pockets for his keys.

"What!?" Laika stepped towards him, pulling her hand free of Evie's grip. "You can't drive. You *just* passed out from blood loss!"

"He wants to go, let him go," Evie argued. She was holding the blood stained paper towels like they were infectious.

"Evie!" snapped Laika. She didn't need this right now.

"What? He's bleeding on the couch and still hasn't had even a flicker of an emotion about it. He should be angry, or hurt, or I don't know, sad?" Her friend shot back, throwing her hands in the air. Alfred looked frustrated; Laika could see words dancing on the tip of his tongue but he bit them back. Instead he pulled his keys from his pocket to leave.

"Evie, you are my best friend and I love you. But seriously shut up," Laika hissed, before she forced herself to hop over the back of the couch to put her body between Alfred and the front door. There was an indignant huff, and then Laika could hear Evie stomp her way towards the kitchen. She'd have to fix that later, but there were more pressing matters.

"I am fine," Alfred repeated as he watched Laika make a human wall out of herself.

"You passed out from blood loss!" she repeated, staring him down.

"I did not pas-," Alfred cut his words off and took a calming breath. Tension had been building up from the moment he'd been startled awake. "I can drive myself home. I have the supplies I need at home to close this injury. I opened it when I unceremoniously jerked my shoulder a few minutes ago."

Laika searched his passive expression, trying to determine if he was lying about the injury or not. She countered, "But you are bleeding now. What if you pass out while driving?"

"You cannot drive my car," Alfred held up a hand to cut off more arguments, "You do not have a license for the camera driving."

"...but I'd be worried about you getting home safe all night," admitted Laika. Trying to fight with Alfred was pointless; he knew his powers and his car better than her.

Alfred sighed.

Laika struck when she saw that opening, "What if I just come with you? Once you're home safe and I know you got that closed up, then I can Uber home? It'll take an hour at most, right?" She'd wanted to offer following in Evie's Saab, but there was no way her roommate was going to give up the keys right now. Laika needed to get her own car sooner or later.

"I suppose that is fine," agreed Alfred. He'd been worn down by her worries.

Laika lit up. "Perfect! Stay right here, okay? I'll be quick."

She vaulted past him and over the back couch, ignoring her protesting muscles. Laika snagged Evie's phone in one hand before taking off towards the kitchen door. She snatched her bag off a hook near the door as she passed.

"Evie!" Laika shouted as she stuck her head through the kitchen door.

"What?" Her roommate replied, a sour look on her face. Evie stood by the sink, clearly having just finished washing her hands. There was smoke rising from the open trash can.

"Alfred brought your phone back, catch!" Laika had the grace to wait for her packmate to react before launching her phone into the air.

"Why did Alfred have my phone?" demanded Evie. She scrambled to catch the device all the same.

Her question went unanswered as Laika added, "I'm taking him home, I'll be back in like an hour!" When Laika got back, she'd talk to her friend about their spat. She quickly headed for the front door before Alfred had time to change his mind.

- ☾ -

November 1st, 2018
Shady Hollows Apartments, Glenwood, CA

The sound of locks disengaging rang through the car, and in a heartbeat Laika was out. The drive hadn't been half as tense as the living room, but she was all too keenly aware that Alfred was still bleeding. Even if her nose couldn't pick out the scent like a normal werewolf, the stain of red had crept into view on his shirt.

"Here, let me help," she insisted as she scrambled around the car.

Alfred was already on his feet though, and while still sickly he looked no more unsteady than he had earlier. "It is quite alright. I can manage myself." He locked the car behind them, then paused to adjust his suit jacket so that the bleeding from his shirt wasn't as visible.

"Are you sure?" Laika wanted to fuss more.

"Quite sure," responded Alfred as he led them towards the lobby.

Laika took a moment to look around the parking garage. She'd been really moondrunk the last time she'd been through here. There were no windows like a normal ground floor parking garage, and she could see a ramp going down to a second level of parking. Despite this, the area was well lit, fighting off any fearful feelings.

He'd parked in the sixth space from the door. The first four spots were labeled for handicapped and the rest were numbered. A little two door convertible was parked in the fifth spot next to Alfred's town car. Laika wondered if everyone had assigned spaces or if it was a free for all.

"Are you coming? Or shall I call you an Uber now?" Alfred stood holding the door to the lobby open.

She realized she'd fallen behind trying to pick out the social structure of a parking lot. Laika hurried her steps to catch up. "Sorry!"

As Laika brushed past Alfred through the open door, her eyes scanned the lobby. She had been a little distracted the last time she'd been through, but now she could appreciate how nice the place looked. The area was as well lit as the garage, with warm tones reflecting off the polished tile floors. A cafe was in one corner of the room, set across from a well-furnished sitting area. If it wasn't for the rows of mailboxes lining the wall to her left, it would have been easy to mistake this for the lobby of a nice hotel.

People were milling about, some waiting by the desk to the front office, probably picking up packages. There was staff swapping signage at the cafe, turning it into a bar before her eyes. Overall it was a pleasant atmosphere, but Alfred didn't linger. He kept moving past the front office, rounding the corner to where the lone elevator sat. Laika followed close on his heels, stepping into the elevator.

As the doors slid closed, Alfred shook a key loose and stuck it into the control panel before hitting the button for the tenth floor.

"Did you do that last time?" Laika asked as she eyed the silver key curiously.

Alfred gave her a curious look before responding. "Yes, the top floor requires a key to access."

"So you live on the top floor?" queried Laika. She wished she had been more in control of herself last time. When he'd taken her to breakfast, Laika hadn't been paying much attention either.

Alfred watched the numbers going up on the screen. He glanced at Laika before responding with his own question, "You do not recall our first ride up the elevator, do you?"

"No," Laika's eyes widened. She'd been so moondrunk... What had she done?

"We ended up stopping at every floor on our way up," Alfred explained.

Laika saw a smirk flitter over his face as he teased her, but she felt relief that's all it had been. She had a bad reputation for being handsy when she overindulged in a run. Pressing all the buttons in an elevator? That was tame.

"Sorry, being moondrunk kinda makes impulse control go out the window." She attempted to avoid a full explanation with a shrug.

"Do not fret. It was late, and I do not believe anyone was left waiting for the elevator." But his eyes stayed watching the climbing numbers distractedly.

The elevator dinged, finally having reached the top floor. Alfred held an arm to hold the door open, waving Laika ahead. As she stepped out, she realized how few doors were up here. There was one immediately to her right, but otherwise the long hallway was empty except for the wooden door at the far end. The floor was hardwood, well kept and free of scuffs. The walls were a soft cream in color, and sconces lit the walkway at intervals.

"Are there only two apartments up here?" she turned to ask Alfred, gesturing to the door to their right.

"Just the one. That door leads to the roof," Alfred corrected gently. He kept walking, keys still in hand. He unlocked the door at the end of the hall, but he hesitated before opening it.

Laika had kept in step with him, and looked up with a concerned expression. "Are you alright?"

His blue eyes met Laika's amber, and there was a long pause. "As you can see, I have made it home safely. I promise you I am going inside to clean this up and then to bed."

She realized what he was doing. Alfred was trying to send her home before they actually went in. Again, she'd been so moondrunk or in a rush for food she didn't really remember more than the dark guest room. Laika disagreed with his plan. "You'll need help with all this blood."

"I can handle myself," assured Alfred.

"You're not getting rid of me until I'm sure about that. You've been bleeding for 30 minutes straight," Laika put her foot down. She wasn't being swept back downstairs. The vampire hesitated for a moment longer before opening the door. As with the elevator, he held the door open so she could step through.

Except Laika didn't. She stood with an expectant look. After a few moments she finally asked, "Aren't you going to invite me in?"

The look of resignation on Alfred's face flickered, and she swore she saw him smile. "The living do not require invitations."

"The polite ones do."

"I am uncertain you count as one of the polite ones," Alfred remarked as he stepped over the door frame. But he continued to hold the wooden door open, "Please come in."

"Thank you," Laika replied, stepping into the darkness of the apartment. There were no lights on in the entryway. She was plunged into total darkness when the door closed as well. Then a click of a switch lit up a few ceiling lamps dotted through the area.

Laika blinked hard, spots in her eyes from the rapid change in light. As they cleared away she was greeted by another door, which was disappointing... Then Laika realized that to her left the area expanded into a wide open living room, the same hardwood floors and cream walls from the hallway continued. The center was almost empty, with a lone couch and coffee table in the middle.

The walls, however, were completely lined with bookshelves. Every inch was covered, except for a few doorways. On one wall were two archways into what must've been the kitchen, with another door tucked in the far corner. On the other wall were two doors, both closed. She was pretty sure the one closest to her had been the guest bedroom, which meant the other must be Alfred's room.

Laika believed you could tell a lot about a person by their car. And their home could tell you even more. Based on the piles of books crammed on every shelf and stacked on the coffee table, she was pretty sure she liked what she saw.

Speaking of Alfred, the vampire had not stopped walking. He was on a mission, heading for the closed door she'd guessed to be his bedroom. He called behind him, "I will go clean this up and then we can get you home. I assume you do not want to miss all of your TV night."

"You don't have to rush; that's the nice thing about DVR," Laika replied as she moved quickly to follow after him. Her eyes fell on the coffee table as she crossed the room, though.

A familiar helmet sat there... except it had been cloven in two.

That distracted Laika. She veered off course, picking it up in confusion. She'd just seen this helmet yesterday and it had been in one piece. What the hell had happened? Her eyes dropped to the pile of leather it had been sitting on top of. Her brain took a moment to piece together what her eyes were seeing.

Alfred's coat was in shreds. The leather was only recognizable by the buckles and buttons that littered the scraps. Reaching out to touch it, she flinched at the sticky sensation. Her hand lifted, and she spotted flecks of dried blood clinging to her fingers.

"WHAT THE HELL HAPPENED TO YOU LAST NIGHT?" Laika yelled before she could stop herself.

Helmet in one hand, she hurried over to the dark opening to Alfred's bedroom. He hadn't put on a light and only Laika's hearing pinpointed him as he opened a cabinet. Again she demanded, "Why is your helmet in two pieces?!"

"Please calm down," Alfred's tone was distracted.

"Calm down? How serious are you hurt?" Laika wanted to follow him into the dark, but she couldn't see more than a foot into the room.

"This looks much worse than it is," assured the vampire again.

Laika looked back at the table, then into the darkness stretching out before her.

She had only been on a few dates with Alfred and so far they'd had fun. Even when every one of them seemed to end with Evie screaming at someone. Laika had admitted to herself she liked this guy... a lot, and it had been a while since she liked anyone like that.

"Are we dating?" Laika called into the bedroom.

There was a clatter as Alfred dropped something. He sounded confused, "What?"

"I asked, are we dating? We've been on a few dates, spent weeks talking to each other, and I'm attracted to you. I am like eighty percent sure you're into me as well. So are we dating or not?" Laika explained her reasoning, but barely kept any annoyance out of her tone.

Silence hung between them for a moment. Before Alfred appeared in the doorway, he had his jacket and vest off, leaving just his blood stained shirt. She couldn't read the expression on his face. "Would you like to be dating?"

"Yes," Laika replied.

"Then yes, I believe we can define this as dating," responded Alfred.

Laika's heart skipped; she'd been hoping that's exactly what he'd say. "Good. You should know I don't put up with dishonesty about how injured the people I am dating are."

"I see," Alfred muttered. He was staring down at her, looking for something Laika couldn't quite place.

"So. Go get your kit and join me on the couch so I can help with whatever mess is happening here," Laika gestured at the now reddish pink shirt, "or when you come back out, I'll be gone and you can lose my number. Fair?"

"Your terms are agreeable," Alfred answered. Still giving her an unreadable expression he continued, "Give me a few minutes to wash the blood away and I will join you?"

Laika nodded. She gave him room to clean up and retreated to the couch. Sitting down, she let out a breath she hadn't realized she'd been holding in. She knew she was being pretty pushy right now. Honestly, if he'd taken the ultimatum and let her walk away, she wouldn't have been surprised. But Laika knew herself well. If they were actually going to date, she would go crazy with him hiding every time he got hurt on a job.

In relationships, Laika needed honesty for important topics. If Alfred couldn't handle that, then now was a good time to end them. Before they really got started and attached...

"Lost in thought?" Alfred asked.

"Just timing you to see if I needed to steal your keys to escape," Laika quipped back.

He laughed in response. "I am glad I beat your time table."

Alfred sat down next to her and placed what looked more like a toolbox than a first aid kit on the coffee table. Laika reached out for the box, but his hand fell on hers. His voice was very careful as he spoke, "Please do not mistake this as reneging on your terms... but I must warn you that this is not pretty by any definition."

"I can handle not pretty," Laika responded without missing a beat. Her hand continued for the box, flipping the latch.

"I am sure you can, but how much experience do you have with exposed muscle?" Alfred asked bluntly.

Her eyes narrowed as she tried to figure out if he was joking. "Really?"

"Yes. Laika, you need to understand that I am dead. Injuries do not work the same for me and this is... rather dire looking. But the only goal is to stop the bleeding as I will heal given time," Alfred pulled his hand back. Laika opened the toolbox to find it was a mix between hardware, arts and crafts, and a sewing box. There were easily 10 different bottles of glue of various types. What kind of medical kit was this? "I will handle putting myself back together," Alfred stated as he started to unbutton his shirt.

"What am I supposed to do then?" she asked. Her frustration threatened to flare, but so far it appeared Alfred was being cooperative.

"Hand me something when I ask," the vampire explained, "and if you feel unwell, then you know where the guest bathroom is."

Laika rolled her eyes at how dramatic he was being. It was unusual for Alfred, but she felt she might regret that thought as more buttons revealed how badly he was injured. He looked like he'd gone through a meat grinder. Chunks of his chest were torn up by hundreds of claw marks. Laika felt her stomach turn. She forced her eyes away from Alfred, looking down at the toolbox.

"Are you alright?" Alfred asked quietly.

"Yes." The word was clipped from Laika. She was not okay. But as long as she took a few deep breaths and focused on handing over requested items, she wouldn't throw up in his living room. Alfred took her answer at face value. He asked for glue, which she gave over. She inquired, "So last night, you were at the center of the fight?"

"Yes, I am the safest person to go on scene as vampires crave living blood over the dead," Alfred explained as he worked. "Once the ritual was dispelled, I contained the frenzying vampires and removed any humans from the scene I could."

"How many of them were there?" She wanted a number.

"I did not count, but many," answered Alfred.

Laika continued to pepper him with questions about the threat containment to pass the time. Thankfully, putting Alfred back together didn't take very long. After about ten minutes he announced, "I only need to wrap bandages now."

"I can help," Laika latched onto the idea. He shouldn't be bleeding anymore, at least.

"Of course," agreed Alfred, handing her the gauze, "Once I am wrapped, will you deem me safe to be on my own?"

"I'm not leaving," the words escaped before Laika could stop herself again.

"I did wonder if that was going to be the case. I will put fresh sheets on the guest room bed shortly then," conceded Alfred.

Laika began to wrap the bandages firmly around his chest. She'd text her friends afterward and let them know the change of plans so no one would worry. "Is that a problem?"

"No, you are welcome to stay. But as you can see, I do not have a TV. I have never needed one before," explained Alfred. He gestured to all the books around them as his form of entertainment.

"Oh that's fine," laughed Laika. They'd find something to pass the time.

"I think I have a copy of Scrabble around here?" offered Alfred.

CHAPTER 7
REVELATION

Evie
November 5th, 2018
Taran Estate, Los Angeles, CA

Evie had taken Thursday and Friday of last week off. Initially, Tony had told her 'hell no' when she called him at 4am on Thursday asking. But she admitted to being on scene for the 'Halloween Frenzy,' as the news had dubbed it. Tony's tone had changed and he'd strictly forbid Evie from coming to work or taking Arik's calls until Monday.

She'd been forced to set Arik to 'Do Not Disturb' by Friday morning. His text messages had started by asking about her health; Evie appreciated that he'd worried if she was hospitalized. But he'd fallen into his usual ways as soon as he was sure she wasn't dying, demanding details of the fight for their screenplay.

She felt a nervous energy flowing through her at the thought of seeing her boss since she'd set him to ignore over the weekend. Thankfully, most of her bruising had faded into light purpling marks and everything on her face was easily concealed. No one would be able to tell the difference, and hopefully he wouldn't be too angry.

When Evie opened the front door with her key, she found Arik already waiting for her. He was sitting on the stairs with two coffees and his laptop, and was dressed for the day. "Good morning," Arik chirped a bright greeting. He held up one of the coffees for Evie.

She was tempted to just take a step back outside and run. What insane trap had the elf set for her this morning? Evie forced herself to perk up. "Good morning; did you have a good weekend?"

"I spent my weekend reading all your updates to our shared document. I absolutely love them!" Arik praised. His good mood was an infectious aura, threatening to sweep Evie up with it.

"My updates?" Evie asked, hoping she wouldn't regret the question.

"Oh yes!" Arik patted the stair next to him and waited for her to join him.

Evie recognized their screenplay on the laptop, but she didn't know the scene she was reading right now. Since when was there a magic fight on a rooftop in the middle of a storm, with lightning going every direction? She snatched the laptop from Arik and went back to the top to read.

The entire screenplay was different. It had morphed from some Elven James Bond monologuer to an Avengers style ensemble with all the races involved in a neat moonlighting unit. Scenes she'd written to make Arik look good had been taken and given to these new characters. The new paramedic witch reminded Evie of Melinda from their short interactions. The vampire was frustratingly similar to Alfred with every line of dialogue.

This was better... a lot better than Evie had written. She hadn't made these updates, and clearly neither had Arik.

Evie checked the revision history. Laika's name was all over the screenplay starting on Thursday night. Instead of joy, Evie felt her frustration start to overflow. She hadn't seen her packmate since

Laika had left to take Alfred home. There had been a few text messages, but otherwise she'd been out of contact.

For a brief moment, Evie considered taking credit for the new script. Instead she frowned. "I didn't write this."

"What?" Arik looked scandalized as he leaned over her shoulder.

"I let Laika read the screenplay last week. I gave her access to the doc and I guess she just rewrote a lot of it," Evie apologized. As happy as her boss was with the changes, he might not be so thrilled to learn that Evie hadn't kept her promise.

Arik's expression went stern and he clarified, "So, you did not spend all weekend rewriting this. Your roommate just took it on herself, with no research or conversations with you? And she produced this screenplay in a weekend?"

Evie nodded.

"How do we get her to finish our screenplay?" Arik's good mood didn't even dip.

"Wh- You're not mad?" The question slipped past Evie's lips before she could even think twice.

The elf had an incredulous look on his face. Arik waited for a moment as if for a punch line and then laughed, "Oh wait! You're serious? This is Hollywood. If you can't do it, then you hire someone who can. It's simply common sense."

There was a sneaking suspicion in Evie's mind that he'd meant himself. Arik had connived his way into this deal to get the screenplay written by an 'authentic moonlighter'. Speaking of the deal... Evie realized she had perfect leverage to get some real answers now. But she had to play her cards right...

"You want me to ask Laika to finish the whole screenplay?" she asked, making sure to emphasize how much work he was asking for.

Arik caught up with her quickly and he took on a serious tone, "Yes. Let's be honest here, you are a terrible writer. Your scenes are B-Action tropes at best. Laika has a flair that we need."

Evie wanted to disagree, but that would be against her own interests. She'd told him day one of this crazy idea she wasn't a writer. There was no point getting offended by the truth now. "Okay, yes, this is a better script. I can get Laika to finish this for you," Evie stated. She'd already started digging her phone out.

"What's the price?" Arik asked.

She could feel his eyes watching her every move as Evie sent a message to her packmate.

> EVIE
>
> I know what you did

> LAIKA
>
> Get your mind out of the gutter!

> EVIE
>
> I'm talking about my screenplay

> LAIKA
>
> Oh!
>
> Yeah, your screenplay was trash I fixed it

> EVIE
>
> I need you to keep fixing it.

> LAIKA
>
> Why? It's not a real movie?

Evie glanced up at her boss hovering over nearby. She had told Laika this wasn't real and she was just filling time until her questions were answered. A little white lie wasn't going to hurt. "Laika says she'll finish it."

Arik's aura lit up like a christmas tree with golds and pinks of pure joy.

"But!" Evie quickly cut his celebration short, "You need to get me all the information you have on elven rituals that corrupt the five elements. And I need it today."

"Is that seriously what she wants?" Arik deflated at the news.

"Yes," Evie confirmed before typing back a message to Laika.

EVIE

I know, but Arik said he'll get us elven
corruption rituals

LAIKA

Really?!

EVIE

Yep, but you need to finish the story for him.

"I have money; could I just pay her instead?" Arik pleaded, sitting back down.

"She says she needs the rituals for the Anarchist case," Evie shrugged as if there was nothing she could do about it. As of right now, Laika did want those rituals for payment, and Arik did want her friend to finish the script. Everyone got what they wanted in the end.

"What about a better job?" the elf attempted as he scrolled through his phone. "I could give her a job here as my other assistant. The pay has to be better than throwing sacks around for a living."

"It's really not," Evie answered.

Arik snapped a glare at her, but the werewolf didn't back down. She and Laika made about the same. In Evie's opinion her job was a lot worse, but it provided health insurance so she stayed.

"The ending better be amazing," scowled Arik as he dialed the phone. Evie could hear him muttering, but she couldn't make out the rest as he turned away. Her text messages chimed again, Evie saw her packmate had responded.

LAIKA

Okay... I really want to help...

EVIE

But???

LAIKA

Alfred helped me write part of it.

He had all the old moonlighting stories that
I used

Evie scowled darkly at her phone. Of course he had to be involved. Couldn't they have anything without Alfred right now?

Arik's call was answered by the gentle sounding voice of an elderly woman, but not a word was understandable. Evie wasn't sure what language they were speaking and she couldn't really follow along.

She went back to her text messages.

EVIE

Can you just ask him to help then?

I'm getting this information for his case

LAIKA

I'll ask, just give me a second

The conversation next to Evie suddenly switched gears, as Arik's voice slowed down. "Grandmama, I need you to speak English... Yes, English. I'm putting you on speaker now." There was a slight crackle as the elf pulled his phone away from his ear. Arik held it between them, finger tapping the speakerphone button quickly.

"Is this clear enough?" asked the woman on the other end. Her English was flawless with a good Californian accent. If Evie hadn't just heard otherwise, she would have assumed the old woman was a native speaker.

"Yes, Grandmama. That's fine. I'm sure Evie can understand you now," Arik answered. He held the phone out to the werewolf.

Evie was startled by the sudden change in plans. "Oh you want me to just ask her?" She'd thought she'd have time to make a list of questions.

"Aeriken, where are your manners? Introduce us properly," scolded the elderly woman.

Evie finally put together what was happening; Arik had called his grandmother for magical advice.

"Grandmama, I have told you a thousand times I go by Arik," responded the elf. He sounded exasperated already. But he did as instructed. "Evie, this is my grandmother, Aerel Taranis, the matri-arch of the Taranis family. Grandmama, this is Evie Belle, she is a moonlighter working on those Anarchist cases. She has a few ques-tions for you about elven magic."

Evie still had no clue what questions to ask, but her phone saved her.

LAIKA

Alfred wants to know what rituals are being offered.

Evie hit the call button, forcing her packmate into this conversa-tion whether she liked it or not. She quickly put on her bluetooth so that she could keep Laika in her ear.

"Hello?" Laika answered, her tone laced with confusion.

"Thank you for agreeing to speak with me," Evie spoke up so Arik's phone would hear her. "I understand you're an expert on elven magic?"

"Oh," cried Laika, "I'll go on break. Give me like two minutes tops to get somewhere quiet!"

"That's correct," Aerel Taranis answered the actual question.

"Do you have a lot of knowledge about the elements used in magic?" Evie tried to sound smart but until last week she couldn't even name all five of them.

"I know enough to answer any question you'll have," Aerel responded. Evie looked to Arik for confirmation, and he nodded vigorously.

"Back," Laika's voice sounded in her ear.

"Okay," Evie answered her packmate before turning her atten-tion back to Arik's phone. She pondered how to ask, without influ-encing the answer. The answer came to her in a flash as Arik fidgeted with his sleeve cuff.

"Would you know a ritual that would increase the air pressure over a large area? A few city blocks for example?" Evie started with the magic that she assumed the woman would be most knowledge-able with.

A cackle rang out of Arik's phone. "Air pressure? Are you asking *the* Skysong Matriarch if she is familiar with our simplest magic?"

"Grandmama, it was more than a little storm front," Arik joined in to explain. "The pressure was enough to crack glass and crush... people."

There was a moment of silence before Aerel replied. "A caster of sufficient strength from the bloodline could pull off a feat like that, but LA suffers from a lack of proper bloodlines."

Laika interjected, "Ask her about the sinkhole? Alfred says a silvertide elf could definitely have caused that much damage if they'd taken out the underground metal supports or a really powerful amberglade could too."

Evie tried to keep her explanation vague. "Do you know of a ritual that could crumble a large portion of the ground out?"

"Do you mean the ground falling away? Or just cracking, like earthquake lines?" Aerel asked for clarification.

Evie wished she could read auras over the phone, because she thought for a moment the matriarch was taking the second question more seriously. So she continued, "The former, an epicenter that radiated outwards."

Aerel admitted, "There are types of elves that could cause that much damage and rituals to allow less powerful ones to generate similar effects. Did this happen in LA?"

Laika cut in, "So that's two for two right now, if these rituals are real."

Their conversation had an awkward pause as Evie used Arik's laptop to take notes. She was quickly updating the chart they'd made a while ago. "I'm sorry, give me a moment to write this down." Arik picked up the conversation to give the werewolf time.

"Hey, Alfred said to ask if there is an elven ritual that combines amberglade and ashfall to invoke chemical imbalances in the dead." Laika sounded like she was reading off a text message. Evie hated the words 'Alfred said', but she knew it was a better question than she had.

"Aeriken, I insist you come up for Christmas," Aerel pestered in a sweet grandmotherly voice.

"Grandmama," Arik tried to push her off, "I've told you the holidays are the busiest times for me. I can't miss the entire Christmas season to sit around a frozen lake with you. Maybe in the new year."

"I'm sorry to interrupt," Evie jumped in at the first silence. She repeated the question from Laika and Alfred.

"As in a Blood Frenzy?" Aerel's pretense of a kind old lady melted away. "Is that what happened at Halloween?"

Evie didn't know how to answer. She went with the truth, "Yes, I think."

"My dear, you have a demon summoning problem," Aerel Taranis declared, leaving no room for argument.

"Demons? Honestly Grandmama, you think it's always demons," scolded Arik.

Evie heard Laika exclaim on the other end of the earpiece. She was probably relaying the revelation to Alfred now.

"Let me guess," interrupted Aerel, "First you had a freak incident involving lightning? Either something caught fire at a temperature that was impossible or there was an explosion of sorts. Next, something metal melted from the inside."

"How did you know?" Evie couldn't stop herself. The old elf had nailed the Fulmino and CorroNect incidents. Maybe she'd heard about them on the news?

"These are called the Corruption of the Elements. You need all five before you can summon a demon. They are usually represented as Lightning for Fire, Rust for Metal, Crumbling for Earth, Crushing for Air, and Blood for Water. The Corruptions must be performed in that order on specific moon phases as well," Aerel explained, but she almost sounded bored by the topic.

"Alfred says he's heard of this and is looking for a ritual book now," Laika supplied, but for once she didn't sound excited. Evie couldn't blame her friend because the idea of someone summoning a demon in Glenwood was crazy. This theory hadn't crossed anyone's mind until now.

"Shit," swore Laika on the phone.

"What?" Evie asked, really hoping it wouldn't be that bad.

There was a short pause then Laika answered, "Alfred says that anyone can summon a demon. You don't need to have magic; it's like universal magic that powers itself."

"Really?!"

"What's that dear?" Aerel inquired, "Did you have another question? Or are you just realizing you've got an elven problem?"

That conflicted with what Evie had literally just learned. "Isn't demon summoning generic- I mean universal magic?"

Aerel scoffed, "I suppose, but Elves are the best at it. A human is more likely to get themselves killed. There is a simple way to determine the answer, though."

Everyone waited for the old woman to continue speaking, but she held her tongue as the minute stretched on. "For goodness sake, Grandmama! I'll visit for Christmas! A couple days at most," hissed Arik on his phone.

"You can compare the summon circle to the depictions in one of the family ritual books," Aerel picked up her explanation. She never acknowledged her grandson's defeat for the holidays.

"I don't have an elven ritual book," Arik reminded. His good mood had flatlined into waves of irritation.

"Elemory has one and she's still living in Los Angeles. Go ask her to see it," answered the elderly woman.

Evie looked between the phone and Arik a few times trying to understand what was happening. She tried to console him with gratitude, "Thank you?"

"Don't thank her. She already got what she wanted," snipped Arik. He gave his grandmother a curt goodbye before hanging up. Laika had already hung up as well, but Evie didn't even remember her saying goodbye.

"So... Where are we going?" Evie hazarded a question, even with the frustration rolling off Arik.

"To Glitterholic..." Arik mumbled in response, turning on his heel to stomp back up the stairs.

Evie looked bewildered. "Shouldn't we go now?"

"It doesn't open until 7!"

- ☽ -

November 5th, 2018
Glitterholic, Los Angeles, CA

Bass shook Evie to the core. How could anyone hear anything with this much noise? Music was pulsing so loudly through this club that she was pretty sure it was vibrating the walls.

Then again, Evie wasn't entirely sure since literally every surface of this place was covered in glitter. Glitterholic lived up to its name. This place could not have been more different from the goth monochrome of Twisted Cross, or even the dive bar feel of Hair of the Dog. The walls, floor, and furniture were all loud colors. Reds, pinks, yellows, and purples swirled around Evie like a vortex.

Arik had marched inside the moment the doors opened, pulling Evie with him. He hadn't paused at the coat check, just made a beeline for the bar with none of his usual dramatics of making a big splash for a club sighting. If anything, Arik's aura screamed he wanted to be out of Glitterholic as quickly as possible.

He'd parked Evie by the bar, set down his credit card, and told her to wait there. She watched him vanish into the growing crowd with a huff. Thankfully, the bar was a little quieter here than the dance floor, allowing Evie to collect her thoughts. She stood impatiently, nails tapping on the glittering plastic of the bar top as she scanned the club.

The crowd was only elves so far; they ranged in colors and dress, but everyone had those pointy ears. Evie also noted that no one looked over 45 in this place. Granted she knew Arik was older than he looked, so that probably held true for the rest of the elves.

"Hi Evie!"

Evie spun around; she'd heard people but hadn't expected anyone to talk to her. Standing just a few feet away was an elf giving her a cheerful wave. She had no idea who this woman was or how she knew her nam-

Eyes widened in shock as Evie realized the elf was Becky. The woman had cut off all her long blonde hair in favor of a short pixie cut and she'd dyed it a raven black. Her nose ring wasn't the only piercing Becky had anymore; multiple studs and hoops spread along both her slightly pointed ears. Plus, the dress she wore must have been black leather with the way it clung to the elf.

Evie realized she'd been staring, or more openly gaping at Becky. What the hell had she done to herself? Why had she done it? Why was it every time Evie was anywhere near something remotely elven she ran into Becky?

"Hi," Evie forced out a moment later.

"I'm really excited to see you," Becky continued. She awkwardly sat down on the bar stool next to the werewolf. Her legs struggled to cooperate with the black leather and she nearly slipped off the seat.

"Yeah, nice to see you too," Evie replied. Where was Arik? Why did this keep happening to her?

"So, we've known each other a long time now," Becky started, making sure she had good eye contact for her speech.

Evie couldn't stop the look of confusion bubbling up. They'd known each other for two months at best? But she didn't cut the elven woman off.

"You've always been so kind to me, especially when I really needed it. I never really got a chance to thank you for that before. By the time I got up the courage you were gone..." Becky trailed off for a moment; she looked emotional.

If they hadn't been in a crowded club, then Evie would have opened up her empathy to try and get a read on this bizarre situation. She tried to soothe the girl, hoping she didn't cry. "It's fine, glad I could help?"

"See, even now you're thinking about my feelings," bubbled Becky. Her tears dried up as she continued, "I've thought about this for a long time and I think I'm finally worthy of it."

Evie was even more confused now, but she couldn't get her mouth to open and stop whatever was happening.

"You're amazing! You're so kind and so good at everything you do, plus you're as beautiful on the outside as the inside," Becky fawned for a moment.

Then Evie realized exactly what was happening. Oh shit...

Becky's face lit up as she asked, "Would you please do me the honor of letting me take you on a date?"

"Don't you have a boyfriend?" Evie blurted out in response. Last time she'd seen Becky, the elf had been all over another guy. Peter or something like that.

"Petronius isn't in a place to be dating anymore," answered Becky. Her confidence from before was shaken by the question. "We weren't meant to be..."

Evie liked that answer even less than she'd expected. She'd been hoping to hear they'd just broken up so she could point out that she didn't like to be the rebound. So she tried again, "I'm not looking for a relationship right now."

"I'm only asking for a date, it's not a marriage proposal," pushed Becky. But the way she said the words made Evie feel even more like it was a proposal. For a moment she again considered opening up her empathy to get a better read on the situation. But as Evie decided she had to be blunt, she didn't want to feel the effects of her next words.

"I'm sorry, you're just not my type," Evie mumbled, "I need to go."

"But-," Becky tried to stop her as the werewolf took off into the crowd.

Evie knew that was going to hit like a gunshot to the heart. What else was she supposed to say? Never once had she felt anything for Becky but mild discomfort. Evie didn't want to destroy her self-confidence, but no good would come from going out with someone so clearly smitten with her when she didn't feel the same way. Leading Becky on would be much crueler than a clean break here.

She forced her way into the dancing elves, hoping they'd be an effective barrier. Maybe Evie could just go wait in the car? Evie looked up, scanning above tall, pretty elves for the red 'exit' sign. She prayed it wasn't too far, and once she got out she'd just text Arik, and-

"Evie!"

She flinched, but it wasn't Becky calling for her this time. Arik parted the crowd as if they were merely paper people. He scolded Evie, "I thought you were waiting at the bar?"

Evie was torn between annoyed and so thankful he'd shown up now.

"The bar got complicated, okay?" she pushed off his reprimand.

Her boss glanced up back to where he'd left her with a curious expression, but he didn't see anything that caused him concern. "How do you know so many elves?"

"Shut up," Evie hissed, a flare of her anger winning, "Did you get the-"

Her question was cut off as Arik held up a manila folder. "Yes. I have multiple photocopies for you, me, and Laika. Shall we get out of here?"

"Please," Evie agreed.

CHAPTER 8
COMPROMISE

Evie
November 5th, 2018
Night Claw Residence, Glenwood, CA

Creeped out was too strong an emotion for how Evie felt, but she did spend the drive back to Glenwood confused. She examined every interaction with Becky over and over. Evie hadn't even been polite the day they met. She practically kicked Becky out while fawning over Tor. There was nothing that could explain that extremely impassioned speech from the half elf.

Becky talked like they'd known each other for years, not months. But that couldn't be right. Could it? Despite the implied Bel Air connection, Evie was certain she'd never met a blonde Becky at her family's parties or school. Maybe she'd find a yearbook to double check?

Evie barely realized she'd parked her Saab on the driveway. Still, she felt guilt creeping up her spine; she'd shot Becky down a little too firmly. She'd panicked in the moment because the date had come out of nowhere. In the light of Evie's dashboard, it was easier to see she should have done better. There was no point dwelling on her mistake now; she'd apologize the next time she saw Becky at coffee.

Sweeping up the folder of papers from the passenger seat, Evie made her way into the house. She needed to focus on her case and not her love life for a few hours. Laika needed a copy of these ritual circles. That meant making her come home tonight. Evie opened the door with her keys, planning on calling her packmate. But there was no need.

"Hey Evie... You're home late," Laika stood by the couch with an overnight bag in hand.

"Hey..." Awkwardness hung from that single word as Evie realized she didn't really know what to say.

Last time they'd seen each other, she'd caught Laika, or at least she thought she'd caught Laika, fooling around in a public space. At that moment, Evie had felt completely justified in her reaction. There was blood on her best friend and a vampire. What else was Evie supposed to think?

Then when confronted, Laika had chewed her out, thrown Evie's phone at her, and ditched her. All less than 24 hours since they'd nearly died at Halloween... Aside from the phone call with Grandmama Taranis, they'd barely spoken in days.

Evie groped around for more words, but she hated how jealous they sounded when she spoke, "Are you finally home?"

Laika shook her head. "No. I needed to pick up some fresh clothes before I headed back to Alfred's. We're going to go look for the ritual circles."

"Seriously?" Evie felt her annoyance surge and wasn't able to hide it. "You've been gone all weekend and you're going back out again? Do you even live here anymore?"

Confusion rippled through Laika's aura, matching the expression on her face. "What? I said Alfred was really, really hurt and I was staying there to take care of him. He's not like us... he doesn't heal as quickly."

"He said he was fine, as I recall," Evie snapped.

Laika glared and set her overnight bag down on the coffee table. "Okay, hold up. What's this really about?"

"It doesn't matter," Evie marched herself past her packmate. She was intent to sulk in her room for the rest of the night.

"Fine," grumbled Laika, picking up her bag again, "It's not like you talk to me anymore anyway. Why would this be any different?"

Evie stopped in her tracks. Why was she doing this again? "Wait," she called, turning around to catch Laika just opening the front door, "Don't go."

"What?" Her packmate paused, but didn't take her hand off the handle. Dark clouds of emotion thundered around Laika.

"I hate Alfred." Evie finally let herself say how she'd been feeling for weeks now.

Laika's frown deepened.

"Just hear me out! He came out of nowhere two months ago and now he's all you're thinking about. He threw our happy life into complete chaos with all his magic and moonlighting. We don't really know anything about him, but you suddenly trust him completely about everything. AND I CAN'T READ HIM AT ALL!" Evie screamed the last part before catching her breath.

Laika stood at the doorway staring quietly. Then she dropped her bag from her shoulder and closed the distance between them to pull Evie into a tight hug.

"You are such a total fucking idiot," Laika proclaimed as she held onto Evie.

Tension melted as all of Evie's limbs turned to jelly. She held onto her friend, returning the hug and using Laika to stand on her feet. Otherwise, she might just crumble to the floor.

"I already know you don't like Alfred and I know why," Laika explained quietly, "I know this has nothing to really do with him. It's about me and you, and how much you worry about me all the time."

Evie felt tears welling up.

Laika held her friend as she continued, "I know it's been a long time since Zach... I know you're worried about what's going to happen to me if this relationship ends badly again, and it doesn't really matter who it is. You not being able to read Alfred's emotions means you can't tell in advance if he's just here to screw around... But Evie, I'm a big girl and I'm ready to try again."

"But-," Evie tried to voice her feelings. She both loved and hated how well Laika could read her, even without magical empathy powers.

"No, you are my best friend and no guy is ever going to come between us. I'm sorry I made you feel that way, but you also don't get to decide who I like or who I'm going to date. That's my decision," Laika cut her off again.

Evie slumped down to the floor as soon as the hug broke.

A moment later Laika sat down next to her so they could lean on each other, shoulder to shoulder. "I love you Evie, but you gotta understand it's my life. I get to make my own mistakes."

"I know," Evie admitted, "I know and I'm sorry. If I can stop bad things from happening to you though... then I can't help but try."

"You can't always protect me from me," teased Laika.

Evie pulled her friend into an awkward side hug, "Says the woman who controls my run schedule. Always forcing me to go when I don't want to."

"Me getting my heart broken is not the same as you rampaging through the neighborhood," Laika shot back with a laugh.

The atmosphere had calmed, all the tension dissipating as the friends cleared the air. That was the nice thing about their friendship. Evie only ever had to open her mouth when there was a problem. They just talked these things out so they could move past it.

"Okay fair," Evie broke into giggles. She wanted to curl up into Laika's arms for the rest of the night. But they had work to do.

She still had the folder of rituals from Arik. Evie cleared her throat and she held it up for Laika to see. "I almost forgot... These are those ritual pages."

"Oh," Laika lit up again, grabbing the folder. She started flipping through all of the papers.

Evie could feel the usual excitement from her packmate... but there was an undercurrent of worry that wasn't normally there. It reminded Evie of when they'd been standing outside Cold Blooded.

"Are *you* doing okay?" Evie nudged Laika in the ribs to drag her attention back up from the papers. The two hadn't really talked about what had happened on Halloween night, or what they'd learned since.

Laika's focus only flickered up from the paper for a second, "Yeah, I'm fine."

"I'm not," Evie admitted, "I'm in full panic about demons marching down the street."

The air around them grew tense again as Laika put the papers down. Her tone was serious when she spoke, "I didn't think when we started digging into break-ins we'd be worried about demons."

"Me neither," the redhead groaned. Evie's head hurt just thinking about what that meant and her imagination kept conjuring up frightful images. Her lack of knowledge was scarier than any truth.

There was a tinge of anxiety to Laika's words as she chose them carefully. "I asked Alfred about demons... but it doesn't seem like even he knows alot about them." A snide comment hung on the tip of Evie's tongue about how there was finally something that Alfred didn't know. But now wasn't the time for that as Laika's next question forced her to push her petty feelings to the side. Her friend asked, " Do you think we're out of our depth?"

Evie took a deep breath as she thought about Laika's question. Were they out of their depth? "Yes, we are absolutely in over our heads right now. We've never dealt with anything more dangerous than a dwarf throwing some glass around until Halloween... But if we don't step up and do something... Who will?" Evie looked up to find her friend's amber eyes.

- ☾ -
Laika
November 5th, 2018
Night Claw Residence, Glenwood, CA

Laika searched Evie's face for any indecision, but found only fierce resolution. But Laika didn't know if she felt that same fire...

They didn't know the first thing about demons. They still had no idea who summoned one. And Glenwood's magical expert was barely getting off the couch right now. Night Claw wasn't rated for this and she really had no idea what she could do to help...

When did that ever stop Laika before?

Her face warmed up with a wild smile, "Obviously, Night Claw is going to rise to the occasion. Think about how jealous Blood Fang is going to be when we stop a demon?"

Evie burst into laughter at Laika's declaration.

The sound egged Laika on. Evie clearly needed a dose of humor to help calm her nerves. "I mean, you saw Randall's face when he heard we were on the case. I think he might actually pop a blood vessel if we are the heroes that save the city."

"I know," Evie managed to say between giggles.

Laika cleared her throat before continuing, her tone taking on a stuffy cadence. "Night Claw could never bust out of the bottom rank! And now they're in the big leagues, competing with Dark Wind for jobs, it's so unfair!"

The peals of laughter coming from Evie were music to Laika's ears. She couldn't help but match her mood.

"Your Randall impression is terrible... And I doubt one job is going to put us on the level with Dark Wind," gasped Evie. She lovingly punched Laika in the shoulder.

"Probably not... but we have to dream big."

Laika meant every word. Halloween had been rough because they'd failed so miserably, and gotten so very lucky at the same time.

But she had her head on straight about what happened that night now. She punched a fist in the air, "Which means we have to figure out how to unsummon a demon!"

"Do you have any idea how we even start figuring that out?" Evie pressed. Her friend was under control again, just leaning into Laika's side.

"Well... As much as you don't want to hear it. Alfred said we need to know the origin of the ritual and the type of demon before we can kick their butt back to the demonic planes," shrugged Laika. She wished she had more to help.

Evie was staring down at the ritual papers scattered around them. "How do we narrow it down?"

"By finding the circle," explained Laika, "I took the week off work-"

"You what?" scolded Evie as she snapped her gaze up to her friend.

"I told my dad I needed the week to process Halloween. He's not happy but he agreed. I'm going to use the extra time to find one of the ritual circles and then we can compare to this," Laika tried to soothe again.

"What am I supposed to do while you're galavanting around without me?" Evie demanded.

"Try really hard not to sleep with our roommate so we don't lose her rent," teased Laika. She was half-joking; Evie hadn't done more than make eyes at Tor for months. But she wasn't going to pass up the opportunity to point out her love life wasn't the only complicated one right now. Laika gave Evie a pleading look, "Or you could make Arik use his LA connections to find any dwarven or witch versions of demon summoning?"

Evie scoffed, "Are you serious right now?"

"I promise I'll spend my days working on your screenplay?" Laika tried to offer a deal.

"Fine... But you need to make sure that Arik looks good at the end of this movie. Or I'll get the blame," Evie negotiated.

"Yeah, no problem," assured Laika.

"Also, I'm not going to sleep with Tor!" Evie added with a huff. But the clear red on her cheeks gave away that her best friend hadn't given up on their roommate yet.

Laika laughed, "At the very least don't sleep with Tor in our bed."

"Oh and one more thing," pressed Evie. She took both of Laika's hands in hers and gave her a very serious look. Laika was growing concerned about what the final term could be. Did Arik want something stupid added to the script like a romance? Or was she about to get a confession that Evie and Tor were already friends with benefits?

Evie took a calming breath then said, "You need to change your ringtone."

"What? Why?" Laika was confused now. What did that have to do with anything?

"The clicking sound is really annoying and I want to hurl your phone through a window every time Alfred texts you," answered Evie.

"Oh... Why didn't you just say so before!" Laika found herself laughing once more.

CHAPTER 9
RITUAL CIRCLES

Laika
November 6th, 2018
Shady Hollows Apartments, Glenwood, CA

"That's not a word!" Laika glared down at the scrabble board that sat between her and Alfred. She was winning, but now he was closing in on her lead during the final moves.

"I beg to differ. 'Hiraeth' is very much a legitimate word," countered Alfred.

They looked comical sitting on the floor and playing Scrabble at 3 in the afternoon. Alfred was dressed in one of his fine suits and used the couch to prop himself up. Meanwhile, Laika hadn't bothered getting dressed after she got up, so she was still lounging in her pajama tank and shorts. A box of poptarts was half devoured next to her.

"No, it's not!" exclaimed Laika. This was the first game she'd actually been in the lead; she wasn't going down without a fight.

Alfred looked smug, like he'd been planning this trap for rounds.

Since they'd started spending time in his apartment, Laika had noticed that he laughed more openly. She didn't know if it was because he was more comfortable in his own space, or with her. Right now that glee was antagonizing her. Laika scowled as she picked up her phone to look it up. Every letter annoyed her as she searched on the Merriam Webster site for anything even close. Nothing popped up. Victory! She raised her gaze back to Alfred, grinning as she turned the screen towards him. "Look, there's nothing there."

The vampire looked unconcerned. He raised a single finger as he recited a definition like he was reading it out of a dictionary. "'Hiraeth' is a sense of longing or homesickness, a Welsh word that has connections to-"

"If it's Welsh that means it doesn't count! And for all I know you're making that up." Laika inclined her head, narrowing her eyes as she studied him. He seemed very prepared if this was a made-up word.

"I assure you I am not. I believe I have a Welsh-to-English dictionary that will support my claim," Alfred answered with a knowing smirk.

"Prove it," Laika demanded. After so many games, she'd realized that Alfred just knew a lot more words than her. He'd even offered to let her use her phone while they played Scrabble. Laika's pride railed against the idea; she was winning this round on her own merits.

Alfred dragged himself up from the floor to get the book and for a moment Laika almost stopped him. He was healing, but slowly. Between that and his wrecked daylight gear, they couldn't go out until the sun was down to look for ritual circles, which had resulted in many rounds of Scrabble. But if she was going to win this one, Laika needed a strategy before he got back. No doubt this was going to be a real word that ate into her lead. She needed to take victory... even if that meant playing a little unfair. But first she'd need to test the waters.

"I believe we will find the answer here," Alfred said as he held out a dictionary to Laika. His smug expression was still in place.

Carefully, Laika rolled her shoulders back and sat up straight. She pretended to look at the proffered book, but kept her gaze on him. She saw his eyes glance down and barely managed to repress her glee. No matter their age or race, a low cut shirt was easily weaponized against a man. At least Alfred had the grace not to openly stare.

"It'll take me hours to find anything in there; you find it," Laika demanded.

As soon as Alfred took his seat on the floor, Laika slid around the coffee table to his side. He'd never disagreed with her physical contact before and she doubted he'd complain now. So Laika slipped under his arm so that she could lean into his side, still being careful of his healing wounds.

He welcomed her contact, but warned, "Keep your eyes off my tiles."

Laika gave him an overly innocent look, being careful not to look at the board, "I would never cheat like that."

Alfred's expression was disbelieving, but he didn't push her away. Instead he adjusted his arm so that he could keep Laika pressed to his side and opened the book.

"Hey," Laika put her hand on the side of Alfred's face, pulling his gaze to hers. Mischief rang in her words, "How would you feel about a friendly bet on the game?"

"A bet? What did you have in mind?" He looked intrigued at the idea; she had his interest.

"One honest answer," suggested Laika. She ran her fingers gently along the side of Alfred's face. Under her touch his muscles twitched and relaxed.

Alfred's answer sounded almost distracted, "An answer... Any question?"

Laika nodded quickly; she bit her lip for emphasis.

"I suppose that sounds like a simple enough wager," agreed Alfred. He leaned into the hand still on his face.

"Even if you get this word, I'm still in the lead right now," reminded Laika. She waited for his agreement before letting her eyes go back to the book. Her hand moved to hold onto the arm she was wrapped in.

Clearing his throat, Alfred opened the dictionary with more force than before. "Give me just a moment to find my word."

"There's not a lot of rounds left, are you sure you can come back even if this 'word' is real?" Laika teased. She watched the C's and the D's flip by. But Alfred paused in the E's as she stretched out her leg so that her toes brushed against his ankle.

A sharp blue eyed look said that Alfred knew exactly what she was doing right now. He held his tongue as he started up the search again. This was too easy. Laika had both the game and the bet won; she just had to go in for the final blow. Leaning forward ever so slightly, Laika's eyes dropped to Alfred's lips. Victory was in reach. "Something wrong?"

"Nothing," Alfred answered. He stopped on a page and his smirk returned, "Here we go. 'Hiraeth', as I promised."

Laika had been paying more attention to him than the book. For the first time, she was up close when Alfred smiled. Her brain finally realized something she'd known but hadn't put to words, and which stopped her dead in her tracks. "You've got fangs?"

"I am aware, as they are attached," Alfred's face quickly dropped into a warm, but close-lipped expression.

"I mean, I knew you did but they're... way longer than I thought," Laika hesitated, her attempt to distract him with a kiss fizzled.

"Do they make you uncomfortable?" His gaze turned back to Laika.

She could tell he was keeping them out of sight now. That really annoyed Laika. She hadn't meant to ruin their fun over something that didn't matter... probably didn't matter. "What? No, I'm fine!" Laika quickly declared.

Alfred's polite expression didn't waver, but Laika was certain that he didn't believe her. He was being far more restrained when he spoke next. "It is alright if they do."

"They don't," Laika snapped back. She was losing this battle and forced them to change topics. "Where is this fictional word?"

They both focused on the dictionary, allowing the awkward moment to pass. Alfred held up his book for Laika to see. "Hiraeth: nostalgia, longing, homesickness, a deep feeling of yearning for something, someone or somewhere."

"Okay... so it might be real, but you still can't use foreign words in Scrabble! It's in the rules," Laika used a teasing tone. She didn't actually know if that was true, but he didn't have any rules in the box.

"If that was the case, then why did we need to look it up?" He raised an eyebrow, clearly expecting an answer.

Laika paused, she looked between the page and the vampire. Then agreed, "You can have the points for this one. But no more words from other languages."

"We may find it difficult to finish the game as half of English is just stolen words from other langua-" Alfred was cut off half way through his argument. Laika snatched the heavy dictionary from his hands and tossed it directly into the center of their board. Tiles went flying in every direction, effectively ending the disagreement and the game.

"I believe that's my win," cheered Laika.

Alfred scowled at her, "How do you figure that?"

She shrugged dramatically, "Because I was in the lead. Do you have a better way to decide?" For a moment, Laika thought he might have an answer. When she shifted to be more in his lap, Alfred reconsidered. "So my victory?" pressed Laika.

Alfred's warmth returned. "I suppose this can be your victory. What is your question, then?"

"Hmmm," Laika made a show of tapping her lips as she considered what she was going to ask Alfred. There was one question that had been nagging at the edges of her mind, more curiosity than actual worry. Tor had said it was rude to ask... but he had agreed to any question... "What court are you?"

His amusement died at her words. Laika felt the air around them grow colder. She suddenly felt worry creeping through her that the question had been much ruder than she realized. But he hadn't pushed her away yet. "I do not tell anyone about my court," Alfred finally answered.

"Why?" The werewolf couldn't stop her curiosity from running away with her mouth. She thought the answer was pretty obvious as he was the 'magical expert' of MOONS. Alfred was either an iris or a rose vampire; those were the only real options left. Just because Laika had never seen him actually do magic yet didn't mean he couldn't.

"Do you tell everyone your weaknesses just because they ask?" the vampire responded.

"Well, yeah. I don't have one," Laika answered quickly, a very serious expression underscoring her words. She hoped if she was open and honest it would help combat the frost that was forming.

Werewolves all had an allergy, something that sapped their powers and made them sick. Most of the population were allergic to silver or wolfsbane, like the legends of old. But Laika wasn't, and she'd never found anything that caused her the same sickness.

"All werewolves have a weakness," Alfred disagreed.

"I swear I don't," Laika replied earnestly, "I'd swear it in blood, if you want?"

His blue eyes scanned every part of Laika's face looking for something. He seemed to find it though as Alfred proposed an alternative. "Please ask a different question. No matter the question, I will answer it as honestly as I can."

Laika scowled, but he really didn't want to talk about the type of vampire he was. She could keep pushing... "Fine," Laika agreed, "But the next one you don't get to sidestep!"

"I promise an honest answer to your alternate question," Alfred nodded.

Her sour expression disappeared as Laika went for the second most important question, "So how old are you?" Alfred threw his head back against the couch and closed his eyes. A few emotions warred on his face from frustration to respect. Laika wasn't going to back down this time. "Well?"

"I do not know," muttered Alfred. He didn't look at her.

Had Laika heard that right? "What?!"

Finally, he opened his eyes to look at her. "I do not know. I have not kept track of my age in a while. It means less as the years pass."

"That's so not fair! You promised me an answer," pouted Laika.

"Yes I did, and I will answer your question. Give me some time to research?" the vampire reasoned.

"You'll tell me as soon as you figure it out?"

"Yes," promised Alfred.

Laika wasn't sure how he'd research his own age, but he seemed sincere. "Okay, as long as you tell me then fine."

"Thank you," Alfred relaxed. All the coldness lingering from before had thawed with those words. Her patience seemed to have soothed him. He looked past her at the ruined game of Scrabble and then to his phone. Alfred added, "We should get moving. The sun will be down soon and then we can go check at Sync Holes for a ritual circle."

"Wouldn't it be better to go to the club? That circle is only a couple days old and with all the construction at the amusement park, that circle is probably gone," Laika pointed out.

"The club is no longer standing and there are rescue workers still on scene. We should not disturb them," Alfred reminded. He'd explained this once yesterday as they made the plan for the week.

"Okay," agreed Laika, "But you owe me one more thing before we leave."

Alfred looked back at her with a flicker of confusion and opened his mouth to ask what.

Laika wrapped her hands in the collar of his shirt to pull herself the distance between them and into a kiss. A small thrill at the contact shot down her spine. Alfred's lips were cool like the rest of skin. But then the tip of one of his fangs grazed her lip, and Laika jumped back before she could control herself.

She expected Alfred to be annoyed with her reaction. Instead he had that smug expression from before. "I knew you did not like my fangs."

"Shut up," hissed Laika, feeling herself blush. She was going to need to figure that out, and fast.

- ☾ -

November 7th, 2018
Downtown Glenwood, Glenwood, CA

L aika couldn't help but be bored. This was not the glorious moonlighting work she'd expected when she got on the Anarchist case.

Yesterday she'd trekked around the edge of a construction zone trying to find a ritual circle. But there was nothing to be found, just twisted metal and heavy equipment. Even Alfred admitted after an hour or two that if it *had* been there, then someone had likely destroyed it when they started pulling the ride frames out of the sinkhole.

Downtown Glenwood, on the other hand, was bouncing back from the pressure ritual. Today there was less destruction as far as the eye could see, and a few people milling about. After the streets and stores were cleaned up, a couple of them reopened with new staff. Usually at this time of night, most places were closed. But Hot off the Presses was lit up like a beacon in the night and had a tacky poster up on the front door declaring them the 'safest cafe on the block'.

Laika held onto Alfred's hand as he walked the streets looking for traces of magic. In Alfred's other hand, he held a small brass compass that pointed them towards residual magic. Runes on the side lit up based on the elements present. The brighter they were, the stronger the magic.

At first she was excited at every flash from the compass, but they were all false alarms. Every security system set off the tracer, which forced them to stop at every door and search around. After what must have been the 25th or 30th door, Laika could tell Alfred's patience was fraying.

"Who uses air magic for a security system? There are a dozen easier ways to use grey or black to reach the same effect. This had to be twice as difficult and much more fragile," muttered Alfred. His expression had hints of annoyance that he was trying to hide.

Laika didn't say anything at first. She just fished her phone out of her pocket, peeking at the time. She shot a quick text off to Evie.

LAIKA

Hey where were you when Pressure hit?

EVIE

Hot off the Presses

LAIKA

Do you know how close to the center that was? Or the direction?

EVIE

According to Owen, I was in the epicenter.

Are you downtown right now? Do you want me to come meet you?

LAIKA

No, that's alright.

EVIE

Are you sure?

LAIKA

Yeah, I'll keep you updated if me and Alfred find anything. Promise

"Come on," Laika reached out to snag Alfred's hand, pulling him away from their latest door. "I have somewhere for us to check out."

There was one last flicker of annoyance at the door that had vexed them, but Alfred's gaze moved to meet Laika's. His hand shifted, lacing their fingers together as she led him back down the sidewalk. "Did Officer Kirkland send an update?"

"Nope, he said GPD is still having no more luck than us. Evie told me where she was when the pressure hit and apparently it was around the center of it." Laika raised her free hand to point down the street towards the tacky sign they had passed earlier.

"That is a wonderful idea," Alfred agreed. He picked up his pace to walk next to Laika instead of being half dragged a step behind.

"I'm glad you agree," teased Laika. She led them back down the street and through the door to Hot off the Presses.

Despite being one of the only places open late at this time of night, it was practically empty. Two couples sat far apart from each other keeping to themselves, and one young girl looked bored at the counter. Above the girl was a menu sporting various news-related puns as the names for drinks.

Laika's eyes scanned carefully, then she saw exactly what she hoped for. 'We proudly serve Moonbeans Coffee!' written on the bottom of the board. She got in line. Next to her, Alfred's gaze was focused on the compass. The runes had lit up like a Christmas tree. He was too preoccupied muttering over the small device to realize that Laika was pulling him up to the counter.

"Hi there, could I get a large Midnight Press with an extra, extra shot of Espresso News," Laika chirped cheerfully at the bored looking barista. Then her attention turned up to Alfred as she tugged on his hand, "Do you know what you want?"

"What?" Alfred's voice was distracted. He took a moment to glance up, assess the situation and where they were standing. "Ah, yes. We will be here for a minute... Please order whatever you wish."

Laika's smile didn't falter as she turned her attention back to the barista, "Make that two please."

The cashier nodded and rattled off the price. Before Laika could pull out her wallet, Alfred had already handed over his card to pay. His attention was still on the compass, but he took back the receipt and folded it away with his card.

"Thanks," Laika cheered. Free coffee always tasted sweeter. Granted, she knew how much moonlighters made. They'd need to be thriftier, so she added, "Next time is on me though."

"If you wish," Alfred agreed.

They stepped to the side despite no one being in line behind them. The cashier started on their coffees behind the counter. That seemed to make Alfred realize something. "We should get you food soon. I recall the standard being three meals a day?"

"Where do you want to go?" Laika asked. She already had her phone out looking for somewhere near and open. With another assessment of the tired-looking vampire, she considered takeout instead. There was a decent Indian place around here. She found a waiting message.

> EVIE
>
> Please just be careful with the sociopath vampire.

"I am not fussed," Alfred assured. He pulled his hand free to flick the compass with a scowl. He continued to mutter, "There is too much air magic around here, I cannot locate anything..."

Laika glared down at her phone. She knew there was more to this than Alfred just not feeling emotions. Every time they were alone, he laughed and relaxed with her. Even now it was obvious he was annoyed with his compass. She looked at the compass then asked, "Is it time to give up?"

He looked up at her and Alfred took in her state. They'd run around all of last night too. No progress was being made right now... "I believe we are done for the night. Wherever the circle is, it is not here and there are too many closed shops for us to do a proper sweep."

"Take out and Scrabble?" proposed Laika. She picked up their coffees from the cashier. Annoyance was still leaking from her about the text message. She led them to a small booth in the corner.

They sat down with Alfred putting his back to the wall and taking the drink skeptically. "You did not need to buy me anything?"

"You bought it," reminded Laika. She laughed at how distracted he'd been the entire way here. "So why did you buy yourself a coffee if you didn't want it?"

"Fair point," Alfred lifted the paper cup to take a drink.

"Why don't you have emotions?" Laika blurted out the question.

The coffee almost spilled on the table, but Alfred managed to recover it. He put down the hot drink to give Laika his full attention. "Why do you assume I do not have any? Do you think I am faking my affection for you?"

"Nope," admitted Laika. She couldn't help the grin creeping up her face. She'd already suspected that she got to see a softer side than most in their short time together.

His eyes narrowed, "Then why do you ask?"

"Because Evie says she can't read you at all. You're the only person who comes out as a complete void," Laika explained.

Alfred paused and she could see him weighing his answer. Finally, he held up left index finger for Laika. She saw a worn bronze ring. It looked extremely old, but well cared for like most of Alfred's possessions. Laika felt like she knew the answer but wanted to hear him say it so she pressed, "What's that?"

"A magic ring. One that blocks all forms of empathy and emotional manipulation from affecting me. This is why Evie cannot get a read on me; she is nowhere near powerful enough to overcome my protections," answered Alfred.

He looked around at the few people in the cafe with them, then slipped off the ring. Laika took it gratefully so she could examine every part of it. There was a faded inscription inside that wrapped around the entire band three times over. The outside looked much rougher than it was. Her fingers found the waves and dips of metal smooth to her touch.

"Where did you get this?" Laika questioned. She wondered if there was any way she could get her own.

Alfred paused a little longer than she liked. But he finally answered, "I made it. To protect myself from chrysanthemum vampires and, by extension, empathic werewolves."

He might as well have said he'd solved world peace, because Laika jumped up from her seat and slammed her hands down on the table. "REALLY?!"

"Please sit," urged Alfred as he waved to her to lower her voice. "Yes, I made the majority of my rings."

Laika couldn't stop herself. She dropped back into her chair, then grabbed his left hand to check the rest of Alfred's fingers. Sure enough, he had another four rings with various metals and gemstones. The right hand contained five more rings as well.

She needed to tell Evie about this, then maybe her friend wouldn't be so weird. But first she should get permission, given how secretive Alfred was. "Can I tell Evie?"

"I suppose you may tell her I have protection against her power. But I would prefer you not mention that I made the ring," agreed Alfred.

Laika nodded quickly. That was fair and should be enough for Evie. "What do all of these do?" she pleaded and held the bronze ring reverently in her grasp. The temptation to try it on was real, but she resisted. There was no way for her to even test the effect right now anyways.

"I will make you a deal then." Alfred held out his hand for his ring.

Laika gave the bronze jewelry up without a fight. "What's that?"

"Pick food, we can go have a meal and when we go back to my place I will tell you about my rings. I prefer not to discuss them in public," suggested Alfred. The corner of his lips turned up with just a hint of his fangs peeking through.

"On one condition," Laika countered.

"Which is?" prompted the vampire.

"Tell me what this one does now?" She dropped her voice extremely low as she pointed to one of the rings. A normal person standing next to the table wouldn't even be able to pick up the whisper.

But Alfred caught every word. His voice was just as low as he held up his thumb with a delicately woven silvery band for Laika to see. "This one protects against most forms of scrying and all mind reading such as lilac vampires."

"That's so cool!" Laika couldn't help but gush. She'd file that away for later, that certain vampires could read minds. At the mention of lilacs, Laika remembered that Evie had told her they were also daywalkers, which meant she could knock them off her list. His confession about making magical items had allowed Laika to narrow him down further and she was thrilled; she'd figure out what he was eventually.

Laika redirected the conversation with a nod to the paper cups between them. "So... Now that you've had good coffee, should we revisit the coffee versus tea debate?"

- ☾ -

November 8th, 2018
Outskirts of Glenwood, CA

"Should we just head back?" Laika pushed for the third time.

She was standing on one of the many hills that surrounded Glenwood. This one was close to all of the cell phone towers that had been destroyed by the rusting attack. From here she could see the new towers that had gone up overnight, powered by dwarven efficiency.

"No... There has to be something here." Alfred sounded intensely frustrated.

Laika swept the flashlight from her phone back and forth across the ground. The light illuminated dozens of boot prints that had trampled through here. She'd put money it was from the same crews that had put up the replacement towers. "I think we're too late to this one."

Out of the corner of her eye she saw Alfred come to a stop. He raised his hand to sweep his hair back. "Are you okay?" Laika pressed. She could barely make him out in the dark. There wasn't even a moon to see by.

"I am fine," Alfred answered, but she could hear suppressed annoyance. He wasn't alright.

"We could go home?" Laika tried again.

Alfred sighed heavily. "I need to at least check before we leave."

"No, you don't. This was the second attack, and then it was a construction zone. You said this was a long shot this morning, plus I can barely see out here. We're more likely to break a damn ankle before stumbling over a months-old ritual circle," disagreed Laika.

She moved forward to lace their fingers together and get a better look at the vampire. Alfred had his usual pallor, but Laika noticed he also had deep bags under his eyes. They'd been growing worse the last few days.

"When was the last time you slept?" Laika teased, "You look like death warmed over."

He attempted to deflect the question, "I need to take at least one loop around here before we leave."

Laika had spent the last eight days just spending time with Alfred. They'd had a lot of fun playing games, working on the screenplay, and researching magical rituals. She couldn't remember the last time she had this much fun with someone who just accepted all her quirks. But in that time, she could remember only once when she'd seen him sleep.

Her expression turned into a frown. "Seriously, when was the last time you slept?" Alfred made a non-committal sound. Laika scolded, "No wonder you're taking forever to heal. It's bad enough you're a delicate vampire. If you push yourself too hard right now you'll just slow down your healing."

"Delicate? I am not delicate and I will be fine," Alfred scoffed and moved to take a couple steps away. Likely to do those loops he'd spoken of before...

Laika didn't let go of his hand. "Nope. I'm taking you home to go to bed. If you really want to come back here to check it out, then we can try again tomorrow with proper flashlights. After you've slept." She tapped into her werewolf strength to keep a grip on him. Then Laika turned herself back to the car. They were going home, even if he didn't like it. Alfred's resistance barely pulled at Laika's arm as her superior strength won out. She could hear him muttering darkly about not being delicate as she dragged him in the direction of the car.

She hoped after a good night of sleep, he wouldn't be too angry with her.

- ☾ -

November 8th, 2018
Shady Hollows Apartments, Glenwood, CA

The car trip and subsequent elevator ride had been quiet. Laika was wondering if she'd overstayed her welcome after forcing Alfred to go home. A week was a long time to crash with someone, especially so early in a relationship. Even if he needed some extra help due to his injuries...

She watched Alfred unlock the door to his apartment. Every movement was sluggish and the bags under his eyes were much worse in the hallway light. Tomorrow Laika would apologize, but seeing how exhausted he looked, she knew she'd made the right choice.

Alfred didn't bother with the lights as he trudged to the couch. Laika flicked them on herself. She'd figured out by now he had better night vision than her, given how often he walked into dark rooms without pause. "Are you upset?" Laika stopped to take her shoes off at the door.

"Not with you," Alfred assured, before he stretched out on the couch.

Padding quietly across the room, Laika sat down on the floor near where Alfred's head was resting on the couch's arm. She could see his phone screen while he texted GPD.

ALFRED

I will need access to the Fulmino Apartments.

None of the other areas still have their circles intact.

KIRKLAND

It's been almost two months!

...but I'll see what I can do!

ALFRED

Thank you, please call once we have permission.

KIRKLAND

I'll put the request in tonight.

Might still be a few days.

"What do we do if the apartments say no?" asked Laika.

"Break in, I suppose," answered Alfred. He let his phone slide onto the couch, every movement sluggish. She laughed. He was far too straight laced to do something as drastic as that. But the joke cheered her up. If he was joking, then he couldn't be too mad. Right?

"Okay, you need to go to bed," Laika pushed. She kept her tone gentle, trying not to be too demanding. He was an adult and this was his house after all. Alfred slid his gaze to her and Laika felt like his eyes were searching for something in her face. He'd done that a lot this week, but she couldn't tell if he was finding what he was looking for or not.

"I have trouble sleeping with someone else in the apartment," he finally admitted quietly.

"What?!" Laika yelled loud enough that the vampire winced. Why hadn't he said something before? She could have headed home days ago if she was keeping him up.

Alfred sat up on the couch patting the spot next to him. When she reluctantly sat down he explained further, "I have superior hearing just as you do, and I have been alone for a long time. Sleep when I am not alone does not come naturally to me. However, I have been enjoying our time together and have been in no rush for you to leave."

"I can be quiet," Laika assured, "No music or TV on my phone. I can just read a book, or head home tonight and come back in the morning?"

The vampire sat pondering on the couch for longer than Laika liked. He did this a lot as well. His thumb found the back of her hand to draw reassuring circles. Finally, Alfred spoke, "I would prefer if you stay... I will try to get some sleep regardless."

Laika let out a breath she hadn't been aware she was holding. "An early night for both of us then."

"Agreed," Alfred nodded. His gratitude was slightly ruined by the heavy bags under his eyes.

Despite the large fangs again making Laika reconsider, she quickly leaned up to press a kiss to his cheek. Then pushed herself up before he could react. "I'll go get ready for bed. You do the same."

Laika made her way to the guest room that she'd been living in for the past week. Pulling clean pajamas from her bag, she made a note she would need to go home to do laundry sooner rather than later. That would have been an easy excuse to get out of Alfred's hair for a night. Why hadn't she thought of it minutes ago?

But for now, Laika decided she was just going to take his words at face value. He wanted her to stay at least one more night. She knew she'd been having an absolute blast all week. A small flutter of emotion in her chest was thrilled that Alfred felt the same. Their silly games had equally amused him. Washing up in the guest bathroom didn't take long. In the name of an early and quiet night, a shower could wait for morning. It was only ten minutes later that Laika padded back out to the living room in her pajamas.

The couch was empty and light shone from the archway to the kitchen. That was unexpected since they'd eaten before going out to CorroNect. Then again, when Laika thought back on the meal, he'd barely eaten anything.

Laika headed towards the kitchen. She considered the door to the master bedroom, but there was no light from there. Quietly she called, "Are you in here?"

Alfred was standing in front of the fridge and looked disheveled by his normal standards. His suit jacket, vest, and tie were gone. The sleeves of his shirt were rolled up and several of the buttons had been loosened. He wasn't even wearing shoes and socks. This was the most undressed Laika had ever seen Alfred, even after spending a week living with him. But all of that was forgotten as she realized what he was doing…

"Are you… Is that a juice box?" Laika tilted her head, confusion on her face.

There was no response from Alfred. If anything, the vampire froze as his blue eyes met hers. He was holding a silver pouch that almost looked like a Capri-Sun. If lunchbox snacks were filled with what she assumed was blood…

His reaction was pure gold, and Laika couldn't help it. She started giggling. "Sorry, sorry! It's just-"

That seemed to break the spell. Alfred set the juice box down, raising a hand to wipe away a spot of crimson on his mouth. "No, it is not. Out!"

Laika stayed in place as she realized she'd been right; she'd caught him feeding while he'd thought she was in the shower. But his expression warned her off from making any more comments.

Laughter followed the werewolf back to the couch as she struggled to regain control. All the fearsome stories of vampires drinking blood from fair maidens seemed comical compared to Alfred sipping from a juice box.

When Alfred emerged from the kitchen a few minutes later, Laika had gotten her giggles to quiet down. His face looked concerned, as if he was on the verge of asking a question, but Laika beat him to the punch.

"So is that how you usually drink blood?" Laika prodded warmly.

"Yes, that is my preference," admitted Alfred. He stayed in the archway to the kitchen watching her carefully.

Laika nodded at his answer, "You drink the artificial stuff then?"

In the years after the Big Five came out of the shadows, multiple advances were made to make the transition easier. One of the most important of those was a cheap blood substitute that most vampires drank. They came in all kinds of containers, and Laika was sure she'd seen that brand at the grocery store before.

Again Alfred nodded to confirm her suspicion.

"Do you not like drinking in front of other people?" Laika scooted to the side so there was room for him next to her on the couch.

He glanced at the spot, then back up to her. "I find most of the living do not enjoy watching vampires feed. There are a few exceptions, like your roommate Victoria."

"Who?" Laika crinkled her eyebrows.

"Excuse me, Tor," Alfred corrected himself.

"Oh," mumbled Laika. That made sense from what they'd learned about Tor and the clubs she hung out in.

"But when confronted with blood drinking, you laughed?" Alfred questioned, his expression neutral.

Laika gave him a mischievous grin. "Sorry. You just looked so shocked standing in the kitchen, half dressed and drinking from a juice box. I can't say that it's a turn on for me, but I mean it's not a big deal."

"Really?" The vampire looked skeptical.

"My mom used to try feeding me freshly hunted rabbits. When I say fresh, I mean raw. My dad says one time he found me chowing down on chunks of blood and guts when he got home. No one's eating habits will ever be as gross as my mom's," explained Laika. It seemed really normal to her, until she learned that non-werewolf families just called that common sense. "By the time I was three, my dad had put down a strict 'no raw meat' rule when feeding me."

The story seemed to settle Alfred down. He uncrossed his arms and took a few more steps into the room. "I have been feeding privately when you shower. But you surprised me by skipping your shower tonight."

"I thought I'd try to keep the house quieter, rather than 20 minutes of running water," shrugged Laika.

He nodded following her consideration for his sleep. Finally, Alfred sat down next to her on the couch, "That is kind of you."

"So we're good then? You don't have to worry about me, and can just drink whenever you need? Even if I'm here?" Laika nudged. He hadn't been kidding about not knowing how to exist with someone else in the house. Games, he could handle. But eating and sleeping were a struggle.

"A fair compromise," Alfred's expression was somewhere between tired, grateful, and confused.

Laika couldn't help but glance at his fangs again. She felt better prepared this time as she leaned in for a kiss. But Alfred quickly pulled back, putting a gentle hand on her shoulder to stop her.

"What? Did I do something wrong?" Laika felt a jolt of panic. How had she messed that up again?

"No," assured Alfred and his smile didn't falter. "You did nothing wrong. As much as I would enjoy a kiss, my mouth will taste like blood right now. I have not had a chance to brush my teeth since feeding."

Laika paled. She had no problems watching him sip a juice box, but actually tasting anything was a nope. She popped up from the couch, embarrassment flooding her features. How many times was the werewolf going to get this wrong?

"Okay, bed time then?" Laika turned some of her nervous energy into a stretch before heading towards the guest room. As she reached the door and saw her ransacked overnight bag, she remembered her earlier revelation. "Also, I will have to run home tomorrow. I need to do laundry, but it shouldn't take too long."

Her ears picked up the sound of Alfred standing up from the couch, bare feet crossing the wooden floor after her. "I do have a laundry room here, if it would be easier?"

Laika looked back to see him standing in the doorway to the guest room. He was always so careful not to invade her space unless she was in the process of invading his. Even that first morning after she'd fallen asleep here, Alfred had never once entered the guest room.

"Really? I kinda assumed you used a laundry service when I didn't see a machine in the kitchen," admitted Laika. She moved her jeans and shirts off the bed by tossing them at her bag.

"That would be annoying every time I needed to wash a shirt, and they rarely know how to get blood out of a white shirt," Alfred pulled on his collar with a few drops of red from when she'd startled him before. Laika laughed before she could stop herself. From anyone else, that may have sounded like a criminal from a movie. But given she'd just caught him drinking blood in a white shirt, she found it hilarious. He continued, "I can show you where it is?"

"In the morning," Laika pushed off the chore until later. She guessed that a loud washing machine wasn't going to be better for his sleep.

She watched Alfred standing in the doorway to her temporary room and found herself wishing he'd come in. He hadn't let their conversation drop since they got back, so clearly he wanted to keep talking too. "Why don't you come hang out over here? It'll be more comfortable than leaning in the doorway." Laika curled her legs out of the way making room for him.

Alfred hesitated for only a few seconds before he entered the room. He agreed, "That does sound more comfortable."

Laika scooted over a few more inches so they had equal space. She had a suspicion even with Alfred still feeling chatty, his exhaustion would catch up to him eventually. Either he'd get up and go to bed, or if he fell asleep here, she could head out to the couch.

"So... How *do* you get blood out of a white shirt? It sounds like you're an expert," she teased, flicking his stained collar. Alfred matched her mood and proceeded to explain in detail the process for both mundane and magical blood. The pair sat talking for well over an hour, not about anything in particular. The conversation wandered across whatever topic came up in the connections their tired minds made.

At one point Laika laid back to stretch out a bit more. Soon Alfred followed so they could continue to talk. The pair lay side by side on the guest bed, just enjoying each other's company.

Laika could see sleep was winning over Alfred as he yawned for the third time in a minute. His tired eyes were half closed as he mumbled out an answer to her last question. Another few quiet moments and he'd be gone. She reveled in the quiet affection, but she needed to get up and to the couch without waking him.

However, as Laika gently placed her hands on the mattress to get the leverage she needed, Alfred's fingers caught her wrist. His words were half asleep mutterings, "You do not need to leave, I can move myself."

"No, stay here. Don't worry about me," Laika assured him with a soft tone. She'd escape as soon as he passed out.

"We can just share then," Alfred mumbled before he drifted off, his hand still loosely around Laika's wrist.

Laika looked to the door, then back down at the sleeping vampire beside her. The choice was easy. She pulled the blankets over them and snuggled up to Alfred's side.

CHAPTER 10
TWO-FACED

Laika
November 9th, 2018
Fulmino Apartment Complex, Glenwood, CA

The call from Glenwood MOONS dispatch had come in during the late hours of the morning. Alfred had the all clear to go to search Fulmino room by room. Laika could see how badly he wanted to charge off to the scene. But his ruined daylight gear and still healing injuries kept him stuck in the apartment until dark, as they had during the previous days.

After a full night's sleep he was less snappy than the day before, but Laika couldn't keep his mind off going out. The afternoon had netted her many victories in Scrabble as Alfred grew increasingly distracted. Finally, he'd gotten up mid-game and warned her to get dressed or he was leaving without her. She'd let Alfred pack them up in the car. He'd be able to get out without gear by the time they arrived.

"Seriously though, how do you not have back up gear?" Laika teased as she unbuckled her seatbelt.

"My coat is very durable and it takes exceptional circumstances to cause damage to it." Alfred was already out of the car and had circled to open Laika's door. Excited energy radiated off of him.

Rolling her eyes, Laika stretched as she got out. She couldn't deny his energy was infectious. "So every time it gets damaged like this, you have to just hide out from the sun for a week? That sounds boring."

"I would not call this week boring. The company has been much more enjoyable than usual," Alfred countered, flashing her an easy grin. He locked the car before taking Laika's hand so he could lace their fingers together again. This seemed to be their new normal.

Laika was thrilled by their new normal and enjoyed their entwined hands more than she probably should. She was aware at some point she'd have to get back to reality, but this week of running from moonlighting scene to moonlighting scene, usually hand in hand with Alfred, had been more fun than she'd had in ages. She hadn't said the word 'boyfriend' yet, but they were a couple. After all, she'd woken up curled up against his side this morning, so the title was accurate.

"Also, I have spent most of my life 'hiding from the sun'. Daylight gear of this nature has only recently become acceptable in public," Alfred added as they made their way up the stairs to the apartment complex's doors.

"So you're at least as old as when every one came out of the shadows?" she teased with a breezy laugh.

A hint of a smile threatened to spread across Alfred's face. "At least. But if this is you angling for your answer, I did say I would tell you how old once I had figured it out."

"I know, but I can still tease you." Laika paused to pull a door open with her free hand. "So... what did you do back when everyone was in the shadows?"

Alfred walked at her side keeping pace. He began his explanation, but cut off as he looked at who waited for them. Laika's eyes had been on him, so she saw his mood plummet as his expression twisted into a frown. He started to let go of her hand, but the were-wolf held on tighter.

"I thought we were meeting at sundown," Detective Gibson demanded. He looked frustrated, standing by the front desk.

"We were, but I was under the impression I was meeting Officer Kirkland, not you," Alfred agreed. His eyes were scanning around the lobby as if he expected someone else to join them. Gibson was not a MOONS liaison, and didn't even like the department or moon-lighters at all.

"Kirkland is out for a while because Leavenworth just got out of hospital. I'm covering for them. Explain to me why I got called down here hours ago then?" Gibson snapped at them. The officer's eyes dropped to their hands.

Laika scowled as Gibson subtly rolled his eyes at the couple. At least he didn't voice his dissenting opinion.

Alfred's tone was polite as he inquired, "If you could enlighten me as to why you were so early, then perhaps we can resolve the issue."

"There you are! I expected you hours ago, Poppet," Hazel cooed as she approached them from the elevator bank.

This time Alfred took his hand back before Laika could do anything to stop him. His neutral annoyance turned into an open glare. "Why are you here?"

"Because I'm on the Glenwood Anarchist case," Hazel laughed like he'd just told a funny joke.

Confusion flashed across Laika's face as she looked between the two vampires. Hazel was a little weird, but even then she didn't deserve this reaction. The strangest part of this entire situation was Alfred. Every interaction, from rude GPD officers and even Evie insulting him, he had been unfailingly polite. Why was he openly glaring at Hazel?

"Hazel was the one who stopped the falling roller coaster at Sync Holes and disarmed the ritual at the cafe," Laika added.

Alfred didn't look amused. She vaguely remembered the only

time she'd heard him speak ill of anyone was about Hazel, at lunch with her parents weeks ago. Then realization dawned on her as she remembered an off handed comment from Owen. That Glenwood's magical expert, who she now knew was Alfred, refused to be in the same room as Hazel. Between the pet names and frustrated expressions, Laika was absolutely certain they had history.

Uncertainty gnawed at Laika, but she forced a greeting, "It's nice to see you again."

"You ignored my advice, I see... Hello Laika." Hazel's gaze drifted lazily down to the werewolf like she'd only just realized Laika was standing there. She must have pissed off the woman again since she was using Laika's name instead of an affectionate nickname.

Gibson interrupted them. "So why was Miss Amadori here hours ago and you just got here? It's been a complete mess that I had to deal with."

"I believe there has been a miscommunication then, as Hazel is not authorized to lead any investigation on this case. She is merely on loan from LA MOONS and completely unneeded on scene. You should have called me when you got here," Alfred explained. He had moved his annoyed expression to the detective.

"I don't have your number," reminded Gibson. He scowled at Hazel, then Laika, as if counting how many people shouldn't be here.

"I do," offered Hazel with a wide grin. "You never asked."

"Officer Kirkland could have forwarded it to you, or dispatch is there to connect you to moonlighters. There is literally no reason you could not contact me before now," Alfred reprimanded, ignoring the other moonlighter to the best of his ability.

Laika wasn't sure whose side she should be taking here. Tension was rising quickly in the middle of the very human-filled lobby of the complex. She reached out for Alfred's elbow to get his attention, then dropped her voice, "What's done is done. I don't care if she was here first, let's just go see if we can find the circle."

Hazel answered before Alfred could, "What a lovely idea..."

Her eyes were fixed on Laika like a hungry predator. Before Hazel had been sweet if confusing to follow, but recently Hazel had been scary. She made Laika feel like prey, which sent a shiver down the werewolf's spine.

"...I already found the circle upstairs on the 8th floor. The door is marked," finished Hazel.

"When?" interrupted Gibson, butting into the conversation.

"Hours ago, I suppose," Hazel shrugged. She twirled in a circle before giving a bow for her grand performance.

Any other day, Laika would have laughed at the odd moonlighter. But the tension in the lobby was still drawn as tight as a bowstring. Especially with Alfred acting so outside of his normal.

"Very well. Laika and I will head up to take a look," Alfred said with a faint frown. His eyes stayed on Hazel while speaking. "I do not believe your assistance will be needed."

Laika felt a small pressure on her back. Alfred had not taken her hand again, but he was trying to steer her towards the elevator. The contact felt off compared to his previous affection. A single step forward and their path was blocked as Gibson interposed himself. The detective looked just as irritated as Alfred as he held his hand up. "Hold on. I don't know how your usual liaison conducts themself, but I can't allow everyone to go trampling through a possible crime scene."

Alfred's voice was restrained, but Laika could feel the frost creeping into his words. "Laika is assisting me on the Anarchist case. Her pack has been officially assigned per my request."

Gibson's eyes flickered towards Laika. She could see the same distaste he had when they met him at the station. "Miss Lowell is not rated for a magical catastrophe of this nature. No werewolf is. I believe the saying is... werewolves are as magical as a rock."

"Looks like it will just be you and me then, Poppet!" Hazel chirped to Alfred, stepping forward as if that was all the go ahead she had needed.

"No." The word came from both men this time.

Hazel drew up short with a confused expression, "But the circle?"

Gibson responded, "Miss Amadori, if you are not authorized to lead the investigation then you have to wait down here with Miss Lowell. No one extra is going upstairs. It's already a mountain of paperwork to justify you finding our ritual circle."

Alfred's blue eyes flashed in annoyance. His mouth was opening to renew the argument with Gibson and he pressed more firmly on the small of Laika's back.

She planted her feet in the ground. Fighting with GPD, even a jerk like Gibson, wasn't going to do anyone any good. Laika reached out for Alfred's arm and gave it an affectionate squeeze. "It's fine, I'll wait down here. You just need to check the circle against the drawing right?"

"Yes," Alfred admitted. He still looked pissed off at the situation, but that didn't leak into his words for her.

"Then hurry up. We can get dinner before going home," Laika squeezed his elbow again.

Alfred's voice dropped to that low sound she could barely make out, "I only need a few minutes and some pictures. I will be quick; stay by Gibson's side while I am gone." Then he was off to the elevators with a curt nod to the detective and a cold shoulder for Hazel.

Not caring that Alfred was still in ear shot or maybe not knowing, Hazel mocked, "He's in a mood today."

Gibson waited for the doors to close before he looked both women up and down, "Both of you go wait by the door. Do not go poking around anywhere. I don't care what the official file says, you're not on the case right now." Then he picked up his phone and stepped back towards the front desk to make a call, effectively cutting off any chance to disagree or for Laika to do as Alfred had asked her.

With nothing else to do, Laika moved to stand by the door. She fidgeted with her phone to keep her hands busy. This was certainly not what she had expected when they showed up. Owen had said Gibson was a racist, but as frustrating as it was, he hadn't done anything out of line.

As for Hazel... The vampire was a mystery. Laika wanted to ask about the familiarity between her and Alfred, especially with the pet name. But her desire was at war with instincts of self preservation after that cold look from Hazel. She couldn't stop herself from stealing glances at the other woman. The vampire was pretty in a classical way, with soft curves and well-styled blonde hair-.

"You're staring." Hazel's gaze was on the elevator doors and hadn't moved the entire time Laika had been looking. How had she done that?

"Uh... How do you know Alfred?" Laika asked quietly.

Hazel turned so she could look directly into Laika's eyes as she answered, "Poppet and I are soulmates, but we're on a break right now."

That was a bucket of cold water over Laika. Soulmates? Those words were a heavy claim... "He... hadn't mentioned anything like that. He said he's been alone for a long time," Laika's words were careful. Was she stepping on the toes of another relationship? Or was she missing something else here?

"Don't worry your pretty little head about that. My Poppet wouldn't want to bother his latest fling with the details of *us*," explained Hazel. She gave Laika a warm smile, but it felt more like she was mocking the werewolf than soothing her. This was maybe the most focused the vampire had ever been in their conversations.

Laika couldn't stop the stupid feelings welling in her chest. Or the way her brain started comparing herself to Hazel. They had nothing in common at all. Was this the type of woman that Alfred liked?

Her phone started to play the Phantom of the Opera theme.

ALFRED

By now Hazel has attempted to invite you to drinks or a meal. DO NOT LEAVE WITH HER! If you have already stepped out, then feign an emergency and get back to the lobby now.

What the hell did that mean? But before Laika could have a reaction...

"I know this is hard to hear; you thought you were special to him. Or at least you were having fun. Why don't we slip out for a drink and we can talk about it? I don't blame *you* for this," soothed Hazel. All of that cold from before was replaced with a motherly warmth, filled with concern for Laika.

How had Alfred known Hazel would ask before she did? Something here wasn't adding up...

When they'd arrived, Alfred hadn't been embarrassed to be seen with her. He'd been annoyed with how rude Gibson was, but he hadn't let go of her hand. Only after Hazel showed up did he get openly hostile. Was this the reaction of a cheater that got caught? Did he just not want Laika and Hazel to talk? Something about that felt off.

Hazel was waiting expectantly for an answer, but Laika decided to risk being rude for another minute. She shot off a message to Evie, desperate for some female advice.

> LAIKA
>
> How do you know if someone is lying?

> EVIE
>
> Their aura doesn't match the emotions on their face.

> LAIKA
>
> Okay how does a normal person tell?

> EVIE
>
> Poke a hole in the story? I don't know!
>
> I was terrible at spotting liars until I got my powers.

Laika gave Hazel an appraising look. Like before, she was well kept and as fashionable as ever. Her sleek black coat had stylish flourishes and easily could have been a designer brand to match the expensive purse hanging off her shoulder. She looked picture perfect like always. All of the work Hazel put into herself daily couldn't be easily hidden away.

If Alfred had a wife, or even a girlfriend like that, there'd be signs in his home. Nothing Laika could think of indicated there was someone else living there. She'd gotten a look in the coat closet by the front door, and there was only one hook set up for his daylighting gear. There hadn't been another toothbrush in the guest room, or anyone else's shampoo. Laika had to borrow soap and toiletries from Alfred the first few days. If he had his wife's soap laying around, why would he have bothered handing her Irish Spring?

This morning Alfred had shown her the stairs down to the 9th floor where he kept his laundry room. Laika hadn't seen a single sign of a second person, nevermind a woman, living there. When she thought about it, his apartment wasn't even well set up to entertain anyone but himself. That was Alfred's home and completely his space.

Laika had growing doubts that Hazel was being entirely honest right now. Maybe they had a more romantic history than she liked, but the werewolf was going to get her answers from Alfred. Because if it turned out he'd made her into the other woman, then Laika was going to break his face before leaving.

"Laika?" Hazel prompted with that same warm tone. She reached out for Laika's arm, fingers gripping with more strength than expected.

That cemented Laika's resolve. She took a step backwards, pulling her arm free from Hazel's grip. Her tone was steely as she spoke, "You are lying."

"Excuse me?" Hazel looked shocked at the reaction.

"I said you're lying. Do you need me to say it louder or slower?" Laika shot back. She was holding her ground on this one. More and more wasn't adding up with the story Hazel had just spun about soulmates. Real soulmates didn't take a break.

"What do you know about lying? You're what, 20? Practically a baby with no clue about the world," hissed Hazel.

Laika could see she'd struck a nerve. She felt like an idiot standing in a lobby fighting about a guy with a stranger. She looked like someone she'd laugh at on trash TV. "I'm not interested in fighting with you. I'm going over there."

She took a step towards Gibson, deciding his terrible attitude was better than acting like a reality TV wannabe. Then Laika froze in place as a horrific sound started behind her. She was reminded of the sounds werewolves made when shifting, but louder and... wetter?

Sensing an attack, Laika spun around to glare at Hazel. But the face that met her was not the same blonde woman. Instead, a brunette with a dark tan and matching eyes glared back, but she was wearing the same coat and bag. "Even if you run away, it doesn't change the fact I'm everyone's perfect woman. My poppet will come back, like he always does."

"What..?" Laika couldn't even find the words to finish voicing her thoughts.

"Hazel." Alfred appeared out of nowhere at Laika's side and wrapped his hand around her arm. His tone and posture was almost threatening.

That's when realization hit her like a shot of ice through her veins. This woman standing there with a face she didn't know... was still Hazel. The vampire had changed her face. If words had failed Laika before, now they'd completely fled her.

"What's going on?" Gibson demanded as he stalked their way. He looked equally confused to how Laika felt.

"Nothing," Alfred answered. His grip on Laika's arm tightened and he pulled her towards the front doors.

"What did you find?" Gibson yelled after them.

"I will email you my report," snapped Alfred. He opened the door with more force than needed before dragging Laika into the night air.

Only as the door swung shut did Laika finally dig her heels in. She didn't enjoy being forced around like a doll, even if she'd wanted out of that mess as much as him. Laika gave Alfred a sharp look, with a hefty dose of annoyance and fear on her face. "What's going on?"

"I will explain at home," Alfred answered.

Laika only narrowed her eyes, still refusing to move.

"Please," he tried again. This time Alfred stopped pulling on her arm.

"If you lie to me, we're done," warned Laika as she stalked past him to the car.

- ☾ -

November 9th, 2018
Shady Hollows Apartments, Glenwood, CA

Another awkward quiet car ride was followed by an equally awkward elevator ride. Now Laika was sitting on one side of the couch evaluating Alfred and the giant red flags that had popped up tonight. Was this going to be a pattern? She wasn't sure if she was supposed to start this conversation and drag her answers from him. Or should she keep waiting?

Before the minutes dragged on much longer, Alfred took a breath. "Hazel is insane. I mean that in a very literal sense of the word, not hyperbole like so many others do."

Laika waited a moment for him to clarify and he didn't disappoint.

"She always has been. Since the day I met her and she called me her soulmate, I have known she was not sane. Nothing since then has ever convinced me otherwise either," he continued.

"How long have you known Hazel?" Laika couldn't help but ask.

He turned pulling one leg up so he could sit on the couch facing her. "Most of my life," he admitted.

"Is she your wife?" Again the questions came from Laika unbidden.

"No, absolutely not. We have never so much as courted before. I do not entertain her advances whenever they hit her. Half the time she does not remember my name, and the rest is that soulmate fiction she spins." Alfred's tone held so much contempt. He really sounded like he hated Hazel.

Laika felt a moment of guilt when a crushing weight on her chest lifted. She'd been so worried at losing this budding relationship. At the same time, it felt horrible to be relieved while being told that someone was out of their mind. She needed to be sure this version of the story was true. Laika sat up straighter and turned so she could meet his level gaze. "Tell me right now that I'm not the other woman, and you're not playing some weird vampire game."

Alfred mouthed the words 'weird vampire game' and the edge of his lips almost turned up into a smile. But he refrained. "There is no game here. I have not even seen Hazel in over a century; I did not believe she knew where I was. You are not the other woman. You are the only woman in my life right now. I told you already I do not date multiple women, nor do I marry one and keep girlfriends. Tell me what you would like as proof?"

Now was Laika's turn for silence. She studied Alfred's face carefully. He'd never lied to her when asked directly. Only once had he refused to answer her questions, the question about which court of vampire he was in. If Hazel was truly his most important soulmate, then wouldn't that protection apply to her as well?

"Tell me what kind of vampire Hazel is? How did she switch faces like that? I know it wasn't an illusion because they don't make... sounds like that," Laika demanded.

She expected hesitation or a deflection given how Alfred had acted about the subject of courts before. Instead he answered quickly with a single word, "Orchid."

"Orchid?" Laika echoed him.

"Yes, Hazel is what is referred to in the modern era as an orchid vampire. They have been called memory vampires previously," Alfred clarified with more detail. Orchid vampires had come up for the whiteboard, but all Evie had gotten from Tony sounded like an urban legend. Laika hadn't bothered putting them on the board in the end.

"So... Orchids *can* actually steal powers? And faces?" Even saying the words sent a visceral shudder through Laika. "How?"

"They can borrow powers from supernatural creatures by drinking their blood. The original owner does not lose their use of the power. Faces are more complicated than that, and Hazel has many of them," explained Alfred. He held out his hand for hers.

She considered taking the hand. Laika's questions were being met with nothing but quick and thorough answers from Alfred. He wasn't dancing around anything. That settled the issue for Laika. He wasn't protecting Hazel from her, so the woman had either been lying or as crazy as Alfred claimed. Her last bits of reservation were slipping away. She wrapped her fingers in his, squeezing them gently.

"So, she would need someone's blood to steal their powers. Does that mean the faces belong to real people too?" Laika prodded to keep the explanation flowing.

"Yes. Her faces come from real people, but to use them she killed the original owners," Alfred answered. He squeezed her hand in return.

The physical reassurance was desperately needed, because at his words Laika went still. "She killed... but you said she has a lot of them... how is she a moonlighter? She should be in jail!"

"Most of them were from before we came out of the shadows. If the government could not prove the crime then and there, they did not pursue it as part of the integration deal." Alfred ran soothing circles on the back of Laika's hand.

This was a lot of information to take in. Laika felt like her brain was splitting in two with panic, or fear, or maybe both. "So she gets away with murder?!"

Alfred grimaced, but he kept talking, "Stopping her would mean killing her. Attempting to kill someone who can leverage an unpredictable array of powers at you is much harder than dealing with a single power set vampire."

"Then what do we do about Hazel?" Laika felt the panic win over fear.

"I will handle her tomorrow," assured Alfred.

"You're going to try and kill her?" Laika wasn't sure she sounded rational right now. But if Hazel was as dangerous as he said, then fighting her was crazy. Whether Alfred was a rose or an iris, it didn't really matter what magic he had if Hazel could just steal his powers.

"No, I am not capable of killing Hazel. Just give me a few days and she will no longer be a problem for us." Again, Alfred sounded as sincere as before.

"Wait!" Laika had been allowing herself to be soothed by his reassuring words. But a very real concern hit her. "When Hazel invited me for a drink, was she going to kill me and take my face?!"

Alfred looked like he wanted to swear, but he kept his patient and calm tone. "There was a possibility that was her plan. She has done so before, which is why I warned you against going with her."

"Bitch," muttered Laika darkly. Not only had Hazel dragged her into the dreaded Girl Fight, she'd literally plotted her murder as well. She needed to pull herself together and stop being a wishy-washy damsel on the couch looking for protection. Laika took her hand back so she could slap both cheeks at once. The pain helped the werewolf center herself.

"Are you alright?" Alfred asked.

"No, but I need time to process what I just learned. Maybe dinner too," Laika responded, trying to take calming breaths. She'd never had someone try to kill her before so casually, and over something as stupid as a guy. Maybe she'd feel better after some sleep?

"Perhaps some delivery and a quiet night in then?" Alfred's warmth was finally back now that Laika didn't appear to be ready to run for the door.

She nodded in agreement.

Alfred found his phone to start an order for them. As he clicked through the delivery app, the whole reason for the trip to Fulmino hit Laika like a bolt of lightning.

"Oh! The circle, did you figure out what kind of magic it was?" She scooted closer to him on the couch. Their knees bumped together in a comforting way.

Alfred relaxed at the contact. "I did. We can discuss the results in the morning. I believe we have had enough excitement for one night."

INTERLUDE - REJECTION

The Anarchist
November 9th, 2018
..somewhere in Glenwood, CA

Rage burned brightly in her eyes. Long ago she'd smothered that flame down into a tiny ember and only fed it when she had to. So many times over she'd changed everything about herself. Even so far as to deform her body, all to be the perfect woman...

But when she'd made her approach, full of warmth and love... that bitch had said *those words* to her...

The pages of their love story needed to be swept clean again... she needed a new plan.

CHAPTER 11
WITCH-HAZEL

Evie
November 10th, 2018
Glenwood Police Department Station #1, Glenwood, CA

Evie sat once more in a plastic chair in front of the receptionist desk of the GPD. She was going over the evidence on her iPad for the tenth time today. What else was she going to do, though?

The burly man behind the desk had given her a sympathetic nod when she asked to see Detective Gibson. He'd directed her to sit and wait because Gibson was already in a meeting. Evie had terrible timing every time she showed up.

Earlier this morning, Laika had uploaded two dozen photos of a dust covered ritual circle. Someone had crudely carved it in the floor of an apartment's living room with a knife, then painted over the etching with white lines. Melted wax and burnt pieces of plants littered the space around the circle. It looked like some macabre arts and crafts project made by moody teenagers.

Evie swiped between the photos and the drawings from Arik's

family book. To her untrained eye the lines looked the same, but the report she was waiting on would confirm their findings.

She let her eyes linger on the beautifully rendered lines of the drawing; whoever had done this had an amazingly steady hand. Jealousy flared in Evie as she wished she had the same precision or even the time to practice. Then again, elves lived to be almost 300 years old. That was a lot more time in general.

Thinking of elves... The last week was one of the weirdest she'd ever had while working for Arik. He'd always been quirky and easily obsessed with new projects, but this was different.

In the entire time Evie had worked as an assistant, she could count the number of times that Natasha had entertained Arik's pitches to the end on one hand. Of those few instances, never had his manager allowed him to move forward. But when Arik had forced Evie to join him in presenting the screenplay, Natasha had read it from cover to cover.

Her first question had been fair. "Where's the rest of it?"

Evie ended up explaining that it was almost done and the writer was actively working on it every day. They needed another week at most to finish the draft. Natasha had given Arik a very stern warning; he wasn't allowed to so much as breathe outside of the manor about this script until it was finished. Evie had been in shock at the almost happy reaction from Natasha.

Then Natasha set everyone with homework if they wanted this project. She'd demanded the screenplay be moved to a proper format, which was a job for Tony. Evie was in charge of keeping her roommate happy, fed, and writing for the next two weeks. There was even a budget for food and anything that would keep Laika motivated.

Finally, Arik was told he had to make some lists by the end of the week. He needed to find a producer who would still be willing to work with him, and an 'actual' action star who'd be willing to help carry the movie.

Evie had really thought that would send him into a spiral. Arik's ego could be fragile and an easy shortcut to a Taran Tantrum when piqued. But to her surprise, he was absolutely energized by the task. He'd spent all week creating lists of people, from close friends to actors he'd never met before.

Even more surprising had been the expectation that Evie would help as well. Arik had been quick to point out that her attention was not really needed with Laika. Her roommate had been working and communicating every day without fail. He wasn't wrong, either. As much as it annoyed Evie, her best friend was doing exactly as asked as long as the redhead let her spend time with her new boyfriend without complaint.

Once the screenplay was done, Evie would pester about getting their boundaries back in order. Including no more skipping of Trashy TV Thursday.

All week, Arik had been showering Evie with random gifts. On Tuesday she'd been fixing the strap on her bag, only to have a new Kate Spade bag dropped in her lap. When Evie tried to give it back, he'd refused, pointing out how he had no use for it. The purse was a few years out of season and likely came from the random gift closet. That's definitely where Evie got her designer jacket and matching shoes that were only half a size too big a couple days later.

She'd worried that her boss was trying to woo her, but it turned out to be a pointless concern. Arik's aura had never touched anywhere near 'dangerous' emotions. Every gift was marked with joy and flares of pride. When Evie thought on it, they usually happened whenever Laika finished a pivotal page or exciting fight. They were Arik's usual over the top way of saying thank you... and to bribe Evie to put up with him.

Arik had dragged her into the process of finding producers and actors. That meant listening to him drone on about why he couldn't work with this man, or how that woman loved him but wouldn't do business. She'd been compiling his notes and helping her boss rank his options into a short list. Actors had been a lot worse than producers because they couldn't be taller, hotter, or buffer when compared to Arik.

In the end, Arik had just needed a friend to stay with him while he worked. Evie had resigned herself to being that person even before the extravagant gifts. She'd done this a thousand times over, all the way back to high scho- Her thought was interrupted by a voice calling her name.

"Miss Belle," the officer at the front desk called. He had a slightly concerned expression, which led Evie to realize he'd likely called her name a few times already.

"Sorry," she apologized while gathering her belongings.

"Don't worry about it. I'm sorry but Detective Gibson just let me know he's not going to see you today," the officer took his turn apologizing.

That was not what Evie had expected. "Did he say why? This is about the Anarchist case."

"I'm afraid not, sorry Evie." His apology had an undercurrent of sincerity. The officer nodded back towards the corner of the department where the MOONS desks sat. Following his gaze, Evie had no trouble spotting Gibson. The blonde cop was herding two young moonlighters towards her at the front desk. She could see the dark clouds of frustration and confusion roiling around him.

His tone mirrored his emotions. "Absolutely not. I don't care what circus that Kirkland usually runs in this department. You are not getting that file."

Keisha was walking backwards, her signature feathery earrings identifiable with every step. She was pleading, "But Officer Gibs-"

"Detective," he corrected without missing a stride.

Keisha huffed but blazed onward, "*Detective* Gibson, we've been helping with research! I found a book that I think will solve everything, I just need to compare notes. I don't know how to get a hold of the lead investigator, which is why we're here."

"We just want to help solve Laika's case," Jaci breezed. She was oddly calm compared to the nervous energy coming off her friend.

Evie noticed she didn't have those huge glasses on, either. For a moment she wondered if Jaci had a superman complex where she was only meek and mild-mannered with them on?

"It's not Laika's case either," snapped Gibson. He didn't touch either of the younger werewolves, but still made an effective wall propelling them to the door. Evie couldn't help but to crack a smile. The girls looked like a younger Night Claw begging for more work.

"Couldn't I jus-," Keisha tried again.

"For the absolute last time, no!" Gibson growled as he herded the pair out of the bullpen. He managed to get them into the same lobby that Evie was waiting in. She tried so hard to keep her face professional and neutral. Since Gibson was standing here, she'd take her chance to talk to him. After all, she *was* on the case.

"I'm way too busy to waste anymore time on this," Gibson pointed at the younger girls then the door. He looked at Evie before including her, "You too, out!"

"Excuse me," Evie shot back. She crossed her arms and straightened up another inch.

"I said get out. I've got reports and paperwork to handle," repeated Gibson.

"No. I have every right to be here. I need the latest report for the Anarchist cas-" Evie started up her argument.

Gibson seemed exasperated, his emotions were a whirlwind of pure frustration. "Why is everyone trying to get that report off of me? You're a werewolf, you don't need a magical findings report. Just go home."

Evie took a step forward and openly glared up at the detective. "Because I'm on the case and I already know that the report says the circle was Elven in nature. I've got the original book of rituals here with me to compare against the report and verify findings. I'm here to do the damn job I was asked to do by the Lead Investigator on the case. You know, when he requested my pack help with research."

Silence reigned through the bullpen and lobby. Bubbles of amusement and curiosity popped up from the other officers. When

Gibson had no answer, Evie pressed again, "I know you're filling in for Owen and Aaron and don't know shit about how to handle moonlighters, but you could at least try to do the job. Or here's a thought: ask for help when you're in over your head."

Again the detective failed to come up with words to shoot her down. So Evie decided to prove her point. She spun to Keisha and Jaci, "Hey! I appreciate that you two came down here to try and help. I know how annoying it can be to get around without your own set of wheels. What book did you bring?"

Keisha pressed her lips together tightly for a moment, like she was trying to decide if she would help or not.

Evie read her like a book; the younger woman was also in over her head. But she had an earnestness about her that just wanted to help. "Look, we both know I can't let you anywhere near this case. Not just because your pack isn't officially on it. Nilani would kneecap the department if anyone allowed you any closer."

That did it. Keisha sighed and held up a book of Elven rituals. It had a sticker for UCLA on the corner and likely came from their library early this morning. Her tone was defeated, "I knew that the rituals had a ton of ingredients, like a bunch of different types of witch-hazel. Since I helped Laika with the original list."

Evie nodded that she was listening.

"Then Jaci told me that witch-hazel is an old elven superstition. If you surround the ritual with an unbroken line of ground up witch-hazel then it keeps the demons inside. We found this book this morning and thought it could help?" offered Keisha. She gave the book to Evie.

"Thank you, this will be really helpful even if we just remove some possibilities." Evie took the rituals in hand. If they hadn't gotten so lucky with Arik already, then Keisha and Jaci would have cracked the case right now. She gave them a sly wink. "Give me a minute to get my report and I'll drive you home. Okay?"

"Yeah, thanks." Keisha didn't look thrilled at being cut out. But her aura was excited that Evie had taken her advice to heart.

Finally, Evie turned back to Gibson and her warm expression cooled. She pressed the textbook into his hands. "Why don't you go log this while you get me the report. So we can both be doing our job for a change?"

Gibson looked like he wanted to say more, but her scene had cowed him into behaving for the moment. He'd failed to disagree with any of Evie's points so far, and now it would be petty. Arguing with moonlighters in the middle of the police station wasn't a good look for anyone during a possible demon crisis. He muttered, "Stay here."

As soon as the detective was out of earshot, Keisha cracked up laughing, "You are one crazy woman. I love it."

Even the front desk officer had a smug smirk as he went back to his crossword. But Evie could read his amusement at Gibson being taken down a peg today. Evie resolved herself to be kinder if Gibson returned with her report. He was so clearly in over his head and she could help him with that. Or at least get the younger moonlighters out of the way.

"Where's Laika?" Jaci asked.

The question startled Evie for a moment; she'd almost forgotten about Jaci. She began her answer, "She's on her way to meet me. She's been stayin-"

Her words cut off as Evie felt another spark of curiosity from the desk officer. She'd literally almost told the entire department that her packmate was dating the lead investigator on the Anarchist case. If that didn't sound like Night Claw was sleeping their way to the top, nothing would.

"Laika's been staying busy with the case. She was supposed to meet me here like 30 minutes ago," Evie recovered quickly.

Jaci nodded, "Oh okay. I thought she'd be with you."

"Hey," Keisha dropped her voice, "thanks for your help with Gibson. It's already so hard to get taken seriously and he makes it so much worse."

Evie's attention went back to the more outgoing werewolf. "I know that struggle. But I was serious that you can't help anymore than this."

"I know," relented Keisha. Her aura swirled into blues and greens of sadness.

"It's not that I don't think you can do the job. But this is mine and Laika's chance to break out of the bottom ranks for real. We got a really lucky break and I can't put my neck out for you right now." Evie decided that honesty was the best. She hoped they could read the regret in her voice, "I'm sorry."

"Yeah, it's okay. Gibson's still an asshat," Keisha teased. Her eyes were alight with joy and Evie didn't think that the Moonscent girls would be holding it against her.

"Your report?" Detective Gibson tapped a manilla folder on Evie's shoulder.

She turned around, realizing he'd snuck up on her conversation. How much had he heard? Judging from the wave of glee coming from behind her and the rush of anger in front, Keisha had made sure he heard the end.

"Thanks," Evie took the folder. The papers felt much heavier in her hands than normal, but before she could do more, her phone came to the rescue. Laika's ringtone was loud and clear enough for everyone standing next to Evie to hear.

"Hello," she quickly answered.

Laika's voice crackled through the phone, with a backdrop of street noise behind it. "Hey! Sorry I'm running late! The buses from that side of town take forever. Are you still at the station?"

"I thought you were getting a ride? Weren't we all doing an early dinner after the station? But yeah, I'm still here." Evie was a little confused; she'd resolved herself to being nice to Alfred all night and not wrecking a meal.

"Alfred had to run an errand and dropped me at home. But you'd already left. He's joining us at dinner, but don't worry, I've got all our notes," Laika was rambling off answers as fast as she could. Then a brief pause and the beeping of a crosswalk warning broke into the conversation. "I'm just crossing the street to the station, I'll be in, in like two minutes."

Evie felt a small flicker of annoyance. If she'd been told then she would have come to pick her friend up. But in the last week they'd been chatting on the phone daily. She'd been kept in the loop about everything with the case and the screenplay was still moving. Before Evie could say anything else...

"What the hell?" Keisha had raised her voice as a chaotic scene unfolded in the lobby.

Jaci had suddenly slammed herself into the front doors with enough force to twist the metal frame. Cracks formed on the glass windows that made up the majority of the doors. They weren't locked, but she was using so much force the frame buckled. Then Jaci started a full sprint into the parking lot. Everyone hung frozen in shock for a few seconds. But between Evie and a room full of police officers, they got moving fairly quickly.

Evie didn't know if any other moonlighters were nearby right now. But if Jaci was frenzying, then Evie was the only line of defense between the girl and bullets. Not to mention how easily a werewolf could tear through humans. To her surprise, Detective Gibson was keeping pace as they passed through the broken doors at the same time.

"Stop," yelled Gibson as he overtook Evie in the chase. He was fast for a human.

As soon as Evie got eyes on Jaci she turned her empathy up... but all she got back was white noise like static on a radio. That didn't make any sense. The only time she'd ever run into that wasn't in an 18 year old werewolf.

"Jaci! Jaci! What are you do-" Keisha had recovered enough to follow them. But her words cut off into a strangled gasp when her friend started to shift.

Evie saw Jaci's form start wavering around the edges. That looked nothing like a frenzying shift... it was almost like her form was melting. Then limbs expanded outwards as the dainty young girl transformed into a gangly creature. Evie nearly tripped over her own feet as a clawed and fanged peony vampire exploded out of Jaci's body. What the hell was happening?

Then fear started to crash into Evie's head like hammers beating on her skull. The cadence of the emotions were too familiar for her not to know them. She screamed, "LAIKA!"

Laika had just entered the parking lot. She'd frozen in place at the sight of peony Jaci, who was on a direct collision course. So much terror was flooding from Laika that Evie almost felt physically sick.

"If you don't stop, I'll be forced to open fire," Gibson commanded, but he was too late.

'Jaci' swung her massive claws at Laika. Her packmate's reflexes kicked in, trying to pull herself out of the way. But nails dragged through the front of Laika's shirt, up her chest and caught the bottom of her chin.

"NO!" screamed Evie. She tried to force her legs to move faster, to close the distance before the next attack.

Then gunshots rang out across the parking lot as Gibson started to unload rounds into the creature's back. As soon as Laika dropped to the ground, she was out of his direct line of fire so he hadn't hesitated any further. Trails of blood began streaming down the peony with each shot that hit. She threw her head back in a roar of pain. Then she lurched around on shaky steps. The peony wasn't bullet proof apparently, but that didn't matter much when Gibson's full clip hadn't put her down on the ground.

Every fiber of Evie's being was demanding she launch herself forward to protect Laika. Her packmate was down on the ground, bleeding, and the monster who had done it was still looming. But the rational part of her brain was straining to hold onto her moonlighter training. She could only help Laika when the threat was contained.

She could hear boots pounding over the pavement as the station emptied. Angry resolve enveloped the air to match the clicks of dozens of gun safeties while the officers prepared for a fight.

Gibson's gun may have been empty, but he wasn't alone anymore. His backup hadn't hesitated to follow him, even against a monster.

A single spot of panic raced forward. Evie knew what it was before she saw Keisha trying to go to Jaci's aid. She threw an arm out like an iron bar to catch the young girl. There was no reason Keisha needed to see her packmate gunned down. Evie pulled her into a bear hug, ready to retreat.

The frenzied peony had more sense than her singled-minded attack had hinted. She kept her eyes on the officers who had drawn on her. That many bullets would likely put her under, and if they didn't, then Evie was ready to force feed wolf's blood down her throat. Her eyes glanced at the prone form of Laika.

No one was giving the peony the chance to do anymore damage. Three of the closest officers opened fire with warning shots. They aimed lower and far to the side.

Again the form of the creature started to ripple at the edges. Evie could see muscles tense and then the peony launched themselves up into the air. Confusion flashed across Evie's face as she saw clawed limbs give way to webbed wings. As quickly as 'Jaci' had exploded into the peony, now the peony had melted away into a slimmer form. The monster wheeled around, wings gaining lift before shooting off into the sky.

"Hold your fire!" Gibson roared, "Carson, get the first aid kit! Garrad, Wilson, stay here and call for an ambulance. Everyone else, get eyes on that monster now. I want to know where the hell it's going."

With the threat escaped and no wings to speak of, Evie didn't have any way to help. 'Jaci' was already out of the range of her empathy as well. So she ignored any thoughts of pursuit, instead releasing Keisha so that she could finally get to Laika.

Gravel stung Evie's legs as she half slid to Laika's side. She had basic first aid training and nothing in that prepared her for all the blood. Deep lines had been cut out of Laika's chest and part of the bone on her face was visible. If Laika hadn't moved when she did, then she'd be dead right now.

"Laika, help's coming," Evie whispered, grabbing her friend's hand. She got a soft groan in response but no real words. Laika's aura screamed pain at her and Evie had no complaints about that. Feeling pain meant that her friend was alive.

- ☾ -

November 10th, 2018
Glenwood General, Glenwood, CA-

"I swore when I left here yesterday that I wasn't coming back unless someone was on their deathbed," Owen griped as he entered the private room at Glenwood General.

"Quiet," snapped Evie. She'd known that Owen was coming to check on her and Laika, but he didn't need to be so loud about it. She hadn't realized he'd stopped to pick up her roommates on the way, though.

"No one is on their deathbed," scolded Shelly. She and Tor followed the officer into the hospital room with a bright bouquet of flowers in hand. Nervous energy spiked off the woman as she ignored the room, heading directly to Laika's side.

"Exactly, and even with her super ears, she can't hear me right now. They have her on so much pain medication a hurricane wouldn't wake her up," Owen waved an arm towards the hospital bed.

Tor gave him a smirk, "Then try being quieter than a hurricane." She moved to Evie's side and nudged her ribs with an elbow in greeting.

Evie frowned in response. She couldn't pull her eyes away from Laika. But as Tor put an arm around her shoulders in a side hug she pressed into the affection. "I'm glad you guys came."

"Yeah," Tor tightened the hug, "I brought her booze for when she wakes up. She'll need more than just a shot to get over this."

Laika was hooked up to half a dozen machines and hadn't regained consciousness. The deep cuts from the peony's claws had been stitched closed and covered with gauze, but Laika still hadn't regained her color. Shelly hovered at the edge of the bed, worried eyes fretting over their roommate.

Evie grimaced before fixing her expression on Owen. The next question came out more accusatory than she meant, "Where were you?"

"Where was *I*?" Owen echoed back. His flippant attitude faded as he moved to Shelly's side checking over Laika.

"Yeah... you've been gone for days and if you were-" Evie couldn't even finish her sentence. She knew that Owen had no fault in the events of the last couple days. No one really did other than 'Jaci,' and no one had found her yet.

Shelly interrupted with a glance up to the officer, and then back to her friend. "Shouldn't these be healed by now? I know that you and Laika aren't fast healers, but normal healing should have closed these up without stitches?"

Tor chimed in, "Wouldn't stitches get in the way?"

"Melinda said they were deep wounds. I don't fully understand what she meant by that, but Laika was hurt more than werewolf healing could handle," explained Evie. She'd been surprised but thrilled to see the witch when the ambulance showed up outside the precinct. The paramedic hadn't wasted a moment as her hand lit up green before she even reached the downed werewolf. Evie was pretty sure Laika wouldn't have made it to the hospital without her.

"Someone took a chunk of her spirit as much as her body," Owen clarified. "Melinda got both bleeds under control before she passed out. There's still a lot to fix, but Laika is stable now."

"Oh, that makes sense," agreed Tor. She looked thoughtful before opening her little black bag and pulling out a sheet of tablets. "Do you think my iron supplements would help? I take them when I'm low on spirit after a long weekend?"

Owen shook his head, "Humans and werewolves don't recover it the same way." He looked like he had more to say but after Evie snorted, he shut up.

Evie had heard this lecture a hundred times before whenever she visited the Lowells. Lavender was a big believer in 'spirit' being the foundation of werewolf magic. However, werewolves didn't have magic and everyone knew that. Her adoptive mother was far into the woo woo magic side of the werewolf religions and would just recommend a full moon run to fix the problem. Not that Laika would be going for a run anytime soon.

There were no tears because Evie had none left at this point. She'd been crying at Laika's side for hours until her tear ducts dried up. That left confusion, frustration, and plain old anger, which had been at war for dominion in Evie's brain all afternoon.

"She's alive and that's all that matters," Owen comforted.

"I know, I know," assured Evie. She leaned heavily into Tor, feeling so thankful that her roommates had shown up.

"I know how you feel right now. On Halloween I was sitting in your place hoping that Aaron was going to be there in the morning," explained Owen. His hand rubbed at Evie's shoulder soothingly. Sympathy rolled off the man, which did help Evie calm down again. Owen added, "So I'm here to do something for you that no one did for me."

Taking a deep breath, Evie asked, "What's that?"

"Make you go home," answered Owen. He was already prepared for her reaction.

Evie pulled herself out of Tor's half hug viciously. "No way in hell! What if Laika wakes up and I'm not here?"

"Calm down," Tor cut in, her calming presence taking on an edge of steel. Evie realized far too late how outnumbered she was. Only a moment ago she'd been grateful for the reinforcements, but Owen hadn't brought them for her. All eyes were on her, but Evie wasn't going without a fight; they'd have to force her out.

"Evie, look at yourself," Owen gestured his hand from her feet to head. Dried brown stains covered Evie's shoes, all the way up her legs and arms as well. Her shirt was torn and beyond saving with a bleach pen. She looked like a horror movie extra.

But she doubled down, "So?"

"Do you really want to be the first thing Laika sees when she wakes up? You, covered in her blood and half dead from hunger and exhaustion?" Owen asked.

"But..."

Owen waited patiently for the rest of Evie's argument, but it didn't come. Frustration swelled up inside Evie because he was right. So annoyingly right that she was a mess. Fear had her thinking like an idiot. She needed some rest and probably food too.

"Come home and get a meal," Shelly pleaded quietly. She'd abandoned Laika's side long enough to take one of Evie's free hands. "Once you get a little rest we can all come back in the morning. Or I can stay and work here tonight so Laika isn't alone." Everyone around her was overflowing with compassion, making it hard to muster a fight.

"Let me drive you home? We can talk about what happened in the car. You can tell me the details and I swear I'll be back in office tomorrow," urged Owen. The unspoken promise that he'd unleash MOONS on finding the attacker was there as well.

Evie couldn't bring herself to say anything just yet, so she picked up her bag. Earlier this week she'd been so excited about her new matching jacket and purse. She supposed they still matched... bloodstains covered both.

Tor tried to cheer her up as she handed Evie the jacket. "Don't worry. I can get blood out of anything. These will be good as new by the end of the week."

"We can stop and get something to eat too," Owen added. There was not a word of gloating about his victory. He held the door open.

"I'll cook," offered Tor. She checked over the room for anything else that Evie might have left behind. Meanwhile, Shelly put down her laptop bag, clearly prepared to stay in advance.

Evie wrote down a quick note for Laika and checked her friend's phone was still plugged in next to the hospital bed. Laika would have it if she woke up before Evie got back. Then she gave Shelly a quick thanks and a hug. Finally, she forced herself to take those steps out into the hall. Owen and Tor walked at her sides, making no attempts to hurry her along.

"That wasn't Jaci," Evie informed the officer when they got on the elevator.

"Gibson said the same thing. He said it looked like Jaci, but there was no way she could do what that thing did," confirmed Owen.

Thankfully the trio were alone so he could speak freely with Evie. "I got caught up on everything I missed before we came to get you. I think you might have just had a run in with the demon. Supposedly some of them are shapeshifters and that would explain all the different forms it took."

Tor opened her mouth but shut it just as quickly to allow the pair to talk.

Part of the explanation made sense given what she'd seen. The rest not so much. "But why would the demon go after Laika?" asked Evie.

"I don't know," Owen shrugged, "Maybe because she was on the right track to figuring out the ritual?"

"But, wouldn't it be better off going after the magical experts tracking it down? Laika and I are doing some running around and research only," Evie pressed again. She could think of at least three better targets without much effort.

"I'd have thought you'd be a better target," agreed Tor. She kept pace with conversation not caring she wasn't a moonlighter.

Owen paused when the doors slid open. "It might have." They'd reached the ground floor and he hurried them into the parking structure where his car waited. He'd brought a GPD cruiser for the ride.

Evie had understood his pause, so she stayed patient until they'd buckled into the car before pushing, "It might have what?"

"No one has been able to get ahold of Hazel since she was at Fulmino Apartments on Friday night. I'm starting to suspect the worst has happened to her, if she doesn't turn up soon," explained Owen.

"What about the real Jaci?" Evie realized that the demon might have been picking off more than just the experts.

"... Let's get you home," Owen answered. He kicked the cruiser to life, trying to avoid the question.

"Owen, what about Jaci?" demanded Evie. She was ready to reach over and shake the answer out of him.

"Gibson set a few officers to retrace her steps for the last 48 hours. They found her body hidden on the edge of Moonscent's run land about an hour ago," admitted Owen. He glanced at her worriedly.

Evie found a few more tears for today.

CHAPTER 12
INTENSIVE CARE

Laika
November 11th, 2018
Glenwood General, Glenwood, CA

L aika's eyes felt heavy, but she could hear people talking close by. She didn't know if it was the conversation or just the pain in her head that made her wake up. Her eyelids were heavy as lead when they struggled open, an odd feeling since the rest of her felt strangely numb.

An aging TV tucked up in the corner of two walls greeted Laika. The screen was dark and so was the rest of the room. She could barely make out the muted colors and patterns of the hospital curtains. Was she visiting Aaron again? No, he'd been discharged already...

Realization hit Laika that *she* was the one in the hospital bed this time. Then pain registered as well, heavily muted behind layers of drugs meant to keep her comfortable. They mostly left her foggy. Still, there were voices in the room with Laika and she needed to find them.

"I need to move her somewhere secure," Alfred explained in that quiet, calm tone Laika knew. He was standing near the foot of her bed. In the dim room she could make out a long black coat but nothing else of his features.

"She's in no condition to travel yet," answered Melinda. She was holding onto a clipboard and light reflected off green gems hanging around her wrists on bracelets.

Laika tried to call out to them, but her jaw wouldn't move. Pain flared across her face, red hot even through all the medicine. She squeezed her eyes shut and after a few long seconds she felt the pain begin to ebb away again.

Alfred spoke again, "If Laika remains here, everyone is at risk. GPD is operating on the theory that she was attacked by the summoned demon. If she was targeted once, then she may be again."

"I can handle a demon," confidence clung to Melinda's words. For just a moment the gems on her wrist glowed faintly, easily seen in the dark room.

"As could I," Alfred rebuffed, "But protecting an entire hospital during such a fight is too much, even for you."

Silence hung between them for a few moments too long. Laika tried to speak again despite her aching jaw. While she didn't make any words, the sound caught Alfred and Melinda's attention.

"Her pain meds are wearing off. Werewolves burn through everything too fast," Melinda complained to the vampire.

She approached to check Laika's vitals quickly. Unlike when the witch was moonlighting, her bedside manner was warm; gentle hands and soft words. "Good evening Laika, do you recall being attacked at GPD?"

Laika felt confusion start welling up as her head began to pound. She'd been attacked? Is that why her jaw hurt so much? Again she tried to speak but she couldn't.

"That's alright. Your mandible bone was dislocated in the fight. It's been set back in place, but it'll be sore for a couple weeks, even with werewolf healing. You're at Glenwood General right now," soothed Melinda. She scribbled down notes on Laika's chart.

Forcing her mouth to move Laika tried to ask, "E..ev..?"

"Evie is back at your home to get some rest. Officer Kirkland and Victoria took her home a few hours ago. Shelly is in the waiting area on a phone call; she will be back shortly," answered Alfred. His blue eyes were watching her intently.

Even just the couple syllables had sent Laika's head swimming in pain. A flash of claws swiping at her face came rushing back. She remembered now... a peony vampire attacked her in broad daylight.

"She's stable," Melinda informed Alfred, "I still don't think you should be moving her right now."

"I will take care of her," he assured in response.

Melinda sighed loudly and her expression pinched up. Then she relented, "Fine. I'll sign her out but it's your ass on the line if she gets attacked again!"

"Thank you." Alfred's shoulder slumped in relief.

"I'll go file this and bring you a wheelchair. But I'm calling Owen and telling him this terrible idea while I do," warned Melinda, "I'll tell the werewolf in the waiting room as well. But you'll need to deal with her if she disagrees." The doctor moved out of view, then the room brightened up for a moment as she opened the door to the hallway..

"I will talk to her before I leave," assured Alfred. In the light from the hall, Laika got a good look at Alfred. Even through her own haze she could see the lines on his face. He looked worried? Or maybe sad?

As soon as they were alone, Alfred moved to the side of her bed to take her hand gently. "I am sorry this happened. Sleep for now, you will feel better next time you wake up."

Laika tried to disagree. She didn't know how much time she'd already lost to being unconscious in this bed. But as his other hand swept her hair out of her face, Laika felt the call of sleep once more. Too much for her to resist...

- ☾ -

November 11th, 2018
Shady Hollows Apartments, Glenwood, CA

This time as Laika found herself drifting to consciousness there was a dull pain lingering, but nothing like the fire she'd felt last time. A cool sensation was sweeping out in circles along her jawline. Wherever it went, the pain was chased away. Maybe someone's fingers? She didn't care as long as they kept massaging the sore muscles.

A lamp glowed on the bedside table, giving Laika enough light to see by when she cracked her eyes open. There was no TV in the corner or distant beeping of machines. She was somewhere quiet and safe. This wasn't the hospital or even her own bedroom, but the guest room she'd practically stolen at Alfred's apartment.

Had she actually gotten up and gone to GPD? Or was her memory of being attacked in the parking lot just a really weird, extended dream? Maybe, since she was still in bed? She shifted to get up when a cool hand caught her shoulder.

"Not yet, please. You should not move for another few minutes, preferably longer," Alfred's voice was just above her.

Laika realized his hand was that soothing touch she'd been enjoying. Her heavy gaze dragged down from the ceiling to find Alfred sitting on the edge of the bed. Her words were slow, "Hey…"

"Good evening. I am glad to see you awake once more," greeted Alfred. His fingers went back to running patterns along the edge of her jaw.

"Evening? What's going on?" She had no idea what he was doing, but speaking was getting easier. Soon she'd be able to move without even the dull pain, so Laika let him keep going.

"How much do you remember?" Alfred countered with his own question. His eyes were following the path of his hands. He looked tired, like he'd been running a marathon with a thin layer of sweat dripping from his brow.

Laika had been laying down too long. Her muscles were heavy from the lack of use. But even pulling her head up was tall order as her neck protested the movement. Nothing was numb, the way her body had been in her 'dream'. Glancing down she could see the neck-line of a hospital gown peeking out from the blanket. So... not a dream... was this why she was struggling to move?

Memories came rushing back.

"I... was going to GPD to meet up with Evie. The bus took forever, so I was late. I remember crossing the street and-" Laika's words died as the image of a clawed monster flashed through her mind. Whatever her face had shown confirmed she did remember everything.

"You recall the entire event then," concluded Alfred. He removed his hands finally and sat a few inches back so that Laika had space. Then he began to unwind brown leather bands studded with green gemstones that were wrapped up his forearms. A magical item of some kind maybe?

"So I was attacked in the parking lot? How long have I been out?" Laika asked. She remembered trying to dodge that initial attack, but she hadn't been fast enough. The vague memory of her night in the hospital was fogged up. How much pain medication had she been on?

Laika didn't remember the conversation, only the warning from Melinda about how long it would take to heal. She had no idea how long she'd been unconscious? Had weeks passed? Given how easily the werewolf could talk now... maybe it had?

Alfred leaned over her to check his phone on the table beside the bed. She could see his frown as he counted the time, "I suppose you have been asleep around 16 hours now."

Less than a day? That couldn't be right!

He hadn't stopped talking, "I am glad you finally awoke as you should eat. Please stay here and I will bring you something easy on your stomach."

"What? That's impossible?" Laika grabbed onto Alfred's arm using him to pull herself up. Her chest heaved for a moment, then dizziness crashed down on her head. She didn't feel anything tear at the forced movement.

"Please be careful," warned Alfred. One hand caught her shoulder while the other checked her forehead, probably looking for a fever. Contact from his cool hand helped Laika push her lightheadedness away. He'd catch her if it came back. Alfred explained, "Magic can accelerate healing, but it does tire the body."

"Magic healing?" Laika echoed back, eyes looking down to assess herself.

Claws had started at her navel and torn a bloody path up to her face. She was going to have one hell of a scar from that. Fear and curiosity tore at Laika. She wanted the mirror in the bathroom to see just how bad the damage was. But she settled for pulling open the front of her hospital gown to check her chest and stomach.

A few pink lines followed the path she'd expected. They looked more like new skin rather than scar tissue, though. "What the hell?" mumbled Laika. Her fingers probed the lines and she felt dull soreness, like it was an old, healing wound. Dragging her attention back to Alfred, she asked, "16 hours, and magic did all this? How? This is amazing!"

"You will be exhausted. Let me get you something to eat," Alfred deflected from the question. He stood up sluggishly, but looked relieved. "I am glad you feel better, though."

The vampire left before Laika could stop him. Which was unfortunate, because now her mind was running a mile a minute. What had attacked her? It looked like a peony, but during the day? And before it transformed there had been a moment of recognition... A sudden jolt of panic hit her like lightning.

"Shit. Evie!" Laika looked around for her phone, hoping it hadn't been lost in whatever shuffle had happened between GPD, the hospital, and here.

Why was she here? Another question for when Alfred returned. But first, her eyes had spied her phone just in reach on the bedside table. She grabbed it and frowned at the big spider web crack on her screen. Thankfully, Evie's number was still easy to find.

After two rings, her friend answered, "Hello?!"

"Hey," Laika replied, glad to hear Evie's voice. She didn't sound injured, but a question wouldn't hurt. "Are you okay?"

"Am I okay? You disappeared from the hospital after Owen and Tor made me leave! Are *you* okay?"

"I'm fine, I swear. So you're home? You didn't get attacked?" Laika let go of the breath she'd been holding.

Evie's tone calmed, "No, I saw everything. You aren't fine..."

"Magical healing," assured Laika.

"No amount of healing can fix you that quickly..."

Laika rolled her eyes as she pulled her phone away long enough to snap a picture of her face. Then her chest and stomach. Evie wouldn't share them anywhere.

A cough caught Laika's attention. Alfred stood at the doorway with a bowl and cup in hand as he looked up at the ceiling. "I will give you another few moments then."

She hit send on the pictures, but by the time she looked back, Alfred was already gone. He was acting much stranger than usual...

"Your face?" Evie sounded shocked, her voice loud enough to cause reverb on the speaker, "You were missing part of your face?!"

"Sorry Alfred- I was what!?" Laika's apology turned into a strangled yelp as Evie's volume hurt her ears.

"Its claws tore- Oh my god Laika! What are you doing!? Don't send people nudes!" Evie scolded, sounding flustered.

"What? They're not- It's moonlighting! And it's just to you!" Laika suddenly realized why Alfred had left so abruptly both times. Whoops... Her hands fumbled to pull the hospital gown closed again. "I told you I was healed and you didn't believe me."

"Don't send nudes to anyone! What if my phone got hacked!?" reiterated Evie.

Laika forced a subject change, "Did GPD catch the monster?"

Evie's voice sobered. "No, the creature grew wings and flew off. Almost like it could shift forms."

"Seriously? So it wasn't a peony after all? Any clue what it was or why it tried to kill me?" Laika's fingers finished knotting the hospital gown shut.

"They're pretty sure it's the summoned demon and it came after you because you knew about it," Evie hesitated before adding, "There are more people missing..."

That sent a chill down Laika's spine. "More?"

"The demon was in GPD with me. I was there talking to Keisha and Gibson. At the time, I thought Jaci was there too, but I wasn't paying enough attention." Evie paused.

"And?" urged Laika.

Again Evie hesitated trying to find words, "GPD found Jaci's body. They're pretty sure the demon... killed her before taking her form."

Laika felt like she'd just gotten punched in the gut. She hadn't known the quiet werewolf long, but she'd grown fond of both the Moonscent girls since meeting them at the UCLA library. Jaci was sweet, and so young... and she was just gone? Like that? What about Keisha? Those two had been best friends... just like Laika and Evie.

"The demon... killed Jaci? But why? She wasn't involved in the case at all!" Laika could feel herself getting wound up. She swung her legs over the edge of the bed, trying to stand. Dizziness took hold, leaving her stuck with her head swimming.

"I know, but it probably took the form to get close to us." Evie didn't sound convinced of her own logic. If a monster had killed Evie just to take her face... Laika couldn't even begin to imagine the turmoil she'd be in. Keisha was living that nightmare right now... because of her.

Laika poked holes in the story with every fact. Evie was hunting down leads as effectively, if not more so, than herself. Alfred was the lead investigator. There were people like Melinda and Hazel who-

Then all the details clicked into place. There may be a demon running around Glenwood, but it hadn't killed Jaci.

"I think I need to rest for a bit," Laika lied quietly. She didn't want to keep misleading her friend, but she had to get answers first. "I might have an idea for tracking down my attacker. I promise I'll let you know as soon as I'm sure, okay?"

Evie let silence go a bit longer than usual. Then she agreed. "Okay, I'm sorry about Jaci. I know you are closer to the Moonscent girls than I am. Rest and let me know where you are so I can come see you?"

"Yeah, I get the feeling that Alfred is kinda picky about who knows where he lives. But I'll ask him and worst case just come home," Laika promised. She knew Alfred could likely hear her. After a full week with him, she'd noticed more than a few paranoid tendencies.

"He wouldn't tell me earlier," Evie growled over the speaker. "If I don't see you soon, then I'm reporting him for kidnapping!"

"I love you too, Evie," laughed Laika. Alfred must've called Evie before she woke up. That explained a lack of calls and text messages blowing up her phone. She waited for an acknowledgement before hanging up.

Alfred had not returned, despite the call ending. While Laika could probably summon him back, she should get dressed first. Especially after she'd accidentally flashed him twice now. Laika's head was still spinning as she got to her feet, but she managed to make it to her bag. A shower would be amazing... Maybe after food, when she wasn't so dizzy. A pair of pajama shorts and a tank came with her to the bathroom.

She studied her face and chest carefully for any injuries. Laika couldn't find anything out of place other than the pink lines that trailed her front. These had been deep at one point, but now were just a foggy memory. She'd been lucky to get this level of healing; even her previous bruises from Halloween were gone.

After dressing, Laika made her way out to the living room. She saw Alfred stretched out on the couch and his head rested against the arm. His eyes were closed. Had he fallen asleep? Laika was tempted to leave him there undisturbed for a few hours. But her meal was on the coffee table and enticed her into approaching. Slow and careful steps carried her silently to snatch up the bowl.

"I should have announced my presence earlier," Alfred apologized. His eyes remained closed.

She had no idea how he'd heard her. Was his hearing really that good? She noticed that Alfred looked tired again, like the day she'd made him sleep. A side effect of his magic perhaps? He'd definitely been using it on her earlier.

Perching on the edge of the cushion, Laika settled next to him. She reached down to brush his hair gently. "It's fine. I might have gotten caught up in the surprise about magic healing... Was that... Melinda? Or you?"

Alfred put an arm on the back of the couch and used it to drag himself up, making space for Laika to sit properly as he did. Then he predictably deflected, "You should eat something. It will help with the dizziness."

That earned him a raised eyebrow from Laika. He kept dodging that question about her recovery. Melinda was a green witch whose magic was used primarily for healing. She'd be easy to point the finger at. But Laika had a sneaking suspicion based on Alfred's state and unwillingness to lie to her, that he'd been helping. His leather bands were probably a magical item of some kind. She already knew he had the skill to make them. So why hide it?

Laika's stomach growled, forcing her to drop the subject long enough to eat. A warm bowl of soup was exactly what she needed after almost a day of no food. This was reheated from some delivery service at best, but it was heaven right now.

Several minutes passed in comfortable silence as Laika inhaled her meal.

"I talked to Evie about everything going on. She told me what GPD thinks, and about Jaci," Laika explained through bites. For a moment, her stomach threatened to rebel at the reminder of poor Jaci.

"I was waiting until you felt better to speak to you about this," Alfred murmured quietly, running a hand over his face. His reaction made the answer obvious.

"So... It was Hazel?" Laika guessed. She put her food down, the warm soup no longer so appealing. Jaci, who wasn't much older than her siblings, was dead because of her. Moonscent had lost a friend and sister because of Laika. How was she ever supposed to live with this guilt?

A complicated expression crossed Alfred's face; frustration, sadness, and anger. "Correct. Hazel assumed one of her stolen forms for the attack. Likely she stole the use of wings from a local lotus in case of escape. That was not the demon."

Laika felt her stomach churn dangerously again. She'd pried the truth of Hazel's powers from Alfred. But it hadn't mattered because the first time she went out, she'd been attacked. Not even 24 hours ago, in broad daylight no less.

"So orchid vampires are daywalkers too? I thought only vampires like Tony could do that." Laika couldn't combat the confusion setting in. There were as many holes in his explanation of what happened as GPD's theory.

"I would not worry about that so much," Alfred attempted to soothe her.

"I have to worry about it! I thought I was safe going out during the day since I'd see her coming a mile away!" Laika declared. His answers weren't helping her calm down.

Alfred looked away, clearly uncomfortable before adding, "Her daywalking is not permanent."

Now was Laika's turn to frown. "How does that work?"

Alfred forced his gaze back onto Laika. He picked up her hand to lace their fingers together. The vampire finally explained, "When Hazel killed Jaci, she did so to get her face and her powers. That includes daywalking, but the ability will only last 2 to 3 days at most."

Silence reigned as another chill crept up Laika's spine. There was a vampire who could just kill someone and walk around in the daylight like normal? How was that fair? Silence reigned as another chill crept up Laika's spine. There was a vampire who could just kill someone and walk around in the daylight like normal? How was that fair? The growing list of vampires who didn't apparently burst into flames in the sun was concerning. Laika had thought there was only one exception, but in the past week she'd learned of two more. What other 'rules' were vampires lying about?

"How... How do we fight against that then?" She stumbled over the question a few times.

"*You* do not fight an orchid vampire," Alfred answered quickly. His hand gave hers a squeeze, trying to soothe her again. "I will handle this in the morning by going to the LA Coven."

Laika felt on the edge of hysterics. "How does that help?"

"Because the LA Coven of vampires are who invited Hazel here. They did so to determine if a vampire was behind the Anarchist case. We now have proof that an elf is the culprit, so the coven will uninvite Hazel and she will leave," explained Alfred. He laid the plan out like it made perfect sense.

Laika knew there was a coven of vampires in LA, but how many could really be in a single coven? Twenty? Maybe thirty? But the earnest expression on Alfred told her he really believed this would work.

She relented, "And they'll make her go where?"

"Back to the east coast or Europe," admitted Alfred.

Anger flashed through Laika, her voice raised, "So she'd get away with killing Jaci with no consequences?"

"I did not say that. Vampires are worse than most at policing themselves, and Hazel's murder of an innocent girl here may get pinned on the demon. However, the coven will not be as forgiving," assured Alfred. He attempted to pull Laika a bit closer with their interlocked fingers.

But she resisted.

Laika thought he was being way too optimistic about the situation. If no one could fight an orchid, then how would they stop Hazel from just coming back? Could they be trusted to get justice for Jaci, one lone werewolf from the west? She nearly pulled her hand back, but fighting with Alfred wasn't going to do Laika any good.

So she nodded her agreement sullenly. Anyone with eyes could tell how unhappy Laika was with this outcome. Still, she went back to her dinner rather than argue more.

"I know it is not what you were hoping for," Alfred acknowledged the obvious. He let her hand drop so Laika could pick up the bowl again. Despite this being his plan, he looked as unhappy as Laika felt about letting Hazel go 'free.'

"No," Laika grumbled, "But it sounds like the best we've got right now."

She wasn't in the mood for food, but she needed to eat if she wanted to be functional tomorrow. Plans were already forming in her mind. There had to be a way to bring Hazel down, even if Alfred wasn't going to tell her.

Now was the time to change the subject. Her mental murder board had gained another point for iris; blood magic could be used for healing if it dealt with the body. Next time they talked about his court, Laika was going to surprise him by already knowing the answer. Between gulps Laika reminded, "I'm not done asking you about your magic."

"I am aware." Alfred leaned his head on the back of the couch and scrunched his eyes closed like a headache was coming on.

"I'm betting that you had something to do with my stellar healing too?" Laika pushed again. She slid so that her legs pressed against his side comfortably. Alfred made a non-committal sound, but the skin contact brought the ghost of a smile to his lips. Laika attempted to lighten the mood. She leaned up to press a kiss to the underside of his jaw. No danger of fangs ruining the gesture there. "Thanks."

"You are welcome," muttered Alfred so low she could barely make out the words.

- ☾ -

November 12th, 2018
Shady Hollows Apartments, Glenwood, CA

Laika had run out of pajamas again. She really wasn't prepared to be spending as much time as she was at Alfred's apartment. Maybe it was time to buy a couple more sleep outfits, so she didn't have to clean them as often. If Laika was at home she wouldn't worry about wearing the same tank to bed a couple nights in a row, but this was still a very new relationship.

Them sharing a bed had happened twice. She wanted to be clean, including her clothing, just in case they ever had the energy for more than sleep. Plus, Laika was trying to pretend she had no plans to go anywhere today, even if she was just waiting for Alfred to leave for LA.

After breakfast Laika had declared it time for laundry. She'd picked up her entire bag to toss in the machine, then slipped out of last night's pajamas. Only then did the werewolf realize she couldn't just go to her room and grab more clothing. Next to an ironing board, Laika found her solution.

She sat on the floor of the laundry room pretending to read a book, dressed in one of Alfred's nice white shirts. He was taller than Laika so it did cover down to her thighs well enough. If found, she'd be a picture of keeping busy, not scheming.

Her gaze was drifting back and forth across the page, but Laika's actual focus was on her phone as she planned. Alfred wholeheartedly believed this could be solved by going and asking the LA coven to send Hazel away. That wasn't justice!

SHELLY

Okay based on the flight number I got from
your dad he'll be here tomorrow.

LAIKA

I thought he was getting here tonight?

SHELLY

I managed to delay him for the night saying
you weren't allowed visitors anyways.

LAIKA

That's surprisingly deceitful of you!

SHELLY

Lying to father figures is a skill I have
honed over two decades of careful
practice.

So what's the plan here? Am I still digging
for information on their corruption rituals?

LAIKA

No, we need more information on vampires.

SHELLY

Isn't that Tor's area of expertise? I can ask
her for help.

Laika frowned; she didn't know how much she wanted every
vampire in Glenwood to know she was after information on orchids.
Then again, Tor excelled at being vague and was willing to help
unlike her more official resources. Laika had considered calling
Owen and confessing everything she knew over the phone. Then
again, GPD didn't have a good track record listening to her. So she
needed more than just a vague explanation of mythical orchid
vampires.

Facts, weaknesses, and proof were required before Laika could
loop in the officers. As loathe as she was to admit it... She also needed
Blood Fang's help. Or at least, she needed their vampire expert's
knowledge because Google knew next to nothing. The wikipedia

page didn't even confirm that orchids were vampires. Her frustration was interrupted by the buzzing of a text message.

> **TOR**
>
> Yo, you have vampire questions?

> **LAIKA**
>
> Do you know anything about Orchids?

> **TOR**
>
> No one believes they're real, but otherwise nothing.
>
> I have a few older friends who might know more of the legends.

> **LAIKA**
>
> I need this to be as lowkey as possible.

> **TOR**
>
> So I'll get them drunk before asking, I'll get back to you when I know something.

It was a start. She felt like she needed to do more to avenge Jaci, but Laika couldn't accomplish that while locked in a tower all day. Getting down from here was the hard part. Alfred's key was used in the elevator to let them reach the top floors. But she'd learned during her week here that it was also needed both to lock and unlock the front door, including from the inside. Even if she got past the door to the hallway, she wouldn't be able to summon the elevator and there was no fire escape down.

Laika grumbled. She'd noticed Alfred was a little paranoid and hadn't given it too much thought. Some people really just liked their space, and lots of people had security systems. Today the wards and spells were proving to be absolutely vexing because she couldn't just dispel them herself.

"Are you down here?" Alfred asked as he approached from the hallway.

Due to both of them having superior hearing, conversations

could be held between rooms without anyone needing to yell. So Laika spoke at a normal volume to answer, "Laundry room."

Even over the noise of the machine, Alfred heard her because a moment later the door opened. "I am preparing to leav-"

Laika looked up from where she sat. She was curious as to why he'd cut off mid sentence, but nothing looked wrong. If anything he seemed surprised. She asked, "Are you heading out?"

"That depends," Alfred answered. His usually calm tone back in place and she noticed he'd stopped walking awkwardly at the door frame.

"On?" pressed Laika.

"On if this is an innocent mistake or an invitation," admitted Alfred.

"Invitation? To where?" Laika repeated, tilting her head to the side. What on earth was he talking about?

"Right," sighed Alfred, "A mistake, I will choose to ignore this then. I am ready to leave for LA. Do you need anything before I go?"

Why was he sighing? Laika was confused, but tried to keep up. She set the book down and looked up at him, "No, are you going to be gone long? Like you were on Friday?"

"Very possibly longer," admitted Alfred. He held up a silver key for her and for a moment he looked like he was going to stay in the doorway. Then he took a few steps into the laundry room and held it out for Laika.

"What's this?" She already knew the answer. Laika lit up as he'd literally just handed her the key to her problems. Her fingers gripped at the cool metal.

"My spare key. As I will be gone long today and I do believe I have impressed on you the dangers of Hazel, I trust you will not abuse this. I am lending you the key in case you need to get out, or allow Evie up," explained Alfred. He'd grudgingly agreed to let her pack-mate know where he lived this morning.

Given how Laika had just been worrying over all his paranoid security measures, she recognized the gift for what it was. Trust.

Alfred was trusting her with the key to his kingdom... at least for today. Laika was on her feet in a flash.

"I promise I will use it wisely." She leaned in to seal the promise with a kiss. Again the brush of lips on lips was thrilling and Laika pressed herself closer. She was mentally prepared for his fangs and refused to do anything as childish as jump.

But as she felt one of Alfred's fangs pressed into her bottom lip again, Laika froze up. She fought so hard against her flight instinct that her muscles all locked up into a tense mess instead.

Carefully, Alfred untangled her arms from his neck and shoulders before taking a step back. He put space between them, and when he spoke his fangs stayed out of sight, "You do not need to push yourself on this. When we have a day not plagued by demons and witches we can talk out the issue."

"There's no issue," Laika tried to wave off the problem. She took a step forward, but it was met with another step backwards from Alfred.

"There is," he disagreed. His patience was worn like armor as he continued, "My fangs make you uncomfortable and ignoring that will not do us any good. We will need to have a real conversation about them later."

"They don't... *You* don't make me uncomfortable," Laika protested but could see the battle was a lost cause today.

"At a later time," Alfred reminded. His fangs were still hidden away.

Laika felt frustration about the whole stupid ordeal. Kissing shouldn't be this hard! She snipped, "Fine, we'll talk about it! But that means we're talking about why you won't touch me or look at me either."

Now was Alfred's turn to look confused, "Because you never gave me any verbal consent you wanted me to touch you. I suppose I could be more aggressive in pursuing that consent, but between my injuries and yours, there has not been a time to talk about it."

"Well... We're dating so..." Laika trailed off, staring at Alfred with a flicker of amusement in her eyes. "You're kind of old fashioned, aren't you?"

"Quite the opposite, an old fashioned type would not care for your opinion on the subject of your body. You will find I am a tad more modern on my views," countered Alfred. He gave her a polite shrug.

Laika wrinkled her nose at his answer. He might have a point, but she still teased him, "So no touching until we talk about your fangs? That's kinda a pity because it might be a while before we handle the demo-"

Her hand holding the key moved to slide it into her jean's pocket. Only for Laika to go fully red as she remembered what she was wearing. Or rather not wearing...

"The penny drops." Alfred shook his head, but he was still smiling at her.

Laika wasn't sure if she should laugh or be horrified right now. She looked like some trashy story out of a dirty magazine.

Alfred soothed, "We can talk about this when I get back?"

"Sure," squeaked Laika. She wasn't sure how much was on display right now, so moving seemed like a bad idea.

"Be safe today," the vampire urged before leaving.

Laika could only nod to him. As soon as Alfred's footsteps hit the stairs back up to the main house she moved. Next to the ironing board there was a mirror hung on the wall. Probably used for changing, given how many of Alfred's suits seemed to live in the laundry room.

Laika stifled a groan just in case Alfred could still hear her from the top of the stairs. She looked exactly as she expected, with buttons not done up enough. And her lack of underwear was probably obvious when she was sitting. No wonder he'd asked if she was inviting him to stay or not...

Whoops.

CHAPTER 13
BLOOD FANG

Evie
November 12th, 2018
Taran Estate, Los Angeles, CA

Evie stared at her phone blankly. When she'd answered, she had moved to the kitchen of Arik's house for privacy. At first, she'd been thrilled to hear Laika's voice sounding stronger than before. But then Evie had gotten a horror story she had never expected.

While there was a demon in Glenwood, it wasn't who attacked Laika. Instead her best friend had been pulled into a possibly fatal love triangle from hell. Just great...

Evie took a few deep breaths to gather her thoughts. She had options, the most appealing being to go hide behind the wards of Alfred's apartment with Laika. But they had just agreed last week not to avoid their problems. Which meant even with all the possibilities, Evie only saw one way forward. She needed information, and that meant working with her enemies.

"Dispatch," answered the voice of Julie after a couple rings on Evie's phone.

"This is Evie Belle from Night Claw, could you please connect me through to Ace Deerling from the Blood Fang pack?" Evie gambled on the moonlighter network having a way to do this. She'd never tried before.

"Hold please," Juile said right before the line clicked to waiting music.

Evie let out a small squeal of excitement that her crazy plan had actually worked. But as the ringing picked up on the line, she wondered if this was a good idea. After Halloween there had been no real fighting between the packs. Then again, they also had barely seen each other.

"Hello?" Ace's voice came through the speaker. He seemed confused, so Evie wondered if it was her number that showed up on his Caller ID.

"Hey," Evie responded, "Thanks for answering."

"Not to be super rude, but who is this?" asked Ace.

Evie frowned, she had been hoping he'd at least recognize her voice. "It's Evie from Night Claw, we had our collective asses handed to us on Halloween by a single vampire?" Silence met her words. She was concerned for a moment that Ace had hung up on her. Their stupid rivalry was getting in the way of her answers. "Hello?"

"I'm still here," Ace's tone was brusque and the words clipped.

"Okay then. I need to borrow Thad for an hour," Evie just got to the point.

"What?" His tone shifted to confusion.

Evie sighed loudly over the phone. "Please?"

"I repeat, what?" Ace snapped back.

"In case you haven't heard, there is a murderer on the loose and I need Thad's brain to solve the mystery," Evie barked, much harsher than she'd intended.

Again there was an awkward pause as some of the frost between them melted. Next time Ace spoke, he sounded like he was trying to be nicer. "Okay, that was my fault. You caught me off guard, because I don't know how the hell you got my number."

"I don't have your number. Julie at dispatch transferred me through because this is about moonlighting," Evie quickly offered up an explanation.

"Julie?" Ace sounded like he was tasting her name for the first time.

Evie didn't need empathy to realize what was happening. She let out a small snort of laughter, "You don't know her real name either, do you?"

"We call her Betty," admitted Ace.

"She never leaves any time to actually ask her name and it's been too long. I would be so offended if someone asked me now," Evie laughed. Their conversation was finally going smoothly, so she tried again. "Laika has a lead that the creature who attacked her wasn't actually the demon. But if she's right, then I need to talk to a vampire expert and the closest I have is Thad." She left off the internal comments that she'd rather ask anyone else.

"What do you mean not the demon?" Ace's voice was curious.

Evie bit her lip without an answer. How much did she actually want to tell Blood Fang? They had never been on friendly terms. What if they went to Owen and Aaron with the theory first? A memory of Laika struggling to breathe in a pool of her blood struck Evie like a bullet to the heart. If she didn't do something, then that could happen again. Hazel had taken a reckless swing once, nothing but some well wishes were stopping her from trying again.

"I mean, that Laika wasn't attacked by the demon. I'm sure that monster is running around somewhere, but I think GPD is chasing the wrong person. I think she was attacked by an orchid vampire," Evie decided on honesty.

"Why do you think that?" Ace hadn't said no, but she could hear his skepticism.

Evie needed to get him in her sights. She could read his aura even through the usual wave of anger. If she tried hard enough, she could convince even Ace to lend his support to this plan. She continued, "I think I should explain in person. I'm picking Laika up from her safe-house and she can fill in some gaps. Can we meet up?"

"Yeah, give me your number and I'll send you an address," agreed Ace.

Evie thanked him before doing as he asked. She hung up feeling a bit more hopeful than before. She only had to get Thad to give them an honest answer. Which meant bringing food with her.

Before leaving Arik's home, Evie charged 4 pizzas to her 'Laika Food Fund' for pickup. She reasoned that if Laika got her answers then she'd write about them eventually.

- ☾ -

November 12th, 2018
Blood Fang Residence, Glenwood, CA

As the Saab's engine turned off, Evie leveled a look at the house they had just parked in front of. Everything about Blood Fang's home was annoyingly perfect. The yard and the building were well kept and easily large enough to house a pack their size. A high privacy fence ringed most of the lot. Evie suspected it probably had a pool with a pool house and all the makings of a fancy yard. Pretty much the exact opposite of the Night Claw's rental house.

She closed the car door and Evie took a deep breath to remind herself that they weren't here to pick a fight. No matter what feelings of jealousy were bubbling in her chest about another picture perfect home, she needed to cooperate with Blood Fang. At least cooperate long enough to get any information Thad had on orchid vampires.

Laika clearly had different ideas as she slammed the passenger door shut. She was a bundle of focus and nervous energy streaking for the door. Again Evie marveled over how less than two days ago, her friend had been in critical condition. Laika shouldn't even be able to walk right now, never mind sprint up the path to the door. Before Evie could retrieve the pizza and catch up, Laika was pounding on the door like a woman possessed.

"Laika!" hissed Evie as she grabbed her friend's arm. "Don't break the door open, there's a doorbell!"

Evie pressed the button while still scowling at Laika. The chime was loud enough to be heard outside. Between the bell and the knocking there was no way Blood Fang could miss them. Still, they stood on the doorstep longer than Evie liked.

"Sorry," Laika had the grace to look ashamed.

"It's fine, I get it. You just want us onto the next step already," soothed Evie. Before she could say any more, the door opened.

Ace was dressed for the gym and greeted them with cautious skepticism. Now that she was standing in front of him, Evie turned her empathy on full blast. She could feel the mixture of curiosity and frustration radiating from Ace. There were edges of tiredness to his movements, like he'd been running for hours.

After a beat, he spoke, "Good afternoon. So-"

"Where's Thad?" Laika cut him off. Her eyes searched past Ace, as if she might spot the pack's vampire expert lurking nearby.

"First things first, I need some explanations before you get anything out of us." Ace's eyes narrowed as his usual sense of anger started to tinge the caution.

Evie stepped forward to cut them both off. "Sorry, she's a little intense today. I did say we'd explain in person and I meant it. Can we come in?"

Ace's face twisted and she could see his anger being reined in through his aura. But Evie could tell he wasn't sold on this and she needed to be careful. His eyes glanced at the boxes of food and he relented. His tone was a warning, "Yeah, come in. If this is an ambush, it's pretty terrible because I could take both of you and you're outnumbered."

"Calling you up and asking to come over would be a terrible ambush plan," countered Evie as she stepped over the threshold.

"Night Claw isn't known for their subtlety," Randall added. He'd appeared from upstairs with a smug look.

Evie turned her empathy on Randall as he reached the bottom of the stairs. His skepticism was like a whirlwind around him, so likely Ace had explained their theory. She could feel his emotions were undercut with a sense of fury and exhaustion. Another tired werewolf?

Randall eyed Laika before speaking again, "How the hell are you walking? From what I heard from Keisha, you were basically dead?"

Unexpectedly, there was no cutting remark from Laika. Just a surge of guilt as she gave a shrug and mumbled, "Magic."

Ace cleared his throat. "Okay, to the living room. You can explain there."

Evie took Laika by the arm and led her the way they were directed. She heard Ace and Randall mumbling about how rich Night Claw must be to afford that level of healing. A scowl threatened her features, but she dragged her expression back under control.

Everything inside of the house was just as nice as the outside. Sitting on the couches, Evie was struggling to find fault with Blood Fang's home. Nothing was like the frat houses from college. There was no tower of beer bottles in the corner or pizza boxes on every surface. At least until Evie sat her offerings on their coffee table.

Randall and Ace considered the tempting boxes, but refrained from taking a slice. They were looking for the strings attached to the pizza. "I've told Randall everything from our phone call," explained Ace. He sat himself down on a secondary couch so he could see both women. "So the real question is, why are you here?"

"What do you mean?" Evie asked. She thought she'd been clear on the phone.

"Why are you here asking Thad and not taking this directly to the GPD?" clarified Ace.

Pizza remained untouched. Tension was building faster than Evie could track where it was coming from. This was quickly starting to spiral as fast as all of their usual fights did. Evie doubled down on known facts, "Because Gibson isn't going to listen to us. Even if I marched into the station in my underwear offering lap dances, he'd ignore anything I have to say."

"Uh..." Ace responded gracefully, her mental imagery had worked to derail his suspicions from solidifying.

Taking the opening, Evie plowed on, "We need to know how we can prove our theory and take it to Owen. Thad's the only vampire expert who might be willing to tell us."

Laika quietly added, "Glenwood's resident magical expert confirmed Hazel was an orchid vampire for me."

"Seriously?" Randall injected himself. He was looming over the back of the couch behind Ace, watching both women with that same skeptical look.

"Yeah, Alfred was watching over me after the attack. We had time to talk about what happened," Laika answered.

"And he just told you that Hazel was an orchid vampire and she tried to kill you? Why didn't he tell GPD that? Why are you coming around to us looking for more information?" Randall rattled off questions one after another.

Evie had to admit they were solid questions too. Things she'd want to know if the situation were reversed. She tried to help, "We don't know for sure that he won't, but he hasn't so far."

"He's not going to," Laika cut in quickly. Frustration was spiking her aura in reds and oranges.

"You don't know that," Ace pointed out.

"Yes! I do!" Laika shot back, her emotions starting to leak into her words, "Because he's just going to go tell the LA Coven about it and have them handle her." That was news to Evie; Laika hadn't mentioned that Alfred had an actual plan during their call this morning or the car ride. Why had she left that out?

Ace raised an eyebrow at Laika with a quizzical expression, "Do we need to do anything, then?"

Evie couldn't help but agree with the sentiment. As much as she felt for what happened to Jaci, if the LA Coven could handle the problem, then let them handle it.

"That's not good enough!" Laika was growing a little hysterical now.

Carefully, Evie put her hand on her friend's wrist. She gave it a little squeeze to remind her they weren't here to fight. Her words were quiet, "Hey, it's okay."

"No, it isn't," Laika argued back. Again she looked like she might cry from frustration at not getting her point across. But she wasn't explaining anything very well...

"The LA Coven is going to sweep this under the rug. They're worse than the mafia and older than any other gang around," explained a voice from the doorway.

Everyone turned their heads to find a rumpled looking Thad standing there. He had a hoodie and pajama pants on, looking like he just crawled out of bed.

"What do you mean?" Evie asked. While she didn't want to pick apart how Laika felt, doing that to Thad was a tried and true pastime for Night Claw.

Thad held up his phone with a yawn, "Ace sent me the rundown before you got here, and as for the rest you weren't exactly quiet. So Hazel, the LA MOONS magical expert, is an orchid vampire and she's trying to kill Laika. You want to know her weaknesses."

"We want to know anything you can tell us," corrected Evie. At least with Thad in the room they might get somewhere now. She'd be able to goad him into yelling answers if she had to.

"Thad," Ace commanded his packmate's attention, "Why isn't LA handling the problem good enough?"

"As loath as I am to side with Laika of all people, she's right. Vampires handle vampires in one of two ways. You don't find the body, or they shuffle the problem out of public view until the current generation is dead. If they have an orchid willing to do work for them, then they'll just hide her for a while," explained Thad. He rubbed sleep out of his eyes then joined them on the couches. Without asking, Thad dug into the pizza.

"And why is an orchid that important?" Ace pressed.

Without missing a beat, Thad gave a shrug. "They're powerful and can steal powers from any other race."

"And they can steal faces by killing people," Laika explained quietly. Her glare stayed cast down on the pizza boxes.

Colors exploded from every direction as Ace and Randall took in the news. Oranges and red dominated over the more neutral and curious emotions Evie had seen a moment ago. Randall moved from where he stood behind the couch to sit down and grabbed a slice of pizza. His actions were so casual and at complete odds with the vivid anger coming off of him that Evie was a little concerned. Then he politely asked, "How do we kill her?"

"Randall," reprimanded Ace, "We don't kill people. We detain them."

Evie could see the lack of conviction in Ace's words as his aura betrayed his real feelings about Hazel. Despite how stupid she believed the members of Blood Fang to be on any given day, right now they'd all kept up. Jaci had died and Hazel wore her face to get close to Laika. Their pack looked at Moonscent like little sisters. All of them were praying for bloodshed.

"I don't know, but if we can get all the information we need to prove our theory, then we can ask Owen to check how Jaci was killed." Evie didn't enjoy their reaction every time she mentioned their dead friend.

"What good does that do?" Randall was on edge. He'd scarfed down three slices like he was trying to make a point.

"If we can get GPD looking for her, then maybe they'll get Hazel before LA and she'll face justice for her crimes." Evie hesitated. The compromise didn't resonate with three men who were barely containing their rage.

Ace stood up. "I need to tell Nilani what we know... She deserves the truth." No one stopped him as he left for more privacy for his call. That was one less angry werewolf for Evie to try and keep in check.

"I don't know much about orchid weaknesses," Thad confessed slowly, chewing over every word. "There aren't many of them out there and they don't tend to live a long time. But I have read that if they steal powers from someone, they steal their weaknesses too."

Evie's mouth turned down into a frown. "What does that mean if we saw her sporting a peony form and then wings?"

Thad twisted his lips to match her expression. "I guess the wings could have been a lotus vampire, so mistletoe and wolf's blood would be our best bet."

"How does any of that help us convince GPD to go look for Hazel?" snapped Randall.

"It doesn't matter," Ace answered before anyone could. He was putting his phone away as he returned, "Nilani is going there now. She's got enough sway with the police; they'll check Jaci for signs of a vampire attack. If Laika and Evie are right, then GPD will be on the trail in an hour."

"Shit," groaned Randall, "By the time she gets to the station, Dark Wind will be hunting for Hazel. They respect Nilani too much to not run down the lead for her."

"Which leaves us sitting on the couch, eating pizza, and not helping again," lamented Evie, realizing the chain of events at the same time.

"Isn't that your status quo?" Thad shrugged as he took another slice.

Evie had been in the process of watching Ace's aura and determining the best way to bring his simmering anger back down. But the insult broke her concentration. "Excuse me?"

"What? It's not like I'm exaggerating. Even back in high school all you did was sit around and make someone else fix your problems. You sat in the middle of the cafeteria like the queen of the school, and let your mouth run with crazy shit all the time," grumbled Thad.

"No, I didn't and you're one to talk. You were such a dick in high school." Evie shot back. She didn't enjoy talking about her years in high school before she'd been able to escape the house. Despite being 'popular' because of who her family was, she didn't have any close friends and serial dated because she couldn't risk bringing someone long term home. During that time, both her sisters had basically run away from home and her father barely even slept at the house. Evie had been alone with her mother and her little brother, who was their mother's golden child. Then she'd had her first shift extremely early due to the stress of home life and everything got much worse.

"What? I was nothing but kind to you! I even asked you to Winter Formal?" scowled Thad. He threw down his pizza.

"Aren't you gay?" Laika cut in. That had been an early subject of debate between Night Claw. With how many hot guys were in the boyband of a pack, at least one had to be gay. Evie had known Thad since high school and always suspected it was him.

"I am, but that's not the point," Thad hissed, "In Junior year, I was still pretending to be straight because my mother wanted me to get in good with the Belles and marry their daughter."

"Wait! Wait! Wait!" shouted Evie, trying to regain control of everything. She could still feel Ace's temper flaring as he silently devoured a pizza himself, but she couldn't focus on that. "You hate me and Laika all because of Winter Formal? You stood me up!"

"No, you sent your little lackey Rebecca to tell me you changed your mind!" Thad yelled back, "At the last minute too, so I had no time to find anyone and had to skip or admit I couldn't find a date!"

Rebecca? Evie remembered her as someone who lived on the fringe of her social circle. They weren't particularly close, and Evie couldn't figure out why Rebecca had done something so Mean Girl to Thad. She defended, "I didn't tell her to do that. I knew you were gay and you were one of like a hundred guys trying to date my family name. But I figured you wouldn't be too pushy for anything more than photo proof of our date. Are you sure it was one of my friends and not someone playing a prank on you?"

"Rebecca. Kinda tall, brunette-from-a-bottle, pointy ears? The only half-elf in the entire school? Your BFF?" Thad snapped back at her.

Evie looked to Laika for help settling this situation, but her friend was busy on her phone. Laika's aura was starting to shift from frustration to anger with every message. She needed to find an answer that would put an end to the conversation. They had a lot more important matters to handle and thankfully her own phone vibrated.

OWEN

Whatever you are doing, stop it!

Sit down and stay put!

EVIE

What?

OWEN

I just got off the phone with the alpha of Moonscent who is pissed we didn't catch the vampire who killed her packmate.

So whatever you're doing, I need you to stay out of this.

Owen was a good cop, he'd tracked the clues back to Evie quickly. But she didn't deserve the lecture, especially when all she'd done was go ask a few questions of other moonlighters.

"You too?" Laika asked sullenly.

"Yeah," muttered Evie. She could feel the eyes of Blood Fang on them.

Ace spoke for the first time since he'd told them about Nilani's plan, "I got told to stay home and out of the way."

"It's not like we're responsible for finding all the connections and clues... oh wait, we are," grumbled Evie. She was starting to realize where all the agitation was coming from in the room. Every one of them had been told to sit down and shut up again. They weren't good enough to go help find Hazel.

"This isn't fair! We can't just let Jaci's killer get away! I say we go hunting," Laika jumped to her feet.

Randall echoed her words, "I think we should go hunt for Hazel."

Evie watched as the auras around the room started to sync up in color as everyone's resolve grew in favor of the plan. This was a terrible idea and she needed to curb it, even if she was pissed at Owen's lecture.

"But-"

"We know she's got peony blood," Ace cut her off.

"That's easy for us," Thad agreed, "A quick cut and we can cripple her with any of our blood."

"We won't be so caught off guard this time," Randall got to his feet as well.

Evie looked at the room and knew she'd never talk them out of it now. But she didn't agree to their insane plan either, even with Laika giving her an expectant look to get onboard.

Ace was her tipping point as he asked, "Do you want to be a puppy who sits at home? Or do you want to run with the wolves?"

"Damn it," Evie swore, "Fine! But we have to call the GPD when we find her so that we don't end up in jail ourselves."

The plan was set.

CHAPTER 14
WITCH HUNT

Evie
November 12th, 2018
Middle of Nowhere, Glenwood, CA

E vie felt ridiculous.

Four hours ago she, Laika, and all the members of Blood Fang had set out to hunt down Hazel. They hadn't made any progress at all. Instead, they were standing in the middle of an empty field with no leads.

"I've got nothing," Thad complained as he pulled his shirt back over his head. He and Randall had just spent the better part of an hour as wolves with their noses to the ground.

"It's all just Jaci's scent," Randall agreed with a frustrated growl. "It's all over the place here, and then it just keeps going off that way back towards Glenwood. But we know that's not right."

"There's a faint scent of blood over there," Thad pointed to a fairly large rock in the field, "But it doesn't go anywhere besides a few circles. There's nothing to track."

Evie frowned as her eyes lowered to the grass. They all knew this was where Jaci had been found, but the field certainly didn't look like the site of the werewolf's final struggle. There weren't claw marks or blood splatter. Just some slightly crushed wildflowers. If there hadn't been police tape on the area, she doubted they'd have found the place.

Shaking herself back into focus, Evie hissed. "What did Hazel do? Steal her scent while she was at it?"

A collective shudder went around the group at the thought. A vampire who could steal your powers was bad enough, but every bit past that was only more horrifying.

"We need to check other places she's been. Maybe we can find a common thread on her scent." Ace had crossed his arms and was looking thoughtful.

Joey piped up quickly, "What about GPD? She was definitely there!"

"No... If we go sniffing around there, Gibson or Owen will ask us what we're up to." Laika sounded as frustrated as ever, her aura still a nervous tangle of energy.

"Okay. Then where else have people run into Hazel?" Ace prompted.

One by one, his packmates shook their heads. None of them had met Hazel during her time moonlighting in Glenwood. Blood Fang hadn't been to any of the crime scenes except the first at Fulmino.

"She showed up at Sync Holes. That was the first time she was around that I remember," Laika confirmed slowly. "And of course she was there on Halloween, but everyone was on duty that night."

Evie ran through the past month, but there was only one other meeting she could remember. "Aside from that and GPD, I think she only came to the pressure attack in downtown."

"What was she doing there?" Ace asked. He paced around the edge of the taped off area, careful not to disturb much.

"Dispelling rituals. She was really good at it too," Evie responded. If Hazel hadn't found her so quickly on the edge of the pressure circle and knew how to remove the effect, then Evie and a lot of other people would be dead.

"That and whatever she did with the roller coaster," added Laika. "Oh, she also found the ritual circle we were looking for at Fulmino! I mean we'd struck out with the other four, so it was lucky she tracked the last one down."

"Are you serious!?" Randall shot them an incredulous look.

Evie was quick to Laika's defense, "What?"

"Are we hunting the Glenwood Anarchist!?" Randall yelled at her.

"I... don't know... We just determined the ritual was elven..." Evie looked stunned but was scrambling to put the pieces together to see the bigger picture. Could Hazel have summoned a demon?

Thad snorted. "That doesn't matter. We've been talking about how they steal powers all day. An orchid could just take the powers from an elf and do the same damn thing. There is no signature orchid magic to track. You look for seemingly impossible overlap between other magics."

"Like 5 or 6 elven bloodlines all working together to summon a demon?" Laika's emotions surged with fear at her own words.

"Yeah." Thad swore. He threw his hands in the air and yelled in frustration. Evie watched as his aura bounced between colors. She knew he was pissed at them for being so dense. The more they talked this out, the more she was growing annoyed at how obvious this was.

"Why would she summon a demon though?" Daniel asked. He'd been quiet during the entire explanation of the hunt, the car ride, and even the tracking attempts. Evie had practically forgotten the mountain of a werewolf was with them until that moment.

"Because she's batshit crazy," scoffed Laika. Her aura flared bright with a surge of anger, and the wolf kicked off her shoes. Her phone was shoved into Evie's hands, followed by a shirt.

"Laika?" Evie scrambled to catch the flying clothing. She had no idea what her packmate was about to do, but Laika had been on the edge of snapping since Evie had picked her up.

"There's a clue here! I know it and I'm going to find it." Laika didn't wait for a response before shifting down to her wolf form. A streak of amber and brown fur took off, nose pressed deep into the grass.

Thad gave a mirthless bark of laughter. "What? Does she expect to find some trail we missed? With her bum nose?"

Evie wheeled around to glare at the man. Before she could start a fight, Ace interrupted the exchange. "Crazy? That's what you say about girls who key your car... not mass murderers."

Shaking her head, Evie folded Laika's clothes over her arm as she tried to explain. "I'm pretty sure she means crazy-crazy... Like a straight jacket, padded room, villain out of a movie."

"Oh..." Ace looked troubled. Skepticism whirled in his aura, clearly not sold on this theory.

"Well that makes sense. Orchids are known for going insane," Thad added in a blasé voice.

Everyone stopped to look at Thad, even Laika, who looked up from across the field her ears pointed their way. Expressions ranged from open confusion to terror.

"What do you mean, go insane?" Evie asked in a careful tone. She was almost afraid of his answer.

Thad had enough sense to realize he'd dropped a bomb with that statement. He cleared his throat to buy time before answering, "Orchids are memory vampires meaning that they steal your memories as well as your blood. After a while, all the memories get too much. So they start to lose touch with reality and who they are. Hazel is probably as crazy as Laika is claiming."

"Then she doesn't really need a good reason, if she's losing her mind," Evie concluded. This whole time she'd been so conflicted, because on one side, Hazel had saved her life at least twice now. But on the other, she'd tried to kill Laika. If Hazel was legitimately going crazy though, then it was in everyone's best interests to stop her.

"We should call Owen and tell him what we figured out," Ace announced. He went for his phone to start the call, but Randall grabbed his arm. Between the two of them Randall would never be able to compete with super strength, but his friend paused all the same.

Randall took his moment, "If we call Owen now, then he'll know exactly what we're doing. Let's just get a proper trail before we tell him."

Evie knew the truth and it didn't match the words flowing right now. Randall was still marred in anger, pushing him to find the vampire first. He wanted to take a swing at Hazel before GPD got involved. She wondered if he'd been closer than the rest of Blood Fang to the Moonscent girls.

"Okay," nodded Ace. He quickly switched to barking out orders for the rest of the pack, "Joey, go shift and take a long loop. If you catch anything that doesn't smell like a friend, then come get Randall or Thad. Daniel, I need you to watch our backs just in case she returns here, even though it's not likely. I'll call a few friends in the LA packs to see if they know Hazel and where she might spend time."

Evie realized she could help as well. "Oh! My roommate knows a ton of vampires! I can ask her if Hazel goes to any of the Glenwood clubs. Maybe we can find someone who knows her."

"Good," Ace agreed as everyone moved to do their job in the new plan. Randall and Thad just stayed by Daniel's side, taking a rest since they'd been trying to catch the trail for a while already. No one stopped Laika from working herself in circles either.

Pulling her phone out, Evie realized she had two on hand. It took a moment to remember Laika had handed hers over. Not the strangest thing, and Evie went to shove her packmate's phone back into her pocket. As if it had been waiting for Evie's attention, the phone chimed and the screen flashed. The banner across the lock screen showed 1 unread text, from Alfred of course.

"Laika! Your boyfriend is texting you," Evie called out, every word felt like acid on her tongue. But she knew her friend didn't want

Blood Fang to know *who* she was dating just yet. A bad sign for any relationship when you were hiding it from people.

Across the field Laika paused, her ears swiveling back to listen to Evie. There was a jumble of emotions swirling around Laika; chief among them were worry and a tiny bit of guilt. Unlike every other time for the past two months, she wasn't running for the phone. Laika's phone pinged again, the counter of unread messages ticking up. As the total climbed higher Evie was surprised he hadn't called by now. "Do you just want me to check?" Evie directed the question at the wolf that was dithering across the field.

"Is that really important right now?" Thad mocked from where he sat on the ground. He was sharing a look with Randall; neither were amused with Night Claw's priorities. There was a huff from Laika, but she started to trek back to Evie.

"Her boyfriend is a moonlighter alright?" grumbled Evie as she unlocked the phone. They checked each others' phones all the time, this wasn't weird. She'd promised to try to be more normal about their relationship as well.

> ALFRED
>
> where are you?
>
> i'm at the apartment and you aren't
>
> are you ok???

Evie made a face at the texts. Who the hell typed like that in this day and age? This was what Laika found so fun? No point mocking her packmate now, that could wait for later. She glanced up to see Laika had reached her. "He's asking where you are. Should I tell him?"

"Can he track?" Randall asked. Clearly, Blood Fang has no plans to stay out of the conversation. No matter how many dirty looks Evie shot them. Randall continued, "If he can then make him come help us. He wouldn't rat us out to GPD right?"

Laika quietly shook her head. She padded the ground worriedly and her aura read of annoyance. But she didn't make any attempts to shift back yet either.

"So he's bad at tracking like you? Just great," mocked Randall.

Ace slapped him on the back of the head, "Knock it off, we're supposed to be working together."

Barcly suppressing a smile at Randall's misfortune, Evie spoke up, "Actually, Laika's boyfriend might be able to help us find Hazel. If she talks him into it." Eyes turned down to the wolf expectantly. Laika shook her head more vigorously this time. "I'm going to ask him, he's a *senior* moonlighter so this should be doable," declared Evie. She started typing up a response.

As soon as her fingers began tapping out that message, a low growl emanated from Laika. Her packmate glared up at Evie balefully. The threat was obvious, even before Laika's lips curled back to reveal fangs.

"Oh hush. You can't stop me," Evie rolled her eyes and hit send.

Laika sprang into the air, on a direct collision course with Evie. But before she reached her target, arms as strong as steel snatched her out of the air.

"Woah, woah, woah! What the hell?" Ace demanded as he got a good grip. He hadn't expected such a vicious attack, but had reacted in time.

Evie danced back out of reach from her restrained friend. She knew how much Laika hated to be handled by human hands while shifted. But telling Ace to let her go was like asking to be bit.

Laika struggled against the arms with both claws and fangs. She drew blood, forcing Ace to let her go. That is, let her go only to hit the wall that was Daniel as he interposed his form between the two women. While he didn't actually try to restrain the wolf, he was an obstacle Laika couldn't easily knock over.

The phone in Evie's hand vibrated a fast response. She'd been hoping that Alfred would be stupidly attentive like usual.

LAIKA

Hey this is Evie, Laika's in wolf form right now. No fingers so I'm typing.

We went to see if we could track Hazel down, but no luck so far.

She wants to know if you can help us find the trail? Please.

ALFRED

sure

where do you want to meet up?

That had been surprisingly easy? Maybe LA hadn't panned out like Alfred had planned, or he'd decided to track Hazel himself already. Keeping Laika closer while he did might be the same as letting them work the Anarchist case instead of working around him? Evie didn't really care what the reason was since Alfred agreed.

"He said yes," Evie called over Daniel's shoulder.

"Yes," cheered Ace. He had a hand over his freshly bleeding wound. This was the new lead they'd all been hoping for when they'd started making calls.

Laika visibly deflated at the news. Her pacing abruptly cut off as she sat down sullenly. Jealousy crashed through her aura out of nowhere.

"Don't be like that," Evie chided her friend, "I told him you were asking. He'd never agree if it was me."

There was no answer from Laika, who was finally shifting back. Her hands reached out to steal her shirt back from Evie, but she snubbed the phone. Instead her attention turned to Ace. There was a slightly embarrassed look on her face. "Sorry... I didn't mean to draw blood."

Ace waved it off, "I'll heal in a minute. These are skin deep at worst; your claws are like paper cuts."

Laika frowned but there was no snap back.

Evie did her best to ignore them as she set a plan up with Alfred.

LAIKA (EVIE)

We are out in the field where Jaci died.

But obviously we haven't found anything yet.

ALFRED

you won't find anything there

she wouldn't have left an easy trail

let me send you directions to a location she
may be

we can meet there

LAIKA (EVIE)

Yeah, sounds good.

Again, Alfred had been so agreeable. The address came through a moment later to the outskirts of Glenwood. The google maps overview looked like an industrial district. Evie wasn't certain what exactly was there, maybe some warehouses?

LAIKA (EVIE)

Are you sure she'd be here?

ALFRED

yes, she needs a homebase

this is somewhere she'd hide

LAIKA (EVIE)

Okay, we're heading back to the car now

We'll be there as soon as we can.

Evie looked up at the sky. She frowned because the late afternoon sun greeted her and it would be dark before they arrived. So much for their daytime advantage...

"I've got a meeting place for us," Evie explained to the group. She put Laika's phone back in her pocket for the moment.

"And Hazel will be there?" Randall pressed. He'd hopped up to his feet ready to go.

"Probably not," admitted Evie, "But Alfred says that places like this are where Hazel likes to set up her homebase. It'll be a good starting point."

"EVIE!" Laika shrieked, "WHAT THE HELL?"

"What?" Evie defended. She could feel legitimate anger directed her way, but Evie shrugged it off.

"Why did you tell them?" Laika stomped her foot, all the tension back in the air.

Evie looked flabbergasted. "Tell them? We're about to go meet Alfred! Do you really think they wouldn't figure it out!?"

"They're kinda morons, so maybe not," hissed Laika, but her righteous anger was already dissipating.

"Alfred?" Thad looked disappointed, "Who the hell is Alfred?"

Night Claw fell silent and turned to stare at Thad. Was he being serious right now? Evie's read of him said yes, he was completely serious right now. But Randall was shocked speechless and Ace was confused. They were such idiots...

"Tall, dark and vampire? Creepy beyond compare, but apparently Laika's type. You were literally there when she met him," Evie reminded. She'd technically been there too, but she'd been exceptionally distracted at Fulmino.

"I thought she was banging Owen so you two got on better cases. You weren't making it out of the bottom ranks any other way," Thad shrugged. His expression held a hint of embarrassment at forgetting their meeting. If he wasn't being so rude, Evie would have given him a pass since he'd likely gone upstairs as well. That would overshadow anything else that day.

"No one wins now," Randall finally found his voice.

Laika shot a dark glare in his direction, "Wins what?"

Thad picked up the answer, "We were betting on the mysterious boyfriend, since he was apparently real and not Canadian. I put money on Owen."

"He's not a moonlighter and we'd already agreed not to call him." Evie couldn't believe how tactless these guys were.

"I put money on Wade," Randall shrugged. He looked mildly uncomfortable and Evie could tell his guess wasn't serious. There was no conviction behind it, had he already known the answer and lied to the rest of his pack?

"Who?" Laika again bristled at the names flying around.

Evie supplied the answer, "He's a total creep who runs a cult pack of moonlighters. So gross and not Laika's type at all."

Scornfully she turned to Ace, not believing for a moment he hadn't been involved in this stupid game.

"Mike," mumbled Ace. He took a breath and added his explanation, "Senior moonlighter, totally capable guy, not bad looking and since he's married I guess that's why all the secrecy about it. For all I know, he and Mary are open or something."

"You're all fucking morons," hissed Laika.

"Everyone get in the car, someone go get Joey," commanded Evie. Irritation laced her every word. There was some grumbling, but everyone did as they were told to avoid a further lecture.

CHAPTER 15
ORCHID

Laika
November 12th, 2018
Outskirts of Glenwood, CA

Laika had stayed silent the entire drive. She was seething, both about Evie ignoring her wishes and over Blood Fang's insulting thoughts on her dating life. Compounded with the anger that hadn't abated about Jaci's death, Laika felt like a bomb ready to explode.

As soon as the car was parked, she was out the door just to give herself some space. Her eyes scanned around and looked for Alfred. He wasn't anywhere in view. This had been an industrial park at some point in its history. Now it was full of rusting machinery and abandoned warehouses. With the sun dipping below the horizon, long shadows were stretching across the ground. Why had Alfred picked here of all places?

"Yeah, this is creepy," Randall complained, giving voice to Laika's thoughts.

The rest of the pack gave a low mumble of agreement, eyes scanning every direction. There were no street lamps out here. Only the headlights from the van lit the area enough for them to see.

"That building over there has lights, do you think that's where we need to go?" Evie pointed to a warehouse that had a faint, yellow glow emanating from its broken windows.

Ace nodded, "Seems likely."

Something about this didn't sit right with Laika. Why would anyone pick such a run down place for their base? Especially without anything to cover the windows?

Laika reached out to tap Evie's shoulder, "Where's my phone? I'm going to let Alfred know we're here."

Evie dug into her bag in the dark. She looked a little awkward handing over the phone. Hopefully she was regretting going over Laika's head on this. This morning Alfred had been clear; he wanted Laika nowhere near anything Hazel related. Who knew what lies Evie had told him to get his agreement to help. While they teased around about texting on each other's phones, neither had ever done something like that before. She only hoped that Evie hadn't pretended to be her.

Laika unlocked her phone and navigated to her latest messages. As she took in each word, a knot grew in her stomach. She felt sick realizing that the short conversation in her messages wasn't with Alfred.

"Stop!" Laika's voice dropped to barely a whisper. She threw an arm out to the side, forcing Evie to stop mid-step. That caused enough confusion that the rest of Blood Fang paused walking as well. All eyes turned to Laika with mild annoyance or confusion.

Evie took the cue to whisper, "What?"

"Alfred didn't send these texts." Laika scrolled up so the screen showed some of their usual messages above the newer ones. She pushed it forward, demanding Evie look at it. "He'd cut off his hand before he ever typed like this. How did you think this was him?"

"How would I know!? I barely talk to him!" Evie's cheeks tinged red, but her eyes looked down at the phone screen. Dawning realization flashed across her face, and she cursed under her breath.

Blood Fang had stopped walking, reconvening where Night Claw stood huddled. With the phone in plain view, they read a few of the messages as well.

> ALFRED
>
> Please do not do anything as foolish as chase Hazel.

> LAIKA
>
> I won't!

> ALFRED
>
> I should be leaving within the hour.
>
> Would you like me to pick up dinner from somewhere here?

> LAIKA
>
> I guess we could just do pizza on the couch?

> ALFRED
>
> A proper meal would be more agreeable if you wish me to eat with you.

These words were night and day compared to the rushed planning from the last couple of text messages. If you looked at them side by side, they didn't sound like the same person at all.

Ace broke the silence. "If that's not Alfred... who is it?"

"I... don't know," Laika admitted as she pulled her phone back to study the messages. Alfred wasn't really the type to let someone else into his phone. She chewed her lip, trying to determine how to find out.

An idea crossed her mind, and before she could talk herself out of it, Laika hit the call button. The phone rang only twice before a chillingly familiar voice answered, "Hello *bunny*!"

"Why do you have Alfred's phone?" Laika bit out the question as she felt her stomach drop. The stupid nickname felt more like a slap than its usual affection.

"We were just *hanging* out, and he didn't seem to need it anymore." A shriek of laughter rang through the speakers as Hazel reveled in her own joke.

Laika flinched at the sharp sound before shooting back with a growl. "Hazel, if you hurt him, I will-"

"Silly bunny! Why would I hurt him? *You* are the problem," Hazel scoffed. The confirmation of who was on the other end of the call seemed to electrify the pack. Phones were being pulled out of pockets, and Laika could hear a rush of whispers around her.

"I'm calling Owen now," Evie hissed quietly.

Ace gave her a thumbs up as he dialed a number, "I've got Nilani... She can send Dark Wind here."

Laika had no more attention to spare for what the others were doing. Hazel was talking, commanding her focus again. "It really is a shame. You just had to ruin things! You could've come for the drink, bunny. Now look at this mess..."

A bristle ran along Laika's spine. "Mess? You *killed* Jaci!"

"Who?" Hazel sounded confused.

"The young girl you killed just days ago!" Laika's voice raised before she could stop herself.

"Oh! I remember now. I didn't have to do that; however, you keep making this so difficult. Hiding behind wards I can't track you through, or surrounding yourself with werewolves constantly. Do understand I needed a way close to you and she seemed like a simple answer," Hazel had begun to ramble on. She'd done this at other meetings as well, like she couldn't help herself.

Every word infuriated Laika. She wanted to march into the warehouse and shove the stolen phone down the vampire's throat. Then Evie placed a hand on her arm in a soothing manner. She held up her phone where the screen read: 'Keep her on the phone.'

Laika swallowed because it meant engaging with this psycho. Her mouth went dry at the thought, but she forced out the words,

"I barely knew her. There was no reason I'd trust her or let her close."

"True, but you liked her, or at least made her feel comfortable. I thought about Evie for a bit too..." Hazel trailed off, her tone becoming more distracted.

"Evie!?" snapped Laika, feeling her anger surging. The casual threat to her best friend had sent her inner wolf practically into a frenzy. "How dare you!? You can't just kill people! This isn't the dark ages!"

"...you are a very sly bunny... I nearly got distracted by all your words." Hazel seemed to right herself. The mad edge to her voice was gone.

"What?" Laika was taken back by the sudden change. They'd just been gearing up into a verbal war, only to fall flat.

"Next time maybe," chided Hazel.

Laika felt her blood run cold, "Next time?"

"You're a very fast bunny, but you will not outrun me. Ta!" The phone line went dead as the sound of shattering glass rang through the empty warehouses.

Laika could not hesitate. She had been caught off guard in the GPD parking lot, with no time. Her shift to hybrid form kicked off, vest already in place since she left the empty field earlier. Heads shot up, the collection of werewolves realizing something had changed. A shudder ran through the group. Last minute directions were barked before phones were tossed and shoes kicked off.

The glass had forewarned the packs, allowing them to shift to hybrid forms in preparation for the impending attack. All eyes were on the lit up warehouse, looking for any sign of their attacker. But they'd been focused in the wrong direction.

A fist the size of a frying pan flew from the shadows to their left. A crack rang out as it connected with the side of Joey's face. He collapsed to the ground with a small gasp.

Shock ran through the rest of the wolves, sending Laika into a small panic as she scrambled back. She needed to reset before coming up with a new plan of attack. Sadly, most of Blood Fang didn't follow her lead.

Ace and Daniel charged into the dark shadows between warehouses where no one could see them. But even with that, Evie's eyes seemed to track them into the darkness, following their auras.

Meanwhile, Thad slid down to the ground checking on Joey. His claws moved as gently as they could, checking for breathing. He didn't try to move the hybrid who was already starting to lose mass as Joey reverted to his human form.

That left Thad distracted when the large terrifying form, a peony, dropped down from above.

Laika recognized the creature from the GPD parking lot. This was Hazel wearing a face from her nightmares. She couldn't just stand around watching as her allies got downed one at a time. Now was the time of action. She lunged forward for the creature.

Before Laika could reach them, Hazel struck. Her massive fist connected with Thad while he tried to cover his packmate. The blow lifted him into the air, sending him flying. There was a gasp of pain as the werewolf hit the ground several feet away. Thad's head cracked against the cement and he didn't rise back up.

After all their careful planning, Joey and Thad were down already.

A warning howl went up behind Laika, summoning Ace and Daniel back. She recognized the sound of Evie. At least someone was keeping their cool. There was no time to pivot though; Laika was committed to her strike. Claws swung high and then crashed down with all the wolf's momentum behind them. The hit connected, leaving a mimicry of Laika's earlier wounds running across Hazel's face and chest.

The problem came when Hazel's body didn't fall backwards to the powerful jump. Instead, Hazel's fist hammered back at Laika, catching her on the shoulder. The power staggered Laika. If it had connected with her skull, the werewolf would've been dead in an instant.

Her shoulder made a horrible pop, dislocating under the force of the blow. She let out a yelp from the assault before her knees hit the ground. Intense pain consumed Laika, making it impossible for her to get her feet back. She could barely move. A foot came stomping down for her head. Just before contact was made, Evie got hands around Laika's calf. She hefted Laika backwards out of the line of attack. The pair unceremoniously scrambled to put more distance between them and the angry vampire.

Then Daniel's colossal form came from the darkness between buildings to take advantage of the distraction. He rammed shoulder first with the power of a freight train. Despite her large stature in the peony body, his momentum forced Hazel back one step at a time.

Laika saw her chance to roll to safety. But she kept her eyes trained on the fight, looking for an opening to attack. In her peripheral vision, she could see Randall and Evie moving their fallen allies from the middle of the battlefield. Good.

Daniel seemed aware of this too, because his clawed feet dug into the ground with every step as he put more distance between his pack and danger. Sensing she was outmatched, Hazel attempted to dodge backwards so that Daniel's strength would turn against him. She'd waited too long. With the vampire's first step, she found a warehouse to her back. Daniel had cornered her with just raw power.

"Vile bull," Hazel spat through the rows of sharp peony teeth. The sound was grating as all her fangs scraped together.

She had more to say but Laika didn't hear the words. A hand landed on Laika's shoulder, the only warning before Ace jerked her arm up without asking. A howl tore from her throat as Ace quickly reset her shoulder before she could tense up. Werewolf healing would numb the pain soon, but in the moment Laika felt like her shoulder was on fire. At least she'd be able to focus again.

By the time Laika got her eyes back on Hazel, Daniel had managed to wrap his arms into a lock, forcing the vampire's limbs to dangle uselessly at her sides. Despite her razor-like claws, she couldn't reach anywhere vulnerable. Hazel continued to swear at the top of her lungs.

If Daniel had been able to shift at Halloween, how different would that fight have gone?

Crazed eyes landed on Laika and that seemed to sober up the frenzying Hazel. Her struggles ceased which curbed the feelings of victory. She was too crafty and it scared Laika. Hazel snarled, and sank her fangs into Daniel's shoulder.

No one had expected her to actually take a bite given wolf blood was her weakness. Daniel let out a strangled yelp and his grip faltered. Their theory didn't seem to be holding up... Why was Thad always so extremely wrong about vampires despite being an 'expert'?!

Ace and Laika were on their feet and moving, but it was too late.

That same sickening sound of wet bones crunching and rearranging reached Laika's ears. It was the only warning they had before Hazel's form shrunk. Daniel's arms had been locked around a much larger peony, and now she could slip free with ease.

Hazel's fangs ripped free of Daniel's shoulder as she launched herself up into the air. The slender batlike form had replaced the razor fangs and claws. Wings beat down, launching Hazel out of reach. This time she had long black hair and blazing green eyes, another new face in the fight.

Below, Ace checked on Daniel. Thankfully the bleeding didn't seem too bad. Daniel's shoulder wasn't ruined, just a bit ripped up.

Laika growled and stomped her foot in frustration. Her target was hovering above them far out of reach again. She searched around for anything she could use to climb up the side of a warehouse. Broken glass and bare walls promised her a difficult time.

"Oh little bunnies, you're starting to annoy me," hissed Hazel. Her eyes scanned over them until they landed on Daniel, "Especially you."

Black veins began to glow on Hazel's face. Laika recognized that as a sign of black magic, but she didn't know what magic was being cast. That is, until Daniel let out a whimper at her side.

His shoulders seemed to be collapsing in on themselves. Bones snapped, limbs twisting as the man fell to his knees. His hybrid shift was reversing rapidly, and painfully by the sounds of it. For a moment Daniel seemed frozen in an in-between form like Evie had been. As he slumped to the ground, his human form won out. Only the slight movement of his chest let Laika know he was unconscious, not dead.

They were in a lot of trouble if Hazel was strong enough to shut down powers with black magic. Laika had never seen it happen before now, but she'd heard of witches who could stop a werewolf in their tracks.

Laika whipped her head around again, praying for some pathway she'd missed in her first scan. If Hazel stayed up high and just shut them all down one at a time, then everyone here was dead. The answer came from an unexpected place.

Blood Fang could create a plan on the fly better than any pack Laika knew, probably from repeated drilling. So when Ace dropped to a knee and laced his hands, she wasn't surprised when Randall began running towards him. However, Laika had more speed than her allies; she reached Ace first. He responded to the change in plans by launching Laika up into the air towards Hazel.

Claws extended, Laika shot through the open sky faster than anyone could dodge out of the way. She dug both hands into Hazel's shoulders and tore down her arms. The leather skin of the fine lotus wings shredded with little resistance.

Together they tumbled back down in a flurry of claws. But Laika managed to keep her body parts away from Hazel's fangs. She had no wish to get bitten today. Their crash wasn't as graceful as the jump. Laika dazed herself for a minute when she hit the cracked pavement. Pain coursed through her temples, causing fog to cloud her vision and thoughts. Once Laika could see straight again, she realized someone had moved her to lean against a wall.

Battle raged on as Hazel hadn't taken a head injury on their crash landing. Ace and Evie were throwing wild swings, trying to keep the vampire off balance. Hazel kept pace with them, throwing up blocks while flaps of ruined skin trailed behind her arm's movements.

Laika realized that Randall had pulled her out of danger this time. His white-furred hands were stained red and even the hard to read hybrid expression seemed concerned. She pushed him away, then used the wall to stand up. Another minute and Laika would return to the fight; her head was rapidly clearing up thanks to werewolf healing.

Evie yelped as Hazel got her hands around the werewolf and twisted her arm until it loudly popped. Then the vampire swung Evie directly into Ace, staggering him back a few steps as well. The pair were open to attack, but so was Hazel with her back to Randall.

He took advantage with only a passing glance at Laika. Since sitting in the living room and learning that his young friend had died by this vampire's hands, Randall had been waiting for a moment to strike.

Randall raced forward at Hazel, raising his claws into a mighty swing. But the sound of shifting bones brought him up short when he ended up face to face with a bruised and bloody Jaci instead of the dark haired lotus. His attack faltered when confronted by his friend, unable to bring down claws.

The vampire masquerading as Jaci didn't have the same problem. Her face spread into a wicked grin as she dove forward. Fangs tore into the soft skin hidden beneath fur on Randall's neck. Laika howled as she tried to push herself off the wall.

Help arrived when Ace got his arm around Hazel's throat. If he had the same concerns about attacking the vampire in Jaci's form, he didn't show it. A crunch followed as Ace turned his supernatural strength to the task of crushing Hazel's neck. He lifted the vampire off her feet so she could only flail helplessly in the air.

She howled against the pain even as the sound strangled in her throat. Hazel's hands started trying to tear away at the muscled arm.

Vampires didn't need air, but she could still panic at the possibility of being beheaded.

With Hazel's fangs out of Randall's neck, Evie stepped in to pull the stunned hybrid out of range. Laika could see a spray of red coming from Randall's wound. There was no time to rush to his aid; she needed to trust her packmate to handle him.

Unable to break free or make sound, Hazel's face was a silent snarl of anger. She attempted to shift her form up to the peony so she could compete with Ace's size. Her clawed feet touched the ground, but the iron grip on her neck didn't let up.

Despite not being the biggest werewolf in Blood Fang, Ace's powers made him the strongest.

Black veins began to snake along Hazel's face as she turned to her black magic. This time Laika saw a flash of light coming from a pendant hanging around the vampire's neck. When she'd been in the air, the minor detail was lost in the darkness.

Even with her head pounding, Laika pushed herself into action. She needed to get her claws into that pendant. It had to be Hazel's focus for her spell.

A strangled gasp tore free from Ace as he fought against the magic trying to force his shift backwards. His shoulders began to violently shake. Bones were cracking, even as he struggled to hold onto Hazel. But Ace's willpower gave out and his hybrid form collapsed in on itself. His limbs twitched in pain as he hit the ground, still conscious but unable to move.

The crushed muscle of Hazel's throat regenerated before Laika's eyes. She realized the vampire must have stolen Randall's accelerated healing. Between that and Hazel's magic, the werewolves were in dire peril.

Laika was too late to stop the spell, but she could prevent that from happening again. She launched forward at the silver talisman swinging loosely around the vampire's neck. Claws dug into the flesh and bone of Hazel's collar as she tangled her hand into the chain. Laika jerked back in a wet tear, pulling the talisman free.

Hazel grabbed at her focus, but it flew through the air out of reach. It smashed into the ground with a metallic crunch. All at once the magic fizzled as the black veins faded away.

No more black magic tricks.

"You bitch," hissed Hazel, her voice was ragged. But as the seconds ticked by her wounds, including her throat, were healing up. Every word sounded clearer than the last, "Why are you making this so hard, bunny? I didn't have to kill them just to take *you* off the gameboard a little longer!"

Laika couldn't follow any of the random babble from Hazel. It made no sense as usual, and there were other more pressing issues. Ace was still crumpled in a heap at Hazel's feet. She seemed to have forgotten about him for the moment.

A quick assessment showed Evie leaning over Randall, hands firmly clamped on his neck. Even from here, Laika could see the mess of red staining her packmate. If Evie moved then likely Randall wasn't leaving here alive.

Laika was alone...

Her rage focused on Hazel, who was still rambling in increasing incoherence. She had no plan and the monster in front of her felt invincible. Every time Laika thought she knew what was going on, Hazel broke out another power. What else could the orchid vampire be hiding still?

No options but forward then. Laika's lips curled back in a defiant snarl. She wasn't going to give up, no matter what.

"Get the fuck out of the way!" A deep voice commanded out of the darkness surrounding them.

Movement picked up on the edge's of Laika's vision. She had no clue who was yelling at her, but she reacted. If they wanted people out of the way, that meant everyone.

Her eyes darted to the prone Ace, then she charged forward.

Hazel didn't care about the voices that started to surround them. She raised her massive hands ready to lock grips like she'd done with the other werewolves.

Laika wasn't sure if she could overpower Hazel like Daniel and Ace, but she didn't even try to mimic them. Instead, mid stride she leapt off her feet and threw her leg up in a kick. Hazel's defenses hadn't been prepared for that maneuver, so Laika's attack connected.

Bones cracked loudly as Hazel gasped in pain. She staggered backwards enough to create an opening. Laika used her attack to repel herself enough to dissipate some momentum. She landed in a practiced roll and her hands scooped up Ace. Then she bolted away at top speed.

Voices started to call back and forth before a sound like sizzling electricity filled the air. But Laika didn't pause to look back right away. She needed to put as much distance as possible between herself and whatever magic was brewing.

Ahead, two complete strangers were looking past her. They were calm and unconcerned about a hybrid werewolf running full tilt at them.

"Hello," called one of the men, raising his hand in greeting.

Laika skidded to a stop, eyes scanned him quickly, trying to determine if he was friend or foe. He was dressed in a nice, dark grey coat that complemented his bronze complexion. The man had an air of someone going to a coffee shop more than a battlefield. His friendly smile and warm brown eyes were reassuring. Laika had no clue who he was, but she was happy to see him and his big friend right now.

His expression unchanged, he lowered his hand. "We haven't met, but we have a mutual acquaintance... who I see is late."

"Time for chit chat later, containment now," the taller man spoke as he moved forward. Each word was accented in thick Russian, and he had the largest fangs Laika had ever seen.

Laika recognized it as the commanding voice from before who had told her to get out of the way. Who they hell were these people? She kept her grip on Ace and skittered off to the side as the russet-haired, mountain of a man stomped past her. Laika's gaze followed him, and her eyes widened with shock at what she saw.

While her back was turned, more people had joined the fight. Three walls of crackling magic surrounded Hazel, anchored by three casters. She pounded a fist on one of the barriers, but it didn't even waver at her attacks.

"Miss Amadori, it's time to calm down," called the man still near Laika. He'd moved to stand next to her so silently, she'd completely missed it.

"THIS IS NOT OVER," screamed Hazel as her form folded down to the original blonde.

The large vampire heaved a sigh while digging through his jacket. He pulled out a set of handcuffs that looked similar to the GPD's for supernaturals. Then he pushed his way into the barrier, passing through it with a little difficulty. A moment later, he snapped the cuffs onto Hazel with a triumphant smirk. "It is over now."

Laika could hardly believe the absurdity of what was happening in front of her eyes. Who the hell were these people?

"Why don't you shift back and then we can talk," offered the friendly man before patting her on the arm. Again he gave Laika a knowing smile, but this time she realized he also had fangs. They were small and easy to miss if you weren't looking. He walked past to where the others were still corralling Hazel.

Realization finally clicked in Laika's mind. This was the LA Coven.

CHAPTER 16
DEBRIEF

Evie
November 12th, 2018
Glenwood Police Department Station #1, Glenwood, CA

Evie's head hurt so much right now. All she wanted was a shower to try and wash away the feeling of blood coating her hands. Even after she'd cleaned off all she could in the station bathroom, patches still stained her arms. Back at the dark warehouses they'd all almost died again. Another fight way over her and Laika's heads. No wonder she had a migraine forming...

Their rescuers had turned out to be a group from LA MOONS and all of them had been vampires. They'd bundled Hazel up into a truck surrounded by people and sped her off into the night before anyone else arrived. GPD had only been another five minutes behind. They'd come in force as well. Dark Wind, Melinda, and SWAT were in tow when they pulled up at the warehouses. Everything had descended into chaos as Glenwood and LA MOONS started fighting over jurisdiction.

Now Evie was sitting between Laika and Ace in a GPD conference room. Across from the trio were Gibson who looked livid, and Owen who looked tired. The only cheerful face in the conversation was the friendly vampire who had introduced himself as 'Bruce'.

Bruce stood at the end of the table, flipping through a packet of paperwork before setting it down. "So, as you can see, since we detained Miss Amadori, LA MOONS will be holding onto her."

"Hold on a minute," snapped Gibson as he slammed his hands down. Evie jumped at the sudden sound. Why did he have to be so loud right now?

"Yes?" Bruce asked, utterly unflappable. His aura never even flickered with anything beside that neutral calm.

"Amadori is accused of murder in the first degree!" Gibson pointed out. He reached for paperwork of his own to throw at the vampire.

Bruce looked thoughtful for a moment, "Do you have any evidence to bring those charges forward? As of right now she's suspected of murder, but LA MOONS found her in the *act* of attempted murder on these poor wolves."

He gestured at Ace, Evie, and Laika with the statement. Everyone else had gone to Glenwood General, accompanied by the tall Russian vampire. While Randall had been critical and Joey seemed unable to wake up, no one was dead.

"We will have our charges soon," Gibson faltered. Owen put a hand on Gibson's arm and they shared a look that Evie didn't recognize.

Usually Owen was energetic and focused. Today though, he'd looked defeated before they'd all been dragged into the conference room. Owen picked up the thread, "No, we don't have any evidence yet. Our investigation into the murder of Jaci Bennet is still ongoing."

"But we know Hazel did it," Ace protested.

"Oh?" Bruce gave him a curious expression, "How do you know that?"

"... Because... she's an orchid vampire and they can steal faces?"

responded Ace, but his words became more of a question than a statement of fact.

"Do you have any proof of this? Any magical expert who can verify this and some kind of recorded proof of Miss Amadori?" Bruce asked. He politely left out saying anything about Hazel wearing Jaci's face around.

Laika answered, "Yes, we have a magical expert. He's who told me about Hazel."

"Where is he?" Bruce raised an eyebrow. Evie narrowed her eyes at him because his aura didn't waver at all. She could tell he was enjoying having the advantage over all of them, but it didn't show in his emotions. They were like a perfect painting surrounding the vampire.

"I don't know," admitted Laika quietly.

Evie watched as currents of worry began to leak into Laika's aura. She hadn't heard from Alfred since they'd left Blood Fang's home. Judging by the text messages between them, he had still been in LA at the time. The realization of this was dawning on Laika, creating a storm of fear and anxiety.

Bruce's eyes were focused on Laika. The gaze was calculating as if he was reading the same emotions that Evie could. Was he a chrysanthemum just like Tony?

"We've called him, but he's not answering," griped Gibson. His sour mood showed through the scowl on his face. Owen sighed loudly, likely unhappy with how much information his fellow officer was giving away.

"As soon as you get ahold of him, then have him contact LAPD with his findings and they'll handle it from there," concluded Bruce. His words were cordial and his breathing even, but Evie knew that was a lie. She'd heard that perfectly level tone before every time Everard Belle said he'd be home in time for a recital, birthday, or holiday, knowing he'd never follow through. Whoever Bruce was, he was an amazing liar.

"Hazel Amadori is the Glenwood Anarchist," Evie said firmly. She tossed a last ditch effort onto the dumpster fire of a conversation.

That pulled Gibson and Owen up short. Their attention snapped onto Evie. This was the first she'd been able to tell them of the theory. Before anyone could stop her, she started at the beginning with what she and Laika had determined about the rituals. Then Evie moved onto her conversation with the Matriarch of the Taranis family about demons. She walked them through Hazel's involvement at each of the crime scenes, and how unusually fast she'd disarmed the rituals.

All eyes were on Evie as she laid out the theory, including Bruce. He was paying rapt attention, and as she stated the final clues she finally felt something beyond that supernatural aura of calm. Worry and concern peeked past it, even if Bruce was keeping his expression schooled. He, at the very least, wasn't sure Evie was wrong.

Owen poked the first hole, "But she wasn't in town at the time of the first attacks?"

"Can we be sure of that?" Evie countered. She'd not really thought about that since she didn't know when Hazel got involved.

Laika quickly came to her defense. "Hazel knew where the original ritual circle was too! Gibson was there when she found it! Alfred and I spent a week going from scene to scene and never found a trace of a circle before that."

"That's true," Gibson grudgingly admitted. He got up and left the conference room without another word. Evie really hoped he was going to go check files and help prove their theory.

Owen wasn't ready to give up. "Yeah, but if she wanted Laika dead, and we can all agree she wanted Laika dead," he paused for a moment to see if anyone would disagree with him, but even Bruce remained quiet, "Why didn't she just let Laika fall to her death at the Sync Holes attack? I read the report, and without Hazel Amadori's intervention then Laika would have died." He wasn't wrong, either. No one could find fault with his logic.

Evie watched as Bruce's eyes bounced around the room with the flow of conversation. It reminded her of herself when she was reading auras. But then again, Tony never even looked up from his phone and knew what you were feeling. Silence hung in the room, waiting to see which side of this theory was going to win. But before another word could be spoken, a sharp knock rapped on the doorframe.

"Excuse me, Captain Corban would like to speak with you." Gibson had returned, his words directed at Bruce. There was a smug aura of victory hanging around the detective matching his smirk. But Evie could feel Owen's emotions nose dive into frustration almost immediately.

Their victory soured as Bruce spoke.

"Ah! Andy! It's been ages, how is Elena?" Bruce beamed widely as he brushed past Gibson, extending a hand to the Captain. He embraced the man in a friendly hug.

"Bruce, it's been ages since you got out to Glenwood. Elena's good, she loved those chocolates you sent for her birthday. This Amadori character must be important for you to take time out of your day," greeted Corban. He slung his arm around Bruce's shoulder leading him from the room. "Come on, we can discuss this in my office. I'm sure I can find us some whiskey around here to drink."

The conference room door closed with a slam, putting that final nail in their defeat.

"What the hell were you thinking getting the captain involved?" hissed Owen as he pushed away from the table. He radiated anger, but thankfully it was all directed at Gibson.

Gibson looked shell shocked. He kept staring at the closed door with confusion written on his face.

Owen didn't let up. "The captain loves LA MOONS! Everytime we let them anywhere near our cases, they swoop it out from under us and he *lets* them."

"But..." Gibson trailed off.

"All our work on the Glenwood Anarchist and you just handed it to LA!" Owen forced himself to stop shouting. Other officers were starting to look up from their desks at the conference room. They weren't going unnoticed.

Red was coloring Gibson's face, his aura a swirl of embarrassment, confusion, and disappointment. He tried to defend himself. "How was I supposed to know that?! You and Leavenworth left me no instructions for keeping the zoo in order."

"Watch your mouth," snapped Owen. He closed the distance between them, getting nose to nose with Gibson. Evie spotted the subtle way Owen looked at them, directing Gibson's attention. Hurling insults at the wolfkin wasn't half as dangerous as doing it in front of three trained werewolves. But she didn't have the energy to do more than frown.

Gibson was at a loss for words like he'd never been corrected before. He looked at the three werewolves who had been sitting quietly. All his emotions converged together into a fury.

"You three are done as moonlighters," Gibson quickly turned the conversation away from his mistake.

Shock ran through Evie. She'd expected to get in some trouble for running off after Hazel without asking. But she'd been the one to call Glenwood MOONS and tell Gibson exactly what happened. She'd even promised him they were trying to retreat before Hazel surprised them. "But-" Evie tried to defend herself.

Ace interrupted, "That's bullshit! We were just doing our jobs!"

"No, you were being *vigilantes*," argued Gibson. He didn't have any fear of the massive werewolf glaring up at him. Evie knew he was right. Owen had even told her to stay put because she wasn't allowed into the field. There was no hope he'd save them right now. Gibson continued his tirade, "You've been nothing but a pain in my ass, making this worse since Halloween. Hell, you took the target of Amadori's murder attempts right to her!"

He blatantly pointed a finger at Laika, who wilted under his gaze.

"But-" Evie tried again, only to be interrupted.

"By the end of the week I'll have all your plastic badges!" Gibson raised his voice.

"Actually, you can't do a damn thing," Owen finally spoke up. His voice was hard, and Evie could feel the barely constrained anger.

Gibson whipped his glare around, "Excuse me?"

"I said you can't do anything to them. First off, you're just a fill-in for the liaison department. You can choose who to call for a job, but you have no say in the hiring or firing of moonlighters." Owen reached down to straighten the papers from Bruce.

"You can't be serious, Kirkland! This-" Gibson's words were cut short as a paper was shoved into his face.

Owen's aura rose to meet his smug victory, "And you can't fire them for literally doing their jobs. Their job for LA MOONS."

The room went so quiet, Evie swore she could hear Gibson's blood pressure rising. She had no idea what Owen was talking about. Before Hazel, Evie hadn't even met an LA moonlighter.

Gibson snatched the paper out of Owen's hand, his eyes devouring the information at top speed. Confusion transformed into annoyance with every line, before he threw the papers down on the conference table. Then he snarled, "What the hell is this?"

Owen shrugged and crossed his arms. "Moonlighters are contractors. They can work for Glenwood *and* LA if they so choose. Dark Wind does, and so do Blood Fang and Night Claw apparently."

Evie quickly grabbed at the papers to understand what was going on. She was greeted by a Moonlighter Consent form with a large approved stamp in the corner. Her name and details were accurate, and her loopy signature was at the bottom. This was dated months ago and even the stamp ink looked faded. When had she signed this? Laika and Ace looked just as bewildered as they read through their own paperwork. None of the werewolves had been part of this saving grace.

"LA wasn't in on the Glenwood Anarchist case as you so kindly pointed out. That paper means nothing," spat Gibson, he looked like he might start foaming at the mouth soon.

Owen gave another unconcerned shrug. His voice dripped with sarcasm, "No they weren't, but as you can see on this form... The

Head of Glenwood MOONS requested assistance with Amadori's capture. What a happy coincidence."

He started handing over paper after paper, showing the requests, assignments, and releases for hybrid forms. Everything looked perfectly in order. Better than any paperwork Evie had completed before. There was only one problem... Evie had no idea why LA MOONS had gone to such lengths to cover for her and Laika. She was certain she'd never met Bruce before today, and given how emotionally confused her packmate was right now, Laika didn't know either.

Evie swallowed, then spoke calmly. "As you can see, we were on the takedown request."

Ace gave her a furtive glance before licking his lips. Then he just nodded without another word. Evie knew if he opened his mouth they'd all be screwed, because Ace couldn't lie to save his life. She'd learned that in year one of competing with him for jobs.

A cold glare met Evie, and she could feel fresh rage run through Gibson. He hadn't forgotten or forgiven her for dressing him down in front of the rest of the station. Then Gibson's glare cut to Owen.

"How you run this department is a disgrace, Kirkland," he spit the words out like acid. Then the detective turned on his heel and stormed out of the room. A slam rang out as he shut the door hard enough to shake the wall, but Owen made no move to follow.

"So we aren't fired?" Ace asked. Relief was starting to flood his features and he put his head down on the table. He still had four packmates in the hospital for the second time in two weeks; Evie had more than a little sympathy for her rival.

"No, only because LA decided to cover your collective asses," answered Owen. He settled back down into a chair. "Don't think for a moment I'm fooled by this pretty paperwork, but someone decided to do you a favor."

Evie knew he was right. She'd never seen these forms before or signed anything with LA MOONS. She couldn't even tell you the names of anyone but Bruce who'd shown up tonight. "I'm sorry," Evie apologized. She looked Owen in the eye before repeating her apology again. "I'm really sorry about this. We weren't going to actually fight her once we realized the danger."

"But she got the jump on us," Ace mumbled from where he was still collapsed on the table.

Laika ignored the forms without any comment. Everyone knew she'd be lying if she tried to claim anything other than a will to fight.

"Thad warned us that LA would just remove Hazel and she'd never face justice for killing Jaci," explained Evie. Her words were hurried, "So we wanted Glenwood to find her first. We didn't realize that she was luring us into a trap until it was too late."

"So you're all idiots," scolded Owen.

"Yes," Evie agreed. She felt shame at what happened at the warehouses. During the fight she hadn't even been that helpful, spending more time dragging others out of the way. Her skin prickled at the memory of Randall's blood again.

"But thankfully you're alive," Owen added a moment later. His tension was starting to fade now that he'd lost the battle for Hazel and won against Gibson. With nothing more to fight and no will to yell at the werewolves, he relaxed.

Evie thought back on what happened to bring them to this moment and her mouth moved before she could think it through, "This was my idea. I said we should go hunting for Hazel and I talked Blood Fang into helping me."

This was partially true, because if anyone had been able to diffuse them earlier, it was Evie.

"If anyone deserves to be fired then it's me," Evie concluded calmly.

"Idiots," muttered Owen as he stood up, "No one is getting fired today. Now go home and clean up. I expect you all back here tomorrow by 9am to do your real paperwork." He opened the conference room door and waved the trio out. The werewolves stayed quiet as they trudged through the station. Evie could feel exhaustion settling over them all now that the dangers, both literal and figurative, had passed.

A few minutes later, they stood in the chilly autumn air outside the station. Three sets of eyes searched the parking lot as they all came to the realization that none of their cars had made it. There was a collective sigh as everyone began to dig their phones out to summon an Uber.

Evie saw Laika also open the app, and opened her mouth to question why they needed two cars. Before she could voice the concern, Ace spoke up.

"Thanks to both of you for saving my packmates tonight. They wouldn't be alive if you guys hadn't helped…" The man trailed off uncomfortably, raising a hand to run through his coppery hair. The words were sincere, but Evie could see he felt awkward about it.

"It's no problem…" Evie trailed off quickly. Blood Fang wouldn't have been in danger if they hadn't brought the pack in on this hunt, so it felt weird to accept the apology.

Laika echoed her thoughts, "It's not like we'd ever stand by and let you guys get hurt. That's just…"

Silence fell as the three shifted awkwardly. Evie was scrambling trying to find any words to fill the quiet. But thankfully Ace spoke first. "So… We should probably sit down and talk," Ace began, directing the words at Evie. "Not today. I need to go check on every-one… But I think we need to get to the root of this whole… rivalry and put it to bed."

Evie gaped.

"We'd like that," Laika answered for them. "When Thad's got his mouth shut, the rest of your pack is almost tolerable."

Evie slapped her arm and gave Ace an apologetic grimace, "What she means is, it's been good working with you, and if we can put an end to our constant fighting then we'd like to try."

"Good," Ace nodded. Again relief cascaded over him as if he hadn't been sure how they'd react. He looked like he had more to say when he was interrupted as Bruce appeared with a loud greeting.

"Perfect! Everyone I was hoping to find right here," Bruce called as he pushed through the station doors. Evie watched him carefully as he approached them with that same perfectly calm aura as before. It was starting to become unnerving that every vampire seemed to have a way to block her powers. "I trust all the paperwork was in order," Bruce commented as he took up a space in the circle between Evie and Laika.

"That was you?" Ace asked, surprise written on his face.

"Who else could it have been? That's twice tonight I've saved you, by my count," laughed Bruce.

"I'm sorry, but who are you?" Evie finally asked the question that had been burning in her head for hours.

"Bruce?" answered the vampire, a mild confusion in his tone.

"No," Laika clarified, "Who are you? That you can sweep in with moonlighters and fake paperwork to clean up a disaster like Hazel."

"Oh! I'm the Head of LA MOONS," Bruce smiled winsomely, as if that explained everything.

Evie couldn't believe her ears because LA MOONS was huge; they had hundreds of moonlighters on call. Witches, vampires, were-wolves, and even some elves were on staff. Getting hired in LA required you to be exceptional, which is why she and Laika had never applied. And Bruce was the man running that moonlighting goliath.

For some reason he'd decided to go into the field to save a few low ranked packs in Glenwood. Nothing was making sense, until Bruce finally played his hand.

"It's been lovely to meet you Miss *Belle* and Miss *Lowell*," Bruce emphasized Evie's last name. He knew her father and would be cashing in on Everard's goodwill for saving his wayward daughter. But then Bruce blindsided them again. "I'm glad I was able to help you both today. Rest assured I'll call in this favor someday."

Evie couldn't stop the breath of surprise from hissing out. He wanted a favor from her?

"Oh, before I forget," Bruce added and held up a cellphone.

She studied the device, but Evie didn't recognize it. All of them had their phones in hand anyway. Then understanding dawned as Bruce offered it to Laika.

"I believe I can trust you to get this back to your boyfriend... If I'm not mistaken, he should be waiting at home for you." Bruce's words were perfectly poised, without a flicker of any emotion breaking that shroud of calm around him.

There was a skeptical look on Laika's face as she held out her hand for the phone. Her eyes widened in shock as the device was pressed into her palm. Evie knew Bruce was telling the truth about the phone...

"How did you-" Laika started, only to be cut off with a wave.

"Miss Amadori had it. I asked after its owner and she told me that she'd left him at home," Bruce explained casually. "I get the feeling he may need a bit of assistance, but is otherwise fine."

A typhoon of relief crashed like a wave out from Laika, but before she could find words of thanks to stammer out, Bruce was on the move. The man looped an arm around Ace's shoulders, and started to steer the other moonlighter out towards the parking lot. "Mister Deerling, let me drive you to the hospital. You have packmates to check up on, and I have moonlighters to retrieve. We can have a discussion about if Blood Fang is ready to move into the big leagues of LA on the drive."

Soon it was just Evie and Laika left in front of the police station.

"Should we be jealous of that?" Evie mumbled to her friend.

Laika ignored her as the relief had washed away whatever tension was lingering. She let out a whoop of joy. "Evie! We did it!"

Blinking a few times, Evie realized that her friend was right. They'd managed to stop Hazel and outed her as the Glenwood Anarchist at the same time. There was still a small issue of a demon on the loose, but that would be tomorrow's problem.

"Yes, we did because we're badasses," cheered Evie. She wrapped her arms around Laika in a bone crushing hug. They clung to each other for a minute.

"I almost can't believe it," Laika proclaimed.

"We are going to celebrate tonight! We need to go out to dinner, get drinks, and expensive food just because. Maybe with a stop at home to cover up our bruises with some makeup," Evie set a plan down for them. She could probably get away with charging the meal to her Feed Laika fund too.

Laika nodded quickly, all signs of exhaustion vanishing to excitement of victory. She added, "I just need to stop at Alfred's apartment. Sounds like Hazel locked him in and stole his phone when she was looking for us."

Evie's confusion overrode any annoyance at the mention of Alfred, "Locked in?"

"Yeah, you can't open the door either way without a key," explained Laika. She finished summoning a ride on her phone.

"Okay, that's kinda creepy. But whatever; it's not a problem tonight. Go let him out and I guess he can come with us. It *was* his case," Evie agreed.

Laika nodded, her voice getting louder, "We can bring Shelly and Tor too?"

"Yes, of course. Nothing could ruin tonight," Evie rejoiced. They were going to finally enjoy a normal meal for the first time in weeks.

CHAPTER 17

COURTING

Laika
November 12th, 2018
Shady Hollows Apartments, Glenwood, CA

L aika sighed contentedly as she leaned against the smooth elevator walls. Her muscles ached from exhaustion, but she was on cloud nine. Today she'd won!

Despite the people recovering at Glenwood General, the bruise encircling her shoulder, and the fact that she'd never get the blood out of this outfit, Laika had stopped Hazel. Even if LA MOONS was throwing its weight around, she didn't get the feeling they'd be letting Hazel free anytime soon. Both Jaci's killer and the Glenwood Anarchist were contained. Laika could work on getting Hazel properly charged later. There was still trouble coming like the demon running around Glenwood, and the looming favor from Bruce, but those were Future Laika's problems.

Party Laika just had to pop upstairs and let Alfred out of his apartment, then get dressed for a night of victory drinking. Evie and she hadn't gotten to go out like this in a long time.

Numbers ticked up as the elevator rose through the floors, then Laika realized she had a more immediate worry. Earlier, she'd been concerned about what Hazel had done to get Alfred's phone. If Bruce was to be believed, her boyfriend was safely at home and just locked in. No big deal... unless he was furious with Laika for going after Hazel. After all, he had explicitly told her not to.

Doors slid open announcing she had reached the tenth floor. Laika cursed. She should've been thinking about how to smooth things over with Alfred. But now it was too late.

Instead of the familiar quiet landing, destruction greeted Laika. Her eyes flew open wide as she took in everything. The short hallway looked like a tornado had torn through it. Holes punctuated the walls, twisted rebar poked out from the broken bricks and drywall, and Alfred's front door was wide open.

Everything became background noise as Laika's attention was drawn to a thick piece of rebar with a person hanging off it. The rebar had been shoved through Alfred's chest, pinning him to the wall. His head rested against the exposed bricks and his feet only barely touched the ground. Red stained through his coat and shirt where the metal protruded.

Panic ran through Laika as she scrambled out of the elevator. Alfred wasn't moving, he wasn't breathing, he just hung there completely motionless. She feared the worst while a scream started to build up in her chest.

And then Alfred lifted his head, and those cool blue eyes turned on her. He was alive!

"I see you are back." His voice was utterly monotone.

Laika faltered mid stride. She didn't know what to make of the cold glare Alfred was giving her. There was such contempt that her feet had just stopped dead. Why was he acting like this? Laika couldn't make her mouth ask the question.

"Nothing to say?" Alfred scoffed, then he put his head back against the bricks. He looked bored.

"How... How are you alive?" Laika managed to stammer the question out as she forced her feet to move an inch closer. He was so angry, but she couldn't just leave him like this.

"I assume because you intended for me to stay here, not die," answered Alfred. He shifted uncomfortably as his feet attempted for better balance. But the toes of his shoes couldn't get any traction. So he gave up, just allowing himself to hang there again. Laika felt her cheeks turn warm as guilt surged. She'd been so angry at his text messages earlier, but she had never wanted him to get hurt.

"I mean, I didn't want you to follow me, but not this..." She waved a hand at the rebar. From this close she could see the metal was bent into a hook, keeping Alfred firmly in place.

Alfred sneered, the muscles in his face twitching in agitation, "Do we have to play this game this time?"

"What game?" Laika knew he was angry with her. Why wouldn't he be after she'd left and done the one thing he'd commanded her not to? In spite of that, Laika felt this reaction was extreme. Nothing he spat at her was making any sense.

She took an involuntary step back to regain her composure. Laika wasn't about to take all the blame just because he was clearly in pain. She countered, "I get that you're mad I snuck out. But it's not really sneaking out if I have the key, is it?"

Alfred shifted his glare back to her. His cold blue eyes were like frosty knives trying to pierce her soul. As he spoke, the tone edged into hatred, "Hazel, enough! I am not in the mood for this."

Laika flinched. All at once the clues clicked together. Alfred thought that Hazel had stolen Laika's face and was prancing around wearing her skin to mock him. No wonder he was so furious right now. "I'm not Hazel. She's been captured by the LA Coven, just like you wanted," Laika steeled herself and moved closer. She stopped an inch out of Alfred's reach and eyed the metal. Given Laika's werewolf strength, she could bend that back into shape.

"How many times have we done this before? Easily hundreds, where you kill off the woman in my life then parade around pretending to be her. I refuse to fall for your act again," snapped Alfred. He went back to sullenly ignoring her.

That pulled Laika's attention off the rebar. Had she heard him right? Hundreds? Hazel had killed hundreds of Alfred's girlfriends? Which meant he'd had hundreds of girlfriends before her... Laika considered leaving him up there as jealousy gnawed at her good sense.

"Are you kidding me? She's killed *hundreds* of people, and you were just going to let her walk away again!?" Laika channeled her jealous feelings into anger. If Alfred hadn't been pinned to the wall, she might've smacked him.

"Please, I know you sound so much like Laika, but I am sincerely not in the mood to pretend she is anything but dead," Alfred barked. Her fury didn't seem to phase his anger.

"I. Am. Not. Hazel!" snarled Laika. Why wouldn't he believe her? Her hands closed around the rebar giving it a jerk. Metal groaned and a hiss of pain escaped from Alfred. Laika paused. As much as she wanted to get him down and straighten this out, he might take a swing at her first.

But cold blue eyes met Laika, hitting her with a glare instead of a fist. Clipped words demanded, "Then prove it."

"How?" Laika challenged, her frustration was starting to build. She was done fighting about how alive she was or not.

"Come closer," Alfred commanded.

Laika was already too close for her own comfort while Alfred was in such a temper. She wanted to believe he wasn't going to hurt her. Normally she wouldn't worry, but he did truly seem to hate Hazel. And fully believed that Hazel was standing here... Her gaze dropped to his lips, and a flash of fear reinforced her concerns.

"Don't you dare bite me," she warned with enough fire in her voice to let him know she was serious. Only then did Laika take that last step. Alfred reached out his hand, gently touching the back of her neck. She relaxed at the affection, only to be jerked forward and off-balance. Fuck! Laika was sure she was getting bit.

No fangs broke skin. Instead, Alfred's tongue ran from her eyebrow up to the edge of her hairline.

"Ew, no, gross," Laika growled, pushing herself away. Surprisingly, Alfred let her go without a fight. Raising a hand to touch her forehead, Laika could feel wetness on her fingers. But when she pulled them away, she spotted red. Maybe from one of her cuts from the fight? The wound must've not closed yet.

He'd stolen her blood? But why? How did that prove anything?

Alfred still had a tinge of red on his lips from tasting Laika's blood. All at once, the cold demeanor melted into surprise. "Laika? How are you alive?"

"I asked you first," Laika rebuffed, exasperation coating every word. He believed her at last! All it cost was some blood... "Can I remove this now? Or do I need to call paramedics?" Her hands went back to the rebar, ready to finish unbending it. She was getting him down before he could make another demand.

"I am alive because I am a vampire, but you were being hunted by Hazel. So again I ask, how did you survive?" Alfred pressed. He didn't relax, which was fair given his position.

That earned him a cool look as Laika mocked him. "I'm alive because I am a werewolf, and we hunted Hazel. Can I take this out, or are you going to bleed out?"

"Wait!" Alfred's hands quickly fell on top of hers. He didn't continue until Laika looked up. "I have had time to think while I was hanging here, and I have decided there is something important I need to tell you."

"Can't it wait until we get you down?" Laika rolled her eyes. He was being exceptionally dramatic tonight.

"I believe it may be best if I tell you first," Alfred disagreed. His fingers curled around hers gently. Laika didn't understand what could be so important right now. However, she relented and let Alfred take her hands in his. The sooner she listened, the sooner she could get back to work. "With everything that has happened recently, I think it is only fair that I explain how I know Hazel..."

Alfred lost his words. He tried to restart a couple more times before falling silent.

After a few long minutes, Laika prompted the vampire to keep talking. "Okay, so? Is this the part where you tell me she's your crazy ex?"

"I know Hazel because she turned me into a vampire a very long time ago," Alfred finally admitted.

Laika blinked as he told her his court, in a roundabout fashion. A secret he'd been willing to promise her any other answer to keep only a week ago. Now it tumbled out in some desperate attempt at honesty.

Alfred was an orchid vampire just like Hazel, with all the same powers. Laika felt so foolish for all the 'clues' she'd thought she'd found so far. She had a whole murder board full of theories trying to puzzle out his court. If anyone had asked her two minutes ago she would have sworn he was an iris vampire. How wrong Laika had been...

Today she'd learned all about how dangerous an orchid vampire was when they stole powers and faces. Alfred was just as capable of every trick Hazel had pulled in their devastating fight earlier. Not to mention that going crazy seemed to be a court trait, according to Thad. Any one of these facts could chill Laika to the bone.

Laika realized the silence had stretched too long. Anxious amber eyes searched Alfred's, looking for any sign he was just like Hazel. She was met with worry and uncertainty. Nothing like the zealous craze she'd fought against today. Laika wasn't in any danger.

"I... see. So that's why you don't tell anyone." She bit her lip and then asked the most loaded question. "Is this... actually your face?"

"Yes, this is what I look like," Alfred answered without any hesitation.

"So you don't kill people, then?" Laika was flooded with relief. He wasn't the same insane serial killer that Hazel was.

"I have other faces," corrected Alfred. He gave Laika an apologetic look, "I am old and it was not always so immoral an ideal to kill.

But I have never been a ripper. There has always been a reason or... accident involved."

Laika appreciated the brutal honesty of his answer. She realized why he'd stopped her from letting him down, just in case she had a panicked reaction. Then the big, bad vampire would be safely contained and she could run away.

"I have not taken a face in a long time," Alfred tried to soothe her growing worries. Laika was still silent as she processed everything he said. There was a lot here to unpack and she had no idea how she felt about it yet. That must have been showing on her face. Alfred sighed, "I understand this is too much for you. I do not tell people what I am for many reasons."

He let go of Laika's hands gently. "You are safe from me. Unlike Hazel, I do not chase after people who have no interest in me. Go pack your bag-"

"What? No. Shut up," Laika hissed. "You're not about to pat me on the head and send me home to Evie just because I need a few minutes."

Laika wanted to know how many times had this conversation happened that straight rejection was his expectation? *Hundreds*? She gave him a hard stare as her muscles strained against the bent rebar. The metal resisted for only a moment before Laika's strength forced it back into proper shape. Then she added, "Stop being dramatic. We need to get you down now and bandaged up."

"Of course," Alfred agreed, but she could read the surprise in his face before he could hide it. Slowly it melted into warmth that chased away the remaining tension.

Laika mirrored his joy. She had always enjoyed spending time with him and their closeness had come easily. Now, an invisible wall between them that Laika hadn't even been aware of was shattered. All the same feelings were there, but a little brighter.

"Okay, so do I pull this out of the wall?" Laika asked. She didn't know how much of the rebar was still buried in the wall. But how else would she get him free?

"No need," Alfred raised a hand to push hers away. "Could you please retrieve blood from the kitchen? I am afraid I have lost a fair amount."

"Are you sure?" Laika looked skeptically at the rebar. She studied the vampire next and he did seem paler than usual...

"Please," repeated Alfred.

Laika knew he had some idea of how to escape, but he wanted her out of the way. She agreed, "Alright, I'll be right back."

She took advantage of her trip to the kitchen to catch her breath. The scene in the hallway mixed with Alfred's confession still hadn't fully hit her. Laika knew at some point she'd have to sit down and deal with everything. Anything that stole faces was terrifying, and she hadn't found a silver lining in the news yet.

Once Laika reached the kitchen, she put her thoughts to the side while searching for where Alfred kept his blood. It wasn't in the big refrigerator she'd taken over during her stay. But there was a mini fridge on the countertop near the microwave. She found it stuffed with rows of the 'juice' boxes. She popped one into the microwave and set the timer.

Was life always going to be as crazy as it had been since Halloween? A small part of Laika hoped so, because the last few years of her life were dreadfully boring. She could do with a little less injury and murder though...

When Laika returned, Alfred was standing on his own feet again. He had one hand braced against the wall for balance. She saw the rebar was still firmly implanted into the bricks, but was now stained with red. Laika couldn't stop the grimace as she figured out how he'd gotten down.

Alfred was checking the bloody hole in his chest. His fingers poked at the torn edges of flesh with a frown. He muttered, "I had just finished regenerating this."

"Did you just- Nevermind, I brought you um... this," Laika held up the juice box. Her eyes were firmly on the open wound through his chest. He hadn't been kidding when he said that vampires had a different definition of fatal wounds. She wouldn't be standing right now, never mind playing with it...

"Thank you. If you do not mind putting that on the coffee table, I will be in shortly." Alfred gave her that same affectionate smile she was growing used to. He pulled his suit jacket closed.

"I'm not scared of a little blood. You didn't have to send me away. I could have helped get you down," teased Laika. She was tempted to poke the injury for effect, but restrained herself.

"I believe you have seen enough gore for the month already," shrugged Alfred, but the motion had him wincing in pain. He needed to go sit down at least.

Laika steadied him with a hand to his shoulder. She'd picked a truly ridiculous man when it came to being maimed. She asked, "Is it normal for you to be crippled every other week?"

A small laugh escaped from Alfred. He responded with a wider grin, "Since I decided to let a particular werewolf into my life, there has been an uptick in how often I am injured."

Laika's laughter rang out, "Are you blaming me? I believe this was *your* evil ex-girlfriend's doing."

"Not my ex," corrected Alfred, matching her mirth.

"Oh, I have your phone by the way. Bruce from LA MOONS gave it to me," explained Laika. She wanted to give it over now, but as Alfred was barely standing, that was one more thing for him to juggle.

Alfred's expression darkened for a moment, "Bruce got personally involved in the fight? And returned my phone to you?"

Laika nodded in response. She could see the answer hadn't made him happy by the way his jaw clenched shut. Was this just a silly rivalry between the MOONS departments? Or was there more here? No follow up explanation came, so Laika pestered with the question, "What's wrong? He's a little smarmy, but he did help us out."

"Bruce is a lilac vampire and likely had a look through your thoughts. I had not told him we were in a relationship or that you knew where I lived. A minor annoyance when he does that, but we can fix that for you," explained Alfred.

Another chill ran through Laika. Bruce had been rooting around in her mind? That was almost as creepy as Hazel...

She opened her mouth to say as much, but faltered when she saw the look on Alfred's face. The annoyance from a moment ago had faded as he gazed down at her. Laika knew she looked an absolute mess, covered in bruises and blood, but clearly he didn't care.

"So I need to get lilac-proofed. Does that mean we get matching rings? That's a bit fast," teased Laika. She wanted him to keep staring at her like this longer. The spell might be broken once they moved inside.

Alfred burst into laughter, even as it made his chest hitch from the still open wound. All of the rage he'd barely been containing when she arrived was gone. He'd been a brewing storm up until he'd licked blood off her forehead. Had Alfred really been that upset when he'd thought her dead? That was sweet, in a way. The atmosphere in the hallway clashed with the debris. They were surrounded by destruction and both of them covered in gore. Laika realized they looked like the set of some terrible horror movie. But the mood was light. Alfred's laughter was infectious, pulling her thoughts towards how happy she should be right now.

Light glinted off his fangs, stealing Laika's attention as they had so many times. Her fear of them was muted compared to before. While they were still as long and sharp as she remembered, she realized that she only saw them when Alfred laughed.

If Laika asked, Alfred would probably let her touch them. What would they feel like?

Laika decided to find out, as she dropped the juice box in favor of tangling her hands in his hair. She pushed herself up onto her tiptoes so she could press her lips to his. His lips were cool and welcoming.

When Alfred's fangs brushed against her lips, Laika embraced the sensation and opened her mouth a little more. Kissing him was like fireworks exploding in her blood. Once she just accepted he had slightly longer canine teeth, then everything else fit into place.

"I told you so," Laika declared when she caught her breath. She wasn't ready to back off just yet, so she stayed wrapped around Alfred.

"Oh?" he smirked.

"I told you I wasn't afraid of your fangs," Laika teased, stealing a quick second kiss.

Alfred leaned to press a few light kisses to her shoulder. He mumbled against her skin, "How lucky I was to be wrong then."

The physical bridge between them crumbled with every stolen touch. Laika realized he'd only ever been waiting on her permission... She was tempted to spend the rest of her night here, but she desperately needed a shower. So she got them moving inside by letting Alfred lean on her shoulder all the way to the couch.

She deposited him on the cushions before retrieving the first aid toolkit and the fallen juice box. Those were handed over, along with his phone, and she stole one last kiss before excusing herself.

Alfred could handle patching himself up, and would prefer it... besides, she could use a minute to gather her thoughts.

Retreating to her room, Laika stripped and turned the shower on as hot as she could handle. Relief coursed through her muscles once she stepped under the water. Today had been a long day, and once again she found herself covered in cuts and bruises. Perhaps she shouldn't tease Alfred about his injuries so much. She wasn't any better.

She started scrubbing away the dirt and dried blood that stained her limbs. Finally alone, Laika let her mind wander to everything she'd learned today.

Laika knew she should be feeling pride for her part in catching the Glenwood Anarchist. She'd literally been the last kick forcing the vampire back into the trap. While she'd been chasing Hazel to alleviate her guilt about what happened to Jaci, nothing she did would bring the young girl back. All Laika could do was give some closure to Jaci's packmates.

Despite the fact that Hazel was stone cold crazy and hellbent on the idea of killing Laika over a guy of all things... That didn't make Laika blameless in Jaci's death.

Hazel was a danger to everyone. Especially if she could wield the power needed to summon a demon. She had to be put behind bars, since no one was willing to stop her more permanently. That annoyance led Laika to thinking about how Alfred had admitted he'd known Hazel most of his life. Now she knew he'd meant that literally. In all her ramblings Hazel had been frustratingly right... She and Alfred did have a bond that Laika wouldn't be able to understand, which only pissed her off more.

Sure, Alfred was hot and had proved he knew how to kiss back in the hallway. But was that worth the destruction Hazel had brought down on Glenwood? Definitely not...

Laika also couldn't ignore that Alfred was an orchid vampire. Right now that was her least favorite type, given what they could do. She hadn't been oblivious to the possibility he'd killed people. Moonlighters sometimes had to use lethal force and he'd been one for a while. Stupidly she hadn't considered all the time before supernaturals came out of the shadows.

How many more red flags did Laika need to walk away?

She should march back into that living room and put an end to this relationship... but she and Alfred had a real spark. Laika couldn't deny the chemistry they had in every aspect so far. Since the first text message, she'd found a hundred interests they had in common and conversation flowed easily. Alfred was the excitement she'd been sorely missing in her life.

Was Laika ready to give that up and go back to nights in front of the TV, with only Evie for company? She needed a few days to decide, and it was only fair to let Alfred know too.

As the last of Laika's grime swirled down the drain, she turned off the running water. Finally she was clean! This was her first shower since getting ready on Saturday. This was perhaps the longest Monday of Laika's life.

She wrapped herself in a towel before heading back into the guest room to dry off and dress in pjs. There was no way Laika was going out tonight. Evie was right, they should celebrate… but it would be better to party when actually rested.

Laika flopped back on the bed and lifted her phone up to text Evie.

LAIKA

I am wiped out

Celebratory mimosas and brunch?

I think it's safe to say we're not going to work tomorrow

Laika waited for a response or even the notification her messages were read. But after five minutes she gave up. She'd hear any reply when it finally came through. Evie may have already fallen asleep if she was half as tired as Laika felt right now.

Freshly showered and dressed, Laika headed back to the living room, only to find it empty for once. That was annoying. She had important revelations to tell Alfred. There wasn't much mystery to where he'd gone since the door to the master bedroom was open. Unlike last time, she could see light spilling from the room.

"Are you in here?" Laika called at the doorway. From where she stood, most of the master bedroom was visible. Every wall was lined with bookshelves just like the living room, except all of these were dusty. Off in the far corner was a bed, likely Alfred's, but given the rest of the room she doubted he used it much.

"Yes, give me a few minutes to finish getting dressed and I will rejoin you," Alfred replied. His voice came from a closed door at the back of the room. Maybe his closet or bathroom?

Laika padded quietly to the door before asking, "Are you sure, can I help?"

"No thank you. I am almost done stitching this up," responded Alfred.

"Stitching?" Laika recalled their first conversation about his healing, "I thought you didn't actually stitch things? Just glue so you don't bleed."

"I have spent too long injured lately so I borrowed some magic to heal myself," Alfred explained. He sounded a little distracted by whatever he was doing.

Excitement shot through Laika. Borrowed magic? Hadn't Hazel done that earlier when she shut down Daniel and Ace with black magic? Maybe there was an upside to orchid powers after all. Questions tumbled from Laika, though she didn't expect answers. "Can I see? Wait, are you using green magic right now? Is that how you healed me?"

However, Alfred answered them as soon as she took a breath, "No, I would prefer it if you wait outside." Before Laika could plead further she heard the bathroom door lock. He was being serious about her staying out. Alfred continued, "I am not using green magic as vampires are resistant to it. I am proficient in it, though, as I used it to heal your injuries."

Laika's mind was going a mile a minute with that admission. She had suspected he did something to speed up her healing, and now it all made sense. Those leather wraps were a focus for green witch magic!

"So let me get this straight. You can steal *any* magic? What magic are you using right now?" She bombarded Alfred with more questions.

"I *borrow* powers, no one loses their magic when I drink their blood," corrected Alfred. The bathroom door unlocked and he emerged fully dressed. His torn white shirt was in hand as well.

"Seems like semantics," Laika teased, not bothering to hide how fascinated she was. He hadn't denied being able to do *any* magic. The possibilities were endless...

Before Laika could distract herself too much on the what ifs, she confessed, "I think I'm okay... Not amazing, just okay with what you told me earlier. I'm still in shock, I think, and I need a couple days to process all of this."

"Understandable," Alfred allowed with a small nod.

"I know that I like what we have, but..." Laika trailed off, searching for the right explanation.

Alfred supplied the words, "This may all be too much regardless?"

"Yeah," she admitted.

"Take your time sorting your feelings," assured Alfred. He curled his fingers into hers before pulling the hand up for a kiss. The gesture was wholly uncool, but Laika couldn't deny she found it sweet right now. "All you need to know is that I will respect your answer and I am here if you need to talk about it."

Laika felt her cheeks go red and her concerns were already fading. She gave him a quick nod before changing the subject. "So how much magic *do* you know?"

From the bathroom counter Alfred's phone rang, interrupting their plans. Laika's began ringing not a moment later in her hand. Why was Tor calling at this time of the night?

INTERLUDE - WAITING

Becky
November 12th, 2018
Night Claw Residence, Glenwood, CA

Becky's attention never left the driveway of Evie's home. She'd been here so many times over the last year, she could close her eyes and tell you every detail of the house. From how many tiles on the walkway, to how often Shelly slept on the front lawn.

That should be Becky's front lawn. But the siren call of 'Victoria' had stolen Evie's attention... No, she wasn't doing this again. She would not get spun up about some trashy woman, especially since Tor and Evie weren't dating. Only a few people were out tonight and none of them gave her car a second glance. It was such a common sight on the street now that no one blinked at it. The glamour charm hiding the passengers from view helped. Becky wondered how much longer she'd need to wait.

"We've been here all day," complained Petronius. Well, the creature wearing his skin whined at her. Her 'boyfriend' was Becky's final sacrifice to summon her demon. She was calling it 'Veks' for the moment.

"I know, just another hour," whined Becky. She wanted to talk to Evie and explain what happened in the club was wrong. Last time Evie had royally messed it up. Maybe Becky hadn't used the exact right words? Or been a bit too emotional? But Evie was supposed to respect her honesty and not run away.

Becky opened the mirror on her sun visor and frowned at the unfamiliar face. She was getting used to the nose ring now that it wasn't irritated; some days she even felt it was cute. But the short black hair needed to go. Nothing about the style complimented her features and that was probably to blame for Evie running away. Agitation started building the longer Becky frowned at herself. She'd gotten the haircut because she thought Evie would like it. But like everything else she did, all of Becky's efforts were taken for granted.

"It doesn't matter what you look like," mocked Veks. He did this whenever he was bored. He tried to push Becky into having a big emotional reaction to minor annoyances. Veks wearing Petronius' body didn't help either. She'd sealed the demon there to bind him to her plane. That had seemed smarter than letting him share her own body like he'd suggested. But she was so over seeing Petronius' face and hearing his monotone voice constantly. It had been bad enough pretending to date the idiot for months.

Becky frowned deeper. "Speaking of looks, do you need to wear that? I thought you could shapeshift, so why do you still look like a wannabe hipster?"

"What's the matter? Feeling guilty that you killed this meat sack? You murdered so many before him, why did this one matter?" Veks smiled for the first time in hours. His grins were always too wide for comfort.

"No, I don't feel guilty," Becky shot back. She hadn't enjoyed the number of people she'd had to kill since September. Their sacrifice was necessary for her future plans.

"Good, because trust me, this meat sack liked you less than even Evie does," teased Veks.

"Shut up," Becky ordered. Putting up with the demon was also necessary for her future plans, but at least he had to follow her commands.

Obediently, Veks closed his mouth.

Becky took a few calming breaths to settle the anger trying to break free. No amount of meditation or yoga had been helping lately. Her temper hadn't always been like this. Normally, she was a docile person, but the last couple months Becky found her patience failing her faster and faster.

She needed to get herself back under control before Evie got home. The sun was already down... Why was she so late?

Less than an hour later Becky found herself complaining again. "Where is she?"

She was met with silence from Veks. He reclined in the passenger seat, playing phone games much like the original Petronius.

"Well?" demanded Becky.

"Well what? You told me to shut up, I'm staying shut up," Veks griped.

Rage rippled through Becky and she held onto the steering wheel trying to ground herself. The smell of burning plastic let her know she hadn't succeeded.

Veks swore as flames came to life on his phone. He quickly patted them out before finally giving her an answer, "This Evie chick knows you're stalking her. She knows you're waiting at her house and now she's avoiding you... obviously."

"I'M NOT STALKING HER!" Becky couldn't control her volume. The air in the car began to heat up. She needed to calm down before she set the whole car on fire. Becky tried counting to ten.

1... 2... 3...

Veks grinned in that creepy way. "Then what exactly is this? You went through all the trouble of bringing me here, and all we've done is skulk in this car as you pine after someone who doesn't want you."

4... 5...

Becky growled. They'd been through this so many times. The words were bit out through clenched teeth, "I brought you here for your magic."

6...

"I could have given you magic without the need for my summoning," corrected Veks, "You didn't even need half of the rituals for that. The first one would have been enough."

7...

Veks groaned, "Can we go now? She's not coming home tonight, probably out with someone else."

8...

"Please! I'm so bored," Veks continued to whine

"NO!" Becky slammed her hand on the steering wheel, "We are waiting here until she comes home!"

"You don't even know *if* she's coming back. You've told me you followed her on a hook up once or twice already," reminded Veks before he continued to mock her. "Evie is out with someone, while you sit here and wait for her. It's pathetic."

Rage was clouding Becky's mind. None of this was fair. She'd put in all the work, she'd put in all the time, and she was the only one making an effort. But Evie just couldn't see Becky, even when she was standing right in front of her face.

9...

An unknown car pulled in front of the house and the passenger side door opened. Becky watched the car intently. Who the hell was this? Laika's boyfriend had a black town car and he rarely came around. Tor was already home, her stupid bike was in the driveway, and Shelly never had visitors. But then Evie climbed out...

Becky's eyes lit up at her Evie! Her anger was stifled by the elation of seeing Her Love for a moment. Only for jealousy to stoke the flames of her temper worse than before.

Who the fuck's clothing was she wearing?

The grey sweatpants and t-shirt didn't fit her Evie. They looked like a man's gym clothes, plus she'd been dropped off by a complete stranger. Had Evie been so cruel to go out drinking and hooking up, while Becky sat here patiently waiting? How dare she!

"See, she's not even thinking about you. Look at her stumbling around in the dark. Go and take her. She can learn to love you when you're her whole life," whispered Veks.

Becky never made it to 10...

CHAPTER 18
OBSESSION

Evie
November 12th, 2018
Night Claw Residence, Glenwood, CA

Evie stepped out of her Uber, so glad to see her house. This had been such a long Monday. She may not have gotten injured in the fight with Hazel, but she desperately needed a shower. She'd feel human after washing away the blood and dirt. Then a meal that didn't come from a vending machine would be perfect.

Regardless, Evie's mood was ecstatic. She and Laika had brought Hazel to justice, stopped the Glenwood Anarchist, and somehow dodged trouble with GPD. They were going to party till dawn if she had anything to say about it. Her thoughts were on which outfit to wear as she ambled up to her door. Probably best not to go all out so she could celebrate with her friends in peace. Then again, if they had a broody vampire at the table it might not matter.

Evie's planning stopped cold as a chill ran down her spine. She hadn't been paying any attention to her empathy. Now it was screaming a warning at her. What the hell was this feeling of malice? She spun around as someone started screaming at her.

"Where have you been!? I've been waiting for YOU! ALL! DAY!" screeched Becky, slamming a car door. She'd been parked across the street. All that hate was coming from Becky. Why was she so angry? While Evie may have owed her an apology, this confrontation was a bit too heated already. "Answer me, Evie!" Becky squared up on the sidewalk. Her eyes glowed in the dark while she glared balefully at Evie.

"Uh... hi. What's wrong?" Evie asked very carefully. She could feel the emotions wheeling around the half elf like a dark hurricane. Her phone was in her bag and she debated if she could reach for it without setting Becky off.

Evie could take down a random angry woman without much issue herself. She was a badass moonlighter who had just captured the Glenwood Anarchist, and Becky was a powerless half elf. But the right call was to text Owen first.

"Are you kidding me? You know exactly what's wrong?" fumed Becky. Her anger was so hot that Evie thought she saw the air around her waver.

"I don't really want to do this right now," grumbled Evie. Yep, this was about how badly Evie had behaved at Glitterholic. She just wanted a shower and to enjoy her night. Not deal with whatever this was.

The aura surrounding Becky was churning violently, flickering wildly with a rainbow of unusual colors. Then it burst into flame, creating a halo of fire surrounding her. Evie realized those were actual flames. She backpedaled fast trying to keep this from escalating, "Or now is good..."

Fire consumed Becky's hands, lighting up the dark street. Her expression hardened as she spat, "Oh! Is *now* okay with you?"

"Yes, if this is about the club, then yes. Now is the perfect time." Evie knew she didn't sound very sure of her own words. What the hell was going on? Hadn't Arik told her that half elves didn't have magic?

Evie needed to de-escalate quickly. Putting on the most apologetic tone she could manage, she explained, "I know I didn't handle things well. I'm sorry about that. I panicked, but running away was a bitch move."

The flame dimmed a little, Evie felt Becky's anger starting to cool. She was on the right path, but she still needed to call for help.

"She's lying," a voice sang from across the street.

"Get back in the car, Veks," snapped Becky. She turned and jabbed a finger at the newcomer.

That allowed Evie to dig out her phone. Before she could dial any numbers the glass on the screen began to heat up, scorching her fingers until she had to drop the device.

"I told you so," gloated Veks.

Evie shot a glare at the car, only to see a second Becky leaning against its door. This one had long blonde hair and wore a prim pantsuit. Flames danced on the woman's fingertips and her expression twisted into malicious glee.

"Who the hell is that?" Evie demanded. Had there always been two Beckys and that's why she seemed to be everywhere!?

"Veks! That was an order!" Becky snarled at her doppelgänger. They really looked identical... Twins?

Veks sighed loudly, "I'm going, but you aren't going to win without me. Evie is lying to you right now."

"About what?" argued Evie. She did feel bad about how she'd treated Becky at Glitterholic. Did the magic being thrown around help her find those words faster? Yes, but she hadn't lied yet.

"Stop making our poor Becky think you care," hissed Veks. This bitch was just trying to stoke the flames. Evie needed her to shut up.

"Veks! CAR!" demanded Becky, all her agitation from before starting to build up again. The halo of fire was growing brighter with each word. Evie could feel the heat radiating off Becky across the yard.

"Fine! But don't say I didn't try to protect you," Veks replied, pulling open the door. She gave them a wink and her features morphed into a mirror image of Evie. Except this Evie was wearing a pink cheerleading outfit that barely contained her curves. Veks kicked a leg up while shaking matching pink pom poms, she cheered, "I'm rooting for you, sweetie!"

Evie paled... Owen had told her that demons could shapeshift. Evie had been wrong earlier... The Glenwood Anarchist wasn't safely behind bars. Becky and her demon were standing in front of her home.

What the hell was Evie supposed to do right now? Her phone was a smoldering pile of burnt debris on the ground. She couldn't risk going for the door either, since the house wasn't immune to fire.

Salvation came in the form of Shelly and Tor's voices. Shelly's words were quiet and mumbled, just on the other side of the front door and explaining the situation to someone on a phone. She was calling for help! Meanwhile Tor's voice had an angry edge to it as she declared she was getting a baseball bat to break the elf bitch's knees. Evie needed to stall, because help would already be on the way. Her stomach knotted up as the only plan she could think of involved the worst kind of lies.

"Becky," Evie's voice sounded scared. She didn't have to fake that at least. "You need to step away from that thing. This is going to sound crazy, but that's a demon."

She felt the confusion flicker in Becky's aura. "But Evi-"

"Please listen to me," Evie cut her off. Of course, this crazy bitch knew that Veks was the demon. But she couldn't let her explain or there was no chance at avoiding a fight. "*We* need to get away from here."

There it was, that flutter of love and affection that Evie had been pointedly ignoring for months. The emotions were marred by streaks of darkness. Everyone had a little dark in them and it wasn't Evie's place to judge. She had plenty of messed up emotions of her own. But the way Becky had been steeped in resentment and rage had made Evie feel sick from the first time they'd met. She hadn't even told Laika this was the reason she'd shut Becky down at their interview. How did you explain feelings as warped as these if the other person couldn't feel it too?

A warm expression spread across Becky's face. The flames around her dimmed as she responded, "... you really do care? Don't worry, Veks won't d-"

"You can't trust that thing," Evie hissed back. If Becky was just going to confess to everything, how the hell was she going to keep this up? She needed to take drastic countermeasures before the demon cut in again.

Evie held out her hand to Becky. With all the sincerity she could muster Evie begged, "Please take my hand. I'll take care of you."

A black supernova exploded in Becky's aura. Evie had said every word perfectly, giving the half elf exactly what she wanted. But Evie felt sicker with every lie. This was one of the most fucked up things she'd done.

"We can take care of each other," Becky answered, taking a step towards the outstretched hand. She looked at it like a drowning woman longing for a lifeline. How badly she wanted Evie's love.

Evie knew she had the woman hooked on her every word. Maybe if she separated Becky from the demon, then whatever power she'd received would fade? Or she could run in the direction of GPD and hope Owen brought Melinda with him.

"You don't need to worry," promised Becky. She was savoring every step up the walkway as if they were the most important ones of her life. "When I summoned Veks, I bound him in contracts that prevent him from hurting me."

"You can't trust a demon not to lie," Evie argued. She kept her voice full of worry and fear. She could hear Veks trying to get Becky's attention, but it was pointless as Evie had the half elf enraptured.

"When I cast the corruption rituals I knew that every life sacrificed gave me more bargaining power. It was easy to forbid him from harming me, and do all he could to keep me alive. I did all of this for *us,*" Becky gloated. She reached out to wrap her fingers lovingly into Evie's.

What the hell did this psycho just say? She'd killed all those people, from Harry at his own birthday party, to everyone she'd seen in the streets downtown, and forced that poor peony to murder... for '*us*'?

"Us?" Evie repeated the word. It tasted like acid as it rolled across her tongue. She couldn't stomach this charade any longer, "There is no us."

Becky's eyes widened in innocent confusion. "What?"

Evie's free hand rushed to cover Becky's, effectively trapping it in place. Stepping to the side to pull Becky off balance, Evie's fingers slid free of the half elf's grasp. Her grip shifted to Becky's wrist, and Evie leaned her weight forward to put pressure on the joint. "And there never will be."

A scream escaped Becky as she fell to her knees. Pain caused tears to start welling up in her eyes. She managed to call, "Veks!"

Shit! Evie had forgotten about the demon in her ill conceived plan to make Becky feel a little of the pain she'd forced on others. That was stupid.

When the creature appeared next to them, Evie recognized the face of Petronius and flinched. Had he always been the demon? She didn't have time to muse further as Veks tore Becky free. He leapt into the yard with an arm around her.

"I told you so," hissed Veks. His expression was wary and his eyes kept glancing up and down the street. "We need to go."

No! Evie couldn't let them leave yet. She reached hopelessly for anything to keep Becky's attention and yelled, "I don't understand, why did you summon a demon for *us*?"

Evie hadn't expected it to work, but Becky raised her gaze like she couldn't resist. Her voice was still choked with pain as an explanation began tumbling out, "So we could be happy? Veks can give me magic and then I can use my magic to protect us from our families.

We don't have to live in fear anymore of our fathers coming around to destroy the life we've built together."

Every word out of Becky's mouth was more insane than the last. What the hell did this psycho know about Evie and her family? Only Laika knew the whole horror story of Evie's childhood. She'd never told anyone else...

Becky was leaning on Veks, holding her wrist gingerly. A bruise was already forming on her pale skin. She reached it back out to Evie while promising, "Your mother will never be able to cut you down again. I'll rip out her tongue for you."

There was no way that Becky was just taking shots in the dark; she knew things about Evie that an online search wouldn't tell you.

"Who are you?" Evie asked. She considered the offered hand and took a step backwards.

Hurt flashed through Becky's eyes, as confusion and desperation tinged the half elf's aura. She pushed against Veks, trying to get free. "What do you mean? You know me! You're the only one who knows me!"

"No! I don't know who the hell you are! You showed up for an interview like three months ago and I've tried to avoid you at all costs since then. We've hardly spoken! We don't know each other!" growled Evie. She felt like she was being backed into a corner, and she had no more patience for this delusional woman.

All of the fury swirling around Becky cracked as she let out a mournful wail, "You... forgot me?"

"We need to go," Veks hissed as he tugged at the wailing woman.

Becky was struggling against his grasp, trying to lunge for Evie. "No! No! You can't have forgotten me! You were the only one- how could you?"

Veks groaned loudly, "Stop being so dramatic. She's not even that pretty! But if it'll get you moving, then I'll help jog her memory."

Evie watched as the demon took on another new face tonight. His masculine features melted into a young girl with dyed brown hair and thick rimmed glasses. She knew this girl! She hadn't forgotten her, but the screaming woman looked nothing like her teenage self!

"Rebecca?" Evie gaped openly. Her gaze went between Veks and Becky looking for similarities now that she could compare them. The same shade of sad blue eyes stared back from both women.

"See, you do remember your high school sweetheart," Becky cooed softly, some of her bristling emotions fading away. Again she strained against Veks' arm, reaching for Evie.

Sweethearts? Evie hadn't even considered Rebecca one of her best friends during high school. She'd forgotten all about her until Thad had been complaining... that Rebecca ruined their date to Winter Formal. How long had she been stalking Evie?

When Evie thought about it, Rebecca Rask hadn't been more than a friend on the fringes of her social group. She'd been someone in desperate need of anyone due to her crap home life. Evie only remembered a few details of the story; Rebecca's father had gotten full custody and stolen her away to the west coast from her mother. Her stepmother had been a real piece of work too, which she and Evie talked about sometimes. Maybe they'd danced once as well?

There was nothing between them that justified a decade of stalking!

"She remembers you, now let's go!" Veks urged, his steely tone was at odds with Rebecca's soft voice.

"No! We're not leaving without Evie!" screamed Becky.

"We'v-" Veks started to argue.

He was in the position of power until Becky commanded, "That's an order! Get Evie and then we'll leave."

Veks swore! He was angry now.

Evie couldn't read his emotions. She knew they were there because something kind of fuzzy existed within her range. But the demon's aura was like trying to read another language when you'd never seen it before.

"Hold up a minute," demanded Evie. She needed to buy time.

How long ago had Shelly called for help? GPD should only be a few more minutes out at most.

"No more stalling," seethed Veks as he took on Petronius' form once more. His eyes shone with a cold blue glow as he stepped towards Evie.

The temperature of the air around them dropped rapidly. Frost appeared on the ground and the air was cold enough for Evie to see her breath. She started to take another step backwards, but felt her shoe slip and she grabbed the wall to keep her balance.

She glanced down. The porch and steps were coated in ice. Even the door frame was half frozen...

Evie had nowhere to run without breaking an ankle now. She guessed that was probably the point. So she wouldn't run, she'd fly!

Using both hands, Evie grabbed hold of the porch railing and vaulted herself over it. She landed into a roll on the frosty grass. The ice hadn't managed to turn the yard into a slip and slide yet. She checked the sidewalk and found it already covered. Damn it!

"Don't get any ideas," Veks warned, drawing Evie's attention back to her actual threat.

Bursts of snow flurried around her. Visibility was dwindling, and Evie worried what that meant for the MOONS backup that was en route. She didn't know how far this extended into the road.

Veks was unaffected by the slick ground. He advanced with sure steps and reached out a hand, "Now if you'll just come along. We can't stay any longer."

Evie had to make a choice: she either needed to fight or run now. There was no more time to stall until help arrived. Frost under her feet wasn't a good surface for making an escape. But she was at one hell of a disadvantage trying to fight Veks alone.

Maybe if Evie could put enough space between them to shift into a wolf? Four paws were always faster than two legs. Then she felt it just at the edge of her range. Evie's fear evaporated, "No, I don't think I'll be coming with you."

Veks seemed to realize something was happening and turned his head to look down the street, only to find Laika's fist slamming into the side of his jaw. Bones cracked audibly with the hit and Veks staggered before falling back.

"Back off, demon!" snarled Laika as she slid to a stop next to Evie. She looked like a goddess of fury dressed for a fight in her vest. How had she known that Evie needed her right now?

"Careful, Becky has magic too!" yelled Evie as she directed Laika's gaze towards the half elf.

Laika's eyes flicked between the pair before landing on Becky. "She seriously summoned a demon?! How?"

"How should I know? You're Night Claw's magic expert," Evie snapped back. Her tone was frustrated, but she couldn't have been more happy to see Laika right now.

She knew that elven ears could hear anything they said. When Evie's silver eyes met her friend's amber, they shared a look only the best of friends could. First opening, they were going to make a move. Evie tensed, preparing to lunge forward. Then the faintest sound of sirens reached her ears, which meant backup was a street or two at most. MOONS was on the way!

Becky raised her arms and fire started to flicker to life in her hands, "Stop interfering! I'm going to kill you!"

"Not today," hissed Veks as he grabbed Becky and all her fire disappeared. He looked worried and his attention wasn't on Evie and Laika as he commanded, "We need to leave now."

"No, I need to kill Laika so that she's out of the way for good," Becky shot back.

"Yeah, overruled," Veks rejected.

"Who cares about some stupid human cops! I am commanding you to let me go!" Becky screeched, trying to pull herself free from the demon's grasp.

Veks pinned her with a sour look. "It's not just some cops you idiot- Nevermind. I'm overruling you for your own good."

His eyes changed to pitch black and shadows pooled under his feet. They began to swirl into a whirlpool that pulled him and Becky down into the street.

"Nooo…" Becky's screams faded as the shadow spirited her away.

Everything happened so fast that Evie couldn't even react. She'd barely moved a muscle before Becky and Veks disappeared. So she cursed, "Damn it!"

Laika let out a curse of her own, jogging to the edge of the street. She took a tentative step onto the asphalt only to find it unyielding. With a huff she turned back to Evie with a weak smile. "So… Hazel didn't summon the demon."

"No shit," sassed Evie, glowering at the street. The surface of the road didn't look like it had just been a whirlpool. There weren't any signs of damage, either.

"I'm so sorry I was late. I only learned on the way that Hazel didn't do it… apparently your stalker did. I just don't know why?" Laika gave her an apologetic look.

"Revenge or love, Becky wasn't very clear about it," Evie griped. Becky hadn't been very clear about anything during their screaming match.

"Maybe both?" Laika quipped. She looked back the way she'd come earlier, then Evie heard it as well. Backup was starting to arrive.

First to appear was Alfred, he jogged down the sidewalk eyes on the street where Becky and Veks had been. "The demon has run?"

"Yeah," Laika called back.

Evie felt a flicker of annoyance; he could have gotten here sooner if he was going to show up at all. But her attention quickly shifted at the crunch of tires when a GPD cruiser cut a path through the slick streets. The lights strobed, but the siren had been cut off during its approach.

Owen was behind the wheel with a few other officers inside. All of them were geared up for a fight. When the cruiser stopped, it was Melinda who climbed out of the passenger seat. She was prepared with charms and knives strapped to her coat.

Finally a howl signaled that more werewolves had joined them from the other direction. Evie recognized two in the front as Mike and Mary from Dark Wind, and they had brought others. Had every heavy hitter from Glenwood MOONS showed up at their doorstep? Evie couldn't think of anyone missing. Owen took control of the scene as soon as his feet hit the ground. He barked out orders to set a perimeter before checking on Evie and Laika.

"Are you okay?" Owen asked as he approached with Melinda at his side.

"No," grumbled Evie, "I just got attacked at my front door by a psycho half elf!"

"Uh... The call said the demon was here," Owen put his hands up in defense.

"Yeah a psycho half elf and her pet demon," Evie clarified. She allowed Melinda to start checking her over for injuries. But she hadn't gotten physically hurt during the assault. The mental scars would take longer to heal.

"Are you sure?" Owen's mouth was just a thin line. He was frustrated at the implication they didn't have the Glenwood Anarchist behind bars.

"I'm sure," confirmed Evie.

She could hear Laika whispering to Alfred at her side. Then her packmate moved, guiding the vampire to the exact spot where the demon had disappeared.

Evie was on her own for this explanation. Right now she had to convince Owen she'd been wrong about who summoned the demon, despite her compelling argument earlier. All she had to do was be smarter than herself... Great...

Taking a deep breath, Evie began, "Okay, from the start then, we got called out to a domestic dispute in September and our moonlighting insurance went up. So Laika and I put out an ad for a roommate..."

EPILOGUE

L aika gave Luca Lowell a firm shove out the front door. "Thanks for visiting, dad! You need to hurry or you'll miss your flight."

"I could call the airline; it's not much hassle to get you and Evie tickets. You can come home with me now. Your mother would be thrilled to have you for Thanksgiving," countered Luca. He'd barely stepped out the door, still trying to convince his daughter to leave.

"No, I need to catch up with work. Evie might get fired if she takes any more time off right now too." Laika forced herself to stay smiling. She loved her father to the moon and back, but he'd been 'checking on' her for over a week now. What she really needed was some breathing room.

Luca stood awkwardly at the door, fixing Laika with a worried look. "Are you sure?"

"Yes, I'm sure. Tell everyone I'm fine and I love them. I will be there for Solstice and Christmas like usual," assured Laika.

"Yeah... okay... Love you kid," Luca gave up. He gave his daughter a final hug before hefting his bag up to his shoulder.

"Love you too, dad," Laika waved. She watched until her father got into his Uber and the car pointed in the direction of the airport. Once he was out of sight, she let out a cheer before closing the door.

Luca was very sweet, flying out from Colorado to make sure Laika was okay. Thankfully he'd taken a few extra days to make the trip, since her siblings were still pretty young and Lavender would need help with them. By the time Luca arrived, Laika was fully healed without even a scar to show. That made it a lot easier to calm her father down and send him back home. He'd been closer than her shadow during his visit.

Laika loved her family dearly, but she didn't want them anywhere near Glenwood while they were still looking for Becky. She needed to start demon proofing the house in any way possible. She'd held off while Luca visited so that he wouldn't try to use it as leverage to force Laika back to Colorado.

She shot off a text message to her magical expert.

LAIKA

You owe me some magic!

ALFRED

I did promise I would set up protection wards.

Once I was allowed over again.

LAIKA

You were banned for your own safety.

But my chaperone has left for his flight

ALFRED

I have met your father before.

> LAIKA
>
> Not as my boyfriend, it's totally different!

ALFRED

I will gather supplies and head over soon.

> LAIKA
>
> It's different!

ALFRED

I will take your word on the subject.

Laika enjoyed how easily they'd fallen back into this pattern. She hadn't actually seen Alfred since the night of the attack. He'd been in contact with text messages the entire time, though. She'd struggled to hide them from Luca during his visit. Now wasn't the right time to tell her father about a new boyfriend.

Boyfriend... The word still made Laika happy just to think about. Over the last week she'd been able to order her thoughts about the status of her relationship with Alfred. Yes, he was an orchid vampire. And yes, he could steal powers from people. And yes, he was capable of terrible destruction, but so was anyone, including herself. Could Laika really hold some what ifs against him? By day three of Alfred's banishment she'd missed their games of scrabble and conversations on the couch with him. At least the break had allowed Laika to make a choice on her own about their future.

In the time she'd known Alfred, he'd never done anything remotely evil. Even drinking blood in his kitchen and the toolbox had been quirky at best. Yes, he'd hidden his court from her, but in the end Alfred had told her the truth about everything important. He'd tried to tell her how dangerous Hazel was and that was on Laika for underestimating him.

Speaking of psychos... How did she know so many maniacal villainesses bent on killing her?

Laika's mood soured as she flipped to the news on her phone. She sat down on the couch to read the latest update in the Glenwood Anarchist case. Hazel's crazed eyes stared back at her from the

LAPD's mugshot that plastered every article. No time had been wasted in publicly charging her with all five rituals and a demon summoning. There was only a minor mention of Jaci's murder in a couple of the initial reports. That was more than Laika had hoped for when the LA Coven got involved.

Sadly, they had the wrong woman locked up for these crimes.

Despite the report she and Evie gave to Owen, no one listened to them about Becky Hargrove, aka Rebecca Rask, being the Glenwood Anarchist. The story was too tidy from the picture Evie painted in the conference room that day. Thanks to countless websites and one terrifying news report, everyone wanted to believe that the vampire behind bars was the culprit. Rocking the boat would just incite the panic that had barely been contained the last couple months.

Laika still scowled about everything. Hazel deserved prison for murdering Jaci, but she didn't deserve to be blamed for Becky's crimes. Until she could find proof for her claims though, the hunt for Becky was dead in the water.

Her phone rang, dragging Laika out of the dark thoughts swirling around her head. If this was her father then she wasn't answering, but 'Evie' appeared on the screen.

Pressing the phone to her ear she greeted her packmate with the good news, "Luca's gone and no, we aren't expected at Thanksgiving this year."

"Thank the moon," Evie replied from the other side.

"I know the food alone would be worth it, but I just need a little not family time. We are sworn in blood to be there for Solstice and Christmas though," explained Laika. This wasn't a big compromise on their part since they usually went anyway.

"I can live with that," Evie agreed to the terms quickly. Her tone was distracted like she was working, but had called anyway. She was probably going over her high school yearbooks or any of the other 'evidence'.

Laika couldn't complain since research was how both of them stayed sane. They'd managed to have a few conversations about what actually happened, too. The attack had left scars on the household. Evie whispered one night to Laika how terrified she'd been of Becky coming back when they were all asleep. So Laika, Shelly, and Tor had taken turns staying up through the night standing vigil in the living room. At least until Laika had found a long term solution to their problems.

"Alfred's on his way over. He's putting up an anti-scrying ward, an anti-demon ward, and an alarm," Laika hoped this would soothe her friend's worries.

That brought Evie's attention back to the conversation. "Will they keep Becky out?"

"They should keep the demon out and slow Becky down long enough for us to kick her ass," Laika paraphrased what she'd had explained to her.

"Good," sighed Evie. All her previous frustration faded into a relieved tone.

"Oh," Laika changed the subject, hoping to keep her friend's stress level down, "Did you give Arik my final draft?"

Papers shuffled on the other end of the phone, "Yes. I gave him a printed copy a couple hours ago. He's been holed up in his room devouring the script. Tony appreciates that you are attempting to use a proper format now as well."

"He's welcome. I had the time since Dad was babysitting me. What else could I do but format pages?" laughed Laika.

She could hear footsteps outside on their pathway. A jolt of excitement had Laika moving to the door in a heartbeat. Only for her to groan as she saw the wrong vampire stomping up the pavement. "Great... The *other* stalker is back."

Jonas might as well have had personal storm clouds over his head. He looked sullen as he marched himself towards the front door, and Laika could feel the scowl etched on his face behind that annoying scarf.

"Seriously? Tor has been ignoring him for months, you think he'd give up," Evie huffed.

"If a decade isn't enough to dissuade an elf, I guess a vampire wouldn't be much different. Give me a minute to handle him…" Laika lowered the phone from her ear as she pulled the door open.

She didn't wait for Jonas to even reach the bottom step before saying, "No thank you, go away."

"You can't drive me off this time. Tor is home, I can see her bike!" Jonas gestured at the driveway where Tor's shiny motorcycle was sitting plain as day.

"She's asleep," Laika feigned a yawn, but she was prepared to square her shoulders. He was never getting into her home.

"Then wake her up!" Jonas hissed. His leather boots hit the steps and began to close the remaining distance to the front door. "This has gone on long enough, I'm over this avoidance dance she's doing. She can't keep hiding behind a puppy like you!"

"Excuse me? Do you want to try that again?" Laika's eyes narrowed as she felt a growl rise in her throat. Who the hell was he to call her a pup? After the peony and Hazel, suddenly Jonas felt so much less scary…

Once Jonas was face to face with Laika, his hand pulled down the scarf so she could see how annoyed he was. "You heard me. This pack of yours is all little pups and you don't scare me. There is serious shit going on and I need to talk to Tor. So go wake her ass up or-"

"Or you'll what?" Laika cut off his threat.

There was no one here that could pull them apart tonight. But fighting in the streets for a second time in two weeks wouldn't go over well with MOONS. She'd narrowly avoided a reprimand with the demon because she'd arrived on scene in Alfred's car.

Jonas gave Laika another scowl. He hadn't been prepared for her to bite back so hard and had nothing to say. Instead, he fell back on glaring at her while trying to figure out his next angle.

"Is there a problem here?" Alfred's cool voice cut through the escalating tension like a chilled knife. He'd appeared out of the shadows of the setting sun almost like magic and managed to startle both of them.

Laika forgot just how quiet he was sometimes, but she was thrilled to finally see him. "Hey!"

Jonas, on the other hand, was practically frozen in place. Laika saw his eyes move between her and Alfred, likely trying to decide if he could handle the pair of them.

"Who is this?" Alfred asked, his question directed to Laika. He spoke past Jonas like he was little more than empty air.

Laika rolled her eyes as she introduced them sarcastically, "Alfred, Jonas. Jonas, Alfred. Jonas is Tor's clingy ex-boyfriend who won't get the message that she's just not into him anymore."

"Uh, hi," Jonas greeted stiffly, "Are you Tor's new boyfriend?"

For just a moment Laika was tempted to answer yes. Maybe save Tor from more visits like this, but she didn't want to start a rumor she couldn't control.

Thankfully, Alfred answered for them, "No."

Jonas brightened up a little bit again, "Oh... good."

Laika saw Alfred pull out his phone and glance down to text, but his attention returned to Jonas as soon as the message was sent. He kept his cool gaze in place. "I believe Laika has made herself clear that you are not welcome in her home."

"No, you aren't," Laika confirmed. She continued to glare at the intruder on her first alone time with her boyfriend in over a week. Silence hung for about a minute then a ringing phone cut through the conversation.

She realized it was Jonas' as he quickly dug it out of his pocket. He seemed surprised by the ringtone and almost fumbled to open it. Avoiding eye contact he rushed down stairs and moved in a wide circle to avoid brushing past Alfred while answering the call.

"Does he come around often?" Alfred asked as he joined Laika at the doorway. He'd spoken in that low whisper that was starting to become theirs, like a secret language.

Laika nodded, "Yeah, at least once a week. He's always looking for Tor but she doesn't want to talk to him. He can't take the hint."

"I doubt he will be a problem much longer," Alfred responded. His eyes were on Jonas's back while the other vampire was retreating further with every second on the phone.

Straining her ears, Laika tried to pick up the conversation, but she'd only gotten a female voice shrieking something like 'Where are you right now?' on the other end of the line. She watched Jonas hurry back to his car and speed off without so much as a goodbye.

"Why's that?" Laika pressed before she remembered that Evie was still on the phone. "Oh shit! Hello?"

But her friend had hung up already.

"Whoops, I'll need to call Evie back and apologize," Laika laughed.

Alfred responded, "I am sure she will forgive you, as you were getting rid of unwanted guests again."

"I think you mean, you got rid of the unwanted guest," Laika pointed out as she met his grin with her own. She saw a look of surprise flicker across his expression and knew her guess had landed true. "How did you do that?"

"I did not make Jonas leave," corrected Alfred.

"But you texted someone who made him leave," Laika elaborated.

Alfred gave her a small smile as he admitted, "Not purposefully, but I should have known better."

The mystery of who he'd texted and how that had resulted in a call could wait for later. After almost two weeks of not even being able to hear his voice since Luca was helicoptering around, Laika had nearly forgotten how much she liked that smile. So, she threw her arms around Alfred's neck and pulled herself up for a kiss that lasted until her lungs demanded air.

Alfred wasn't some big, scary orchid vampire to Laika; he was just someone really interesting, who had a job she aspired to and treated her well. Was he the smartest decision she'd ever made?

Probably not, but Laika was willing to gamble her heart again with him.

"So what are you doing for Christmas this year?" Laika asked once she could find her breath.

- ☾ -

Evie
November 21st, 2018
Taran Estate, Los Angeles, CA

"Just call me back," Evie sighed as Laika tried to tell her to hold on.

She didn't know how long it would take to get Jonas away from their front door this time. He was extremely insistent for someone who was getting a 'no' from everyone who answered the door.

Evie sat in the kitchen of Arik's estate, organizing all her evidence against Becky. She'd even gone as far as to dig out old yearbooks and get all mentions of Rebecca Rask for her collection. Basically, she was tracking everything from their initial meeting to the events last week. She kept copies here at work, locked up in Tony's office at night, and a set in her closet at home.

This was the only place Evie felt safe right now. Arik had a myriad of magical protections around the house to keep out crazy fans and rabid reporters. He'd even hired a little extra security to come around during her shifts. They weren't like the moonlighters she knew, but more like paramilitary werewolves and witches who took up posts along the outside of the estate. Nothing was getting in or out without them knowing.

That was another good reason to leave a copy of all her documents here. Plus, Evie could dig through them in her downtime at work. Since she'd started 'writing' a script for Arik she'd had a lot more time to work on moonlighting at her day job. Maybe today would be the day she had a breakthrough on the Becky case.

Tony had called her obsessed a few times already. But if Evie didn't do something to help keep herself busy, then fear was going to swallow her whole. Granted, Laika getting wards installed at their home meant she'd get a good night's sleep tonight.

Evie was going to start at the very beginning of high school again and work her way through. She'd eventually find a clue that proved Becky was behind the demon and then GPD, LA, and everyone would have to listen to her. Or re-listen to her.

She'd discovered that since high school, Becky had liked literally every single post or update on every platform she'd had. Looking back through her social media for the first time with her new outlook had been terrifying.

Evie had even dusted off her Mythic account to check all the old posts back when she'd been in contact with her family. This was the most supernaturally inclusive social media around. It had everything Facebook had, but more options and better guidelines. Sure enough, Rebecca Rask was there and tagged in a few photos too.

Annoyingly, as soon as she came online she'd received a lot of old messages through the website. Evie had barely given them any attention since it was all notes from her sisters. Like Josie wishing her a happy birthday every year, even when she never got a response. Or her other sister, Colette, apparently had been sending family updates and pictures to her monthly for the last decade. There were photos of weddings, ultrasounds, and nieces she'd never seen before. Even her idiot brother, Tristan, had sent a message years ago asking if he could turn her room into a personal gym. He was always a terror when they were growing up since he was their mother's golden child.

Most frustratingly of everything Evie found on the ancient account was a brand new message from her father.

No more than five minutes after she'd gone online for the first time since she was 18, Everard reached out. Like he'd known Evie was going to sign in before she did... More likely he'd paid someone to watch for her or a sister had ratted her out.

Evie was pointedly ignoring the message and refused to give him the satisfaction of the small check mark icon letting him know she'd seen it. Meanwhile, Sylvia Belle hadn't sent anything to Evie ever. That hadn't changed since she ran away, either. Curiosity forced Evie to check and see if she and her mother were even Mythic friends. She discovered they weren't anymore...

Her mother's account was still public and a quick scroll showed that any sign of Evie had been scrubbed from Sylvia's page. That included removing mentions of her from old posts even before Evie ran away. At least the woman was thorough when she wanted to cut contact.

"EVIE!" Arik yelled. He'd materialized at her side while she lurked down memory lane.

"What?" Evie shot back. She'd managed to not jump three feet in the air, despite how startled she'd been. Instead, all the anger at her family channeled into a glare at her boss.

"I finished the script," Arik declared proudly as he put the loose booklet down in front of her, completely oblivious to any anger directed at him.

Forcing her emotions back into check, Evie tried to smile. "Is it any good? Or do you want Laika to make changes? She's going back to work after Thanksgiving, so I'll need to know right away."

Arik nodded like he understood, but his aura buzzed with so much excitement that Evie doubted it. "This is amazing! The scene at the end when everyone appears out of the fog is perfect!"

"I'm glad you like it then," Evie pushed thoughts of her family away so she could indulge in Arik's pleasant emotions and forget her problems for a bit. When he was in a mood this good, it was easy to bask in the joy.

"We have no time to rest," continued Arik.

"We?" Evie felt her stomach drop again. How could this be another 'we'?

"Of course, I wouldn't leave my partner behind now. You're my moonlighting expert and think about this, soon you could be a producer on this movie... well, junior producer, but still." Arik wrapped an arm around Evie's shoulders and threw his hand out in an arch in front of them. "Imagine it, your name up on the big screen in those closing credits."

"That's insane. I'm not a movie producer," protested Evie. She could see the hint of madness weaving through Arik's aura. He was so excited that he wasn't thinking straight.

"But you could be. Instead of being an assistant to the stars, you could make them," he countered quickly.

Evie opened her mouth and closed it again. She was completely at a loss for words right now. But she better find some fast or she'd be signed up for another crazy plan.

Her silence only encouraged Arik. "This is perfect! I'll promote you to being the first producer at my studio."

"You don't have a studio," Evie pointed out. She needed to derail his budding plans now or it would be too late.

"Golden Age Productions," Arik didn't falter. He kept going like she'd never even interrupted him. "I'll have the paperwork in place by the end of the week. Between you and me, we already have star power, a producer, and a studio."

Evie leveraged her superior strength to get out of Arik's embrace. "I don't know the first thing about making movies."

"I know, I know. That's completely fine. We'll get a Senior Producer and they can show you the ropes," assured Arik.

His eyes sparkled, making Evie regret her next question before she even spoke. "Natasha already told you to make a list of producers and none of the ones you've worked with before are still working. Half of them passed away from old age years ago. So who would gamble on this crazy idea?"

"I'm so glad you asked, because we've got enough buzz that someone has already reached out to me about the project. Evie Belle and Bruce Kamau produce a Golden Age Production, 'Project Moonlighter'," Arik gave a bow at the end of that mouthful.

Evie was at a loss for words because her boss was out of his mind as far as she could tell. No one was supposed to know about this movie and somehow someone had already reached out. How was that not concerning?

When Arik demanded they write a movie, she'd thought it would die like every other project he'd ever started working on himself. But this Moonlighting phase wasn't going away any time soon. She had enough problems in her life right now... maybe this could solve one of them.

"How much does my promotion pay?" she sighed.

Want More?

Check out the rest of the Moonlight in Glenwood series!

Join the Night Claw Pack!
https://moonlightinglenwood.com/

About the Authors

Aynsley & Lita are a collaborative duo that have worked together for nearly a decade. Their creative projects span from art to role-playing games, and now the world of urban fantasy literature. This is their 1.5 attempt to write a book that ended up being book two. No, they are still not a couple.

- ☾ -

Join the Night Claw Pack!
https://moonlightinglenwood.com/

www.ingramcontent.com/pod-product-compliance
Lightning Source LLC
Chambersburg PA
CBHW060406260626
47160CB00006B/2447